# Ministry.5

*Jarg.I*

## TONY NUTTALL

Edited by Matthew McKeown
Liverpool Literary Agency


ISBN: 978-1-5272-5100-7

*To Emma,*
*Whose hard work created a space, a book of empty pages,*
*waiting to be filled.*

# CHAPTER 1

MINISTRY.4

The spray emerged in slow motion; twisting, contorting, globular shapes, deforming then reforming, an expanding universe of Type-O, common as muck.

'Same thing happened last year,' Meg complained, drawing me back to the filthy white tiles of the pub toilet, trying to subdue the fury betrayed by her voice.

'Yeth.'

'Your birthday,' she continued, manoeuvring, trying to catch an eye as she wiped my face before dropping another disc of rusty-brown cotton wool into the black bag.

'Jutht unlucky,' I muttered, focussing on *Becky's a slag* scrawled across the wall, seeking distraction, trying to keep my thoughts away from my special day; done for another year.

The angry brushing intensified, each stroke violence; naked torsos, tattooed bodies, blood and laughter in the flickering firelight, before thoughts shifted to the traveller's chariot, careering down lanes at breakneck speed, the exhilaration of the galloping horse returning me to the stasis and routine of the village, as the oncoming dawn gave the merest hint of light.

I recoiled with fright as her skin touched mine, an involuntary reaction, quickly hidden; the honesty of muscle memory overcome as I returned to this version.

'How are you going to explain that eye?' she asked, standing over me, mouth hanging open, tongue lolling out to the side.

'I'll thay ith a stye or thom-thing,' I replied, feeling repulsed.

'You're not going to tell me, are you?'

'Jutht unlucky,' I repeated as her shoulders dropped and she relented, for she had secrets of her own.

The loaded silence continued as she applied smears of expensive delusion: moisturising balms, foundations, then layer upon layer of makeup, a mask to conceal my purple blush of savagery, though not enough to obscure the swelling now deforming my features.

I'd allowed Meg in, slightly, knocking on the back door of the Waggon, knowing she'd be there with her mop and bucket, cleaning up the puke and piss as the lock-in ended and the next day began. I'd studied her face, watching it crumple as I smiled and said, 'Lovely morning.'

She grinned, standing back, surveying her handiwork before holding up a mirror for me to consider my reflection, with its closed eye and swollen lips.

It looked like two faces melted together as I offered a crooked smile to this latest version of me.

'Them lot won't bloody notice anyway,' she declared with a shrug, screwing lids back onto bottles. 'What time are you there?'

'Ten-thirty,' I sighed. 'Always ten-thirty.'

They did notice as I returned to routine; sat around the garden centre table, with its overpriced everything, an audience of wrinkled faces and grey hair observing me, a slight trembling and scent of lavender permeating the air.

'What happened to your eye?' Pauline asked, frowning, the dip of an eyebrow behind her thick-framed glasses contorting her features.

'Bee sting,' I replied, forgetting about the stye.

'On your eye?'

'Yes, one of Pete's, I think.'

'How can you tell?'

'Just feels like one of his.'

'Did you not see it?'

'I was asleep.'

'I didn't know they came out at night.'

'He imports special ones – from Germany.'

'Thought we'd stopped all these bloody immigrants,' Masie joined in, spouting the usual harmless xenophobia, popular in these parts.

'Your lips have swelled,' Pauline kept pressing, overlapping, not letting go.

'And your face has gone a bit orange,' Becky added.

'Anaphylactic shock,' I said, my lips curving into a smirk as I wondered how long the graffiti in the pub toilet had been there.

Withdrawing from the conversation, I sat back, watching their wrinkled mouths moving through the usual rota of subjects, expressing opinions relative to this physically and psychologically isolated village of multiple truths. It was the same every week.

'At least we got our country back,' Carla declared, to a flurry of nods around the table.

'Isn't that your Michael?' Iris asked, her words tinged with excitement at something new interrupting the flow.

'It is,' Doreen groaned, as the others shuffled in anticipation.

'Not working, then?' Iris continued, relishing the chance for one-upmanship, even at her age.

A shake of the head was Doreen's mortified response, as Michael ambled towards us.

I knew who he was: weed psychosis, walking in circles from the swings to the tree house, to the forest and then back again, day after day; one of the trapped youths bored out of their heads, tottering trance-like, seeking escape through screens.

I sat biting my tongue, wearing a smile as I contemplated Michael on trial, wondering why they never asked what he was doing here. *Buying bedding plants perhaps*, I thought, as contrary to popular belief, I knew he was working; dealing to the underage, underpaid staff; the victims of broad brushstrokes and tainted policies, their only means of bearing this existence in a chemically-induced other, until the next shift arrived.

'What are you doing?' Doreen asked, channelling Iris's disdain.

'Nothing, Grandma,' mumbled Jesus to Pontius Pilate, before wandering past, shoulders slumped.

It was the correct answer. They didn't want him to speak; they wanted him to remain silent, sucking up all that fear and shame, for they were safe in the silence, in maintaining their illusions.

I left them to it, taking a detour to the toilets to tax Michael under the guise of moral authority, pretending to flush them away before leaving him to consider an eternity in hell.

I popped one under my tongue as I walked down the lane, my afternoon taken care of as I tried to escape from myself.

I'm thinking, always thinking, spending hours in front of the cracked mirror, perfecting Meg's response as she opened the door, her eyes wide in shock before rebounding into a frown. Tears threatening, I let them spill in an attempt at feeling emotion as I lay naked on the floor, considering my split reflection.

My current version is rounded, rough edges smoothed by pleasantries and nature, perfectly attuned to this place. But, I'm also frustrated, anxious, walking in circles; like an animal in a cage.

I lie on my back and stare at the ceiling, knowing what such deliberation means; this reflection on reflections. I can feel it creeping up, that familiar feeling; it was ever thus, my path leading to the next place, and then the next, adapting, changing like a chameleon, repeating the same story again and again.

∞

I walked quickly, opening the gate; it's loud creak failing to draw me from memory as I continued along the narrow path, operating on two levels, engaged in two realities. My body was reacting as if still there, in the past: shallow breathing, heart pounding, soaked with perspiration until the monotony of ritual, that stealer of dreams, saved me from myself, slowing down thoughts and smothering impulse as I crossed the threshold, finding normality in a silver flask of tea and row of white cups waiting patiently on the wooden side table. I continued through the stone-framed doorway into a room lit by a single florescent tube, gently buzzing, occasionally flickering.

It was cool inside, despite the summer heat. A permanent sense of dampness and decay lingered, not quite hidden beneath the overbearing smell of bleach and furniture polish, a synthetic pine.

Small sounds echoed loudly off thick stone walls and magnolia-painted render, as I took my tea to the table in the centre of the room and chose a seat towards the edge of the arrangement; off-centre, the chair screeching in protest against the wooden floor, filling the chamber as I sat. I focussed on the cup, taking a noisy slurp, leaving trails down the side and a ring on the table.

There was tension, always tension when alone as I tried to stay calm, keeping memories at bay, seeking distraction in the mundane; considering biscuits, a centrepiece of Rich Tea arranged in a circle, offsetting the rectangular pink wafers stacked like Jenga blocks in the middle.

Marion must have set up today.

The silence was broken by approaching footsteps echoing through the Chapel. Fr Webb came hurtling in, filling the room with movement and life, ignoring me as he advanced straight to the table, taking three wafers and cramming them in, one after the other, mouth open and red cheeks quivering. I watched as he transformed them into a bright-pink mush, making a wet slurping sound instead of the typical crunch, sending pink dandruff drifting down to rest in his white beard, covering a flabby set of chins.

'Evening, Peter,' he said, as he sat his portly frame down on the opposite side of the table. 'Nice stroll over?'

'Very nice, Ted,' I answered. 'It's glorious this time of year – the long nights, flowers blossoming and wheat turning in the sun. Saw a few deer up on the meadow on the edge of the woods – just beautiful.'

'Ah, God's glory revealed,' he exclaimed, reaching forward for two more wafers. 'You don't get this in your inner city – each season more beautiful than the last. I love the frost myself,' he continued, sending another cloud of pink cascading down to the table below.

I nodded and smiled politely, agreeing with the point if not the sentiment, as he struggled to get up out of his seat to distribute the minutes, his breath rattling with exertion.

'Should be a good one today,' he joked, placing the papers around the table and patting me on the back, grabbing a couple of Rich Tea as he went by. He winked, and the corner of his mouth rose into a smirk, red rising into his cheeks as he tried not to laugh out loud – and his laugh was loud.

In truth, Ted was right. It would be the same as all parish meetings there had been and ever would be, seasonal variation notwithstanding, of course.

I flicked through the minutes, feigning interest, reading the text without digesting any of it, before being drawn out of despondency by the sound of Alf and Paul clattering through the stone doorway, their silhouettes reminding me of Laurel and Hardy as they stepped towards the light. They were the perfect reflection of the village and its underlying tensions, with the old dwellings of blacksmiths, gamekeepers and farm labourers now inhabited by commuters. Fragments of a traditional life remained, and a few farmers, such as Alf, were hanging on through the gentrification, but the villagers no longer understood the changing of the seasons or rituals of the land, the feel of dirt beneath nails. There were no longer shared stories to be passed down; the oral histories forgotten as centuries of accumulated knowledge joined piles of rusting equipment in abandoned barns, all meaning lost.

Alf banged into the heavy oak door after tripping over the raised threshold, as he did every week.

'Fuck,' he shouted, just about managing to keep his false teeth in, though a few globs of spit caught in his ginger stubble. 'Sorry, fathers, but that fucking dog – oh, sorry, fathers,' he spluttered, as his Jack Russell followed him in and curled up in his usual corner, silently taking the blame before looking around the room as if to apologise for his owner, then resting his head on his paws.

My eyes returned to Alf, who was so squat and broad that he found it difficult not to crash into things, better suited to working the fields, where he couldn't cause any damage. He looked anywhere between fifty and a hundred, wearing a weathered look with a red face and deep pores, his nose pointing off at an angle as he strode over and shook my hand with the usual briskness. My own digits disappeared in his massive, heavily calloused palm; the consequence of a lifetime working the land, like generations of family before him.

Paul entered with a more dignified bearing; tall and reed thin, with red-rimmed eyes and dark, lank, greased-back hair, his skin pale from spending most of his life inside an office. He was one of those cryptic businessmen who had migrated from the city, buying up farmland and creating his own utopia, straight out of Country Life: stables, horses, alpaca, weekend shoots, golf clubs, two Range Rovers and all the rest. Despite his obvious wealth, his most discernible feature was his trying too hard to fit in, swapping a black business suit for his assumed ideal of the country gentleman: Harris tweed jacket and moleskin trousers, all ironed and pressed to perfection, not a crease or stain in sight. Then, of course, there were the Hunter wellington boots, whose two white logos confirmed him as an imposter. He was a walking caricature, fitting all the stereotypes, an urban fox out amongst the flock; the something new changing the dynamic of the village.

Where Alf brought chaos, Paul brought calm, but it was an uncomfortable, claustrophobic calm, unpleasant to be in. I watched as he floated slowly towards the table, each step of his sorrowful gait the same length and speed, as if he practised walking in straight lines.

I stood as he reached the table, receiving his soft hand; the pressure not too slack nor too great, measured and precise after many years spent in meetings and conferences, whilst Alf bustled his way around to sit next to Ted.

'Evening, Father,' Paul squeaked, in a voice that always caught me off guard; too high-pitched for one so morose.

'Evening, Paul,' I replied. 'Finished work early today?'

'Yeah, still loads to do, though. Going to be a late one, I'm afraid – burning the midnight oil.'

'No rest for the wicked, eh?' I plucked from the standard range of responses, adding a practised, almost natural laugh. After two years, I still had no idea what he actually did for a living.

'Looking forward to the weekend. Got a shoot in the morning, and then the fair in the afternoon.' he smiled, looking genuinely excited. 'Do you fancy a go at the shooting, Father? Are you allowed to fire a gun?'

'Not for me, I'm afraid, Paul,' I summoned the appropriate facial expressions: frown-smile-nod, frown-smile-nod. 'God's creatures and all that, but thank you for the offer.'

'*Fuck off!*' Peter cursed, as I continued smiling.

'Surely, there's no problem shooting something if you're going to eat it?' Paul droned, frowning as he pulled up a chair alongside mine.

Somehow, he even managed to do that without making a sound. I felt the strong urge to touch him, to make sure he was really there.

'Uh, yes, the Church is a bit on the fence with it all. Some think of them as God's creatures, others think that nature and Christianity are completely independent. To be honest, it's just not for me,' I said, reinforcing the facial expressions with upraised palms and shrugged shoulders, to further emphasise the point. 'John "Jack" Russell would've jumped at the chance, though,' I added, nodding at Buster in the corner.

'Ah,' he murmured, clearly not understanding.

We all turned as Roy stepped into the room.

Staying near the doorway, hand resting on the stone frame, he shouted in his mock Irish accent, 'Ah, let's see. I'll have the Hindu curry, steak and chips, and a glass of Coke, thanks.'

Laughing, Ted stood up and, in his slightly better accent, replied, 'Do you know where you are? You're in a police station.'

'Oh, right. Well, in that case, I'll just have the satay chicken,' Roy answered, before creasing with laughter.

It was the same every week, a Father Ted routine always raising a smile; mine remaining fixed as I observed their shared glances, studying the tiny expressions and mannerisms. They'd grown up together in the village, with Ted joining the clergy and Roy the police force, so between them they knew everything there was to know about the place, good and bad. They'd spent their lives together, stories interwoven, their friendship uplifting, everything I was not. I'd had friends, and these were the cast of my current adaptation, but in my life, friendship was shallow, fleeting. I'd never stayed in any one place long enough for it to be anything else.

Roy sat to the other side of Ted and began chatting across him with Alf. I couldn't hear what they were saying, as the formerly silent room became filled with the echoing voices of the other Parish Council members who were now arriving. In came Steve, covered in bee stings, and then Anthony, bringing up the rear with his familiar red wine smile.

Marion popped her head around the door, and in an Irish accent called out, 'You'll have some more tea? Ah, go on, you'll have some. Go on, go on, go on, go on, go on,' in keeping with the running theme.

'I'll have a skinny dry cappuccino please,' Paul responded, smiling, trying to move on from Father Ted, his attempt at humour falling flat.

'No cappuccinos, frappuccinos, macchiatos or lattes – skinny, fat, wet or dry – I'm afraid, just tea,' Marion replied, this time in her normal voice.

Ted knocked on the table and I switched off, my mind moving on from this place, seeking out the future as it passed in a blur.

I was momentarily coaxed from my stupor as they tackled foxes living within the church boundary, condemning them to the same fate as the rest of God's creatures. Badgers? Kill them. Squirrels? Kill some. Crows? Kill them all.

It wasn't unusual. Upon arriving in the village, I'd quickly realised that the most beautiful landscapes were in fact a front line; killing fields in the struggle between man and nature, with villagers the foot soldiers in a guerrilla war of traps, ambushes and chemical weapons. I glanced up to find the headmaster standing naked in the corner.

'What is it?' Paul asked.

'Sorry?' I answered absently.

'What is it? Your head just jolted over there.'

'Oh, nothing – a mouse,' I said, my gaze still fixed upon the naked form, writhing, for my eyes only.

'I can't see any mouse,' Paul went on, perhaps sensing something.

'Need to get some traps,' Ted suggested, sensing nothing as usual.

'Kill them all,' Alf added for good measure, as Paul remained focused on the empty space.

The meeting moved on, voices rising as always when discussing the imminent death of the village, and how it was about to be swallowed whole by the adjacent town and its identical, undersized, rubber-stamped houses of central government policy. For all their anger, it seemed inevitable, the people and place becoming a memory; photographs of characters that would fade over time, just sepia images on the pub wall alongside shire horse brass. There was a brutality to the policy, a social cleansing with a blunt, unimaginative and destructive solution, designed to attract investment and make the country competitive, but, as Alf rightly said, 'It's what's most profitable for the developers, and fuck everyone else… Sorry, Father.'

'Anyone fancy a drink in the Waggon?' Ted asked, putting an end to the usual hand-wringing and head-shaking, and for once everybody was in agreement, with the exception of Paul, who was going home to do something with numbers.

I gazed around the church, feeling melancholic as the lights went off, before the still silence was broken as Alf clattered into the pews, followed by the thump of his body hitting the hard floor. There was no 'Fuck,' just a hiss, causing me to shout 'Fuck,' turning in panic as Ted switched the lights back on, repeating, 'Sorry, sorry, sorry,' at the sight of Alf on all fours, blood dripping from his nose.

'With me teeth – with me teeth,' Alf hissed, bare gums shining in a contorted grimace, as we helped him up and pushed a tissue under his nose to stem the flow of blood that was already soaked into the stone. 'With me teeth,' he shouted again. 'Butter! Butter!' his voice becoming increasingly panicked. 'Butter! Butter!'

I wondered if he was concussed, as Paul and Roy joined the huddle, and we began bombarding him with instructions.

'Sit down.'

'Bend over.'

'Pinch it.'

'Put your head back.'

'Butter, butter,' Alf kept muttering, his stubble full of spit and blood, pink gums smooth and glistening.

Paul suddenly broke into laughter, and Ted soon followed suit, his booming cackle echoing through the cavernous space as I followed the direction of their eyes to find Buster sitting down in the aisle, Alf's false teeth set firmly in his mouth, a toothy grin of perfect pearly white teeth smiling back at us.

I took a sharp intake of breath before the laughter overwhelmed me, so powerful that it was soundless as it emptied my lungs, leaving me gasping for air before I eventually regained control, only for Buster to cock his head and set me off again. Our hysterics were feeding off one another, Alf joining in, rasping like Muttley, relieving the pressure that had been building up, and which we knew would increase over the coming days, weeks, months and years, as the insular village was assimilated into the outside world, piece by piece, field by field.

Alf put his hand into his pocket, the smile pausing and then bobbing closer until Buster dropped the teeth onto the floor and collected a biscuit. He cupped his hand around the dog's head, rubbing his ear affectionately before picking up the teeth, flicking off a piece of grass and placing them back into his mouth. 'Stupid dog,' he whispered, as he walked out through the arched doorway, tripping on the step with a customary, 'Fuck,' and then meandering past the wonky headstones towards the church gate.

The lane was dark, overhanging trees blocking out the moonlight as we walked silently down the middle of the road, a hunched over posse avoiding the stinging nettles protruding from the hedge. Despite the recent dry weather, it was always damp along here, the rotting leaves giving off a mild scent of decay, leaving the ground slippery underfoot. Occasionally, I'd stand in something more substantial.

'Why is it okay to leave horse shit lying in the road?' I asked the darkness, to no reply, the answer probably obvious, but still evasive after all these years; something about meat.

A rustling in the brambles suggested fauna, the night shift, fleeing our approaching footsteps as bats did their fluttering dance overhead, their world a different reality, stirring me from thoughts of violence as they pinged in frequencies, taking moths on the wing. I loved this, wondering if the others even noticed as we successfully navigated the elbow in the road, an arch of light appearing in the distance marking the end of the tunnel, where village meets world.

A set of headlights came down the slope of the hill as we reached the main road. The junction between ground and sky was indistinguishable in the darkness, making them appear supernatural, like alien craft descending as another flickered over the crest. Alf shuffled past, a beagle catching the scent, making a beeline across the road and then pushing open the heavy wooden door, its creaking hinges leaving behind the quiet of the countryside for the sound of voices intermingled with laughter, echoing off the low timbered ceiling. Everything paused, slightly longer than usual, as they looked up to see the strange appearance of the new interlopers. Alf's face was still streaked in blood and spit, and Ted's white beard was decorated with fragments of pink wafer. I glanced down at my shoes, completely covered in horse shit, until finally the flood of noise came crashing over us as they returned to their conversations, no doubt speculating about what had just arrived.

Ted pushed his way through the crowd at the bar; lads from the cricket team just finished training, I presumed. Pin and Jamie gave polite greetings as we shuffled past offering the standard handshakes and small talk. I found myself observing their tight friendships and camaraderie with an acute sense of envy. It was something I'd never experienced, the idea of a team, bonding and caring for one another. It was difficult to mix with people my own age, the collar making them pause and scramble for a safe subject, as if placed before a judge. The laughter, the swearing and the lowered inhibitions would grind to a halt – the reasons people went out drinking in the first place – so I avoided imposing myself, often loneliest in the busiest of places.

Ted reached the bar, ordering three pints before looking around and arching an eyebrow. 'Gnat's Scrotum?'

'What?' I mouthed.

'Gnat's Scrotum, do you want a pint?'

'Stella.'

It was always Stella, though perhaps he was hoping my palate had matured overnight, and I'd go for something more civilised, like Gnat's Scrotum.

'Didn't know gnats had scrotums,' Roy said, a slight crease between his eyebrows suggesting that he was giving it serious consideration.

'Of course they do,' Alf replied with authority, a playful upward curve coming to the corner of his mouth, 'except for the Jewish ones. They cut theirs off.'

'That's foreskins,' Roy shouted, attracting glances and tuts from surrounding groups, before quietly adding, 'Imagine, a religion that makes you cut the end of your cock off.'

I backtracked quickly, not wishing to be drawn into the conversation, whilst at the same time trying to minimise any further staining of the heavily patterned carpet as I returned to the darkness outside. Finding a picnic table cum bench, I removed my shoe and proceeded to batter the floor with it.

'Jesus wept,' I mumbled, as the deep grips held the shit in place, sending me hopping around in search of a stick until a musical giggling stopped me mid-hop.

I turned to find Paul's daughters amongst a group of girls wearing barely enough to contain them, like children in grown-ups' clothing, all squeezed cleavage and awkward, coltish limbs; high heels, long hair and makeup. Amy and Chloe had been attending the youth club for around six months. They were twins, sixteen years old and generally good, attentive kids.

'Had a bit of an accident there, Father?' Amy laughed, the gaggle dutifully giggling along. 'I'd love to help, but maybe not today, eh?'

'You're OK, Amy,' I replied, keeping my eyes fixed on my stick. 'I must have done something pretty evil to deserve this.'

'Have you been naughty, Father?' one of them asked boldly, a brunette hiding behind her friends as they all giggled again.

'I'm never naughty,' I answered quickly, trying to stop any double entendres, still popular in these parts, my face throbbing as capillaries filled with embarrassment. 'Where are you all off to, then?' I asked, eager to change the subject.

'The pub,' Chloe answered, stating the obvious.

I continued flicking, letting the silence stretch out until they felt either uncomfortable or bored.

'See you in there,' Amy pouted, like they do, imitating ducks and celebrities, all puckered lips and sunken cheeks as they spun around in formation, giggling as the creak of the door announced the latest arrivals, leaving me to clean out my grooves, which I eventually achieved by abandoning the stick and standing in the pond.

I returned inside to find that our posse had broken up and were intermingling with other villagers. I considered each group, deliberating over which one to join, but I knew that it didn't really matter. Evenings in the pub tended to go the same way: standing awkwardly on the edge, more observer than participant, smiling a lot and taking small, regular gulps, trying to think of something witty to say, then deciding not to say it.

I spotted Ted with the cricket team, so wandered over, nudging in, saying hello and retrieving my pint, which I finished quickly before offering to buy another; politely declined in case I hung around. A sense of relief washed over me as, having satisfied the demands of etiquette, I moved myself to the wall, where I could watch what normal people do whilst propping up the bar.

Meg was on tonight; the reason the men were standing next to empty tables and chairs. I watched them order, talking to her breasts, glancing for a view of her bending over to pull packets of crisps from the box on the floor, sending savoury sales through the roof.

'Another bag of Quavers please, love.'

'That's your third tonight.'

'I know, I'm starving.'

'How are Quavers going to fill you up?'

She didn't look at me or ask what I wanted; she just placed a Stella down on the mat in front of me. 'A donation to the church,' she said, smiling, before going off to serve the next customer. Crisps again, no doubt.

I liked her. She didn't go to church, so didn't see the collar as a reason to act differently; to change her personality. Ted had warned me off her the first time I'd come to the pub.

'Bit of a wild card that one,' he'd said, pausing dramatically before raising an eyebrow and whispering, 'Divorced and had an abortion, they reckon.'

Not that she cared what people thought or said. She was from the village, but her mentality didn't fit the standard model, and though some of the stories were true, most were just rumours given credibility by her appearance behind the bar, where she faced drunken locals trying a variety of seduction techniques as alcohol made them braver. There were whisperings of a sweepstake running amongst the cricket club, but the prize would remain unclaimed.

She came over between servings, placing another pint of salvation before me as she recognised the stage of the evening I was going through.

'Football's on in the other room,' she suggested, providing the excuse I needed to move.

A couple playing darts and the Amy and Chloe group were the room's only occupants, with the underage girls taking up a table in the centre, drinking Aperol Spritz and blue WKDs, engrossed in one another, chatting noisily. I slinked into a corner, hoping to avoid detection, perching myself on a stool at the bar to watch the highlights, or in this case, lowlights. My presence was noted, however, as one by one they drifted over, laughing and talking loudly, full of youthful courage and exuberance, as I posed for selfies and joined in conversation whilst trying to watch defeat play out over their heads. Their conversation was becoming increasingly risqué, their touches to my arms and thighs more frequent, as they egged each other on.

Another Stella appeared on the bar as they got more pissed, the talking and touching becoming more intense as they closed in around me. I stretched my neck higher, feeling on edge, using the football to avoid eye contact as I recoiled from their pats and taps, trying to block out their words as phone flashes joined the blinking of the fruit machine, leaving purple spots in my vision as the questions became more direct.

'What can a priest do?'

'What have you done?'

'Are you a virgin?'

They started going through the 'bases,' trying to outdo one another with carnal tales, their minds shaped to view everything through a sexual filter.

'Time please, ladies,' Meg rode to the rescue, placing another beer down on the bar, 'put him down.'

Much like their parents, the girls found the barmaid slightly intimidating, and so they returned uncomplaining to collect their belongings from the table.

'They had a bet on,' Meg said, as she closed the door behind them, leaving a fragrant taste in the air, a heavy cocktail of perfumes, 'see who could pull the priest.'

'I'm not allowed,' I murmured, watching the Speaker of the House in the corner, stroking himself through his shorts.

'That just makes it more of a challenge,' she grinned wickedly. 'Would give them massive kudos at school.'

'At school?'

'School,' she repeated, as a laugh escaped.

I looked up at her and shook my head. 'I don't know where to start with that.'

'Now you know what it's like for me.'

'Eh?'

'Every night, they think I don't notice. "Bag of Quavers," bag of fucking Quavers – they're just fresh air and cheese dust. The topless lady on the nuts used to distract them, but that's long gone. They just didn't consider the consequences.'

'Yeah, it's the cross we must bear, I'm afraid. The price of being incredibly attractive.'

'Fuck off,' she grinned. 'Can I walk you home?'

'Aren't I supposed to ask you that?'

'I'm not the one who needs an escort.'

We linked arms as the door creaked shut behind us, and took a moment to admire the stars as we stepped out into the silence of the night. They were glorious, and I was drunk.

I was focussed on trying to control my breathing, keeping the panic at bay, as we walked back through the tunnel of darkness, Meg's heels clattering against the road.

The cocktail of fresh air and alcohol had my head spinning as we arrived at the gate to the vicarage, a small one-bedroom brick cottage that didn't quite stand up straight. Gravity had taken its toll over the years, it looked pissed, like me.

'Are you going to invite me in?'

'One for the road?' I conceded, feigning reluctance as I pushed the gate open.

She took the key from my hand, since we both knew it would take me a while as she propped me against the wall and opened the door.

'Stella, Stella or Stella?' I shouted from the fridge, as Meg made herself comfortable in the lounge.

Our friendship was finely balanced, unlikely, clandestine and exciting, picking the pieces of our personalities that fitted whilst withholding those that conflicted. She couldn't be with a priest, with its abstinences and virtues, and I took reassurance in that, my faith a barrier, an invisible wall that we could press up against without breaking through.

Look, but don't touch.

A smile crossed my lips as deep bass went coursing through the ancient stone and timbers, the sash windows vibrating in their frames, showing disapproval; would have preferred Chopin or Satie, no doubt.

She was dancing when I returned, gyrating, her hands expressive as I turned the light off and Peter joined her, moving and laughing in the middle of the living room for what seemed like minutes, but was probably hours. It felt uninhibited, pagan, allowing us to escape the tension present every time we met; that huge white elephant, but it was also deceptive, carefully managed, a cold heart hiding behind our apparent spontaneity, as I dared myself to touch the fear, push that line a little bit further before retreating back to safety behind my wall, within my shell, as the beats went on.

# CHAPTER 2

PROTESTANT

I awoke on the sofa to sunlight streaming through the yellowing net curtains of the living room. Outside, the birds were singing cheerfully, contrasting with the vibrating bass still booming from the speakers. Standing gingerly, I switched it off, returning the house to peace as a slight whistling appeared in my ears, a protest for the abuse they had endured.

I didn't need to search for her; she'd gone, sneaked out, a thief in the night, only red lipstick around the rims of the beer cans leaving any indication that she had been here at all. Quite a few beer cans, I noticed.

Negativity beat down on me, as it always did whenever Peter supplanted the priest. A disappointment, a feeling of revulsion and self-loathing coming through, hitting my mind in symphony with the hangover, assaulting my body. I was trembling, struggling to form lucid thoughts against a backdrop of anxiety and confusion; delirium tremens as I knelt at the sofa and prayed, atonement for my sins, unclear what I was offering penance for, since the evening was still blurry. Regardless, I knew that most priests don't do what I do, behave how I'd behaved, drinking and then dancing around the living room with the local barmaid. The self-flagellation felt justified; I despised myself. Our Lord must remain ascendant.

Agitation had me moving from the floor to the shower, cowering under the cold water, purging negativity, refining thoughts, though the self-loathing would only recede with the hangover, I assumed.

Shivering, I put on new robes and checked the cupboards for something to eat, finding nothing, just hair of the dog sitting lonely in the fridge. I forced it in and held it down, feeling its calming chill spreading through my stomach, my spirits rising as it entered my bloodstream. It was a big day for the village, one I was looking forward to, our moment of protest, a bespoke rebellion through the lens of village politeness. It was the first surge of adrenaline in the streets for years, as David took on Goliath.

Until now, they had been bystanders in the 'Age of Protest' – or 'Impunity,' depending on social classification – watching from the sidelines as subtle signs of dissatisfaction grew. In retrospect, the warnings were everywhere: the return of raves in farmers' barns, graffiti on the village bus stop, the resurgence of football hooligans in the towns, now political, aligned with government policy; and a racism that hadn't really gone away.

Here, they'd quietly shook their heads. It all seemed so far away, a passing phenomenon, as the country listed under a government and political system no longer fit for purpose. They'd scan then turn the page, looking for crosswords, Sudoku, distraction, as parties they'd trusted became fragmented before reforming into extreme versions of themselves, loose coalitions of self-proclaimed Grand Wizards and Spartans, breaking down as Etonians called out Wykehamists whilst blurting out Kipling and burying themselves in history, the glory of an empire where the sun never set, living out their boarding school wet dreams.

To the majority, they were an insurgency, their takeover swift, whips withdrawn and positions filled based upon allegiance to obsolete ideologies. The foreign-owned media provided a platform, a soapbox for projecting their truths, saturating the masses, blaming benefit cheats and immigrants for the current malaise. The free press, meanwhile, painted a different picture, labelling them 'Gammons,' useless, fatty lumps of meat, their angry red faces becoming subject to derision and ridicule as they filibustered and spouted rhetoric, speaking in military metaphor whilst reminiscing of days spent serving Her Majesty in the Territorial Army.

The village, however, liked gammon, so they continued to read and believe, stoically hanging on as the stories that built the nation were hollowed out or placed in managed decline. All the while, they looked the other way, watching the horizon for an approaching army of foreign invaders, as elsewhere, people just like them died waiting in corridors and committed suicide in care homes, as private companies, with their non-executive directors, waited in the wings to take over, zero-hour contracts at the ready. It all seemed so distant.

In a parallel world, protesters had appropriated the Gilet Jaune and were marching through city streets, smiling and distributing flowers, dancing to music. The government turned away, cutting itself loose from the population and blaming Fancy Bears for the populist propaganda, rule by decree now in place, yet still, here they'd believed; remaining on the sidelines, parroting slogans, condemning protesters as anarchists and terrorists, buying into the narrative.

Until now.

The faceless money had arrived, and they were startled, like a rabbit in the headlights, finding no reward for their staunch loyalty as the City cashed in for the good of the nation.

I arrived at the village hall to find people milling around outside in spotless Gilets Jaunes, everybody animated, louder, a bit more alive. Nervousness and excitement filled the air, catching, as dogs ran about impatiently, circling the group, tails wagging as horses whinnied, stamping their hooves and nodding their heads. It felt like the prelude to a hunt.

A number of 'Morning, Fathers,' were expressed, barely discernible amongst the background chatter, as I made my way through the crowd, the smell of bacon sandwiches making my stomach growl, reminding me it was there. I followed the scent trail into the main hall, where shafts of sunlight acted like translucent screens, making the contrasting shadow seem darker as dust motes danced. I could just make out Ted and Roy, deep in conversation at the far end, talking urgently in hushed voices. Ted saw me as a flicker, temporarily illuminated before disappearing again as I walked through the slices of light, beckoning me over in a moment of reappearance.

'Morning, gentlemen. This looks a bit serious,' I said, perhaps a bit too light-heartedly.

'Just a heads up,' Ted's voice was low, drawing me in, 'Bishop Gordon is on his way here, and, in a nutshell, he does not want us attending or supporting the protest.' He held out his palms, a sharp intake of breath proving his irritation, jowls wobbling as he gently shook his head. 'Secondly, he is very concerned about the direction of your youth initiative. He has received a few phone calls recently from some concerned parents, as well as one from the archbishop.' He raised his eyebrows, to emphasise the importance of the archbishop. 'Any idea what that could be about?'

'Nobody has said anything to me,' I shrugged. 'How are you, Roy?' I asked, redirecting the conversation, but he also looked annoyed. 'I take it you'll be protesting today?'

'You wouldn't believe it, but I've got to police the event. I'm to stop these people from "overstepping the mark." The right to peaceful protest, and nothing else. It's a stitch-up,' he exclaimed, his body language, clenched fists and shaking head, making sure we knew he was upset. 'They cancelled my leave, and the powers that be have told Ted that he can't protest, either. We've lived in this village all our lives, and now we're not allowed to fight for it. Meanwhile, I've got to ensure that the diggers get full access to the fields. It's town hall politics, and it's not even our town hall.'

I grabbed a couple of bacon rolls as the tray came past, a palpable feeling of relief emanating from my stomach. 'You don't *have* to comply, do you? Can't you – I mean, *we*, make a stand? I'm going up there, I don't care what they say.'

They glanced at each other, and then off in different directions, feet shuffling nervously.

'Let's see what the bishop has to say first,' Ted murmured quietly.

I gave a smile, hoping the rest of them were not going to be so pliant, as Alf entered the hall.

'Right, everybody, time we were going – get the placards. The ladies will meet us up there with flasks of tea and a lovely spread,' he announced, with a nice bit of gender stereotyping. 'Let's show these bastards that nobody messes with the Village," he screamed, shaking his fist in the air. 'Sorry, fathers.'

I followed his shuffling form outside and addressed the crowd, giving a blessing and a prayer to set them off on their crusade, this motley band of pensioners and middle-aged rebels, around forty in total, our home guard, trudging towards the battlefield with placards over their shoulders.

Anarchy wasn't the first word that sprung to mind.

Ted and I followed up the road a few minutes later, past the horse shit I'd trodden in the previous night, as Nobbler strode by in the opposite direction, covered in mud. He was the local gamekeeper, and one of Alf's closest friends.

*Must be preparing for the weekend's shoot*, I thought.

'Fathers,' he nodded with a smile.

'Are you not joining the protest?' I called over. 'Alf's leading them up to the fields.'

'Nah, they'll be back soon enough,' he replied over his shoulder, not breaking stride. 'I'm going to get my head down for a bit. Up at the crack this morning.'

We entered the coolness of the church and waited for Bishop Gordon to arrive, Alf's blood stains still visible in the aisle. What the place lacked in size it made up for in character, with its thick flint walls, worn stone floor and exposed timber roof; remarkably atmospheric, particularly when alone in the silence of the night, candles flickering in alcoves, casting their deep, dancing shadows. I'd close my eyes and feel its ghosts, eight hundred years of ritual before the potent symbol of the cross, finding peace in a deep meditative state, numbed, sedated, floating, not thinking.
But today was different.

I was agitated, full of child-like impatience.

'I'm going to the field,' I declared.

'Just wait,' Ted said.

'We're going to miss the protest.'

'It'll be on all day. Just wait, will you?'

He was nervous, pacing about and looking behind things, retrieving yellowing pieces of paper from the ends of the pews, old orders of service, and putting them into the bin before searching out others.

'He sounded very angry,' he said.

'Small man syndrome,' I replied, getting a smile. 'Anyway, what right does he have to be angry? It should be you getting angry. Who is he to tell you not to protest against something you and the congregation feel so strongly about?'

He just shrugged. He looked fed up.

The creak of the door, and then quick footsteps echoing through the chapel announced his arrival. It seemed to last an age.

*He isn't walking that quickly*, I suspected, *just has short legs.*

I was about to crack a joke when the bishop entered the vestry and closed the wooden door behind him with a heavy clunk, before turning to flash us an anguish filled smile. He was mostly bald, with a neat trim of grey hair around the sides; an egg in the nest, decorated with a constellation of liver spots above a pointed face, with its small, puckered mouth and lack of chin giving him a slightly cruel look. He offered us a hand that was so limp, I didn't know whether to shake it or get down on my knees and kiss the rings.

'Right,' he began, once we were sat around the table, 'I propose that we break the meeting into two parts, to cover the two urgent matters we must discuss. Although, it's not so much a discussion as it is me explaining to you both what is happening and why.'

Ted and I both nodded, as we exchanged furtive glances.

'The first matter is the protest. We cannot be seen to support it.'

'Why?' I asked.

'Why would *you* be bothered, Peter?' he snapped. 'You are not even from around here.'

'Because they are my – *our* congregation,' I said, looking to Ted, trying to get him involved, 'and it will adversely affect this parish. We have a responsibility to–'

'You need to understand the bigger picture,' Bishop Gordon butted in. 'Since they won the legal case repealing the right for us to allocate places in our schools based upon church attendance, the congregations have disappeared. The churches are empty. We expected a slight drop, but nothing like this.'

'Well, it was a form of blackmail,' I said.

He took a second to glare at me before continuing. 'It appears that many were only attending church to get their children into a good school, without actually having any religious inclination. At the moment, we have an average age of sixty attending our services, and they are diminishing slowly as people pass away.' He paused for dramatic effect. 'This is one of the reasons why we have decided to support the extension. It gives us seven thousand more households, a reservoir of new people to refill our pews. The other–'

'I don't think it's a lack of people in the area that is keeping church attendances down,' I interrupted, repaying the compliment. 'It's the demographics across the country – across the Western world. Attendance has been going down since the nineteen-fifties.'

'The *other* issue,' he raised his voice, ignoring my point, 'is that we have been in high-level discussions with the local authority, who have suggested that they will look favourably on our tender to run the two new schools that will be built as part of the extension, but only as long as we are seen to be in favour of the proposal. The demographics argument is null.

The children will be taught in our schools and will start attending our churches as a result.'

He leaned back in his chair, a smug look on his face.

'And the existing residents will just have to accept it?' I asked. 'I think I know what the majority will think if the Church fails to support them on this issue. You're supporting the institution as opposed to the interests of the congregation. What are we supposed to say when they ask why we're not standing alongside them?'

'I wouldn't expect a village priest to understand,' he shook his head. 'It is simply a matter of scale and futureproofing. What looked like a bad situation for the Church may turn out to be a great opportunity for spreading the word of Our Lord. Not that it will be something you need to concern yourself with once our next item has been addressed.'

'I'm attending,' I insisted, with more than a touch of defiance. 'I couldn't look them in the eye if I didn't.'

He shrugged his shoulders as though he didn't care one bit, which was worrying. 'Now, Ted, could you please leave us,' he said. 'I have a rather unpleasant matter to discuss with Father McKay here.'

'I'd rather he stayed,' I said, wondering what rabbit he was about to pull from his hat.

'It's up to you, but you may wish for as few people as possible to be privy to this information,' the bishop smirked. 'I think you know what I'm talking about.'

I was confused, but I could see he was relishing this power trip, which only hardened my resolve. 'Ted stays,' I repeated, 'if he doesn't mind.'

Ted nodded, his face bright red. He hadn't said a word all meeting.

The door opened, and Paul's wife Sarah came in. I stood up to greet her, smiling, holding out my hand as she strode over and punched me square on the cheek, her engagement ring digging in, drawing blood, followed by a second shot hitting me in the ear. The ringing sound blocked out whatever it was she was screaming at me, 'dirty bastard' and 'pervert' definitely in there, as I reeled back, spinning away from the table, trying to get my bearings. Everything came into focus in slow motion, Bishop Gordon restraining her, guiding her to a seat as tears ran down her face. She was shaking with fury as she spat at me from across the room. I had an irrational hatred of spitting.

I retreated, as I always did when confronted with violence, allowing Peter through as Ted snapped out of his shock and moved towards me when I stepped forward, fists clenched. He placed his hand on my chest, enough to bring the sounds and surroundings back into focus. I looked at him and let out a long exhale, regaining control. I was trembling.

'If Paul was here, he'd fucking kill you,' she screamed.

'Wha– what?' I stammered, lost for words, 'I don't know–'

'Pervert,' she screamed again, sending a metal candle stand clattering off the table, clanging violently as it bounced on the hard stone floor, the sound reverberating around the small space.

Bishop Gordon took control, placing a pink phone on the table. It looked slightly improper in his hand, with its diamante trim catching the light, reflecting spots around the room. Ted picked it up as Sarah slumped down, crying.

'Give the phone to Father McKay,' Bishop Gordon instructed mechanically, like a Dalek.

Ted handed it over quickly, as if it was a burning cinder.

'Look at the pictures,' the bishop said, in the same automated tone.

I started scrolling through the photographs until I was faced with an image from the night before, of the girls cuddling and looking at the camera, their eyes big and red. They'd obviously been drinking.

'It's the pub,' I became incredulous. 'I'm sorry, but I don't see how it's my responsibility to–'

'Keep going through the pictures,' Bishop Gordon commanded.

I flicked through more of the same, more of the same until… there it was. I paused, shock washing over me. 'But…'

I was sat on the stool at the bar, mouth agape, looking up, eyes red. Amy was stood to the side of me, her top lifted, revealing her breasts; her friend stood squeezed in next to her, revealing a single breast of her own, both pouting at the camera.

My face turned red. I could feel my heart beating, hear the blood thundering in my ears. 'But I – I didn't see any of that. I was watching the football. I wouldn't ever–'

'She came home at three in the morning with love bites all over her neck,' Sarah hissed. 'You disgusting–'

'It wasn't me!' I shouted. 'I was talking to them. I was watching the football, having a drink on my own in the–'

'Liar!' she screeched, her face contorting as the rage resurfaced.

I felt Peter squirming in my mind, drawn to the emotions, the violence; locked away, but always there, as I took a breath, trying to subdue my rage.

'Have you asked Amy herself?' I asked gently, a drip of blood running down my cheek, like a red tear.

'She said it wasn't you, but they always say that, don't they? She probably thinks she's in love with you. They've been groomed in that club of yours. Look at the photo. If you've fucking–'

'I haven't touched your girls or any others,' I yelled over her, my fist slamming on the table as anger overpowered restraint, fuelled by the barbed comments, spreading like fire. I was furious. 'I wouldn't do that. I didn't know what they were doing. How could you think I would?'

'Well, you did do it. Look, it's there,' she jabbed a pointed finger towards the phone. 'Fuck you, I'm going to the police.'

'That's ridiculous, I haven't even–'

'You'll see how ridiculous it is when you're locked in a fucking cell,' she snarled. 'Do you know what they'll do to you in prison?'

With that, she snatched the phone out of my hand and stormed out of the vestry, her fading footsteps echoing through the chapel until they disappeared.

The silence was deafening.

I looked at Ted, and then to Bishop Gordon; one shocked, the other smug, before slumping down in my chair, placing my head in my hands. The adrenaline was wearing off, and now I was starting to feel tired, though at least the hangover was gone.

'It's not how it looks,' I said desperately. 'They were stood by me while I was watching the football. I had no–'

'The Ministry,' Bishop Gordon muttered. 'We've been hearing some worrying things about this club that you're running for the youth of the area. What happened last night has pretty much confirmed my suspicions. They play pool, they play chart music with no filtering of content, no censorship–'

'They are listening to this music every day,' I said quietly. 'They are all fifteen and sixteen years old.'

He took out a piece of paper before continuing. 'Instead of Bible readings, you have been talking about Canny West, an American whose songs are full of foul language and extreme references to sex and drugs, amongst other things.'

'I ask them what they want to talk about. This week it was Jesus Walks, a golden oldie by Kanye West–'

'Of course he walks. Couldn't call a bloody Uber, could he? Could walk on water, could–'

'We spoke about it for nearly two hours. Twenty children for nearly two hours. Some of them are inspired by it, some of them, it turns out, are not.' I leaned back on my chair, feeling exhausted. This didn't seem important. 'We discuss a different subject every week, usually inspired by modern culture. I give a priest's view. I'm not preaching or forcing sermons down their throats, otherwise they wouldn't come here. I'm just bringing Jesus and God into the conversation.'

'Oh, and what about prayer, hymns or psalms? What about learnings from the scriptures – the apostles? Do you not think we should be teaching these lessons to our children?'

'We discuss whatever questions they have, mostly about modern culture and science. Last week, they wanted to talk about Richard Dawkins. These kids are bright. The discussions are challenging.'

'Dawkins is an atheist. Why are you discussing the beliefs of an atheist in a church group?'

'Because that's what is relevant to them. We've had the woman's place in religion, evolution, consumerism, Islam, the migrant crisis, even abortion. They are not giggling children. They have views and opinions. They also have many questions.'

'And do you speak for the Church on these matters? You don't have a set of approved answers, since the Church itself does not have a single unified response to such questions. Do you chat about Dawkins, and how he attempts to disprove the existence of God?'

'I tell them what I think as a priest and a man of God – my own personal opinions, formed through my learnings from the Bible and other life experiences. I say that Dawkins is a reductionist. It doesn't matter how intelligent the man is, if God does not want to be found then Dawkins will not find him, whether you look up a hippo's arse or down a giraffe's neck. What are they even looking for anyway, a little bearded man?'

'But you shouldn't be–'

'How did one of the children put it again,' I cut him off, trying to recall the exact words. '"It's like opening the bonnet of Dad's car, and then saying there's no such thing as Jaguar because they've figured out how the engine works."'

'Well–'

'There's a bunch of them,' I went on, 'new atheists, who sell a lot of books offering some sort of proof of a non-existence, but they all end in disappointment, just a loop of self-referential logic – pop science. They are like evangelical preachers for their own religion, but are essentially parasites feeding off others, dependant on the survival of their host for existence. Good sound bites, though, and they sell a lot of books.'

'Humph,' Bishop Gordon sighed after a long pause, placing his palms on the table, having evidently failed to understand what I was saying. 'It's irrelevant anyway,' he wafted a hand dismissively. 'Here's what is going to happen.'

This time, I stopped to listen.

'There is a procedure we must follow. I'm going to accompany Sarah down to the station, and offer her support throughout the whole process. We don't know where this is going to end up, and the Church has to be seen to be supportive of her from the outset. You are suspended from all Church activities with immediate effect, until we have more details. The Ministry is to stop permanently, it is finished. Ted is to take over the youth group.'

'And what, you go back to four children singing around a guitar?' I scoffed. 'No disrespect to you, Ted.'

Ted just shrugged his shoulders.

'It's the way it has got to be, Peter,' Bishop Gordon said. 'You created this mess, and now you've dragged the reputation of the Church down with you.'

'But I'm innocent–'

'My job is to limit the damage that your actions will cause,' he continued, revelling in his role. 'Once we ascertain the severity of the charges against you, we will decide internally whether a moral sin has occurred. In the meantime, you will go home and wait, reflect on your sins and pray, though I must admit, I fear for you. I will pray for you also.'

'Thanks,' I replied, making no effort to mask the sarcasm, 'but you seem to have passed judgement already.'

Bishop Gordon put on his jacket, saying nothing else other than goodbye as his quick footsteps took him out of the vestry and through the chapel.

I glanced at Ted, who had a tear rolling down his face. He was only just holding himself together.

'I didn't do anything,' I said. 'I didn't see what they were doing. It's just not me.'

'I know,' he nodded. 'You wouldn't do that, I know. It was the violence that shocked me – I'm not used to it, and what do we say to people about the development?'

He started sniffling, and then he couldn't hold back the tears any longer, his body trembling as he tried to catch his breath. I held him as he started bawling and nestled in, making my shoulder wet, until his breathing gradually settled and the crying stopped.

I wondered if he had fallen asleep. It felt a bit peculiar.

'It'll be OK, Ted,' I reassured him, prising myself away from his grip, 'it'll all come out in the wash. She's got a good punch on her,' I joked, trying to lighten the mood as I began gathering my belongings. 'That boot camp training obviously works. Right, I'm off to join the protest. I'm in trouble anyway, so it can't make my situation any worse.'

'But–'

'Don't worry, Ted, it'll be OK,' I called back over my shoulder, trying to convince myself as much as him, as I walked along the aisle before hesitating, and then listening.

An unexpected hum of voices penetrated the room, faint, but getting louder; the sound of an approaching crowd.

I spun on my heels, hearing footsteps coming towards me. Ted was running over, his robes fanning out behind him, cheeks and chin wobbling as he stopped alongside me and we stood frozen, waiting, both thinking the same thing.

'Has word got around already?' he whispered.

I replied with a shrug as the noise increased, a chanting that we couldn't make out, the words indecipherable as voices intermingled. It was getting closer, appearing to stop outside the church yard, my heart pumping as adrenaline entered veins, hands clenching and reopening.

'*Perhaps we're about to see a bit of fire in the belly of Middle England,*' Peter giggled, disappointed when the sound continued its journey past the gate.

Ted opened the door a crack and peered out before opening it fully, finding the crowd of crusaders returning to the village from their field of battle, placards waving in the air, their chanting joyous, victorious.

Curiosity overcame fear, forcing us out to the church gate.

'What happened?' I shouted to Noddy, another village character whose real name I didn't know.

'They've gone,' he answered. 'The planners turned up, and after a meeting in the field with the contractors, they were instructed to vacate the site. There were a few suits down there that looked furious.'

Alf came across, wearing a broad smile on his face. 'Bloody hell, what happened to you? Ted been knocking you about?' he laughed, pointing to the blood on my cheek.

'What's going on now?' I asked, ducking his question.

'Turns out they didn't clear the site of wildlife before starting work, so they've had to stop.'

'But they did clear the area,' I said, a frown creasing my forehead. 'We saw the reports.'

'Well, they can't have done a very good job of it,' he placed a heavy arm on my shoulder, leading me to one side. 'As it happens, there's a badger sett in the hedge.'

'They had all the setts removed.'

'It appears there is a new sett, recently dug. They must have got through the wildlife fences somehow.'

'But–'

He raised his eyebrows as a big smile broke out across his face. 'You didn't really think we'd been shooting badgers, did you?' he sniggered with a wink. 'We also happened to discover a colony of great crested newts in the pond, an endangered species, though we might have overdone that one a bit – they were fucking everywhere. Sorry, Father. They could get into a bit of trouble over that one, trying to hide evidence of an endangered species. It should push them back for a few years anyway.'

For the first time that day, I laughed out loud. 'Alf–'

I suppose we have the Lord to thank for this, eh, Father? Must have been raining newts, or maybe the village should just buy a pint for Nobbler, who seems to be managing the wildlife wonderfully this year. Are you coming down the pub?'

'I'm afraid not,' I replied, despite wanting nothing more than a drink. 'There are a few things going on here.'

'Ah well, see you later, then. You know where we are if you get a thirst. We'll be there for a while, I reckon.'

He waved as he turned down the hill, kicking up dust on his way towards the village, enjoying his victory.

I turned and smiled at Ted, who was beaming, the extension problem solved, or kicked down the road at least. They were overturning centuries' worth of regulation, so I expected their reprieve to be brief, but there was a subtle brilliance to their protest.

Next, Roy and two police constables came by, making sure everything remained peaceful, no doubt all the way to the pub. He came over for a word.

'What's going on?' he asked. 'I've had a call through. I've got to go down to Paul's place to untangle one hell of a mess by the sounds of it. She *is* sixteen, so unless you forced yourself on her then you are legally OK, but–'

'Whoa,' I interrupted, 'I haven't done anything. I haven't been near her. They took a photo whilst I was unawares, which has been misinterpreted by Sarah, putting two and two together and getting five.'

'Well, I'm going there now. Where will I find you?'

'I'll be at home. I've already had enough of today.'

It wasn't even lunchtime, but more had happened in the last twenty-four hours than in the previous two years, and as I lay on the sofa staring up at the ceiling, I gave a small nod of acknowledgement, sensing the work of another. I felt better than I had in a long time, despite the allegations hanging over me, like my life was on play again after a long pause, lifting me out of my repetitive stupor.

Ibiza Chillout was playing, much more suited to the house and the mood; the opening bars of Barber's Adagio for Strings filled the room. It was beautiful, uplifting. *Perhaps the Church could do with a remix*, I thought, as I fell into a deep sleep, wondering if priests ever holidayed in Ibiza.

It felt like I'd only just drifted off when I was awoken by an urgent rapping of the front door. A pause, and then off it went again, *clack, clack, clack*, penetrating like an ice pick, forcing me to jump up quickly, grimacing as my neck protested about sleeping on the sofa.

I realised that it was dusk; I'd slept for most of the day. My mouth felt dry and furry.

*Clack, clack, clack*, the knocker drummed again, spurring me to move, to hasten towards the door, opening it slowly to find Roy standing there with the pale shape of Paul behind him. I held the door where it was, not open or closed, neither welcoming nor repelling, an involuntary reaction to seeing Amy's father, waiting to see how he would react.

'It's OK, Father,' Paul said, poking his head around Roy's shoulder, 'there'll be no trouble.'

I stepped back, opening the door fully as Roy removed his hat and walked through, solemnly followed by Paul. Taking their coats, I ushered them towards the sofa, offering tea, which, to my relief, was gratefully declined. I'd thrown last night's beer cans away, and the place looked fairly tidy, all things considered, as I sat in the upholstered armchair and leaned forward, hands together. It looked like I was praying.

There was silence that I had no intention of filling, so it was left to Roy to begin.

'Well, I've spent the afternoon getting to the bottom of what has gone on, and I'm glad to say you are not in trouble – not at all. Indeed, you have been a victim, if anything, Peter, so if you have any worries then please let them go.'

I felt a weight lift off me, even though I'd convinced myself I wasn't concerned.

'Good,' I said, offering very little, waiting for them to continue.

'We spoke with Amy, and she confirmed that it was nothing to do with you. Then, she got a bit emotional and, uh,' Roy turned to face Paul.

'You can tell him,' Paul said to his hands. 'He has a right to know, and it will stay inside these four walls.'

'Amy's affections are directed towards,' Roy cleared his throat, '*another* person, whom we have spoken to, and they have confirmed her version of events. We looked through further photos of the evening on another phone, and found one of Amy, uh,' he glanced at Paul again, getting a nod of assent, but he was clearly uncomfortable saying what had to be said. 'Kissing her friend. The other friend, who was, erm, exposing herself in the photograph.'

My mouth dropped open. 'You mean, she's a–'

'I think the word is experimenting,' Paul interjected. 'It's a bit of a long story, Father, but essentially, I brought the family out here looking for the good life, and it turns out that myself and my family have different ideas of what the good life is. They were enthusiastic enough at the start, but the reality is Amy and Chloe are bored. Their friends aren't here, and they were raised in London, shopping on Kings Road, visiting cafes, going to shows, galleries and the rest of it. The combination of their age and the change of scene means they are going off the rails a bit, I suppose, rebelling. I'm never here, so it's difficult for me to provide guidance, and Sarah is of pretty much the same opinion as them. I think they are trying to get at me by doing this sort of thing.' He looked traumatised by the whole affair. 'Also, I'd just like to say that I'm sorry, Peter, for what's gone on and, uh, Sarah's reaction. She should've thought it through before going off like that. She thinks the girls can do no wrong, so strikes out. It's always somebody else's fault. She's used to having things her own way, and the girls are growing up no different.'

Roy leaned closer to me, hands clasped. 'I have explained to Sarah that you have every right to press charges, for assault and–'

'No, no, no, I don't want this to go any further,' I said, holding up my hands like a pair of stop signs. 'I just want it finished. Let's not spoil what's been a great day for the village.'

'I thought you'd say that,' Roy sat back, his relief palpable. 'Great, now let's just get on with our lives – in the pub.'

'That bishop of yours looked a bit disappointed about the whole thing falling apart,' Paul added, lightening the mood. 'I think he was looking forward to a bit of drama. I'm not sure he's too keen on you.'

'Oh, he's alright,' I lied, 'we're just very different people. He thinks we should do things one way – I think we should do them another. We're chalk and cheese, but his heart is in the right place.'

'You should have seen his face when we found out what the girls had been getting up to,' Roy laughed. 'He nearly fell off his chair.'

'He kept saying, "the Church can help with this – the Church can help with this,"' Paul joined in, mimicking a jerky, panicked Bishop Gordon.

'Amy will be what she will be, and there is probably not a lot anyone can do about it. I'd love to watch the bishop giving a talk about sexuality, though,' I grinned, pleased to see smiles on all faces.

'Right,' Paul said decisively, as though drawing a line under it all, 'I insist on buying you dinner at the pub. We've ruined what should have been a good day for you, so please join us. I'm buying for you as well, Roy.'

I started to decline, but my gut told me otherwise. It was important to accept, show there was no animosity and stop the rumour mill before it started. Plus, I did not want to spend the evening alone with my thoughts.

We left the house, the walk beautiful as always. I pondered the two years I'd spent treading this same path, a neat triangle of home, church and pub, until we finally entered the latter, noisier and more raucous than I could ever remember. Most of the patrons had been there since lunchtime, and it showed.

'I think you need to go and have a chat with that lady,' Roy suggested, pointing to the bar, where Meg was sitting on the wrong side, looking bored as one of the drunken villagers talked at her.

I checked my shoes, an unconscious act, before I walked over, greeting everybody as I passed.

'Sorry to interrupt,' I announced myself. 'Any chance of a bit of service around here?'

'Ah, made it, did you?' Meg laughed. 'Wondered where you were.'

'Not working tonight?'

'Collateral damage, I'm afraid. I got sacked,' she grinned, 'always the sign of a good night.'

'What?'

'Sarah came in shouting an hour or so ago, showing Trev pictures of the girls in here drinking last night. Accused us of getting her daughters pissed, threatened us with the police, the usual. So, Trev laid me off, only for two weeks, between you and me, until the next drama comes along in the mad bitch's life, and she forgets about it.'

'But they've been in here buying alcohol for the girls themselves before today. "Better than them doing it in some field," were their exact words.'

'I know, but it's the easiest route for everyone. I feel a bit sorry for her, to be honest. She made quite a scene, screaming and shouting. The whole village was here, and I could feel them closing ranks. It's not the way people do things around these parts. The only thing more sacred than the church is the pub, and she stood right there defiling it, baring her teeth like a dog.'

'She spat at me.'

'What?'

Paul came floating over, making a point of focussing on me as Meg looked away. He knew, I could see it behind that practised smile, allowing me a glimpse behind the highly-polished façade of Paul and Sarah, a double act attacking on one hand and all conciliatory on the other; good cop, bad cop; Jekyll and Hyde. Somebody did have to take the blame for Amy's erratic behaviour, and their compulsion was to go straight for the heart of the village, the church and the pub, without a second thought; to scoop it out, to show their dominance. He was political, adept at deflection, manipulation, misinformation and covering up inadequacies by shifting blame, lashing out instead of looking in. Aiming for the priest, they'd missed, but they did bag a barmaid at least; not a bad day's shooting. The laughter and camaraderie of our little tete-a-tete earlier seemed stage-managed now, fabricated.

'Are you ready to order?' he asked, waving the menu a bit too cheerfully.

'I'm fine actually, Paul,' I replied without cheer, looking at him, making sure he knew that I was more than a little perturbed.

His eyes flicked to Meg, and then back, meeting and holding mine for a brief second before looking away, understanding, as the corners of his mouth turned up and slowly formed a smile, that urban fox out amongst the flock, changing the dynamic of the village.

'Ah, OK, then. Maybe tomorrow,' he shrugged, all contrived cheerfulness gone as he placed the menu on the bar and disappeared into the swaying crowd.

'I think you might have been a sacrificial lamb, I'm afraid. It may be my fault that you got the sack,' I confessed, turning back to Meg. 'Well, not my fault per se, but I was involved.'

'What are you going on about?' she asked, inquisitive creases materialising on her forehead, though the smile remained.

'Do you fancy going for something to eat? It's on me – I'm starving. Also, I just need to be away from here, truth be told.'

'Only if I can get you out of those robes – spend time with Peter for a bit,' she said, arching an eyebrow, unaware of what she was asking.

'I do have a casual section in my wardrobe,' I answered proudly.

Not to suggest that priests are tasteless or unfashionable, but we very rarely get the opportunity to wear nice clothes. Opening my wardrobe felt like stepping back in time, viewing in monochrome, black and white, probably the same garb clergy were wearing hundreds of years ago. A row of identical black clerical shirts, one for each day, hung next to a row of identical black trousers, with a small pile of plastic dog collars in a tray on the shelf completing the day-to-day outfit. On occasion, something a bit different was required, calling for a long cassock, surplice, tippet, alb and cinctures; my uniform to cover any eventuality, all in black, of course. It was only a long stole that brought any colour to proceedings, picked from a selection of white, gold, red, purple or green, depending on the season.

Where dogma ended, bright colours erupted from the hangers next to the monolithic block of black. It was predominantly jeans and shirts, lots of shirts, most only worn once, some still with labels attached. I'd often spend time browsing through clothes shops, the attendant, usually confused, asking, 'Are you buying for somebody, Father?' I found it difficult to resist, often spending a small fortune on a shirt that I'd probably never wear, logos a weakness, a residue of my upbringing.

I returned to the living room wearing jeans and blue-check Lacoste, its tiny green crocodile making me feel a little coy.

'*Woo*, look at you,' Meg teased, standing up and pulling my shirt out of my jeans – physical contact. 'Very nice. There's a man in there after all.'

Colour flushed my cheeks, as I reached for a drink to cool myself down. I didn't know what to say; I was unprepared.

'Is that aftershave I smell?' she asked, my face glowing again as I quickly brought the can to my lips, saved by a beep outside, telling us that the taxi had arrived.

'Thank you, God,' I whispered, as she made her way out and inelegantly clambered into the back of the waiting car, trying to maintain her modesty in a short dress, whilst I paused to recompose under the pretence of finishing my drink, which was already empty.

I climbed in alongside her, thighs touching, stress levels rising as we sat close together. I focussed on breathing. We'd spent many nights in each other's company, but this was the first time we'd gone out in public, going somewhere, together.

I was calculating, thinking about how I was supposed to feel; probably nervous. Convincing myself it meant nothing, but finding that feeling of hope, those butterflies they talk about, difficult to sate, it hit me that of all the men who had tried, it was me in the car with her. I should have experienced a swell of pride, of honour, of achievement; all those things, as I started anxiously bouncing my leg, wondering if I was acting it out right. It was a complex blend; the primary emotions much easier.

'Town please, mate,' she shouted, and then sat back with a smile.

It was already getting dark as the car began winding its way along the country lanes. I was looking out of the window, trying not to feel travel sick on my empty stomach, as the driver sped between tall hedges, around blind corners and over lurching humps, trying to get this fare finished and then on to the next. The droning voice on the radio was making me irritable.

*One of the pirate stations*, I presumed. *Out of their control.*

'This capitalism has to be continually reordered, otherwise it will consume itself,' the speaker was saying. 'It's a vital, inevitable process once the balance becomes so skewed to the benefit of a minority. Who knows what it will look like on the other side? Hopefully, the economy can become subservient to society again, not the other way around.'

'Can you turn that off please, mate?' I asked, but everybody was politicised as he held up an index finger, allowing the sermon to continue.

'The wealth is spread only to very few, there is no cycle of prosperity, the money is taken over seas, hoarded or invested in the next profit-making venture. Trickle down is probably the right phrase, a mere trickle to nourish the millions.'

'Mate?'

'This is important,' he complained, getting in a huff.

'I know, but just one night off.'

Meg seemed more relaxed, taking it upon herself to assume control of the conversation, chatting about her day and the scene in the pub. 'So, what happened to you?' she asked, once she'd finished telling her story.

'Patience, patience,' I said. 'I'll tell you when we get there.'

'Tease,' she grinned, squeezing my leg. 'Better be good, making me wait,' she stuck her elbow into my side as we came to the checkpoint, handing over our IDs as they inspected the boot.

I glanced out of the window at government #StrongerTogether slogans peeling off their boards, #underclass scrawled over them in thick sweeps of youthful energy.

The taxi dropped us off next to the Old Market Square, an attractive expanse of cobbles surrounded by Tudor and Georgian buildings, with a few shops and cafés tucked into the ground floors. It had a slightly continental feel, if you ignored the grim colonnaded sixties building at the bottom. The place was bustling with young people, walking from pub to pub, their voices loud, laughter ringing out.

Groups of boys moved with a swagger, boisterous, physical, pushing one another around, laughing, whilst the girls clattered about in heels on the uneven ground, holding hands or linking arms, trying to stay vertical. I was so used to the village, I felt on edge, as if violence could flare up at any moment.

*'You've been there too long,'* Peter complained. I found it hard to disagree, realising that I'd become cocooned in its established patterns of

life and behaviour; its predictability providing safety from people acting rash.

'What do you fancy?' I asked, looking around, feeling lost.

'Anything. We could just grab something quick,' she said, pointing at a mock Tudor van in a far corner of the square. 'What about a kebab?'

'Sounds good,' I smiled, almost laughing out loud, having pictured a sit-down meal in a nice restaurant.

We linked arms and wandered over, me conscious of her touch as I gazed up at the cylinder of grey meat getting a tan from the red heating elements, a crispy skin forming with clear fat dripping off into a stainless-steel tray. There was no queue; nobody in their right mind ate a kebab whilst sober.

Sitting on a mock-Victorian bench under the mock-Georgian streetlights, we scooped most of the salad into the mock-Tudor bin and started eating. It brought back memories of nights out, the inner city, a younger me, lonely. I glanced across at Meg, winking at me as she sucked her fingers, savouring the last bit of flavour. I laughed, offered her my tissue, which she wiped across her mouth, smudging her lipstick. There was no elegant way to eat a kebab, it was always primal, the plastic fork useless as the bread fell apart. You had to get your hands dirty.

'That was amazing,' she groaned, leaning back against the hard wood.

She was right. I could have sat there all night, watching, learning what they do.

'Pint?' I suggested, pointing towards the Rose, another shit-hole.

'Pint,' she nodded in agreement. 'You take me to such classy places.'

The pub didn't need bouncers as not many people went there, and those sitting around the bar didn't look capable of trouble. The aroma was stale beer, the décor minimal, and not in a sleek designer sense; they just didn't have any, which gave the room its own character.

'Do you want to go somewhere else?' I asked.

'Nah, this is fine,' she said. 'Nice and quiet.'

A large man was sat on a bar stool, taking up most of the serving space, forcing me to the end of the bar, near the wall. The top of his arse was peeking above a low-slung waistband, his stomach flopping over the front. I was surprised that he could fit on the one stool.

I concentrated on catching the attention of the bored-looking barmaid, holding a note between my fingers until she noticed it twitching and took my order. My eyes were irresistibly drawn towards the large man as his sweaty fragrance reached my nostrils, building up to an unbearable crescendo until the pints clattered onto the bar and I scurried off to our table, almost gagging, leaving a trail of drips as I went. There was something unnatural in that stench.

'Here's your change,' the barmaid called over.

'Keep it,' I replied, wiping my eyes. I couldn't have gone back over there.

'Very generous,' Meg pouted. 'Why don't I get nice big tips like that?'

'Because you're the lucky barmaid who gets to go to the pub with me,' I replied, as she arched that single eyebrow in response.

The empties started to pile up, and I started to relax. We talked about the day's occurrences; she thought the photo was hilarious, and sat, mouth agape, as I told her about Sarah, pointing to the cut on my cheek, and how I'd also been laid off for improper conduct.

'She's even madder than I gave her credit for. Maybe she does belong in the village after all,' she laughed. 'Didn't you tell her that you had an alibi?'

'No, I kept you out of it,' I said, feeling a bit of colour return to my cheeks. 'I knew it was rubbish, so I didn't see the point of dragging you into it, even though you did end up involved somehow.'

'A dirty little secret, am I?' she tilted her head, acting demure, like they do.

'I'm not sure they'd believe me if I'd told them you came around for a disco,' I laughed, the truth stranger than fiction.

We each looked down at our drinks, and then up at each other, no smiles, just looking, a long pause where the sounds, smells and sights of the pub disappeared, leaving just us. The last orders bell rang, breaking the silence.

'One for the road?' I asked, our usual catchphrase.

'I'm not sure I want to go home just yet. Shall we go for a dance? It's not like we've got work tomorrow, and the place over the square has a late licence and some cheesy music.'

I remembered the negative feelings I'd experienced that morning, the self-loathing. *I'm a priest*, I thought, as a wave of guilt washed over me.

*'And here you are again,'* Peter whispered.

'Don't worry, I'll look after you,' she assured me, sensing my hesitation. 'There'll be no photos of scantily clad teenagers with their tits out tonight.'

'Oh, well in that case, I'm going home,' I joked nervously, predictably; observing, calculating.

Dancing it is.


The club was half empty, with few hitting the dance floor; mainly groups of girls and the odd couple of guys dancing in their vicinity, moving sideways, trying to edge their way in. The music was loud, nineties cheese, difficult to talk, so we just danced, beers in hand, bathed in multi-coloured lights shining through the clouds of smoke that blew out every two minutes. There was something desperate about it, that stage before everybody is pissed enough, as a strobe went off like a lightning bolt, the club's own internal weather system. I watched Meg as she disappeared, becoming just a silhouette, before reappearing as the smoke drifted away, ready for the next cloud to blow over.

It started getting clammy as the place filled up, alcohol lowering inhibitions and more men daring to dance. I looked up at Meg, saw that her silhouette was changing, getting bigger with each flash of the strobe. Then, as the smoke cleared, a man became visible, arms wrapped around her, holding her from behind with his chin resting on her shoulder. I stopped dancing and stared, unsure of what to do as she beckoned me over to the side of the dance floor, the man walking alongside until we got to a quieter part of the club.

'This is Dan,' she shouted.

I offered him my hand, which he accepted with a smile. *Must be a friend*, I thought.

'He's my boyfriend,' she continued, no smile on her face as she explained to Dan who I was, back to being the village priest, with no mention of Peter.

I wasn't listening anyway, I was feeling something, like I'd been winded. The smile remained as I nodded along, but inside I was getting it right, collapsing piece by piece, the feeling compounding, getting worse with each minute, becoming a physical pain, a weight, a sickness in the pit of my stomach.

Dan reached over to give me another handshake. 'Great to meet you,' he said.

'You too,' I replied, as he kissed Meg on the cheek, her eyes fixed on me, staring through the smile until she turned around and he led her to the dance floor, disappearing into the smoke.

'*Fuck off,*' Peter hissed.

She beckoned me to follow, but I stayed still, feet planted to the ground, trying to capture the sensations, wondering what physical reactions were appropriate.

'*This is where you go and smash his face in,*' Peter suggested helpfully. '*It's what normal people do.*'

Alone again, I edged my way through the crowd, returning outside to the cool air. It had just gone midnight, couples were kissing in doorways, and I fled the shadows in pursuit of the light of the square, feeling overloaded by my only emotion, rage, which I turned on to myself. A thousand questions and told-you-so's battled for dominance; there was nothing positive, as all pointed downwards towards disappointment and capitulation.

A drunken taxi queue wasn't the place to be in this frame of mind, so I decided to walk, as I often did after drinking. There was no point getting home quickly, no way I'd sleep, so I followed the winding, cobbled streets past striped canopies and the illuminated tower of the flint cathedral, before continuing into the urban sprawl, suburbia, a characterless expansion of identical houses on straight roads, a portent of the future.

Walking quickly, head down, deep in thought, my shadow flipped from front to back as I passed under the evenly-spaced street lights until  the rows of houses ended, giving way to industrial units, hulking sheds with empty car parks covered in broken glass, glistening as the movement-sensitive lighting clicked on, a glittering path now showing the way. No fuzzy edges or soft boundaries, it was a dead, soulless, clinical piece of zonal planning, finishing as abruptly as it had started.

I climbed over the stile into a field, away from the streetlights, away from people, into the darkness, my thoughts becoming more rational as I walked along the edges of the grass, away from the town now a hazy glow receding behind me. Anger gradually lost its potency, replaced by acceptance. This was, after all, the path I had chosen, and she was just the latest, but then at the same time, she was different than the others; she had inspired feelings, perhaps even real emotion. Rage became relief, providing comfort; it was just a game really, walking to a line and daring myself to cross it, knowing that I would not, desperate but terrified of the love that God could not give.

The moon was bright, helping me to make good time as I concentrated on avoiding rabbit holes or furrows in the ploughed fields, putting thoughts on the backburner and feeling a sense of peace again, alone in the darkness. I knew the route without thinking, placing one foot carefully in front of the other, occasionally slipping over or tripping on a divot or tree root, as stinging nettles and brambles brushed against my hands and legs, not painful enough to merit concern or hinder progress. There were beautiful moments, unique to the countryside at night; the sound of horses galloping unseen in the fields as they sensed an intruder, the barn owl flying overhead, looking for its next meal; and the rustling of deer, descended from the safety of the forest to feed amongst the farmer's crops. I forgot myself for a while.

After walking for an hour, I found myself on Alf's land, and as I came over the crest of a hill, I stopped to look down at the village. The church stood, illuminated in the valley, the only source of light, houses imperceptible within the dark mass of surrounding trees and hedges. Everybody would be asleep; all the politics, personalities, egos, tensions, jealousies, loves and hates on pause until consciousness returned in the morning, when the status quo would resume in this rural bubble.

My eyes looked up at the past, at constellations painting the clear sky, wondering if any sort of sign would appear, like a shooting star telling me that I'd be OK, but nothing, just points of light that had travelled for millions of years, ending their journey here, now; what a waste.

'Evening, Father.'

I let out a frightened yelp, as a voice came out of the pitch-black bush to my side, sending me stumbling on the uneven pathway, until I fell to the ground in slow motion.

'They have to be on fire before they start talking,' I cried out, as a shape slowly emerged from the darkness, a pair of glistening eyes, the rest of the features blacked out, the body detaching from shadows, like Virgil coming to give me a guided tour of hell.

It was holding a gun.

'Erm,' I said, not sure of what to do next, my mind racing, trying to think who I may have upset as it stared at me silently, blinking occasionally.

*'They've found you,'* Peter warned, as a cold shiver passed through me.

'Shooting foxes, Father,' it whispered softly, before smiling, showing a set of teeth to go with the eyes.

There was one tooth missing. It was Nobbler.

'Fucking hell!' I let the back of my head sink down against the dewy grass.

'Didn't scare you did I, Father?'

'Just a bit,' I managed a laugh, my heart feeling like it could burst out of my chest as he bent over to offer me his hand, pulling me up off the ground.

'Glorious, ain't it, Father?' he proclaimed, pointing up to the sky as I dusted myself off. 'I saw you stargazing.'

'Yes,' I replied, still trembling, 'it's incredible.'

'Most people don't even bother looking up these days. Too busy watching reality TV or the talent shows.'

'Or staring at their smart phones.'

We both took a moment to stand quietly, just looking.

'God's work?' he asked after a while.

'I think so.'

'It doesn't really fit with the Bible, though, does it? The world created in six days and all that. I'm not religious, as you probably know.'

'Yes, everyone goes for that, Genesis, but if you read it allegorically it does make sense. The original word, used in the Hebrew Bible, just means a period of time. It can be a day or a million years, or anything in between. If you look at it literally, as in an earth day, like the creationists do, it obviously doesn't work so well. "Day four populates the darkness and light with sun, moon and stars."'

He produced a hip flask from his pocket, taking a swig before offering it across. 'Something to keep you warm?'

'Why not,' I replied, taking it from his hand and swallowing a gulp, wincing at the taste, feeling the whisky warming my insides before handing it back. 'Thank you.'

'I spend a lot of time up here with the stars, so I've done a lot of reading about them, about the universe. It's amazing to read about it, and then to come and look at it, to think through the enormity of it all.'

'I agree. Whatever your beliefs, you cannot fail to be humbled by its magnificence – its vastness.'

'And here we are, two tiny specks in a field on our spinning rock, amongst millions of galaxies, hurtling through space and time in an ever-expanding universe. Cheers,' he saluted, before taking another mouthful.

'Blows your mind,' I replied, the whisky kicking in, topping up the Stella.

'I thought science had taken God out of the story.'

'It's pretty much the opposite, actually. They all point to the Big Bang, an explosion of light and energy, a singular event where everything was created from nothing. "God said, 'Let there be light!' so there was light." I think that points pretty conclusively to the possibility of a creator.'

'There's no proof, though, is there? I'm more into the scientific solutions myself. None of this metaphysics nonsense.'

'I only said the *possibility* of God. There's no proof of anything before the Big Bang, but at the same time, you can't make something out of nothing, and every effect has a cause. Two good scientific principles for you there.'

'But science suggests that God is just man's way of understanding everything we don't understand.'

'Or, science is just man's way of figuring out how God did it.'

'All of this could have just happened by chance.'

'It could have, but that doesn't sound very scientific, does it? None of the scientific reasoning is any more proven than the idea of God. It's impossible to prove anything before the Big Bang, since space, time and scientific laws didn't exist. It's metaphysical, beyond physics, but consider this. Life could never have existed if there was the tiniest variation in the properties of the Big Bang. A change in the law of gravity by one billionth, for example, and none of this would be here,' I waved my hand across the sky for effect. 'It would have imploded on itself, or flown apart, never forming molecules.'

'Well, yes, but–'

'And then there's the density parameter. If it varied by more than one part in a million billion, just one second after the Big Bang, the universe would not still be expanding. Plus, the fact that spacetime has just three physical dimensions, and that if the measure of nuclear efficiency varied by even a minute amount, there would be no hydrogen, meaning none of this.' I was waving my hands at the sky again, and then pulling the head off a stalk of corn, showing it to him in my palm.

'The Anthropic Principle?'

'Yes, that's it. There are some other things, but I just can't remember them right now. Something about unevenness in the Big Bang and density in the universe. I read a lot, too. An armchair scientist.' I swayed slightly, realising I was as drunk as he was. 'Where was I?'

'Unevenness in the Big Bang.'

'Oh yes. What I am trying to say is that the Big Bang was perfect for life in too many improbable ways for it to have just been chance.'

'There is the multiple universe theory, where we are constantly in a cycle of big bangs and big crunches, as the universe expands and collapses back in on itself,' he said authoritatively. 'If it happens infinite times, the perfect combination will come up at some point.'

I nodded, acknowledging his point, a good one. 'That sounds similar to the Hindu Vedas,' I said, 'where the world is in a constant cycle of creation and destruction every eight billion years or so. A day and night of Brahma.'

'There's also the parallel worlds idea – parallel universes.'

'Doesn't the parallel universe idea click in neatly with God, though? Heaven and hell, all of that stuff?' I shrugged. 'I'm sure there are an infinite number of theories you could put forward, but aren't these just overcomplicated guesses? Isn't science supposed to be based on the simplest explanations? Stephen Hawking says there must be trillions of other universes, and nobody bats an eyelid, everyone says OK, because that is what he needs to make his theory work. Anyone mentions the G-word, and everyone shrieks in horror.'

'I'm just saying, there are viable alternatives to God.'

'I agree, all are as viable as each other. At the end of the day, we may just be the other side of a black hole. All of that stuff must go somewhere.'

'Makes sense. Everything moving away from a point, expanding as more stuff is sucked up.'

'The Big Bang could just be a black hole,' I said, the idea dawning on me for the first time. 'Once you get past the event horizon, all of our laws of physics no longer apply. Nobody knows what's on the other side, and surely, if there is a black hole, according to scientific reasoning, there must also be a white hole, where things appear. All of that material must go somewhere.'

'That could be it,' he exclaimed, joining me in pissed-up epiphany, 'there are millions of them. It's not multiple universes, it's multiple black holes, like bubble bath, each unique, this one suitable for life.'

'Could all be suitable.'

'Oh, so we're not God's only pets?' he laughed, taking another nip of whisky, our eyes never leaving the sky.

'Who knows?' I smiled. 'God might have lots of little projects on the go. Given the vastness of the universe, I'd say it's improbable, almost impossible, that we are the only life.'

'Didn't expect you to say that,' he grinned.

The conversation went into a lull as we both stared.

'I'd better get back,' I broke the silence, 'get my head down.'

'Yeah? I'm gonna hang around for a bit. The foxes are long gone – I'll just have a think about our chat. It's the best place to do it, with the subject matter in front of me.'

'I've enjoyed it,' I said, patting him on the shoulder. 'We should talk more often. It's not all about God with me, you know. I'm interested in pretty much everything.'

'Me too. You've surprised me tonight, I'll admit.'

'You're surprised?' I replied quickly. 'Not nearly as surprised as I am, believe me.'

'A lot of people have this preconception of me as a gamekeeper, but I just let them get on with it,' he shrugged. 'Alf knows the truth, though. I have no interest in money, I just love what I do. Even if I had money, I'd still be doing this.'

'Then you're very lucky. There are not many people who can say they're happy with what they've got – content with their lives.'

'Including you?'

'Sometimes,' I admitted, looking back towards the village.

'You might consider going out of that gate, Father – walk down the lane. You never know, you could see something interesting.'

Those were his final words, emanating from the black as he returned to his three-legged throne.

I considered going to sit in the church for a while, in the darkness, so I could feel at peace and think, but then the church hadn't been calm of late, its ambience tainted by anger and rage. I continued towards the cottage, down the dark lane, like Nobbler suggested, almost walking past the overgrown entrance to one of Alf's fields before a reflection of the moon caught my eye.

I stopped and walked back, taking a second glance. It was one of Paul's Range Rovers, barely visible, black and hidden behind the overhanging branches. Strange. I took a step towards it, hearing giggles inside.

'Shit,' I whispered, retreating back into the shadow of the hedge, glancing around to make sure I was alone and not part of some dogging engagement.

*'What are you doing?'* Peter complained.

I wasn't sure, but curiosity kept me there until the car door opened and Charlotte, Alf's daughter-in-law, climbed out, adjusting her skirt and buttoning up her blouse as I stood in the hedge, frozen. I could hear my heart beating as sex permeated the air, the surgeon now wandering naked in the field next to me.

Paul leaned over and kissed her, a long kiss, as he turned the key in the ignition, the lights coming on, bathing the surroundings in red as the light inside flicked off, casting him in darkness. I slowly pushed myself back further into the hedge, trying not to make a sound, the crack of the odd snapping twig concealed by the smooth humming engine.

Charlotte walked past quietly, facing forwards, in the direction of the farmhouse that she shared with her husband and two children, as Paul reversed out and drove the other way, to his sleeping wife and three children. They were both very similar in many ways: from the city, ambitious, materialistic.

'*What an incestuous little place*,' Peter chuckled as I clambered out of the hedge.

I slid the key in the lock and entered, thinking how different things had become since I'd left only hours before, a starry-eyed idiot full of hope, like a teenager. Nobbler and Paul had been a distraction and negative thoughts and emotions were now creeping back, starting with a whimper, and then kicking and screaming as I sat on the sofa in darkness, entombed behind the thick stone walls.

I remained awake, too frightened to surrender to the vulnerability of sleep, as the alcohol began its slow withdrawal from my system. My eyes were dry, red, my thoughts a flood of negativity; deep, dark currents, a turbulent swirling, sluggish and massive. It was tortuous as time dragged, the hands of the clock travelling agonisingly slow, memories from another life fighting for ascendency as the faint light of the new dawn came creeping in, turning all colours sepia.

A gentle tapping permeated my thoughts, pausing the currents as I was drawn from my history, breaking the surface, gasping for air as the memories quickly fell away, leaving only fear. The tapping started again; it was the front door.

'*Paul*,' Peter cursed.

I clambered off the sofa and staggered into the hallway, using the walls as support before pausing, scrutinising the dark silhouette standing motionless behind the patterned glass panel.

It was Meg.

I opened the door, my heart thumping.

'Hi,' she said, pausing as we considered each other. 'Can I come in?'

I nodded, standing to one side to let her pass straight through to the living room, the dance floor, turning on the light as she sat down. She had been crying; her mascara smudged down her cheeks.

'Are you OK?' was all I could think to say.

'Yes, you?'

I nodded, as fear starting to rise within me. I'd been primed for this last night, but now I was vulnerable, unprepared. 'Stella?' I asked.

'I owe you an apology,' she began, speaking quietly, looking down towards the floor. 'I didn't know Dan was going to be there.'

'I think it's me that owes the apology,' I replied, 'I – I...' I moved to sit next to her on the sofa, like a tongue-tied teenager, not knowing what to say.

'He's – Dan's a good guy, but he's just a boyfriend,' her words tapered off into a whisper, as a teardrop fell onto her hands, clasped tightly in her lap. 'That's why I didn't tell you about him.'

Another teardrop fell.

'He seems nice,' I said, both angry and thankful that Dan existed; another barrier, another excuse.

'He is, but he's not...' she looked up at me, her eyes wide, trembling slightly. 'I don't love him. Well, I do, but...'

The tears were freefalling down her face, out of sync, I observed, as her eyes returned to her lap. I wondered if I should be feeling guilt for this collateral, but love was to blame.

'It's not your fault,' I said reassuringly, handing her a tissue out of my pocket, already covered in lipstick and kebab. "There's nothing wrong with you having a boyfriend, a normal life. I'm the weird one that lives by this set of rules.'

I'd started erecting my wall, curling down safely behind it, but she looked over it and shook her head.

'There's something else,' she said. 'It's *you*. Why can't I just say it? I...'

I held my breath throughout the pause.

'I have feelings for you, Peter,' she got it out, smiling through the tears, giving a self-depreciating shrug, as if it were a personal failing.

My heart jumped, like it's supposed to, as I placed a conciliatory hand onto her shoulder, a lump forming in my throat as a feeling of achievement flushed through me.

'Me too,' I blurted out unexpectedly, each word sounding strained and high pitched as I stood before the barrier, stress levels rising, sensing the approaching danger.

Game on.

Her smile grew, blissfully unaware of the battles within me. 'I thought it was just me,' she said. 'I didn't want to spoil anything. It's difficult to know what to do with your... well, you're a priest.'

'I know. It's complicated, and I'm naïve,' I said, wondering where this shit was coming from. 'I thought I'd been seeing things that were not there. Things that I wanted to be there.'

Her hand found mine, our fingers entwining, my mind screaming run as I strained every muscle staying still, convincing myself that I was in control.

'I've never had a girlfriend,' I said. 'I'm like an inexperienced teenager when someone pays attention to me. I don't know what to do.'

She leaned over and kissed me on the lips, her hand going around my neck, holding me. I paused, flinching as I did everything I could to stay there, waves of panic washing over me as my hand reached across, touching her arm, feeling that feeling, that I was leaving my body. She pulled back and looked at me, leaving a long pause, like they do in the movies, before placing her head in my lap and letting out a big sigh, exhausted.

'Will you just hold me?' she asked.

I nodded, unable to speak, a scream stuck in my throat as I felt the weight of her on my thighs. I tried to become rational, scientific; to categorise the sensations, feeling the warmth of her body, detecting the smell of old perfume, before glancing down and then turning away from the curve of her breasts disappearing into her top, rising and falling with each breath. We were both silent, careering between happiness and panic; mostly panic.

'It's messy, isn't it?' she murmured. 'I love you, but I can't be with you. You're married to the Church. We don't fit.'

'Let's just have this night,' I said, relieved that she'd provided the get-out. 'Stay where we are for now, and think about the rest tomorrow.'

I was starting to relax. I'd pushed the barrier, but we wouldn't go any further. I could enjoy the moment, take satisfaction in her words, knowing that I was loveable, even though it was a fiction, a delusion, a social construct.

After a long silence, she sat up. 'Can I stay?' she asked, flipping me back into panic.

Not waiting for a reply, she stood up from the sofa and took my hand, leading me upstairs to the bedroom, my body hesitant, mind racing, looking for an escape. Peter was prowling, contemplating violence.

'I can sleep downstairs,' I said pleadingly, tripping over my tongue as I paused in the doorway, relieved that the bed was made at least. It had been so long since I'd slept in it.

'It's OK, I'm not going to jump on you, Peter,' she laughed. 'I know you have your vows, and I don't want to be the one to make you break them. I just want to be with you tonight.'

She walked into the room, lifting her dress above her head and letting it drop to the floor before turning to face me. I watched as it fell in slow motion before looking up at her, standing in black lingerie. She was beautiful.

I let out an audible gasp, the terrors flooding over me, forcing me to avert my eyes, not sure where to look.

'Erm,' I began to stammer, like a computer with a glitch, 'Erm, erm, I'll sleep on the sofa.'

'No,' she lay down on the bed. 'Turn the light off if you're nervous.'

'Not nervous,' I said, having gone well beyond nervous, now approaching terrified, as I tried to hold myself together, 'just not a normal Friday night. More like a Saturday.'

This was the moment, the test where I had to prove myself to myself, summoning all of my strength as my hands moved to my belt buckle, fighting to stop the trembling as I undid my trousers, letting them fall, trying not to trip as I moved to my shirt, where I fumbled nervously with the buttons. I hadn't done this in front of a woman before.

There was a sharp intake of breath, held, followed by a long exhalation as it dropped to the ground. An emotion filled 'Peter' was all she said, as she sat up, no longer confident and sensual, just staring, her eyes moving up and down, taking it all in.

'What happened to you?' she asked.

I stood silent, unable to speak, shaking my head side to side like a child, as my arms instinctively folded across my body. It had gone badly. I wasn't ready. I wanted to run.

'You're covered in scars,' she said, our eyes meeting. "There's hardly an empty space. Who–'

I shook my head, no, my eyes returning to the ground, where they stayed for what seemed like an eternity before she reached out a hand, which I hesitantly took, switching off the light and climbing in next to her, lying still, my senses alert to the slightest movement or sound. I felt her foot slowly move across and place itself on top of mine. I held my breath, and then let it out slowly as she left it there, touching, our bodies coming together as I lay, tears streaming down my face, cowering before the images in my head.

# CHAPTER 3

PUPPET

I was awoken with a start by the crack of gunshot, as the sunlight streamed through the window. It went again, *crack, crack,* echoing through the valley as another cumbersome pheasant broke cover, fleeing from the beaters and flying for its life over the line of waiting guns.

A spray of lead and puff of feathers; the shoot had begun.

I looked across the bed at Meg, on her side, propped up on one elbow, looking at me, smiling. 'I wondered when you'd wake up.'

'What time is it?' I asked, feeling self-conscious. I couldn't imagine I looked particularly attractive whilst sleeping.

'Not sure.'

'How long have you been awake?'

'About an hour.'

'You could've put the kettle on,' I joked.

'Too busy looking at you,' she grinned, gently punching me on the shoulder and biting her lip. 'Are those initials?' she pointed at one of the crude markings on my body.

'Yes,' I replied, remembering the moment, the blade and the blood. I covered it up, not wishing to engage, as I lay silent, looking away.

'Quite a night last night, wasn't it?' she changed tack, laying her head on the pillow.

'I can't remember anything after the pub,' I teased, staring up at the ceiling as she punched me again, this time a bit harder.

'I'm glad it happened,' she said. 'I was gutted when Dan turned up. I nearly started crying there and then.'

'Yes, I didn't see that coming,' I said, before pausing to consider my next words. 'At least we know where we are with each other now.'

'It's not just you,' she sighed, 'I've tried to say it so many times. I don't know how it will work out. I love you, but I can't… well, you know.'

'I know,' I turned to face her. 'I'm a priest, and I carry the baggage that comes with it, but, as mad and antiquated as it seems, I believe in it. Last night, I wished I didn't. I don't believe in sex before marriage, and although I don't know Dan, I could never go behind his back – it's just not me. What's that quote from the Bible again – "never touch another man's rhubarb?"'

'I wouldn't want you to change, Peter,' she smiled, and then after a pause added, 'Well, maybe just a bit. You're the only man I know with real morals and beliefs, and whether I share them or not, it's one of the things I love about you, even though it keeps us apart. We've slept in the same bed, and you didn't try to touch me. Not even a cheeky elbow in the tit,' she tipped me a wink.

'Waited till you were asleep for that,' I smiled back. 'Surprised they're not black and blue.'

'I just hope it's not because you don't want to?' she arched that eyebrow again.

'Of course I want to. You're the most beautiful thing I've ever seen.' It all seemed easier to say in the morning. 'Although, you *are* the first woman I've shared my bed with, so I've no comparisons to draw. You might be rubbish.'

She leaned across and prodded me, and then started gently mussing my hair. 'I love you, Peter, but I don't love the priest, and it's such a huge part of you.'

Two more cracks outside, and another one bites the dust.

'You couldn't see yourself living here, with me?' I asked, with a hint of sarcasm. 'Life wouldn't be so different. You wouldn't have to change, become all pious.'

'Is that a proposal? Aren't you supposed to get down on one knee?'

'Nah, I already know what the answer would be.'

'You don't belong here anyway. You'll move on soon.'

My insides jolted as I considered just how transparent I actually was, whilst two more cracks reverberated around the valley, another life lost.

'So, what now? What do we do?' I asked. 'Just carry on as normal?'

'I suppose that's all we can do,' she said, climbing out of bed and standing in front of me in her black underwear, the pale morning light illuminating her skin. 'See where we end up.'

Nervous, my eyes returned to the ceiling.

'You can look at me, Peter,' she frowned. 'I know you can't touch me, but you can look.'

I sat up. The terror, fuelled by alcohol and darkness in the night, had since diluted, and as she slowly unclipped her bra, letting it drop to the floor, revealing full white breasts. I stared, my mind completely empty as she then slid her knickers down over her thighs, letting them drop silently and stepping out of the pile they made with her bra on the floor.

She stood straight, looking at me, bold and confident. I looked away again; couldn't help it.

'Look at me, Peter,' she urged, gently.

I did as she asked.

'Wherever we end up, I want you to remember me,' she said. 'I love you more because you didn't touch me, but maybe one day things will be different. One day, I hope you will.' She smiled, and then turned to leave the room. 'I'm going for a shower. Put the kettle on.'

I lay there for a while, thinking about how much I'd achieved with Meg, the situation having developed much further than I'd dared anticipate, as against all instincts, I'd stayed. Peter remained silent, never one for giving credit, as I found last night's clothes crumpled on the floor and quickly pulled them on before descending the stairs to make some tea. I gave the smiling crocodile a kiss, feeling slightly euphoric, savouring the moment.

Ten minutes later, Meg followed me downstairs, drying her long hair with a towel as she entered the kitchen, where two hot cups sat waiting on the table.

'What are you up to today?' I asked, choosing small talk, unable to think of anything more significant to say.

'I'm probably going to meet Dan,' she answered.

A pang of anger, and then relief, passed through me before easing away. I nodded; it was the way it had to be.

'How about you?' she asked. 'Are you going to the fete?'

'Not sure,' I said, realising that I'd completely forgot about it. 'I'm still suspended, I think. I'll just see where the day takes me.'

The doorbell rang, and we both jumped up with a start, each looking to the other for direction.

'Upstairs,' I eventually mouthed, flicking my eyes to indicate the way, which she duly followed, leaping two steps at a time.

I entered the hallway to find Ted's face squashed against the glass of the front door, deformed, cheeks red and puffing. I let him in, and he fought to catch his breath as he bustled past and picked up Meg's tea, taking a mouthful.

'I've just come to make sure you're OK after yesterday's dramas,' he said, 'and to apologise. I think I should have stood up for you more with the bishop. Lovely tea,' he took another sip. 'I need to be a bit more like you. I need to be stronger and speak my mind.'

'I'm fine,' I said, 'and you have nothing to apologise for. It came as a shock to everyone, not least me. I'm just glad it's all done and dusted now.'

'Are you coming to the fete?' he asked, his eyes scouring the table and worktops for biscuits. 'I've got you down for judging the vegetables.'

'As exciting as that sounds, I'm still suspended. The bishop hasn't made contact, so you're going to have to do all of the services on Sunday, I'm afraid.'

'But he knows you didn't do anything,' Ted scowled. 'What's he waiting for? How am I supposed to get around three churches in one day?'

'Who knows what goes on in that man's head. Anyway, I was just about to get a shower, if you'll excuse me,' I nudged him towards the door as he finished off the tea, oblivious. 'Hopefully, the bishop will be in touch sooner rather than later, and I'll be able to share the load.'

I closed the door behind him, and then opened it again to retrieve my cup from his trembling hand.

Meg reappeared at the bottom of the stairs, her hair now dry. 'I don't even get a cup of tea, eh?' she smiled. 'Treat them mean, keep them keen, is it?'

'I think living with a priest may be too fast for you after all.'

She laughed, giving me a hug and a kiss on the cheek. 'I hope I've left you with some nice memories,' she whispered, before following Ted out the front door.

The house was silent again as I sat in the armchair, feeling content with my performance. Things were messier than ever, but a woman had feelings for me, felt some love, though apparently not enough. The creak of the garden gate intruded, opening and closing, the latch carefully put back into place. I would usually hear footsteps on the gravel before anyone made that far along the path, like an early warning system, so I placed my cup down and hurried to twitch the curtains in time to see without being seen.

It was Paul.

I'd forgot all about that particular predicament, and now my thoughts were back on last night. The affair raised a new set of problems, as I asked myself, *Where do my responsibilities lie? Do I speak to Paul? Do I speak with Charlotte? How will Alf feel if he knows I withheld information from him?* By saying nothing, I was allowing it to continue before all the sordid details eventually came pouring out, as they always do.

'This isn't confession. There's no right to confidentiality,' I mumbled to myself.

'*Fuck him,*' Peter recommended.

The metal knocker rapped on the door, a short machine-gun burst, disturbing both the peace and my mood, but I had no choice but to transform my frown into a painted smile and offer a cordial greeting.

'Morning, Paul. What can I do for you?' I asked, standing back, blinking rapidly. He'd really gone for it with the tweed this morning, a new outfit for the shoot, difficult to bring into focus. *Maybe if I stare long enough, a three-dimensional image will appear*, I thought, choosing to keep him on the step. 'How was the shoot? I heard you banging away.'

*Did I really just say that?*

'Morning, Father,' he replied. 'It was a good morning – bagged a few birds.'

*Did he really just say that?*

There was a momentary pause before he continued. 'Father, Ted told me you might not be coming to the fete, which shocked me a bit, if I'm honest. I hope the events of the last few days haven't dissuaded you from attending. It wouldn't feel right if you weren't there.'

'I was temporarily suspended from my duties, Paul, and the bishop has yet to tell me that I can return.'

'But it was just a misunderstanding, Peter. I thought we'd cleared it up.'

He placed his hand on his forehead, as though in the midst of a tragedy; an actor, like me, dramatically enhancing the spoken word. 'Ah, I'm so sorry about all of this – what a mess. Could you not come anyway? Come in your normal clothes, as a normal villager, if you can't come as our priest.'

'*Normal villager,*' Peter giggled, amused at the idea.

'If you are angry with me or my family, I completely understand, but please put that to one side for today. It's the village fete, not Paul's fete, and we are raising money for the church.'

'I'll pop around later,' I capitulated with a shrug, 'show my face and give my support.'

'*Pathetic,*' Peter snarled, disgusted.

I walked into the village that afternoon with a slight skip in my step, greeting a few neighbours as I made my way to my fate.

'Morning, Alan,' I waved cheerily. 'Morning, Margaret.'

People looked twice at the sight of me in shorts, my pale, almost blue legs seeing the sun for the first time that year; for the first time in a number of years, come to think of it.

The gravel crunched underfoot as I entered Paul's front garden, or rather his forecourt, to give its proper title. It was the biggest house in the village, our Versailles, with a courtyard framed by a terrace of aged red-brick stables on one side and open-sided tithe barns on the other, their matt-black timber weather boarding and corrugated metal roof providing a beautiful contrast to the bright flowers of the borders and exposed timber structure of the interior, like the skeleton of a whale. Despite the obvious beauty of the surroundings, there was something unpleasant in their arrangement; the terraces drawing me in, feeling like they could close and ensnare me at any time.

The huge rickety farmhouse formed the backdrop, with its bent, aged roofline, exposed timbers and layer of lichens giving the appearance that it had always been there, grown from the ground itself, but inside it was clinical, minimalistic, spotless; Wi-fi and Bluetooth, contradictory, a reflection of its owner.

Crowds were bustling between stalls set up to form a narrow street down the middle of the courtyard, complete with hanging baskets and bunting that zigzagged its way all around the place. Bright pendants fluttered in the breeze, leading to Range Rovers shining outside the front door, parked at jaunty angles, like the front cover of Country Living.

Marion spotted me and made her way over, chirpy as always, her dog Esther by her side, carrying a tennis ball that she dropped at my feet, wanting to play.

'Morning, Father,' she said. 'Hardly recognised you without your work clothes. Are you off today?'

'I am,' I said, 'even priests need a day off occasionally. It looks great,' I exclaimed, feigning enthusiasm as I gestured towards the stalls. 'How's it going with you?'

'It's pretty awful, actually, Father,' she whispered. 'Between you and me, looks can be deceiving. We couldn't bring anything along or help with the setting up, nothing. They had the whole thing designed, like a set, and all the catering has come from Borough Market, but they've got the cheek to call it homemade. Sausage rolls are four pounds fifty – sandwiches six pounds. Who is going to pay that around here?' She shook her head and crossed her arms. 'He's invited plenty of his own from the city, who would probably pay it, though of course they don't have to – they have their own buffet. They had a shoot this morning, and now they're getting drunk over there, but the village people are pretty much just walking in and then walking straight back out again.'

*'Village people,'* Peter smirked, picturing a Red Indian, a cowboy and a builder

Bidding farewell, Esther dejectedly picked up her ball and followed Marion out of the gate. I walked along the street of stalls, confirming that what Marion had said was true; there were no mis-shapes, cornflake cakes or smarties running in the icing. Vendors were stood behind counters looking bored, no doubt feeling awkward, picking up on the clear mismatch between themselves and the villagers, who walked by aimlessly as professional photographers clicked away at Paul's vanity and ego, dressed up as altruism for the day.

I found him and his group at the end of the stalls, standing separate in small circles of conversation, drinking spirits or champagne, cordoned off like a VIP section, exclusive and self-important. Ted was in there, awkward amongst the tweed of the men, whilst the ladies looked like they were going to the races, wearing high heels and beautiful hats topped with bright plumes of feathers.

'Father,' Paul called out as he saw me approaching, 'just in time.'

A crowd of Hunter logos turned to look at me as I waved and walked over, deciding not to join him on the other side of the rope.

'Thank you for coming,' he said, 'I've been waiting for you to arrive. You're just in time for the announcement.' He gently tapped a microphone, which his wife Sarah, resplendent in white, had handed to him, sending a dull thud reverberating around the forecourt. 'Ladies and gentlemen, may I have your attention please,' he began, as faces turned towards him, surprised at the high-pitched voice that came from the speakers. 'First of all, thank you for coming out and supporting the fete, which I think you will all agree has been a resounding success. It's been my pleasure to facilitate it this year.' As if on cue, his friends gave a token golf clap. 'Now, I'd just like to make a presentation to the church, if I may. I know there are a few strange faces here today, but at this morning's shoot, we managed to raise seven thousand, five hundred pounds, which I would like to present to the church, to pay for the much-needed repairs to its roof.'

Again, a small smattering of applause, as I began to feel nervous. Without the right clothes or words, he'd caught me off guard.

'And to accept this donation, it is with great pleasure that I invite…' he paused, eyes fixed on me, '… Bishop Gordon to join me and receive the cheque.'

I took half a step forward, and then stopped. Ted and I shared a glance as the bishop's bald head emerged from between the tweed jackets and tight-fitting dresses. He, too, glanced at me before taking one side of the novelty cheque in hand and smiling for the flashing cameras, as I stood clapping, both relieved and confused.

'But we can't just let them have the money without joining in the fun themselves, can we?' Paul baited jovially, snatching back the cheque. 'I propose that a member of the clergy should be fixed in the stocks and soaked. Five pounds per sponge, and I'll buy twenty-five to get the ball rolling.'

Paul's friends cheered and laughed, as did the children. Indeed, everyone was smiling, the villagers warming up a bit.

'Unfortunately,' Paul continued, 'Bishop Gordon is looking immaculate today in his robes, but luckily, Fr McKay has turned up in his civvies. Fancy getting a soaking for the church, Father? The new roof will stop you getting wet inside at least,' he smiled, as I became the focal point of this world.

I smiled back, uncomfortable. 'Of course,' I nodded, pushing the smile a bit wider.

'Lead him to the stocks!' came the rallying cry, as the children ran over, laughing and pulling me towards the barn, where the ground was still wet from earlier soakings.

It looked like fun, bending over, placing my head and hands in the recesses as the top timber was placed over my neck, fixing me into place. I could pull my hands out, but my head was stuck, trapped and prostate before the crowd. It felt like a Biblical stoning was about to take place, when I glanced up to find Sarah walking towards the bucket in her tight white dress.

*'She who is without sin may cast the first sponge,'* Peter whispered, as she pulled a soft yellow missile from the bucket and sent it spinning, bouncing off the edge, missing my head, but drenching me all the same.

*'Bit of venom in that one,'* Peter observed.

Paul provided a running a commentary as his friends took turns throwing, streaks of water flying through the air, and then an explosion if it hit either me or the stocks. I relaxed, laughing as they cheered whenever one hit me square on, water spraying the crowd. Even Ted had a go, gentle but accurate, before the children collected the sponges, pausing the action whilst they refilled the water buckets. I was soaked through, water dripping off my nose and hair, but there was a smile on my face as I looked down at the white marble gravel on the floor, feeling refreshed in the stifling heat.

'Of course, Fr McKay probably wishes that Sarah or I were in the stocks, after we accused him of sexually molesting our teenage daughter earlier this week,' Paul laughed into the microphone, causing the crowd to fall silent. 'She says he didn't touch her,' he went on, as I tried to look up, not breathing, the timber across my neck blocking any movement as the barn became abuzz with chatter. 'Don't worry, it was all just a misunderstanding, though he is something of a lady's man.' He laughed again, that fake laugh, holding the listeners in the palm of his hand.

'Who?' his audience shouted, like a pantomime whilst Peter roared inside.

'He's been seeing our Meg from the Waggon, haven't you, Father?' Paul giggled. 'I think most of the guys here are probably a bit jealous. Nobody tell her boyfriend about it please,' he finished in a mock whisper.

I froze still, not that I had much choice, whilst everybody stared at me until a slight gasp signalled for the gossip to begin in earnest.

'Shall we let him out?' Paul asked, getting only silence in reply as he placed the microphone down on a table and came over to undo the trap.

It took an age to release three of the four clips, before he bent down, bringing his face close to mine, as he fingered the last one.

'I paid her five thousand pounds to fuck you last night,' he said under his breath. 'I hope you enjoyed it.'

My stomach dropped as my eyes looked up to meet his. He was still smiling.

'Do you know what you call a woman who you pay for sex?' he paused, watching my face turn red, the veins pulsing in my neck. 'She's a whore. You've been fucking a prostitute.' He glanced around, making sure nobody was in earshot. 'I could have fucked her myself for a tenth of that, but you couldn't pay me to touch that bitch,' he purred softly, before turning and smiling to the crowd whilst releasing the last clip.

I stood up quickly, the huge piece of oak falling to the ground, clattering as it bounced, breaking the silence, and immediately stepped towards him, closing the distance as he walked away, hands by my side, fists clenched, mind empty, feeling completely calm; Peter ascendant. I reached up to grab his shoulder, to turn him around, knowing what I was about to do, when a sponge hit me in the face, soaking wet and cold. I paused, and then another hit me, the crowd laughing as a third shot narrowly missed; the splash of water enough to bring me to my senses as the next one flew by.

I saw panic etched across Ted's face as he grasped for another sponge, which I stepped back to avoid when the latest arc of water came flying by.

'Have you been naughty, Fr McKay?' he shouted in a jovial voice, hoping to turn it into a joke, a Punch and Judy show.

It was working; the crowd laughed as I looked again at Paul standing next to his wife, laughing along with his other guests, the fake laugh I'd seen on his face many times before. He'd wanted me to hit him in front of all these people, but I simply joined in with the laughter as another sponge hit me on the side of the head. I was in control now, all passive-aggressive confidence.

His smile faltered, and he braced himself as I walked towards him, lifting my hand and scratching my head as he flinched and jumped backwards, closing his eyes, the children giggling in recognition of that old playground staple, no doubt hoping to see a wedgie next. My other hand went to the microphone as another sponge was launched, missing me and hitting Paul on the top of the head, spraying his friends, a roar of laughter erupting from the villagers behind me.

I switched on the microphone and held it to my lips, my eyes fixed on his as I paused, enjoying his discomfort.

'Firstly,' I began, 'thank you, Paul, for this wonderful event you have staged. It's very generous of you, as was the cheque for the church roof. We won't have to buy umbrellas to hold a service anymore,' I laughed, my voice echoing around the quieted barn and courtyard, bouncing off the surrounding buildings. 'Thank you also for the soaking I received – I'm just glad you're all such bad shots. The pheasants must be overjoyed.'

Slowly, the crowd began to laugh along, clearly unsure about what was happening.

'With regard to village gossip,' I went on, 'I'm not in a relationship with Meg, I'm afraid, or anybody else for that matter – though you are right, I'd be a very lucky man if I was.'

The smile remained fixed on Paul's face, but he was clearly hating this.

'We're friends, that's all,' I continued. 'There are certain things I don't believe in doing before marriage, and in front of everybody here, with God as my witness, I can tell you that my beliefs remain intact. I also believe that a man and a woman can just be friends.'

This drew a round of applause, with Noddy shouting, 'Amen, Father, me as well,' and getting an affectionate clip around the back of the head from his wife Mel, which brought a few more laughs.

Paul's smile was faltering as he looked around at the growing laughter and good-natured chatter. He'd lost control of the situation.

'You, on the other hand, appear to have a problem in this regard, Paul, which I'm available to help you with,' I clasped a friendly hand on his shoulder. 'My door is always open, as they say. Working off-site last night, were you? Just up the road, in the layby, I think?'

The laughter and chatter rose again, as I handed the microphone back to him. The smile had gone, the façade fallen, and he turned to his wife and shook his head, silently mouthing 'No' whilst she stared a hole through him.

My smile was real this time as I walked through the crowd, one person patting me on the back, followed by another, as Sarah chased after me and grabbed me by the arm, her sharp nails digging in deep.

'What do you mean?' she demanded. 'Who was he with?'

I stopped and looked at her, half expecting another punch to arrive, but it didn't. She knew, her shoulders dropping as she let go.

'It's Charlotte, isn't it?' she asked quietly, almost meekly.

I nodded, trying to muster sympathy as her face crumpled in grief before quickly switching to rage. She let out a guttural roar and turned back to face Paul, sending a glass spinning towards his head.

Another strong hand came through the crowd to seize my arm tightly; its owner, Alf, stepped forward. 'You mean my daughter-in-law Charlotte?'

I nodded again.

'I'm sorry, Alf. I saw them at it last night.'

He patted me on the shoulder. 'It's OK, son. Nobbler told me already, but you've just confirmed it. I'll take it from here.'

He followed Sarah towards Paul, and a volley of yells and blows erupted behind me as I walked off past the stalls on the pop-up street. I turned around to survey the destruction as Alf and his sons worked their way through Paul's guests, who had stepped forward to defend him. Flying fists were interspersed with the odd shriek, as Sarah sat astride her wayward husband, pummelling him with her shoe, the red flash suggesting Louboutin.

Stalls tipped over as the fighting spread, their bunting dragging down the others in a domino effect, leaving owners desperately trying to protect their produce. It looked like a battle scene as the villagers started throwing food at Paul's guests, the overpriced sausage rolls proving particularly popular, along with scotch eggs. Baguettes flew like javelins, whilst some used them as makeshift clubs, and then a huge puff of icing sugar flew up into the air, creating a billowing cloud before it settled and fell, covering everybody in fine white dust. The children had flipped the vegetable stand and were using it as a barricade, as Amy and Chloe threw prized tomatoes, lettuces and radishes at their father's friends, who had gone from Kings Road glamour to a motley shower of broken hats, ripped dresses and smeared lipstick.

The backdrop of anger was giving way to enjoyment, as villagers emerged from combat streaked in food and dust. It looked like a celebratory festival, Tomatina or Holi. In the VIP section, Paul's friends had acquiesced, standing helplessly with their backs to the house, watching Alf drag him across the gravel by his ears, screaming, Sarah kicking him as he went. Alf shoved him into his car, banging his head against the door and shouting, 'Go – now, and don't come back.'

Paul said nothing, gratefully slamming the door closed behind him and clicking the lock, no doubt relieved to still be in one piece. He started the engine and accelerated, launching a spray of stones across his guests, shattering glasses and sending people diving for cover as they were strafed by white gravel. The car was pelted as it made its way towards the exit, scones making a particularly large bang as they made contact and exploded, covering it in whipped cream and jam. Even the stall holders were joining in, having realised that they were not going to make any more sales today.

He glared at me as he drove past, out of the gate and onto the road, a gaggle of children following, throwing missiles and screaming with excitement. I pushed through the crowd at the gateway, finding two police cars with lights flashing and Paul climbing out, the tweed almost indistinguishable beneath its rich patina of food and blood. Roy gave me a smile and a nod as he walked towards him with a breathalyser, a gesture I returned before heading up the road towards the cottage, my exit.

I walked home with a lightness in my step, savouring the scenery for the last time before swallowing one of Michael's pills with a grimace, and then lying down in the cornfield to look up at the blue sky, its criss-crossing contrails pointing to exotic locations. A butterfly fluttered by, changing my focus from the global to the immediate; to ladybirds eating aphids, spiderwebs floating and swallows swooping dramatically from above, as waves from the breeze moved through the field, turning it liquid. My mind felt open, fixing images and memories as I absorbed the richness of this world, smiling, thinking back on the scene at the fete. Riot would be inaccurate; more of a rampage in a style unique to the village, all clotted cream and bunting, violence reserved for the wildlife in this gentle place.

My mouth was dry, head buzzing, as I left the solitude of the corn, taking a well-trodden path before turning up the track towards the cottage, the final leg, when I stopped, sensing something amiss. In the shadows, creeping behind me, was a black mass, its gentle hum barely audible beneath the cacophony of nature.

I remained still, facing away, as the Range Rover sat quietly, observing, thinking, whilst I assessed my options, finding them limited. I was hemmed in by thick hedges on both sides, blocking my only escape routes; I'd never make it.

*'Credit to him,'* Peter said, *'he's picked a good spot.'*

I turned to face my adversary, obscured by tinted windows, nothing visible behind reflections of trees and sky as I pictured that smile appearing on his lips. Time moved slowly as I waited, watching the car whilst birds and insects carried on their business around me, oblivious, as another aeroplane drew a line overhead.

Gravel crunching, he started edging towards me. I was tense, hearing voices from my childhood, shouting, 'Stand, don't run.' I didn't move, obeying their command, like I always had as the car came to a halt, no more than six metres in front of me now, Paul still invisible.

It started moving again, agonisingly slow, leaving me with no recourse other than to wait for the scream of the accelerator and the car to come flying towards me, but the speed did not increase; it just kept crawling until the bumper was brushing the hairs on my legs, the engine still idling.

The passenger door eased open, an invitation, my heart thumping as I accepted, making my way around the car, wondering if he would shoot me instead as I pulled the handle and looked inside.

'Sarah,' I exclaimed, letting out a sigh as she looked at me from behind the steering wheel.

'Get in,' she barked.

'I thought you–'

'I was bloody tempted, believe me,' she growled, cutting me off, before repeating the order to get in, a bit calmer this time. 'We need to talk.'

I clambered in and closed the door, noticing the feel of luxuriant leather on my bare legs. It felt cold with the air con blowing, my hairs standing on end and goose bumps forming as she accelerated too quickly down the track before stopping outside my cottage with a jolt. She turned off the engine and sat facing forward, keeping her hands on the wheel, staring into an uncomfortable silence.

'I am going to say all of this just once,' she spoke at last, 'and I will not repeat or admit any of it before anybody else. I'll deny everything. This is between you and me, and I'm only telling you because I feel a tiny bit of guilt, and maybe a bit of fear because you are friends with him upstairs,' she pointing at the sunroof. 'I do still have a shred of conscience, believe it or not.'

She'd found that difficult to say.

'After today, we are leaving the village,' she said. 'We shouldn't have come here in the first place. As you could probably tell, I don't like it and the kids hate it, so we're going back to the city and I'm going to sell the house.'

'Is that Paul's decision–'

'He can fuck off,' she interrupted. 'We're only here because of him and his stupid plans, dragging us all into this sorry mess.' She turned to face me and sighed. 'Paul is not what he seems, and our reason for moving here is not for the "good life," as he calls it. He's a very powerful man, with fingers in many pies.'

*'Fingers in pies,'* Peter scoffed.

She looked ahead at the front windscreen, and then up at the mirror, checking, her hands still on the wheel. 'He is very good at what he does – he makes things happen. Need a license to sell arms? Paul will make it work. Want to make a case for invading another country? Paul will make it work. Want to discredit someone in the media? Paul will make it work. He shapes public opinion, a manipulator, a spin doctor for the rich, who operate above morals.'

'Not all of them,' I argued.

'All they are interested in, at the end of the day, is finding ways to get what they want – more money and more power, and Paul helps them achieve it.' After a long pause, she added. 'He wasn't always morally bankrupt, He was a normal, doting father in his first marriage, but the more time he spent with these people, accumulating wealth, the more like them he became. "I see how the world really works," he often says.'

'So, what's that got to do with me? I'm just a priest in a little village, and he tried to destroy me in front of everybody – for what?'

'He certainly didn't see that coming,' she allowed herself a hint of a smile. 'He'll be offering you a job if you're not careful, once he's calmed down, of course, which will be never. He's worked with some pretty horrendous people in the past – people who nobody else will deal with, and he's come out without a scratch, yet he takes on the village priest and gets beaten up, cream-caked and arrested for drink driving.' She suddenly burst out laughing, letting out a loud snort.

'I didn't ask for it, any of it,' I said, failing to see the funny side. 'From you, Paul or your children.'

'I know. This is more like a hobby to Paul – something to play with outside of work. He's heading up an investment vehicle from the City, which gets access to ministers in order to influence government policy. He has put a large chunk of his own money into it, so is putting a lot of effort into lobbying behind the scenes. Basically, he has input on planning policy on things like the expansion of towns in huge blocks, for the construction of houses. He then either takes this knowledge and buys up the land himself, or sells his intel to developers for a large sum.'

'They bought the other farms, didn't they?'

'Yes, and now they're after the rest, to "maximise opportunity," as he puts it.'

'"For what shall it profit a man if he gain the whole world and suffer the loss of his soul? Or what shall a man give in exchange for his soul?" said Mark eight thirty-six.'

'Oh, please don't start quoting that shite. Anyway, we moved into the village, and Paul managed to get straight on the parish council. You were identified as a possible threat by Bishop Gordon, who is also involved, using his influence where he can.'

'What?' I began to protest, but she held up a hand to stop me.

'Fr Ted is bendable, so was not considered a threat,' she continued. 'You, however, are a different creature all together. They know your history. They know about your father. You're confrontational, a potential risk, so they had to get rid of you somehow.'

I detected an indirect compliment in there somewhere.

'Paul was looking at putting on a spectacle today, in front of some of his fellow investors, a show where they could all appreciate his talent, the puppet master pulling the strings. They all knew what was supposed to happen as you walked through the gates in your shorts, and the rest, as they say, is history,' she laughed again. 'He'll be furious.'

'What about you? Will you leave him?'

'Probably not. We'll go back to London, I'll have the life I'm accustomed to again, whilst he disappears and earns lots of money somewhere for a couple of months, and then comes back and promises that he'll never do it again. It's happened before with other women, and I didn't walk away then, either. I thought Charlotte was my friend, but Paul can spot them a mile off – power hungry. Her mistake is that she probably thinks he likes her – even loves her, but knowing Paul, he's probably just using her to chip away at Alf, putting a few fractures into the tight family unit, hoping it will disintegrate in the future. Then, he'll step in and reap the rewards.'

'He, erm, mentioned Meg, the barmaid.'

'Yes, he paid her five thousand pounds to sleep with you. He wanted to discredit you, but first he made sure that she lost her job, and then he threatened her with the police unless she took the money. She's looking after her father on her own, and Paul whispered all sorts of poison into her ear. He creates a weakness, and then exploits it.'

'So, she didn't really have a choice,' I mused aloud.

'She wasn't *forced* to take it. There's always a choice.'

There was another long pause as I considered what she'd just said. She turned towards me again, placing a hand on my thigh.

'I know something that would really piss him off,' she bit her lip as she eyed me.

I stared straight ahead, flinching as she slowly moved her hand up under the edge of my shorts.

'What perfect revenge that would be,' she leaned in close.

'What are you doing?' I asked flatly, meeting her hungry gaze.

'I've heard some interesting rumours about you down the pub,' she purred, closing her eyes and bringing her red lips nearer to mine.

'I'm sorry,' I shouted, jerking away.

I'm not sure why I apologised, it felt like sexual assault, but she just opened her eyes and removed her hand with a shrug and a smile, before sitting back and giving a little a sigh. She didn't seem angry or upset; easy come, easy go.

'Looks like you were telling the truth back there after all,' she murmured, using the rear-view mirror to touch up her lipstick, gurning, pulling her lips over her teeth to make sure she'd covered all areas. For a moment, she looked like a corpse, her skin pulled tightly over her cheekbones, her mouth a puckered hole, a reminder of mortality before she let her face return to its normal shape, a battlefield of injections, serums and snake oil.

She looked across at me, as if she had just remembered I was there. 'Right, I'm going to leave, if you'll please fuck off,' she brought the meeting to an abrupt close.

I watched the car vanish behind the bushes at the junction as she reversed down the path, and listened until the crunch of tyres and drone of the engine had disappeared before closing myself off from the world.

I sat in my armchair, exhausted, waiting, ignoring the banging on the door and Ted calling my name through the letter box. I didn't know if Bishop Gordon was with him, so I sat quietly until I heard footsteps fading down the far end of the path. I was tired of having to explain my actions, of defending myself whilst people picked holes. The lights remained off as the world kept spinning, day becoming evening, the sunset projecting flickering silhouettes of trees on the net curtains and back wall.

The front door tried to summons me again, but I continued to ignore it as Meg started shouting my name. My stomach flipped, but I remained still. At this point, she was just another person who I didn't want to speak to, though I knew I'd have to think about it at some stage.

*No doubt, she's heard about the day's events in the pub*, I thought, as a piece of paper slipped through the letterbox. *Tomorrow*, I decided, my focus switching to the laptop, its backlight an island in the spreading darkness as I composed my farewell to Bishop Gordon, short and sweet:

*I have left the village with immediate effect, and do not know when I shall return. Please confirm disciplinary process when you are able. Kind regards, Fr McKay.*

I copied Ted in, feeling he had a right to know, and then typed out another message, this time to Dad. A first step whilst I figured out what I was going to do next.

Preparations complete, I opened the whisky and washed down my prescription, keeping me balanced, chemically numb, staring into space, trying to block out thoughts as I waited for the planet to complete its half-turn, my mind taking me to the same old points, breaking me, again and again as I prayed and repented, mouthing and then shouting the words. It felt endless, infinite, until shafts of orange light pierced through the window of the back room, announcing the salvation of the next day.

My body protested as I slowly climbed out of the armchair and looked out of the window. I began to interrogate myself, questioning my actions, but there was no change of heart. If anything, the past week had been the highlight of my two years there, reawakening me after I'd become dormant under the safety and predictability of village life. I felt conscious; the outside world suddenly mattered again.

Like a burglar, I rushed around the house, emptying wardrobes and ransacking drawers, stealing my own belongings, all of which fitted into two large kit bags. It didn't take long – I didn't have much – but the bags, like my life, were heavy.

The new sun sat low in the sky, so it was still cool and hazy outside, or fresh, as Alf would say. I closed the front door behind me, turning the key and then posting it out of reach before stepping onto the lane, my shoes already wet with dew from the overhanging plants and grass that lined the path. Pausing, I looked at the wonky cottage one last time, doubting that I'd ever see it again, and it wasn't without feeling that I finally started walking, already nostalgic about a place I hadn't yet left. It wasn't unpleasant; it was a sensation that I could wallow in, thick and luxurious, a beautiful melancholy, if there is such a thing.

At the bottom of the lane, I turned to take another last look, my sadness now tempered with excitement for the future.

'Need a hand with your bags, Father?' a voice called from the thick bushes to the side of me, where the lane met the junction.

'What is it with this place and grown men hiding in bushes?' I shook my head, as Roy emerged from the greenery, Ted following close behind, inflicting an immediate pang of guilt.

'Can we help?' Ted asked, a big smile filled his face, as though he'd been on an adventure.

'I've booked a taxi to pick me up outside the pub,' I said. 'You could give me a hand, if you like.'

It was the only landmark in the area, and there would be nobody about at that time of the morning; no lock-in with Meg still suspended.

'I'll give you a lift,' Roy offered, indicating a police car hidden in the layby as they each took a bag and control of the situation, whilst I procrastinated, trying to find words, feeling ambushed. I'd hoped to slip away; there one day, gone the next, as if I'd never been there at all, but I'd been outmanoeuvred, underestimated them, as everybody always did. I followed along to the car, clambering into the back, where the naughty people go, with Ted turning to face me and Roy watching in the mirror.

'We knew you were still up there,' Ted was smiling excitedly. 'Nobbler saw a glow from your window last night, so we got down here early, to make sure you wouldn't leave without saying goodbye.'

'I'm sorry, I just…' I couldn't finish the sentence.

'Is it *goodbye*, or just, you know, goodbye?' he asked, softening his tone on the second one, and flicking an eyebrow for emphasis.

'It's the first one, I'm afraid, Ted,' I replied, watching his shoulders drop.

'But we can sort out the issues with the bishop,' he said pleadingly. 'I mean, yesterday was hardly your fault. I thought you handled it very well – much better than I would have.'

'It's not just about yesterday, or the even last few days,' I confessed. 'The problem is, deep down, I just cannot bring myself to care about a lot of the issues in the village. I keep scolding myself about it, but the thing I keep coming back to is that this place doesn't need any help. It's middle class, safe and... beautiful – the perfect idyll of winding country lanes, cottages, fields, horses and pubs. It has its problems, like the extension, not to mention a few wayward characters, as we've seen recently, but they're not really problems that I can help with. I'm from a city, which is where the people and issues just seem more relatable to me.'

Ted smiled and nodded understandingly.

'It's only now, with things becoming a bit messy, that I've started caring. It's been a wonderful two years here, but it's time to move on. The bishop has actually done me a favour. Don't tell him that, though.'

Ted was still smiling that fixed smile I knew too well, as the door to my side opened and the huge frame of Alf struggled in, banging his head on the rim.

'Fucking door. Sorry, Father,' he mumbled, pushing me further across the back seat. 'Morning, Father. I was watching from the field – sorry it took so long for me to get across.'

*A military operation*, I thought, smiling, as they all looked to one another, proud as punch. *Maybe I could stay, become something more – one of them...*

'*No,*' Peter protested, directing my thoughts to Meg.

He was right.

'You all need to know a few things that I discovered yesterday,' I announced. 'Paul is with the group that bought the other farm, and he's after your land, Alf. Yesterday was all about getting rid of me, and trying to chip away at your family.'

Alf sighed. 'We'll deal with Charlotte the way we deal with everything,' he said, 'as a family, behind closed doors. The company that bought the other farm is registered in the British Virgin Islands, so it's impossible to know who's involved, but they certainly won't be getting my land. I don't think he'll come back anyway. He's a coward.'

'He lobbies MPs to fix planning policy,' I explained. 'Then, his company makes a fortune from buying and selling on land at the most opportune times.'

'I'm not completely surprised to hear it,' Alf replied. 'The government is rotten to its core – people like Paul the beneficiaries of their policies, like pigs in a trough. It is an illusion of democracy – all the parties are from the same social class, the same demographic, probably the same school class, and they are all offering the same thing. They've got it stitched up. All policies from all parties point to the benefit of the same people, the one percent, a political monopoly, pretending we have a choice. Elections change nothing.'

'We can vote for whoever we want,' Ted countered; the first time I'd heard him disagree with anything.

'Ah, but you can only vote for what's on offer,' Alf said, waving his hands to emphasise his point, 'and when what's on offer from both parties only benefits the same few people, you don't have a democracy. Why do you think so many people don't bother voting?'

'Good point,' I agreed, as Ted shrugged. 'If it was truly democratic, the one percent wouldn't exist, since they are far outnumbered by the ninety-nine.'

'There will always be a one percent,' Roy put in. 'It's impossible for everyone to be equal. It doesn't mean they're bad people.'

'It's incredible to think that a company from a tiny tropical sandspit could be the biggest threat to our village,' Ted hit the nail on the head.

'It is how they operate,' Alf said matter-of-factly, 'behind a screen of confidentiality. That's why these tax havens are allowed to exist by elected people, whose prime motivation is to line their own pockets. The government could close them all tomorrow if they wanted to, whilst making a fortune in the process. Why don't they? Because we are just a red square on a map – numbers on spread sheets that need to get from column A to column B. That's all that matters to these people, but at least now it's the devil we know.'

'Are you leaving, then?' Alf asked me.

'Yes, I'm going to see my dad first, and then I'll see what happens,' I answered.

'You only seem to stay in a place for two years,' Ted blurted out, 'and then you move on. You're like the Wandering Jew. Why can't you settle? Why do you keep drifting?'

He was right. Since I'd been ordained, I'd served in four different parishes, each one going the same way, feeling empty after a time, getting itchy feet, having to move.

'Is it because of your past?' Roy asked.

'What do you mean?' I was caught off guard.

Everybody went quiet.

'I've, erm, seen your records,' Roy said sheepishly. 'I know the gist of your upbringing, and the, erm… current situation.'

'Me too,' Ted admitted.

What they were talking about was confidential, but no anger rose in me. It was difficult to be upset with these people; they were only trying to help, however misguided it might have seemed.

'*At least it isn't a Father Ted sketch*,' Peter consoled.

'I don't know.' I replied, unable to suppress a smile. 'Definitely not on a conscious level, but subconsciously, maybe I can't settle because of my past. Perhaps I'm destined to wander until the Second Coming.'

Ted grinned, as the awkward silence returned.

'Maybe you need to go home?' he eventually suggested.

I didn't answer, didn't think about it; remained quiet, drawing a line. It was not a subject I was willing to discuss.

'Can we drop you at the station?' Roy asked, changing the subject, relieving the tension.

'I've already ordered a taxi to pick me up at the pub,' I said. 'I need to drop a letter off as well.'

'Then we'll go to the pub and take it from there,' Roy concluded, starting the engine and driving quickly down the narrow, single-lane roads, past dense hedges, becoming transparent with speed, allowing views into the surrounding fields.

I jumped out at the pub and posted a letter to Meg; the question I could not answer. Perhaps this was running away, but the status quo filled me with loathing. She was different than the other women; she'd made me feel more than just standard emotions, but it was time to stop. I wasn't ready to push further, despite the panic I read in those few handwritten phrases, saying she was so sorry and that we needed to talk, to let her explain, pointing towards love and the pain that always follows.

'I did warn you about her,' Ted reminded me as the village disappeared behind us.

# CHAPTER 4

ANYWHERE, SOMEWHERE, NOWHERE MAN

*God is dead. God remains dead. And we have killed him. How shall we comfort ourselves, the murderers of all murderers? What was holiest and mightiest of all that the world has yet owned has bled to death under our knives: who will wipe this blood off us? What water is there for us to clean ourselves? What festivals of atonement, what sacred games shall we have to invent? Is not the greatness of this deed too great for us? Must we ourselves not become gods simply to appear worthy of it?*

It was an impressive speech from the lunatic on the soapbox, Nietzsche, flavoured in local nasal tones as people walked by, ignoring him. It provided distraction, something to ponder as I walked from the station in the rain; more of a drizzle, not enough for an umbrella, but enough to get me wet. It always seemed to be raining here.

The journey had passed slowly, the windows streaked with rain, blurring the slice through England, obscuring views. I'd tried to read, but couldn't focus, Dawkins and Hawkins would have to wait. Instead, I'd closed my eyes and tried to sleep, unsuccessfully, as the train gently swayed to its own rhythm, announcements jolting me awake whenever I was about to drift off.

I wasn't happy or relieved to arrive; it required action, movement, away from the stasis of the train. The checkpoints were tortuous, the inspectors self-important, but then it was a familiar walk, one that I'd undertaken many times, leaving the station and turning my back on the city centre, its dark satanic mills now gentrified apartments, restaurants and bars, interspersed with gleaming glass towers. The place was thriving, but there had been a price to pay, wholesale change obliterating the culture and creativity of the people, disarming a music and club scene that had fed off the edginess of inner-city deprivation to create something unique, now replaced by chains and concessions, the cultural sterility of the branded thematic experience: Tiger Tiger vs Hacienda.

Was it wrong to mourn deprivation?

*We've never had it so good*, the tattered sign suggested.

My thoughts felt denser here, compressed; deeper, darker, more important. Perhaps it was the proximity of buildings limiting views, limiting light, closing in, or the rushing of cars and people, an assault on the senses as noise rebounded erratically off the hard surfaces. Maybe it was the constant stopping, looking around, judging velocities, before starting again.

As I walked, the streetscape started to deteriorate gradually, subliminal warnings to visitors that they were going the wrong way, urging them to turn around and head back towards the shiny towers. Only the canal distracted me, its beauty in the interaction of man-made and natural, stationary and fluid, the stationary becoming fluid as I stepped on a tilting flag, sending up a spray of dirty water, rousing me from my reverie. One leg was soaked, and my shoe now squelched with each step.

I'd arrived at the boundary of the 'Anywhere,' where the granite paving and mock amphitheatres gave way to cheap tarmac, dug up and continually relaid in patches and strips by utility companies.

The gateway was formed by three railway bridges, the last remnant of an industrial aesthetic that gave the city its identity. Curved iron arches, streaked with rust, spanned the road, carrying lines above, its monolithic walls permanently moist, stained with algae, ferns growing wherever they could get a foothold. It provided a temporary respite from the rain and weight of my bags, where an acrid stink of piss lingered, soaked into the porous stone over decades, a regular pit stop on the way home from a night out. I was on edge as my shoulders throbbed, wary of the pigeons, their tails visible as they cooed and spun above, streaked spatters of white on the walls and pavement betraying their presence.

'*Piss and shit,*' Peter scorned; it was a sensory experience, an emotional recalibration, dragging hopes and expectations to the bottom.

There was no magical world awaiting once you passed beyond the gateway. The Victoriana became a defensive landscape of blank walls, chain-link fences and tattered billboards, an in-between place, where people drove through to get somewhere else, the faded double-yellow lines reminding them not to stop here, as if they'd want to. It felt appropriate that I was in this man-made purgatory, with nothing to focus on, just cars passing by.

I put my head down and walked, feeling low, drifting aimlessly in the knowledge that one chapter of my life had ended, leaving me waiting for the next to begin, again, rinse and repeat. Only, the next chapter was not laid out before me; I was in a place between chapters. I could do anything, go anywhere, which was the most frightening thing of all.

My beliefs remained resolute; I had no doubts about my faith, about God or religion. He had saved me, but I was starting to question the Church, wondering what good I could really do in it. Like me, Christianity was drifting, unsure of its next chapter as society evolved. The young no longer believed in gods and deities, their brave new world letting go of the religion that had made sense of life for centuries, finding its traditions no longer applicable, behavioural codes and belief systems superseded as freedom replaced duty. There was nothing to fill the God-shaped void, no new story to replace the old; it was a materialist world with material joys, the flip side being a spiritual vacuum of depression, anxiety and loneliness, epitomised by this place. Money was their new God, the Church merely a museum of saints, hanging on.

'*It's dead,*' Peter whispered. '*There won't be a next chapter.*'

I kicked a can, sending it clattering across the pavement, distracting me for a moment as I glanced up to see the hotel looming closer. I walked through the final puddles to my halfway house, an out-of-scale interlocking of grey metal and concrete blocks with punched hole windows, alone, dominant and modern alongside an expanse of empty car park, softened by leftover patches of grass and unhealthy saplings strapped to posts, barely living. It had a fortified feel, as if designed to repel a siege of battering rams, trebuchets and towers rolling forward, covered in screaming men, trying to breach their defences.

It was difficult to be optimistic in this place.

The rooms were all identical, standardised en-suite cells either side of a long central corridor, repeated on each floor, repeated in each city. It seemed appropriate for the location, a temporal place, where people stayed for one night, a place for the lonely, but it was good to drop the bags at least.

I showered and put on some dry clothes, before practising emotions and checking emails, an angry reply from the bishop, saying I should have remained whilst my superiors decided my fate, guilty until proven innocent.

'*Fuck him,*' Peter giggled.

I didn't really care what happened. The village already seemed so long ago, and my mood was improving with the weather, which now only looked like it might rain as I left the glazed lobby and found a place to stand between the puddles; their smooth surfaces reflecting clouds amongst the fractured paving. I opened a chocolate bar I'd bought from the vending machine inside, the only source of sustenance that didn't give change, and looked up at a Victorian tower rising in the distance, a landmark pointing to Dad.

The urban context had not improved, but I was seeing more as the dark cloud lifted from my mind. A surge of serotonin with a splash of endorphins allowed nature to be observed everywhere, waiting in the wings for us to look away long enough to cover all trace of human endeavour. Tufts of grass forced their way between cracked paving slabs, displaying a desperate will to live, hanging on to life as people walked all over them, grinding them down, whilst a patch of scrubland housed a Darwinian survival of the fittest, difference fighting difference. No place for the docile here, it was nettles and brambles all the way, alive with insects, a miniature ecosystem, with butterflies fluttering in places they had no right to be, around industrial units, railings, CCTV and razor wire. Even in this vacuous, man-made desolation, I could see the beauty of God.

The sun had broken through the dark grey clouds, sending shafts cascading through the gaps like a Biblical scene, the metal railings creating a strobe effect as I continued walking towards Dad. I arrived early, strolling further up the road to admire the building's original entrance, a Grade II listed Victorian ensemble of stone bands and frames, set within deep-red terracotta brick, constructed when people still believed in higher ideals. The grandness and solidity of the building hinted at an omnipotent power; its recessed entrance sat between imposing towers, as humbling as any cathedral. It was the gateway to an internal world, a monastic community, isolated in their deliberation and reflection; a sombre and powerful architecture for a powerful institution, rebranded, but still known by its original name, emanating from the Anglo-Saxon *Strang* and *gewæsc*, 'a stream with a strong current,' or Strangeways. It was Britain's largest maximum-security prison, home to murderers, rapists, thieves, gang leaders and terrorists; hell re-branded, and home sweet home to Dad.

I arrived at the new modern entrance block, hit by the smell of disinfectant as I entered, that synthetic pine triggering memories, a bit different than the village church. Switching to autopilot, I submitted to the standard procedures, checking in with ID, electronic fingerprint and visiting order, and then placing my belongings into a locker and sitting down to wait for my allotted time. I was surrounded by mute, silent people, the only noise coming from children running around excitedly, about to see Daddy. There was a strange contrast between people and setting; the room was filled with ladies dressed in slinky short dresses and tight-fitting clothes, bright red lipstick and tanned flesh incongruous with the sombre waiting area. It felt surreal, as though music could start at any moment, the room going dark and coloured lights starting to flash, as arms waved and bodies writhed, like some abstract game of musical statues, but nothing happened; the clock carried on ticking, the children playing, feet and fingers tapping. There was a nervous tension.

When my time slot was called out, I joined the security queue, like an airport, only without the exotic destination at the end. Empty pockets, take off shoes, belts and watches, and walk through the metal detector; raise your arms, spread your legs, lift your feet and open your mouth, as hands run up and down, feeling, probing into pockets, brushing against genitals. It was uncomfortably intimate, intrusive, touching under the pretence of security whilst maintaining market share. Mine was mercifully quick, the guard looking past me at the svelte figure to my right, blonde hair cascading over bare, tanned shoulders; no bra under her skin-tight top, being rubbed down by a female officer, sex everywhere.

I patted the Labrador on the head as he came over and sniffed, receiving a stern look from the handler in return, and then sat in the second waiting room, same as the first, all fluorescent lighting and polished lino. I studied the fire escape plan on the wall; the prison was shaped like a snowflake, like something for children to colour in, a starfish perhaps, with six legs radiating from a central core, Bentham's Panopticon, all areas visible from a single point.

'McKay,' shouted a hoarse, raspy voice, pulling me back into the moment.

I stood, following a stocky, well-built officer, who silently escorted me down a corridor to the kiosks, a row of windows between vertical partitions, each sparsely furnished with a small counter and moulded plastic chair. Everything was magnolia, apart from the linoleum floor, which squeaked as you walked, the synthetic smell still dominant, concealing the stench of thousands of locked-up men.

Dad was sitting under a single spotlight that cast ghoulish shadows down his face, making him look pale and drawn, like Hannibal Lecter. He was behind the glass screen, waiting, a big smile creasing his features when he saw me approaching, and I couldn't help but smile back, wishing I could reach through the glass, to hold him. He looked well with his hair in a crew cut, despite a few more flecks of grey than last time. There was a new scar forming down his cheek, to go with the rest of his collection, his mark of Cain, but his eyes were full of humour.

I sat down and picked up the black handset fixed to the wall, placing my palm on the glass.

'What happened there?' I asked. 'Handbags again?'

'Yeah, something like that,' he laughed. 'A shiv, two blades melted into a toothbrush.'

'Good for removing plaque?'

'So that you can't stitch it back together.'

I felt sick to the pit of my stomach, I'd already known what it was.

'Who did it?' I tried to keep the anger out of my voice, knowing he wouldn't tell me.

'Doesn't matter – could have been anyone. It just happens.'

'But why you?'

'No reason. Violence is a currency here, you give as good as you get. Hurt them when they hurt you, and you'll be OK. Don't fight, and everybody knows about it. You become a target, for bullying, for sexual abuse – there was even a rape a couple of weeks ago. You grass them up, and you may as well be a nonce – you're a dead man, so you just get on with it.'

It never failed to shock me when he spoke of such things, as if they were normal; as if everyone lived like this.

'Apart from that, you look well,' I said. 'Looks like you've put a bit of weight on.'

He'd found his niche in the prison, like a shop steward, an interface between the prisoners, with their grievances, and the authorities, though it appeared to be one way traffic most of the time. At least his mind was active, that was the most important thing. Boredom could kill, a slow, conscious death.

'What else is happening? Has it improved any?' I asked, hopeful, despite knowing the answer.

'No, it's getting worse, or maybe I'm just getting old,' he smiled wryly. 'I really don't know how they think this thing works. Did you know that fifty-five percent reoffend within a year of leaving this place, and end up coming straight back? How can that be right?' he shook his head. 'I keep seeing the same people pass through again and again – some of them are good mates now. There's no rehabilitation, just concentrated aggression. They're wound up and then let out, like snarling dogs, destined to find themselves back in the cage, wasting more money.'

'Well, you'll be alright. I'll look after you when you get out,' I said, making light of it. 'You won't be coming back.'

'I know, and I've got parole in two years – it just frightens me. Why can't they stay out? Have things changed so much? Are we better off in here?' he shrugged his shoulders.

'Our two worlds are getting closer every day,' I said. 'We're practically on a war footing. The problem is, the so-called terrorists and anarchists are just normal people who disagree with the government.'

'This place is full of them, called terrorists for protesting – refusing to stay quiet. The far-right nutters are making their life hell in here.'

There was a pause, a slight awkwardness, as there always was when our two contrasting worlds came together.

'I'm fine,' he eventually murmured, random words to break the silence, before smiling again, nodding. 'You know me, I'm alright.'

The smile gradually disappeared from his lips as he looked down to the counter top, his hand moving side to side as if feeling for the grain. I nodded back, feeling anger, frustration, a slow-motion movie scene running through my mind. I wanted to break the glass, put my fist through it, sending a shower of crystalline cubes flying through the air alongside splinters of wooden frame, spinning and then dropping to the ground, leaving only bent nails and an open portal to Dad. Instead, I just sat, acting, nodding and smiling, rage contagious in this place.

'Looks like you've had a bit of trouble yourself,' he remarked, indicating the scab on my cheek.

I'd forgot it was there.

'Like I said, it's no fairy tale on the outside,' I said, smiling, drawing a laugh out of him at least. 'Anything back from the MPs? On the suicides?' I changed tack, bringing up something he could get his teeth into.'

'There have been four deaths classed as suicides in the last two months alone. A lot of them shouldn't have even been in here – they are mad, genuinely mentally ill, and they usually go one of two ways. They either break down or become ultra-violent, completely unpredictable, thrashing around.'

'But surely there's a structure in place–'

'I'm still sending letters to the governors and politicians, and still not getting any replies. I'll carry on, it's all I can do, but it's only going to get worse in the long run, with government cuts on the way, meaning less screws. They just keep chipping away, saving money, as the number of deaths rise. I'm actually starting to feel sorry for the people working here. They couldn't do their jobs properly if they wanted to.' His eyes were looking bright again. He was on a roll. 'There's a real feeling of resentment bubbling away just below the surface – it's a pressure cooker. We're overcrowded, packed two-to-three in cells designed for one. They cancel activities due to lack of staff – library visits, gym sessions and even religious services are withdrawn, so we're locked in for twenty-three hours a day. Self-harm is going through the roof.' He was shaking his head again. 'It's going to get to a point where it will explode, and when it does go off, it will be worse than the last time. There will be too few staff to contain it. Bear in mind, the place is also full of mobile phones, in contact with other prisons. If they synchronised action, the whole system could be brought down to its knees, all for the sake of a few extra quid.'

'It's the same on the outside,' I said, 'every public service the same story – the police are being decimated. They rely on specials to make up the numbers, all to save money. We'll end up with the army on the streets if something big goes off, and we both know where that leads.'

He leaned forward and lowered his voice. 'Day-to-day violence is spreading, so we usually end up in emergency lockdown most days, but with less screws there is more opportunity for the bad guys. There are power struggles all over the place – each wing has its own hierarchy, its own rules. One wing tries to get a foothold in another, and all hell breaks loose as allegiances switch and gangs break up into factions, wannabees. Lots of slashings, stabbings – nobody gives a shit. They get pissed on hooch or high on Mamba – they have no hope. They don't think they will ever get out. A bloke got jugged the other week, first time I've ever seen it.'

'What's that?' I asked, regretting the words as soon as they left my mouth.

'They mix sugar or bleach with a kettle full of boiling water, and then throw it into someone's face. The sugar makes it stick and burn for longer,' he explained matter-of-factly. 'Strips the skin, like napalm.'

I felt sick again. *Is this really happening in this century?* I thought. It sounded medieval. 'Don't the guards get involved?'

'Not really. I've seen groups of blokes go into a pad, and then come out minutes later, the occupant slashed up, cut to bits. A bloke lost his eye the other week. The officers watch and know what's going on, but a lot of the time they don't get involved. I don't know if they are scared or just can't be arsed. Either way, it makes their shifts easier.'

Grimacing, I nodded. 'Why does it never get reported? Why does it never get into the news?'

'Most of it gets classed as "concerted indiscipline," which covers anything from two prisoners refusing to do as they are told, to the whole place going up in a riot. Nothing to report here, just lots of concerted indiscipline going on. Change the semantics, and everything's fine.' He sat back and sighed, probably realising that he'd said too much. 'Anyway, believe it or not, most people in here just want to get their head down, get through their sentence and leave. It's not all bad – there are some genuinely good people here. You've just got to work your way around the problems, same as anywhere else. I'll be alright… Tell me, what's going on with you? You usually give plenty of notice before you visit.'

It all seemed so petty compared to what he was going through, but I knew he enjoyed hearing about my life, and the issues that existed outside of prison. Most of it actually sounded quite funny when I said it out loud, and we laughed together as I told him about the pictures of Amy and the food fight at the fete. I loved seeing him like this, assembling pictures in his mind. He clearly needed a release.

'Well done for not swinging for him, though we've probably got Ted to thank for that,' he said, when I explained about Paul, before moving on to Sarah trying to seduce me in the car, and what had happened with Meg. I didn't mind going into detail with him. We'd spoken about sex and relationships before.

'You're allowed to have a relationship before marriage, you know,' he counselled quietly. 'How can a man and a woman celebrating their love for each other be wrong? It's love – you're allowed to be happy. I mean, the Sarah incident I can understand, but you've spoken about Meg a few times before. She sounds great, and you light up whenever you say her name. Don't let her slip away.'

'But my beliefs prevent me from–'

'Are you sure?' he gently interjected. 'Your religion allows for sex before marriage, am I right?'

'I'm just scared of it all,' I confessed, always more honest with him than I was with myself, 'and religion does get in the way. I just… it's easier.' I shook my head, unable to put the feelings into words.

His smile became a frown as I continued, telling him about my leaving the village.

'Where are you going to go?' he asked, his knuckles turning white as his hand tightened on the receiver, helpless, stuck behind the glass, unable to be a dad and sort things out.

'Not sure,' I answered quietly.

His eyes looked down at the table, and then flicked back up to me, thinking, as I explained my disillusionment with the Church.

'Is this temporary or permanent?' he asked.

'I don't know,' I said, another honest answer.

Speaking to him was soothing. I was putting thoughts into words, confessing to the only person I could truly trust, as he listened intently to my reasoning, relieved to hear that my beliefs remained intact.

'Maybe I could work in the chapel here,' I suggested, trying to lighten the mood, but he'd replied before I could finish the sentence. It was a mistake to joke about this place.

A voice came over the tannoy, announcing that visiting time was coming to an end.

*So quickly?* I thought, my stomach flipping and the anger ratcheting up a couple of notches, returning to frustration and rage.

I placed my hand back on the glass, Dad reciprocating, even though neither of us could feel anything but a cold hard surface.

'I want you to go see Yoda,' he said quickly, making sure he got it in.

*'No,'* Peter responded vehemently, and for once, I agreed, as I stood frozen, looking at him.

'I haven't seen him in years,' I said, my head shaking, a sense of panic starting to rise within. 'I haven't been back there for years. I don't even know where he lives now.'

'He lives in the same place,' Dad said. 'I never ask you for anything, but please promise me you'll go to see Yoda straight from here, before you make any decision on your future.'

*'No,'* Peter repeated, not just a single word, but a thousand at once, echoing from all directions.

'Promise me,' he implored, becoming more forceful as he saw a guard appear behind me. 'Do it for me.'

'No, I…'

We were both standing now. I could sense panic in his voice.

'Please,' he said.

'But–'

'Please, Peter,' he whimpered, his façade of machismo crumbling.

I acquiesced, nodding, murmuring yes, Peter screaming within; I couldn't bear to see him like this.

A large hand tapped me on the shoulder, and I was gently ushered away, my eyes locking on to Dad's before he disappeared from view behind the partition.

It was a lot quicker getting out than in, doors opening with the scan of a fingerprint, ensuring I was ejected in mere minutes, whilst Dad was escorted back to his box. I was emotionally exhausted, drained, shaking with anger and self-pity, as memories and thoughts broke free, rioting. It was worth it every time, though; giving him hope, a morale boost, a link to the outside world, but it also left me in a state, as if I'd absorbed every raw emotion rampaging about the place.

I took deep breaths before turning to look at the high walls topped with their rolled metal profile; judgement on earth, home to sinners. They had to be punished, to serve their sentences for the crimes they had committed, but the barbarity inside had no place in a civilised country. Its stories painted fantastical images in the mind, of mythical monsters, Hieronymus Bosch, applying various torture techniques to the fallen, who waited placidly in line. The prisoners' victims would no doubt approve, but there had to be a better way, one where they could come out better people, genuinely repentant.

*Perhaps heaven and hell are actually here*, I thought. *Not just some abstract idea for the future, but metaphors for now, for our being, our lives, our state of mind.*

If so, that had to have been hell itself before me, a concentration of rage, fear, anger and hate, surrounded by this buffer zone of nothingness.

Other visitors emerged from the entrance, walking in the same direction before breaking off, each alone with their thoughts, the scraping of high heels and cries of children the only sounds for miles around. One by one, they disappeared, not wanting to be associated with 'these' people, resuming their lives as I walked towards my cell, unsure whether I should stay or go, checking emails, one from Ted:

*Hi Peter,*

*You are the talk of the village at the moment, but in a good way. You are being credited with removing Paul, though there is a bit of confusion around why you have left – lots of gossip and rumours circulating, which goes down very well around here! I've said your two-year placement was finished, and now you have gone off to decide on your future – the truth(ish).*

*The village fete has been declared the best one ever, and shall go down in local folklore. There are plenty of nightly re-enactments in the Waggon. Paul's house has gone on the market, the boards have gone up, so hopefully we have seen the last of him and will have more pleasant neighbours in the near future.*

*Meg is a bit of a mess, I'm afraid. She's asked me for your number, which I have not yet given to her. Should I pass it along?*

*I hope you are safe and well, and I look forward to hearing from you soon, once you decide on your future. There is always a place for you here.*

*Regards,*
*Ted.*

Even at this most vulnerable stage, the village felt foreign to me; Ted already distant as I replied with reassurances, whilst denying Meg my number, the break always clean. I was nowhere, but I still preferred it to that somewhere, even as I looked around the standardised solitude and decided to leave. I wouldn't sleep well in this place, never did; lying awake, trapped by the usual fears, my mind not releasing me until the following morning. Liverpool would be no different, but I had to grasp the momentum that Dad's words had created before I had time to erect barriers and contrive reasons not to go there at all.

Again, I became automated, preventing thoughts from interrupting my impetus, quickly packing clothes drying on radiators, the dirt of the streets making them stiff, baked into the fabric, and then handing in my key and treating myself to a taxi, partly because my shoulders couldn't cope, but mostly to keep moving; to prevent me from dissuading myself. Besides, I was going to a different station, serving a different part of the country, a journey I never thought I'd make, back into my darkness.

∞

The black cab came to a crawl, and then a frustrated stop in the traffic, which seemed to go on as far as the eye could see.

'How close are we, mate?' I asked.

'Couple of hundred yards, pal,' the driver replied.

'I'll jump out here,' I said, leaning forward to pay.

I lugged my bags out and joined the flow; groups of men moving, full of urgency and tension, heading towards the distant sound of chanting, as the crowd became denser and police numbers increased, drawn like bees to the concentration of emotion.

I arrived at the rampart leading up to the station, a relic of the old rising gently to meet the new, a conglomeration of metal cladding and glazing, with the usual WH Smith and M&S at the forefront, the standard pallet. Liverpool had played United, the government overlooking its policy of unlawful assembly to maintain the modern opium of the masses, and all the societal divisions it maintained. How could the people of Manchester and Liverpool unite whilst a ball was being kicked?

A line of police separated groups of fans halfway up, mostly just spectators, apart from a few young agitators, all wide eyes and arms held out before them, fuming, beckoning to the enemy. Most ignored them; they were all testosterone, yet to fill their bodies, performing mock charges before turning back, pacing around, nostrils flaring, and then charging again, ranting vitriol.

'Fucking *scum*.'

The police looked bored.

There was no way into the station; I became frustrated, wondering what it was about football that turned people primitive, chimp-like, as I went back the way I came, entering an empty café; most of the customers on the pavement, pointing phones at the football mob, voyeurs hoping for a bit of action.

I headed straight for the toilets, where I changed into my clerical outfit, immediately gaining status, an elevated place in society, before returning to confused glances, as if a superhero had emerged in their midst. The agitation on the rampart had descended into scuffles, the police line fragmenting as pressure was applied to different points. Batons were out, occasionally swinging towards a shaven head as they backed away, leaving the middle ground clear. It had become more serious, no longer merely shouting from juveniles, but also big men on a collision course, the police squeezed in between, darting out of the way of the inevitable. It must have been like looking into a mirror as they faced each other; the same haircuts, designer labels, trainers and social class, identical save for their respective club regalia.

*Any other time, they'd probably get along like a house on fire*, I thought of these obvious kindred spirits, who had everything in common except allegiance to a particular franchise. Football was their outlet for primal emotions, with its battle cries and war dances; traditions of face paint and lager before combat with the neighbouring tribe.

They met with a crunch, supressed feelings initially finding release through kicks, but then the pressure pushed them together, limiting space, leaving a mass of shaven heads angrily bobbing, like potatoes boiling in a pan, grunting as a punch was thrown or received. They couldn't really hurt one another, bouncers fighting bouncers; they didn't seem to notice the blows, remaining calm, churning out punches like automated machines as they released their pent-up anger and escaped the mundanity of their day-to-day lives. I found the whole thing difficult to resist, appealing to something deep inside me, where Peter lived.

I stepped forward, alongside the flash jacket of a police constable embedded within the front row of a gawping public, stationary, as they watched the writhing mass in front. My next step took me into the gap between the crowd and the melee, the constable putting her gloved hand on my shoulder, before registering that I was a priest and pulling it away, unsure what to do. I convinced myself that I was there to make peace, but that was a lie. I was captivated by the violence, drawn to it.

'Excuse me please,' I said to the nearest two, their faces bright red as they grappled with each other, spittle flying. 'EXCUSE ME PLEASE!' I repeated, shouting this time, gaining their attention as they paused, looking at me as if I were a mirage before turning back to each other, confused. 'Could I just get through?'

They both smiled, showing a kind of mutual respect, before letting go of each other and standing back.

'Sorry, Father,' they mumbled in turn.

The next two combatants had also paused, looking at me with the same confused expression, top lip lifted, creating wrinkles on the nose, a pair of buck teeth. They did the same, withdrawing, one catching the other with a blow to the chin as he shuffled back.

'That was out of order,' I chastised, stopping, giving a stern look.

'Sorry, Father,' he replied, a trickle of blood running down from his nose. He tried to wipe it away, but only succeeded in smudging it clumsily across his beetroot face.

'It's not me you need to say sorry to,' I said.

'Sorry, Gav,' he called over my shoulder, waving apologetically to his opponent. 'I just got carried away.'

'It's alright, Don. Happens to the best of us,' his victim replied, as if he had accidentally stepped on his toe.

*They know each other*, I realised, incredulous.

The other nearby potatoes had also stopped, only the ones on the far side still grunting away.

'Let Jesus through,' one shouted.

'Stop fighting – the vicar wants to get through.'

Although the Church was losing its relevance, people still had respect for the collar, more so than for the police, it appeared, as they gradually stopped and let go of one another, silent but for the heaving of breath from their exertions, as if they had just completed an aerobic workout; bums, tums and thighs, or maybe Zumba. I smiled at an image in my mind, of bald heads facing an instructor, upbeat music and synchronised routines, thrusting and jumping in bright Lycra, feeling the burn.

The Red Sea parted down the centre, leaving a clear path, voices coming from either side as I passed through – 'Father,' 'Reverend,' – pleasant greetings, as if I was back in the village, amongst more genteel folk, making me question why they were here at all. The answer was simple; they just didn't know it. They needed to be part of something, to belong to a cause, the demise of religion having left a void that football had filled, its players the new Gods, setting one denomination against another.

Most had their eyes to the ground, slightly unsure, the adrenaline tapering off as I walked through with a swagger, emerging out the other side to see the spectators also parting, allowing me to continue walking towards the station as they closed ranks behind me like flowing liquid.

'Macca,' a voice called out.

I stopped, a freezing sensation creeping over me. I hadn't heard that name for years, not since Liverpool, as I hesitated before turning, reluctant to find its source, but the whole scene had kicked off again, as if somebody had knocked it off pause. Four police horses now approached from below, making their way up the concourse through the crowd, all different colours, a big white beast leading the way, snorting and shaking its head behind a Perspex visor, giving off steam and frothy sweat as it was restrained, anticipating the action to come.

*Conquest,* I thought, as I finally entered the station, filtering through the checkpoint before walking between the various food outlets. *It will be over soon enough.*

The train was crowded with football fans singing, their spirits high from alcohol and not getting beat. I'd managed to get a seat, tight in the corner, where I unclipped my dog collar to avoid the usual barrage of jokes. I was feeling comfortable; these were people I understood, like an army returning from enemy territory, warriors in high spirits, draped in colours, flags and standards, shouting battle cries and victory songs, their plunder a solitary point. It was tribal, knitting together disparate people into a cohesive family, strangers acting as one, with songs spreading down the carriage as the revellers bounced up and down along the aisle, arms waving in the seats. Their characters were amplified, louder, bolder, saying and doing things they could never do in their everyday lives, in front of everyday people. The shackles were off; monkey see, monkey do.

I looked through my reflection at the landscape passing by; the industrial green between cities, with its forgotten villages and the characters that lived in them, as we sped across a bridge, the water below giving a flash of brilliant orange, a last salvo from the departing sun. I was seeing analogies, metaphors, from football to the murmuration of starlings now decorating the sky, forming amorphous shapes, twisting and folding in clean, fluid movements. It was everything that religion should be, a continually changing blur, a joyous, connected sharing of emotion as they simultaneously moved as one.

'God,' I mumbled to myself, attracting a glance from the fan sitting next to me.

*'Flowery shite,'* Peter scolded.

The fields gave way to suburbs as the train approached its destination, providing glimpses of urban scenes, people walking and cars driving, oblivious to the fact that they were being watched. The tracks slowly descended, becoming enveloped in shadow as we slowed and then juddered to a halt in the cut, its walls an intricate patchwork of brick and sandstone, again, the manmade and the natural; the foundation the city was built upon, its richness barely visible in the darkness. It had a Victorian feel, like steam trains had recently plied the tracks, their coal dust and smog staining the surroundings, coating everything in shades of black as I stared out of the window, my reflection staring back, elongated, pale and gaunt, jerking with fright at the sight of a face emerging from a tiny black house, imperceptible in the gloom, before disappearing again as he closed the door behind him. A devil taking a cigarette break.

We proceeded to lurch forward again, into darkness then light, darkness then light, as the journey continued below arched bridges carrying streets of life above, before finally emerging from the shadows into the bright, artificial light of the station, slowly coming to a halt between the long empty platforms.

'This is the final destination,' the tannoy announced. 'Please alight, and remember to take your belongings with you.'

*Home*, I thought, the word loaded with meaning, filling me with dread as I remained seated, sweating, letting the carriage empty until I sat alone, the sounds of football fading, their effervescence diluting as they broke up, mixing with outsiders. I tentatively followed, begrudgingly leaving the carriage and walking up the concourse, a tiny speck in a vast, empty space, my steps echoing, bouncing off the hard surfaces and decorative iron beams sailing overhead, supporting the dirty glass roof, allowing the last hues of sunset through a filter of grime and pigeon shit.

It was quiet, a brief lull whilst they checked my documents, waiting for the next trainload of foot soldiers, though I welcomed the delay. As they waved me through, I became self-conscious, sensing people close, their steps in rhythm with mine, feeling vulnerable as I turned to see random stragglers, whose boisterousness and camaraderie was gone for another week. The nearest of them was almost upon me, head down, hands in pockets; just the dome of his shaven head visible as he glanced up and our eyes met, holding each other's gaze for a split second, enough to send a message, before his face went back down behind his scarf.

*'Paranoid already,'* Peter scoffed.

I exited through a stone archway filled with sleek glass, delivering me on to a raised terrace, steps cascading below. The expanse of St George's Hall loomed before me, a mass of Portland stone, with a portico of uplit columns breaking up its bulk, sitting like a temple on a broad plinth. A smile touched my lips; it felt like I'd chanced upon an eccentric old friend, somehow forgotten. Most civic buildings reinforced power, but this was a celebration of eighteenth-century hedonism, created for festivals, dinners and concerts; it still suited the culture of the city today. The plaza in front gave it breathing space, afforded in recognition of its stature and the importance of decadence to the city, guarded by stone lions resting on high plinths. As a child, I imagined that they awoke at night, walking down to the tunnel, protecting us from the *Woolybacks* and *Plazzies* trying to get through. The smile spread.

*How the young mind can accept such ideas*, I thought, *believing in the remarkable before the realities of life are forced upon them.*

There was a crowd, silhouettes gathered around an illuminated red shadow made up of ceramic poppies cascading down between the columns, before oozing off the plinth like liquid, a falling tribute to the fallen in an appropriate location. It was here that the Pals met, Lord Derby's quota, filled with propaganda and bravado before shipping off, their flesh and bone meeting the mechanized war machine, less than half of them coming back. If the crowd turned, they would see the Duke of Wellington stood on top of his column, cast from melted-down bronze cannons captured at his

Waterloo, a perch for the pigeons. Memories were flooding back.

'Don't look at the man on the top,' Dad used to say, 'Look at the column. They are the bodies of the dead, lost in battle, the common man – unidentified, anonymous, raising him up.'

I preferred the poppies.

A group of girls walked past below, raucous and laughing, drawing me from my introspection, their voices loud, actions dramatic, wearing very little, as was typical in these parts.

'*Fuck off*, you *slag*,' one screeched, shoving her friend, and then placing a protective arm around her.

'*Eeee*, you dirty bitch,' came the reply, as the others laughed hysterically, scattering across the pavement before coming back together, like the starlings, beautiful, shimmering and unrefined, reacting to each other's movements and sounds, travelling in a flock to the next bar.

I realised that I still hadn't entered the city, remaining rooted at the top of the steps, surprised to find I was glad to be back as the anxiety and fear dissipated. I glanced down at my heavy bags on the floor.

'*There's a lot more baggage than that,*' Peter reminded me, seeking to nip any optimism in the bud.

The girls' voices drowned him out, though, as I picked the bags up and descended, stepping over the threshold, passing an invisible border, and allowed the city's memories to rise back up into my mind, flooding over mental barricades carefully placed to maintain sanity and some semblance of happiness.

It was all coming back, its sounds, its smells; the feel of the pavement underfoot, the streets still imprinted on my subconscious. It had changed since I was last there, but it was also the same as I walked along Lime Street, an area I remembered well, where the old had been replaced by a characterless new. There was an honesty about it at least, the new development apologising for its blandness, carrying drawings of the architectural richness it had replaced upon its monotonous elevations, as takeaways and pubs continued to illuminate the terrace with neon-tinted life en route to the Adelphi, slightly out of my budget.

The streets were getting busier as I continued into the city. I called at the usual chains, but they were all full; no room at the Premier Inn. My shoulders were complaining as I looked to the pub across the road, its neon-green lights hinting at an Irish bar, whilst the décor pointed towards the Beatles.

*McCartney's*, I read above the door. *Could be either or both.*

A sign on the wall said hotel, worth a try as I picked up the bags and stepped into the nightlife, a wave of noise and warm air hitting me as I opened the door.

It was bustling, but not so busy that I couldn't get through; just right as I leaned over the bar, shouting to the barmaid, not loud enough for her to hear over the music as she ushered me to the end.

'Have you got any rooms?' I asked.

'We have,' she said. 'Do you want a double or a single?'

'Just a single,' I replied, relieved.

'You might need a double, you know – good-looking lad like you,' she smiled, giving me a wink. 'Where are the rest of you?'

'What?'

'From the stag do. Where are your mates?'

'I'm not on a stag do.'

'Then why are you dressed like a vicar?'

'I'm a Priest.'

'Behave,' she slapped me on the arm and pointed across the pub to a group of nuns, a hen night, raucous in the corner. 'I suppose that's just Mother Superior having a night out with the girls,' she cackled, and then shouted out, 'Eh, girls, the stripper's arrived – stripper vicar.'

The nuns all jumped up at once, hollering, waving an inflatable man and a variety of dildos in the air, apart from the bride-to-be, who looked panicked at the thought of me removing my clothes in front of her. We both went red.

'You're hilarious,' the barmaid grinned, hitting me again before opening a door and ushering me through.

The room was small, but fine, slightly garish, with a bottle-green carpet, magnolia walls and matching green duvet; clean at least, with a small window to let in a bit of daylight. I was surprised at how quiet it was, considering the music booming below.

She handed me a key on a huge, heavy fob before leaving me alone, my initial optimism disappearing as I thought about where I was and why I was there. *This time yesterday, I was in my cottage in the village*, I thought, glancing around pensively, the place suddenly feeling too small, slightly claustrophobic. I had to get out, so quickly changed and went back downstairs, seeking the comfort of alcohol to delay the inevitable.

'Never sit with your back to the door,' I heard a cowboy say, as I took a stool at the end of the bar. The hen night had moved on, replaced by a Where's Wally-themed stag do; men dressed in stripy red tops and bobble hats, with blue trousers and thick-rimmed glasses, drinking shots, having a good time. They were the latest on a conveyor belt of stag do's and hen nights, passing through in a variety of costumes, occasionally coming together, bouncing off one another, flirting, adding to the richness of the atmosphere.

The highlight were the Spartans, most of whom had let themselves go somewhat. *No more Persians left to fight*, I supposed. Hairy ale guts hung over loincloths, swaying, man boobs trembling, but they didn't care, and with cries of 'Sparta!' shots were downed. The groom stood exposed in the middle of the pub, at the mercy of his warriors, as his Sambuca-coated nipples were ignited, flames of blue and yellow flaring up as the pub laughed hysterically, turning off the lights, the flash of camera phones giving frozen stills of the scene. It felt depraved and decadent, much like the actual Spartans.

'No smoking in here, love,' the barmaid shouted loudly, sending the pub collapsing into another wave of laughter as the nipples went out and the lights came back on.

The rest of the clientele was mostly middle-aged, either couples or single-sex groups, becoming increasingly boisterous as the evening wore on, moving off the carpeted areas and on to the wood, an impromptu dance floor, courtship displays taking place wherever groups intermingled, seduction techniques unleashed; the women immaculate, the men more varied, all talking animatedly, enjoying themselves. Meanwhile, I propped up the bar, drinking pints, an observer, always an observer. I was last man standing as the pub gradually emptied, the barmaid shouting time and ringing the massive brass bell, leading me to thoughts of Meg. I wondered what she was feeling.

*Regret, pain or disappointment? Something? Nothing?*

*'Dan?'* Peter suggested.

Heading back upstairs, I hoped the drink would take the edge off, but the room felt tighter as I closed the door behind me, the usual sense of panic starting to rise as I saw the police chief lying naked in the corner. I continued calmly, like they'd told me to – routine, routine, routine – getting undressed, folding clothes, brushing teeth and climbing into bed; breathing steadily to try to keep the feelings at bay. I felt sick, contemplating the night ahead.

My mind wouldn't stop, taking me down negative tangents as I looked at my whole life in two bags on the floor, jobless and homeless, alone with nowhere to go.

*What do other people see?* I asked myself. *What do they see when you take away all possessions and distractions, get rid of everything, their home, their job, their friends and family – stripped right down to the core, to the ultimate meaning of their lives? What do I see?*

'God,' I mouthed silently, 'in everything,' knowing that without God, it must be a void, a massive, meaningless void, an accident called life until death, and then nothing; no soul to carry on to the next stage, no future.

*Does day-to-day life insulate people from such massive thoughts*, I wondered, *or do they just not go there? Maybe they do see it, but they're able to just accept it.*

I drifted off into a shallow sleep, floating in and out of consciousness, my dreams vivid, indescribable, sliding just out of reach whenever I was about to get a grip on them, to comprehend them, my emotions lurching. They were invaded by a sharp knocking, a banging, as I sat upright and looked at the door, but it wasn't the door.

*Am I still asleep?*

The banging continued, a long, steady rhythm, complemented by low moans.

*No, please no.*

I felt the four walls rushing in on me, the weight of the ceiling pressing down, and I started to panic as I looked at the rectangle of light around the door, an angular halo, my guardian angel showing the way to escape, to run, but I stayed, even as the terror started to rise within; to wash over me.

*Bang… Bang… Bang… Bang…*

I could hear their breathing, panting through the walls, getting faster with exertion; my breath matched it, gasping, moaning as I struggled to fill my lungs, the sounds of my fear matching the sound of their pleasure, their sex.

*Bang... Bang... Bang... Bang...*

The low moans started to get louder, turning to high-pitched yelps, becoming more regular, whilst I concentrated on my breathing, getting in sync with the headboard, trying to stay in control of my emotions, to stop my mind from breaking free, running wild. It seemed to go on forever.

*Bang... Bang... Bang... Bang....*

Drenched with sweat, I felt like I was choking, suffocating. I needed to get out, but was determined to stay, so I lay there, my heart racing, gripping the sheets tightly, nails digging into palms; breathe in, breathe out. *Got to do something*, I thought.

I stood up too quickly, the room spinning as I staggered over to the sink and vomited, dropping to my knees, my body continuing to heave, twisting out of shape till it felt like it would snap. I fell down against the toilet, tasting the acid in my throat, in my nostrils, spitting it out before the next set of contortions set in, sending tears running down my face.

*Bang... Bang... Bang... Bang....*

They were speeding up, the bangs coming closer together, flesh hitting flesh, loud wails of ecstasy forcing their way through the wall, not caring who hears, lost in each other before a final crescendo as my body twisted in a silent scream, and then all quiet, their cries fading and breathing slowing until there was only stillness, followed by the gentle hum of talking. We had reached very different climaxes; my head resting, panting, on the cold porcelain. I was exhausted and empty.

I felt like I was floating as I returned to my sweat-drenched bed, my body tingling, feeling detached, heart still thumping, but I knew the worst was over; descending from the peak as the panic retreated until the next time.

*At least I didn't run*, I thought, seeking consolation. I was still there. *Not going to run anymore.*

I lay awake, thinking, my mind getting quieter as my body counted the cost of its exertions before giving in, letting sleep take over.

I woke up confused, drenched in daylight streaming through the thin curtains. For a second, I was still in the village, but then I sat up, recognising my surroundings, relieved that the night was over, whilst also feeling a sense of achievement after not ending up walking the streets. They'd started again next door, banging and moaning, not thinking of anything past their own four walls; just each other's bodies, their own intimate pleasures. It didn't seem so fearsome in the cold light of day, free from the effects of darkness and alcohol.

I jumped in the shower, the sound of the cascading water drowning out the pinnacle of the performance before stepping out when silence had resumed.

I was the first arrival at breakfast, interrupting the barmaid who was setting up. It was the same woman who had welcomed me the night before.

'You must be knackered,' I called over, reminded of Meg.

'Dead on my feet,' she replied. 'What would you like, love?'

'Erm, I don't know,' I said, drawing a blank.

'Well, what would Jesus have?' she grinned, evidently still convinced I was on a stag do.

'Probably a full English with scrambled eggs,' I said, returning the smile. 'Brown toast, obviously.'

'There you go.'

'Sounds great. Oh, and a coffee please.'

My stomach was growling, hollow after last night.

'Good night's sleep?' she asked brightly, placing a coffee down on the table in front of me, instant.

'Not really,' I answered, thinking I must have looked like shit.

'Noisy neighbours?'

I nodded as she smiled involuntarily, as though trying to hold in a much bigger laugh.

'Sorry,' she said, 'I thought you'd be out late, with you being in fancy dress and all. I thought you'd miss them.'

I looked up, raising an eyebrow as the laughter broke through. 'They gave an encore this morning,' I said. 'In case I'd missed the premiere.'

'They come here every couple of months. A special night to keep the flame burning bright, they say.'

'You could have warned me. I thought they were going to start yodelling at one point.'

She laughed out loud again, as she set out my knife and fork.

'I won't be hanging around for the matinee,' I said.

'They're not always like that,' she said. 'They do role playing, so it depends on what characters arrive each time.'

I spluttered on my coffee. 'I think Genghis Khan was in there last night,' I closed my eyes and shook my head, hearing the noises again as she continued laughing.

I was just glad to be talking to somebody.

'You'll meet them in a minute,' she said. 'They're the only other guests here, and they're usually early.'

I wasn't sure that I wanted to put faces to those sounds as a full English landed in front of me, my stomach growling in anticipation, but then the door opened just as she was topping up my coffee, and we both glanced up.

'Morning, Margaret. Morning, Stan,' she greeted them warmly.

I almost choked on my beans when Margaret walked into the room and turned to hold the door open for Stan, who came wobbling in behind on his walking stick. Margaret was clearly the younger of the two, probably somewhere around seventy, but bespectacled Stan had to be at least eighty; definitely no Genghis Khan, his silver hair slicked back, whilst she still had her rollers in. I looked to the barmaid, who gave me a wink and a smile, and all I could do was put my head down, trembling, trying not to laugh; holding my breath and clenching my teeth, concentrating.

'Good night last night?' she asked.

'It's always a good night here,' Margaret answered, before adding, 'Full English with everything please, loved. I've earned this.'

'How do you want your eggs?'

'Unfertilised,' Margaret cried, exploding with laughter, Stan joining in, the old ones are the best, as they say.

She had a laugh that could break through walls, loud and infectious, demanding company, providing the opportunity to join in, to relieve some of the pressure. The laughter eventually faded, leaving behind a warm residue that I basked in as I continued eating, sensing something beautiful behind the humour of it all.

# CHAPTER 5

IN MEMORY SANE

I leaned my head against the glass, feeling a strange buzzing in my ears, until the bus moved up a gear and the vibrations intensified, making me pull away. I was seeking distraction, dissecting my surroundings; anything to stop me thinking about my destination as we travelled against the flow, the bus silent, my only company hollow-eyed loners coming off the end of a night shift, crowded busses passing the other way.

The road was straight, direct, cutting a section as the centre gave way to the city that day trippers didn't see, a cityscape shaped by war and the slum clearances that followed, although the weed-filled plots, still empty after the Luftwaffe's bombs, suggested nothing about their history.

*How beautiful it could have been*, I thought mournfully, as we passed clusters of industrial units, strung like a choker around the city centre, moving on to blank red-brick walls and fences, behind which people lived in a maze of cul-de-sacs and dead ends. It was an environment created by politics, socialism in bricks and mortar, a nice enough idea, a council house with garden for all, but somehow it had ended up lifeless, soulless, dispirited and defensive. The road continued, past smashed up bus stops and speed cameras; past derelict Victorian factories, waiting patiently as they fell apart, ripe for regeneration in any other place, but not here, a step too far.

Where the clearances had stopped, the terraces began, a regular toast rack of streets coming off the main road, each a village with its own tight-knit community beneath a multitude of satellite dishes poking out like Mickey Mouse ears, suggesting flats, DSS. The main road was now shops, people, fast food, sun tans, phone covers and vapes; some open, most with roller shutters closed. Classical buildings were interspersed, a throwback from wealthier times, now left to rot, too expensive to maintain, cursed by their special distinction.

I felt hairs stand on end, goosebumps rise, as I caught a glimpse of the sandstone church in the distance, its spire tall and elegant, pointing to the heavens, concentrating thoughts and prayers and beaming them up. I stood, but had to look down, focussing on a young boy surfing, letting go of the bar, knees bent, swaying with the movement of the bus, everything evoking memories as we juddered to a stop.

The beeping of nearby traffic lights drew my eyes from the ground, as a grey wave of the elderly came travelling towards me in slow motion, pulling their tartan trollies. As they crashed silently around me, I stood, trembling, until the green man's flashing spurred me into action, breaking into a run as the lights flashed amber, before slamming to a halt as I arrived outside the church, my story set in stone.

My head felt like it was expanding, deforming, as it tried to contain the volume of thoughts. Trailing a finger along the rough stone wall, I continued on, placing one foot in front of the other, following it around the corner, my stomach lurching as the house came into view from behind the trees; more history, more meaning. I was struggling to maintain my composure, feeling the dam straining, about to break.

Placing my hand on the metal gate, I paused for a second before opening it, hearing that squeal as it closed behind me, rust biting into rust. Everything was familiar, the forgotten instantly recalled, each detail a trigger: the gate, door knocker, overgrown privets, chimney pot planters still empty, the cracked tiles on the pathway; overwhelming as repressed memories returned, reclaiming me. I didn't remember when I first arrived – I'd been unconscious – but the rest of that day was fixed in my mind, vivid, as if I knew something important was happening.

The sounds of the place were missing. Outside our room, it was silent, the normal routine disrupted, the usual people gone. Everybody could feel it as we nervously glanced at each other, apprehensive, saying little as we watched the clock slowly follow its path. Tick followed tock, as they say. I remembered every detail of that clock for some reason, its thin red hand trembling on every second before going onto the next, our faces looking up at its minimal, clinical face. It didn't seem to be going fast enough that morning.

We all turned and looked towards the door when we heard the handle rattle before it slowly opened inwards, blocking our view, shadows of feet reflecting on the polished floor through a tiny gap at the bottom. The shadows moved forward and a man appeared, a man we did not know, dressed like a civil servant: brown trousers, brogues and a blue pinstriped shirt with a light-blue tie and cufflinks. He didn't introduce himself, there were no pleasantries or explanation; he just took out a list and started to read out names, baritone, well spoken, southern, with a military demeanour, each name pronounced like a command.

Some stepped forward compliantly, following other men through the door to who knows what, whilst others ran, hid, looking to find another way out. I was a runner, following instinct, though there was no secret passage out of that place. It was just a matter of time as they ticked off names then turned the place upside down looking for the others, like a grown-up game of hide and seek, without the laughter; without the fun.

They found me under the bed, behind a pile of blankets.

I'd heard the scuffles and wails getting closer as others were caught; the footsteps approaching as they systematically pulled the place apart. There was a long pause, a sliver of hope, or cruelty, before the sheets in front of me started to move. I'd inhaled and held it, feeling my face flush as I tried to make myself smaller, become an ant, an atom, but then the sheet was pulled out, revealing three men's faces looking at me, curled up, foetal, until I was pulled out by my arms and legs, and dumped in front of a group of strangers.

'That's him,' I heard one of them say.

I was soon to learn that this was Yoda.

Then, the tall man came towards me with a syringe as I backed into a corner, lashing out once I touched the wall. All I could hear was Yoda's voice saying, 'It's OK, it's ok,' as I slipped away.

I remained at the end of the path, staring at the front door. This was where he saved me; took me under his wing and gave me shelter, a life, when it all came tumbling down, scattering us in different directions.

A tear ran down my cheek; I wiped it with my sleeve. I was just standing, nothing was moving, no hall lights switching on, no signs of him as I looked up at the small bedroom window, the one on the left, my room, where I'd woken up, disorientated, at my most vulnerable, outside of the world I understood.

I was not suited to society, my mind shaped by mistrust and fear, violence the only solution I knew as I punched holes in the plasterboard, splintering the door in an attempt to escape. I felt like a wild animal taken from its natural environment and introduced to a cage, the animal metaphor appropriate. I was uneducated, feral, and it felt like a prison.

The first month was virtually a blank, and the following period hazy at best, spending most of the time sedated, awake but not awake, barely conscious, just lying there, eyes open, no thoughts, no feelings, but at least the anger was kept at bay. I took the pills happily, craved them, some sort of addiction, rooting around when he wasn't there, taking one and then drifting off, not wanting to be awake, to face it all. I was afraid, but I also knew I wasn't going back to that place.

There was a blur of concerned professionals, doctors and psychiatrists trying to unpick me with their soft and gentle voices as I sat there, dumb, silent, locked in. It felt like they were talking to somebody else about someone else, and I'd just listen, my mind numb and floating, suspicious of people I didn't know, finding their softness stressful, like a caress, an attempt at seduction; turn over and we'll tickle your belly.

'You need to talk, to open up. 'You're like a dam holding back huge pressure,' they would say, along with other idiomatic phrases.

'A problem shared is a problem halved.'

'Light at the end of the tunnel.'

'Take the bull by the horns.'

And so on.

Probably useful advice at times, but not in this context. It was too painful, and I was too wary, wondering if they were testing me.

'If you'd rather not speak, try writing about your feelings,' one suggested, but I couldn't write.

They were watched closely by Yoda, with quiet conversations following each session. They would ask about my feelings, but nobody would question me about that place; no visits from the police, government officials or social workers. I was off the radar, and I was glad. I didn't want to think about it, let alone talk.

It took months for me to accept Yoda; to accept that I was safe and this was not some elaborate hoax; that he was not going to hurt me. I felt lonely, alone, missing friends, but they weren't coming back, I understood that. I'd come to accept solitude and the safety it offered. I'd seek it out, sitting for hours in its silent caress, no questions, no judgement, but bit by bit I was changing. From my initial rejection, I'd gradually swung in the opposite direction, becoming dependent on him.

I smiled the memory, even though it was embarrassing; clingy, like a dog, pining whenever he left the house, sitting at the top of the stairs, waiting for his silhouette to appear at the front door. When he wasn't there, I was at the mercy of my mind; it would run, telling me I'd have to leave soon. He'd find me shaking and would hold me, stroking my hair, telling me I was safe, settling me like a baby before giving me a pill to sleep, to forget. I was being deconstructed and then reconstructed, I understand that now, but as a teenage boy, it was a mix of feelings that I could not comprehend; my history, medication and age creating a complex soup of permanent imbalance. My memories, my core personality, had been obliterated, driven from me. I didn't know who I was; just some hollowed-out shell, lacking thoughts or opinions on anything, conditioned to do the opposite of thinking, to forget. I still felt fear, but it was a different type than what I was used to. This was not physical, it was a fear that I could do nothing about, a fear of losing what I had; the feeling that some call love.

I'd never felt love before, not even for my mother or father; I'd been too young to understand what it was. I'd heard the word, but I had no idea if it was real or just something invented; what people said, a fantasy. My feelings for Yoda were not love, but obsession. I was lost, and he was the answer to everything. He filled a void in me that I didn't know existed; worked out a path for me, helping me take the first steps into Christianity, setting up a framework, a routine for life as we'd start and finish with prayers, the rest of the day occupied by the demands of the Church, directing me towards God.

At first, I was like a wraith, helping with the preparations before services, and then disappearing whenever strangers appeared, returning only once these intruders had left. Over time, though, the voices would become recognisable, and I would start to catch glimpses of the speakers. Simple greetings followed, leading to slightly longer conversations; 'Hello' became 'How are you?'

It was the same in the house. When people visited, I would find it hard to breathe; hiding, listening behind doors until, eventually, familiarity began to draw me out, and I started to welcome people, keen to listen to what they had to say, looking for company in the church.

He invited tutors into his home and introduced me to the Bible, and whilst my initial reaction was, as always, silence, I quickly opened up once I started to learn. It gave me purpose, and I was voracious in my consumption, my mind having been starved until that point. It wanted more: theology, science, maths; I craved it, spending my days alone in books, soon catching up and then overtaking children of my age, doing exams a year earlier than required and getting the grades without stepping foot inside a classroom.

I became a part of the Church, part of its community, swinging incense and carrying the cross, taking part in services and holding conversations with anybody that wanted to talk. He'd given me a doctrine to live by, and I threw myself into it, accepting what I should believe in, how I should behave and what makes a good person. It made me feel part of something bigger, with values and beliefs based on something good. I was no longer autonomous, I didn't have to think for myself; I was being re-educated to think the right way.

I'd been socialised into becoming a functioning member of society, and yet there were depths that the indoctrination could not reach; my inner monologue, constantly talking about the past I was trying so hard to repress, sometimes violently, but still it remained.

'*We are all infected and impure with sin,*' Peter would mock.

I started running, to get out of the house and empty my mind; to stop thinking, but I could never outrun the voice; only quiet it for a limited time, until the run was over. I needed something more.

The answer was Stanley Park.

I'd run through the manicured gardens, past the wrought-iron bandstand, with its glasshouse and sandstone structures, and then around the lake, where fishermen cast lines to catch leviathans living between shopping trollies and traffic cones; running hard till I was panting, out of breath, on the edge of the football pitches. There, I'd find two large packs of adolescent adversaries, watched over by uninterested police, chatting and joking as the groups moved backwards and forwards, ebbing and flowing in a contorted dance, like the starlings, as they hurled rocks and abuse at each other before coming together in a crunch of flying fists and kicks.

It was Walton versus the Breck, and this was where they relieved their boredom and frustrations at the monotony of their teenage lives, through battle. This was where Peter would find freedom, his voice rising with the adrenaline, taking over as the fists flew and blows landed, revelling in the cries and the blood until the police would get bored with the entertainment and move us on. I'd wash in the lake, wiping the blood off my knuckles and face before running back hard, pounding the pavement, no longer fighting myself as Peter was sated.

Once home, I'd seek forgiveness; confess my sins whilst pulling a blade down my arms, watching the blood rise in lines, the droplets getting bigger and bigger until they ran down my fingers into the sink or the bath, joining the water and contorting into beautiful twisting shapes, diluting and fading before the next one arrived.

*Forgive me, Lord, for I have sinned.*

I'd often look at the vulnerable underside of my wrists, the pale blue, but suicide was never in my thoughts, and the cutting wasn't a cry for help. It was a distraction, an outlet, absolution; my private conversation with God.

*What would have happened if he hadn't picked me up?* I thought, rolling up my sleeve to look at the white lines crisscrossing my forearm, barely perceptible now, but still a permanent reminder of my salvation.

'Are you going to stand there all fucking day?' a voice asked from behind.

I spun around and then looked down, finding Yoda looking up at me. He didn't seem a day older than I remembered, all four-foot-ten-inches of him; little bald head, and sticky-out ears with clumps of grey hair protruding out of them. He was possibly wearing the same clothes, too, a knitted tank top of chocolate brown and light-blue diamonds above caramel cords.

It was only in seeing him in the flesh that I realised how much I had missed him, feeling embarrassed about not keeping in touch, but thankful, relieved that I was here now.

A broad smile spread across his face.

'Peter,' he said, in that deep but gentle voice, as he beckoned me forward, putting his arms around me in a tight embrace, his shiny scalp just below my chest. I hugged him back, awkwardly, trying not to squeeze his head, placing my hands on his shoulders instead.

'Sorry for turning up out of the blue,' I said, before adding sheepishly, 'and for not keeping in touch as much as I should have.'

'No problem, I knew you were coming. I thought you might have got here last night.'

'What?'

'Your dad told me.'

'Eh?' I frowned.

'He called me yesterday, after your visit. He was worried. Told me the gist of it in the minute he had.'

'But–'

'We've been in touch since he went to prison. Well, on and off since your mum died actually – not necessarily as clergy and congregation, more somebody to talk to. We get on. We're mates, I suppose.'

My mind was racing. 'I didn't–'

'He's the reason that you and I met in the first place. He asked me to come and find you.'

I was staring, mouth agog, trying to think, wondering where to start. He had me, and he knew it.

'I had no idea,' I spluttered.

He always had a way of knocking me off balance with a sleight of hand, a turn of phrase; those Jedi mind tricks. You could never turn up to speak to him prepared. He would spin you around, disorientate you, opening you up, leaving you vulnerable.

'Come in, come in,' he gestured excitedly, pulling his keys out of his pocket as he squeezed past, no doubt delighted with how things had gone so far. 'What are we doing talking on the doorstep?'

I followed him inside, and as he closed the door behind us, everything came rushing back. It still looked the same, smelled the same, like old books, a smell I'd missed; something resembling home. I hung my jacket on the newel post, the usual place, and then opened the door into the small living room with the same worn armchair, the same two-seater settee and the electric fire, with its red light revolving under fake coals. The rest of the space was taken up by books, always books, plus a small TV balancing on a haphazard pile of hardbacks in the corner. It was like a normal house, only smaller, fitting perfectly around him.

*Did he grown in proportion with his surroundings, or did the place shrink to fit him?* I wondered. *He's a stubborn old goat, so it was probably the house that had to yield.*

Scruff came over and sniffed around me. He was a wiry terrier, blind now, with just the three teeth jutting out of his mouth at different angles; talk about dogs resembling their owners. There had been a continual line of Scruffs since I'd known him, all identical, like he'd had the original cloned, with new ones ready to take out of the cupboard once the previous replica had expired. They were old from the beginning, with a temperament to match.

He gave a little growl, demanding that I offer my hand up for him to smell, and then he sat by my feet, seemingly accepting me, yet still angry after all these years. I sat on the sofa looking around, taking it all in, receiving memories, until Yoda entered with a tray of coffee and biscuits.

*Garibaldi*, I thought. *Always Garibaldi.*

He produced a little fold-out table and set it up between us, before placing down the tray and taking the seat opposite. He then got straight down to dunking, letting me wait, closing his eyes in mock ecstasy as he ate the soggy biscuit, savouring every mouthful; the same old routine.

'You look like shit warmed up,' he finally said, not one for empty pleasantries. 'You haven't slept, have you?'

'Not really,' I laughed.

'Your dad says you're leaving the village, or that you've left it already.

What's the score there?'

'Just the usual,' I shrugged. 'Itchy feet.'

'It's more than that, though, isn't it?' he prodded, reading me like one of his books.

'I've been suspended.'

He jerked upright, nearly spilling his coffee. 'What for? Who did that?' he demanded, outraged.

I smiled. He loved a fight, and was still protective as ever, even after all these years. I explained what had happened, the sorry tale becoming lighter with each telling, like harmless fun a lifetime ago; shits and giggles.

'Sounds like a Carry On film,' he quipped, laughing aloud at some parts, and he was right; Barbara Windsor's saucy cackle, Kenneth Williams's nasal tones and Sid James's dirty laugh could easily have been transplanted onto the lead characters. I was struck again by the gentleness of village life.

The joviality stopped when I told him about Bishop Gordon and his involvement with Paul.

'That little gobshite,' he shook his head. 'Grown a pair, has he? I'll ask around, see what he's up to. Don't worry, I'll sort that out.'

He couldn't hold back the smile lifting the corners of his lips.

*Right up your street*, I thought. *Like Scruff, looking for something to sink your teeth into.* 'I still would have left. I wouldn't let him push me out if I wanted to stay there,' I added, perhaps a little too defensively.

'I know,' he nodded, 'you don't need your tough guy routine with me. He's a man who needs a system and rules to hide behind. He does what he's told, and he thinks everybody else should do the same without questioning anything. He's like a fucking robot.' He started laughing at that, moving his arms in little jerky movements, looking across to check if I was laughing along. I was, I knew the script. 'So, what pushed you? You usually have something lined up before you move on.'

'I'm having doubts,' I said. *Something else to get your teeth into.*

Everybody doubts their faith at some stage, Peter,' he sat forward, looking concerned. 'You wouldn't be human if you didn't. You wouldn't have a pulse. God gave us free will – we choose our own direction.'

'It's not my faith,' I answered quickly, 'I still believe. It's about the Church.'

'Go on.'

'There's a split inside me. I feel like two different people at once, Peter and the priest. At the moment, they just feel so far apart.'

'That's quite common, believe it or not,' he shrugged, as if I'd just described the symptoms of a mild cold.

'I stand at the pulpit, saying the words and carrying out the actions, but it feels like I'm acting, like a performer on the stage, putting on a costume and reading a script.'

He was listening intently, pausing only to pick up a Garibaldi and inspect the currants. God and biscuits.

'I thought maybe it was because I was working somewhere else,' I went on, 'where I was an outsider, but it's not just that. The split isn't an external thing, it's more internal. I've been moving for all the wrong reasons.'

'At least you understand yourself – you can see the issue,' he said, seeing the positive in everything. 'That's good. It's rare.'

'The Priest exists solely on the surface,' I confessed. 'There's a barrier. I feel like Peter impersonating a Priest.'

He picked up the last biscuit and then sat back in his chair, thinking. 'I see that people are struggling,' he said. 'They sense that there is something missing, but they go shopping instead of looking to religion to resolve their problems.'

'But that's not really–'

He held up a finger, cutting me off mid-sentence.

*'He's on the 68, taking the long way around,'* Peter groaned, as I prepared to listen. He never gave a short answer, always preferring the scenic route.

'Their world is being stripped of meaning,' he continued, 'replaced with desires, the next mobile phone, thinking it will fix everything until the next must-have piece of bullshit comes along. Don't get me wrong, some of these items can improve lives, but plenty do just the opposite.' He studied the biscuit, counting currants, talking to it, turning it. 'It's different than it was years ago. People just don't seem to think for themselves anymore – they are told how to think. They don't do what they want to do, or take risks to get where they want to be. The characters and eccentrics are disappearing. They're becoming standardised – the same clothes, the same haircuts. Where are the men who went out on ships? The men who fought for their beliefs, for the country? They've been replaced by call centre workers, middle management and clerical officers.' He looked over and smiled. 'Sounding old, aren't I?' he laughed, as he popped the biscuit into his mouth, crunching it quietly, deep in thought. 'They work to buy the things that will fulfil their desires, but most people who come to see me are getting nothing from their jobs except money. They don't do what they like, they do what is lucrative, or sometimes not, and this is where it touches on what you are feeling. They are employed in roles that they have to act out, becoming someone else.'

He looked down at the plate, seeing it was empty.

'But that shouldn't be me,' I said, wondering where this was going. 'Being a Priest is different. It's religion, faith, me speaking God's word to the congregation. I shouldn't have to act.'

Again, he held up a finger, signalling that the lesson was not yet over. 'Don't you see all the smiling faces everywhere? Masks that people wear, even in the shittiest jobs? Their employers want them to act a certain way, be happy whilst you get a minimum wage for wiping a pensioner's arse, or selling some old shit to somebody who doesn't want it. Eventually, work and life become inseparable – something created by the employer. People don't know who they are anymore, their personalities distorted. We are all air stewardesses now, hiding what's really going on inside, an all-smiling society.'

'But I *need* to become something else,' I countered. 'It allows me to escape. I need to put on the mask and become a better version of me, a smiling face.'

He was sitting forward, nodding, mind-reading.

'It means I can hide something of myself,' I smiled, almost apologetically, 'presenting the version of me that's required for the role, concealing the bad bits. Maybe everybody is the same,' I shrugged my shoulders. 'Maybe we all need work to make us normal. Maybe once we're away from the humdrum, the normal human condition comes through – the chaos.'

'But that's not a natural human condition,' he argued, voice rising slightly. 'We are in a dumbed down, non-thinking era. The latest thing they're worried about is deep fakes, but we're already there, individuals are deep fakes. Fuck artificial intelligence, it's this artificial stupidity I'm worried about.'

'We're as advanced as we've ever been,' I objected. 'The highest quality of life in human history.'

'Depends how you define quality of life,' he laughed bitterly. 'Behind all the smiles and talk of how "we've never had it better," everyone seems to be on pills to maintain their act. Anti-depressants, tranquillisers, anti-psychotics – you could hear them rattling along the road if you listened close enough, those pill boxes with the days of the week on. We're mentally weak all of a sudden, vulnerable. There's an epidemic of phobias, depression, anxiety, loneliness… mental health issues all around us.'

'The past wasn't some perfect utopia, either.'

'True, but society has changed. The idea of community has gone. They're all individuals now, separated and isolated, shaped to fit society's needs in their own lonely, self-consuming worlds. They seem to be bound without realising it, tied up and conditioned, limited in how they act, how they think. We're not designed for that. We're social beasts, so much more vulnerable on our own.'

'Surely, things aren't that bad? I'm not sure most people would agree that they are pill popping zombies.'

'If it's not anti-depressants, it's recreational drugs, or getting pissed off their heads at the weekend. They need to get out of their lives of ritual and habit – wanking, working, washing, sleeping and eating. They overindulge, vent their anger. Frustrations come out in violence, stabbing one another –

shootings over tiny little things, a look or a misplaced word, escaping life until Monday comes around again and the mask goes back on.'

'So, you're saying I'm normal. We're all just schizophrenic now?'

'Well, what do you think you are?'

I paused, finding it difficult to put my thoughts into words. 'I'm not much of a consumer,' I began, thinking of the two bags that held all of my belongings, 'and though I need the escape of ritual and habit, my mind doesn't let me rest there. It's as if I'm composed of layers, like an onion, each one a different version of me, with different, contradictory viewpoints. There's the fully conscious me, which operates day to day – the one that wants to be the Priest,' I hesitated before adding, 'and then there are the others that emerge.'

'Go on,' he softly urged.

'There are internal dialogues,' I glanced down to see my palms held open, almost pleadingly. 'I argue with myself. Is everybody like this? Am I actually schizophrenic?' I heard the desperation tinting my words, as I finally gave voice to an unspoken idea that was constantly going through my mind; the starting point of many a sleepless night.

'You're not schizophrenic,' he grinned.

'The problem is that the personalities are so at odds with one another. When the priest speaks, people think there's more truth to my words, due to a perceived status. Deep down inside, though, there is such anger, such rage, that I keep a lid on. There are demons there, pure evil. I imagine myself fighting, punching, kicking – hurting people. I feel like a fraud standing in front of a congregation, spouting God's words of love and truth, when I'm not even able to be honest with myself.'

He reached over and put his hand on my knee, causing me to jump, unconsciously, a natural reflex.

'There are valid reasons for your feelings of rootlessness, your directionless wandering – your anger,' he said, speaking slowly, looking me in the eye. 'You're different. It's not money or desire that's responsible for the way you are, it's your past. The other life still being lived inside you, if you like.'

I nodded, feeling a sudden pain in my finger, a bubble of blood rising where I'd bit my nail down to the quick. I clasped my hands together on my lap.

'Religion doesn't have all the answers to your questions, Peter. You need to look for them yourself, but you don't have to leave your job first. What would you do, become a clerical officer like the rest of them? May as well get a lobotomy.' He smirked, trying to inject some levity. 'Your weaknesses are actually your strengths. I can't stand the idea of you becoming sanitised, turning into a Bishop Gordon, gutless, chinless, toeing the line.'

I felt exhausted, my body heavy, tired, like I had just completed a long journey. He spoke softly, quietly, but there was real power in his voice. His small frame seemed to fill the room.

'You have your own personality, which needs to come through,' he said, using his hands to emphasise his points. 'There is no reason why your anger can't be your greatest asset, as long as it's used correctly.'

'Wait, what?' I didn't understand.

'Break down the barrier, and let Peter come through the priest, as opposed to the priest subsuming Peter, and we will have something very strong,' he said, as if stating the obvious. 'That's how you will heal the split in yourself. The priest needs to become Peter, not the other way around. This is where everybody is getting it wrong.'

*'And that's why they call him Yoda,'* Peter whispered, a hint of triumph detectable. *'Let me past the priest.'*

I couldn't speak, and instead just sat gawping at him.

'Where are your bags?' he asked, seeming to sense my tiredness. 'You can stay here tonight, even though you've eaten all my biscuits.'

I hadn't touched one, of course. It was one thing for the Garibaldis to be seen, but another thing entirely to manage to grab one.

'Back at the hotel,' I answered, 'in town.'

'What were you going to do after this? Where were you going to go?' he frowned, a pattern of deep creases sinking into his forehead.

'I don't know,' I said, knowing how stupid I sounded. 'I hadn't planned that far ahead.'

'Go and get your stuff,' he said, feigning exasperation. 'Your room is ready upstairs. It's up to you how long you stay, but I won't have you wandering around homeless. There's somebody I want you to meet tomorrow. Speak with him, and you may get a clearer idea of what you want to do.'

'Who is it?'

'No one important. Now, go and get your stuff.'

With that, I was outside, the door closing behind me. I didn't remember leaving my chair.

*'Fucking Jedis'* Peter whispered.


I returned later that evening with my bags, lugging them through the hallway and up the narrow stairs as Scruff worried my shoelaces, shaking his head, growling and gumming me, wishing he still had teeth.

'Scruff!' Yoda shouted. 'Scruff!' but it didn't seem to register as I added going deaf to the dog's list of ailments.

My body remembered this place, with its uneven treads, the third one creaky, the slightly shaky banister and the smooth painted spheres of the newel posts, which I used to swing around. I tried it with my eyes closed, walking up the last few stairs and then along the landing, reaching my hand forward and gripping the door handle, its feel familiar, exactly where I expected it to be.

Opening the door to my room was like stepping back in time, though I felt more like I was staggering backwards as familiar objects, long forgotten, reasserted themselves; relics from my childhood, the defining period of my life, which still had its hooks set deep inside me.

*How different it was back then*, I thought. *How different I was back then.*

I laughed as I sat on my Sergio Tacchini duvet, lying down and smelling it, searching for a long-lost trace of me. My Head bag was in the corner, and even my posters were still up on the walls: U2, Simple Minds and Pink Floyd covering the woodchip wallpaper.

I looked around, and the laughter began to subside. It now felt slightly disconcerting, as if a mother had lost a child; preserving their life and sealing it off, a capsule frozen in time.

*That's not his style*, I thought. *Surely, it hasn't been like this since I left – a shrine to me?*

'Well, you didn't run.'

I turned around to find Yoda in the doorway, leaning on the frame.

'What are you up to?' I smiled.

'This is where you left off,' he said. 'I wanted you to see it, childish as it may seem.' He walked over and sat next to me on the bed. 'I want you to think of everything you've achieved since you were last here – places you've been to, people you've met. The boy that was here could never have dreamt of those possibilities. His mind was closed, possibly never to open, but then it did, and now look at you.'

'Yeah, living out of a bag.'

'I'm very proud of you,' he said, after a pause. 'You've been away for so long, afraid to come back, which is why it felt important that you should see this.'

'It all seems so trivial now,' I shook my head. 'It meant everything at one point.'

'The memories of that snotty-nosed child of the nineties, who lived in this room, dictate your behaviour now, as a grown man. The point I want you to understand is that it's not just place that you need to consider, it is also time. It is always a combination of both. A place does nothing to you. The city is just a backdrop, a stage, if you like, upon which life takes place. It is fixed. It is people and time that are temporary, fluid – coming together and drifting apart, intertwining, creating stories, creating memories. It was over twenty years ago that you were last in this room, and your memories of the city are also from that time. What I'm trying to say is, you have nothing to fear by being here. Everything looks the same, but it's completely different. The past is in the past.'

'Somewhere long ago, in a galaxy far, far away?'

'Yes, I suppose you could say that,' Yoda flicked his eyebrows. 'Now, I don't want you hiding behind the door while you're here, whether it's for a day, a week, whatever. This city is your home. Go out and get to know it again. Get to know the people you once knew.'

∞

A forgotten fear was re-emerging, as I sat nervously tapping my fingers on the table. Dinner was always traumatic; he only knew one way to cook, everything boiled until completely drained of flavour, and tonight would be no different. I remembered retching, faced by another meal of boiled meat and vegetables, the only point of disagreement we'd had ever really had.

'Don't eat it, then,' his usual reply to my protestations.

Tonight's fare was boiled potatoes with boiled bacon, and half a tin of runner beans. I found myself flinching as memories, lodged deep in my subconscious, tried to trigger my gag reflex and evacuate my stomach, as I looked at the gelatinous white fat of the bacon.

'Don't you want that?' Yoda asked, his fork hovering.

*'You can't stay here too long,'* Peter whispered.

We were talking and drinking, keeping an eye on the empties of strong Polish lager, from the German supermarket, that were accumulating on the sideboard. Considering his size, Yoda was probably the best pound-for-pound drinker I had ever known. He could put away vast quantities seemingly without effect, or perhaps with effect, but I was too far gone to notice. He was telling me how he'd been forced into retirement two months earlier because of Fr Williams, who was currently facing charges for the sexual abuse of minors over a ten-year period, after one victim had the courage to come forward.

'I felt physically sick when I heard,' he said. 'I didn't suspect a thing. He was well liked, popular, with a steady congregation. Then, I received a telephone call from the police, telling me he'd been arrested.' He necked his can before reaching for a fresh one. 'I headed down to the station, and Fr Williams admitted to everything there and then, in front of me, as if admission would go some way towards absolving him of sin, a confession to cleanse his soul. The police had to go and see parents whose children he might have abused, to tell them everything that had happened. It was horrendous.'

'But why did you have to take the fall?' I asked.

'It was on my watch, so I resigned immediately. I couldn't believe I'd missed it – there must have been clues that I just hadn't picked up.'

He sat shaking his head, clearly still in disbelief. It was the first time I had ever seen him doubt himself.

'You can't keep an eye on every church in Liverpool,' I said. 'You can't take responsibility for one bad apple.'

'I couldn't live with myself if I didn't. The Church has made grave mistakes with similar cases in the past, and I wasn't willing to be a part of that culture of not listening to allegations, or priests being brought back into the system, as if he could repent and be repaired. Fuck that. Hang him out to dry, I say.'

*What a way for such a remarkable man to finish his career*, I thought, shaking my head slowly, *dragged down by another's misdeeds.*

'You know what it's like,' he sighed, 'we have to show it's not a Church problem, but a Fr Williams problem – the opposite of most organisations. The Church has done it many times, we are probably more guilty than most, but the more you look, the more you see it happening. It has become ingrained in our society.'

'What do you mean?'

'Look at the police, for example, and what happened with the newspaper seller just walking home, or that Brazilian guy, standing, waiting for the train. They did it with Hillsborough, they'll do it with the next, and the next and the next.'

'What's that got to do with the Church?'

'It's not just the police,' he continued, ignoring my question, 'there was the academic who wouldn't toe the line with Blair's policy on Iraq. Look at the government for that one. How many bankers have faced a jury, despite clear proof of illegal activity?'

'None?' I answered, wondering how he was going to pull these disparate threads together to make a point.

'Not far off, yet if somebody claims extra benefits, they can end up in prison.'

'I still don't see what that's got to do with–'

'They deflect blame from the individual on to the system when it suits, because how can you arrest a system, be it a religion, the government, the police or a bank? You can't. It's impersonal, centreless, just an abstraction, and so they all get away scot-free. I couldn't be a part of that. The Church can no longer be part of that.' He sat back and let out a sigh, rant over. 'Besides, I'm getting on now. I had to stop some time,' he lamented, draining the last of his beer and giving the can a little shake, to make sure it had all gone. 'Right, I'm off to bed – early start tomorrow. Are you staying up?'

'No, I'm shattered,' I said, the previous night catching up with me. 'I just want to say thank you. I feel a million times better today than yesterday. I can't believe I stayed away for so long. I'm so sorry.'

'Nothing to apologise for, lad. I was watching over you, speaking to people about you, and you really do have to give yourself a bit of credit. You are an incredibly strong, bright young man.' He stood and placed his hand on my shoulder, smiling down at me, the light from behind catching the few remaining grey hairs on his head, creating a halo effect. 'Take Scruff out for a shit, and make sure you turn the lights off after yourself.

I'll see you in the morning.'

# CHAPTER 6

ABC

I slept better than I had in years, deep and dreamless. The sheets were undisturbed, save for the indentation of my body, not soaked with sweat or wrenched from the corners; no signs of struggle or anguish, of twisting and turning; just calm and peace. I muttered a prayer of thanks to the Polish lager.

Voices were coming from downstairs, a different bass vibrating through the floor as I checked my watch: nine-thirty. I'd slept in; unheard of.

*'Probably drugged the butter beans,'* Peter suggested, as I quickly pulled my clothes on, trying to remain quiet, though Yoda would know exactly where I was, the creaky floorboards betraying my movements.

I crept down the stairs, avoiding the third from bottom, stretching over it, pirouetting on the newel post and landing quietly before pushing open the living room door. There I froze, blinking. I'd let my guard down.

'Good– good morning,' I stammered, after a long pause, considering the bizarre scene of Yoda sat in his armchair, holding his coffee, grinning widely, whilst across the room was the former Archbishop of Canterbury, the ABC himself, taking up the sofa.

He was massive, accentuating the small scale of the room which made him appear even bigger that he actually was. They looked so odd together, like Gandalf and Frodo, Hagrid and Dobby; two different species of human being. His white beard and frizzy hair gave the impression of an eccentric wizard or mad professor, the glasses and cowlick eyebrows reinforcing the image, pointing to God.

'Hello,' he boomed amiably, standing up and offering me one enormous hand, whilst the other directed me to a space next to him on the sofa.

His voice was hypnotic, difficult to say no to, and I shook his hand firmly before squeezing in alongside him. It was tight, so I made room by leaning forward to drink a coffee offered by Yoda, who was still grinning at the cafetière on the table in front of him.

*I didn't know he had a cafetière*, I thought.

'I've heard a lot about you over the years,' the surprise visitor smiled, turning to face me, 'your name keeps popping up. There's nothing to worry about, by the way. We just want to discuss what you're going through, and your thoughts on the Church.'

'Is that all?' I asked, suspicious.

'John's been chewing my ear on the telephone,' he said, placing his cup down onto a coaster.

I was so used to calling him Yoda, I'd almost forgot his real name.

'But, first of all, let me reassure you that you are not under any sort of disciplinary process, suspension or anything else. Your work to date has been exemplary, and the issues leading up to your suspension were misinterpreted.'

'Have you told Bishop Gordon about this?' I asked.

'Yes, but he is now busy with a disciplinary process of his own, thanks to the information you provided regarding the proposed housing development, which was not Church policy. We are not in bed with these ruthless investor types,' he put his index fingers behind his head, making devil horns. 'Bishop Gordon has been doing the wrong thing for the right reasons. I believe his aim was to protect the Church, not to line his own pockets – it's just unfortunate the way he's gone about it. He is a good bishop, very well organised, and he runs his parishes smoothly. He is, how should I put it? Business-like, yes. Functional and professional.'

He took a noisy slurp of his coffee, and we all sat looking at one another as I wondered about asking for an autograph.

'I, erm, assume you've discussed my issues – what we talked about last night?' I said, looking to Yoda, breaking the silence.

He nodded in reply, mouth full of biscuit.

'It's slight overkill, you turning up,' I said sheepishly, turning back to the archbishop. 'You really needn't–'

'Not at all,' he dismissed the notion before I could fully express it, opening his palms like giant scales and glancing at Yoda, 'it's an opportunity for all of us. You're concerned about your position in the Church. It's a very challenging role, and tell me, who doesn't have doubts? You'd have to be dead not to have the occasional wobble. What is it about the organisation that you're struggling with, since Yoda reassures me that your beliefs are solid? I want to hear everything, cards on the table. Come on, let's have some beef,' he declared, waving his fists in the air, far too jolly, winding up Peter.

'Beef?' I didn't quite understand.

'You know, some *beef*,' he repeated, leaving that residue of awkwardness that appears when the old dip into youth culture.

*'The Archbish of Banterbury,'* Peter said mockingly.

'Well,' I began, 'I find that it's too closed off from the realities of life in our society, only catering for a small demographic, ageing and middle class, the rest only attending services when they have to, for christenings, weddings and funerals, or when they have to pretend, to get their children into a good school.'

'Here we go,' he flicked his eyebrows towards Yoda, before returning his gaze to me. 'Surprised you're not calling them madrasas, indoctrinating innocent minds. Go on.'

'I find it to be closed-minded in regard to modern life, and unwilling to try to integrate – to accept new ideas. It won't even discuss them, nor will it defend itself. There are remarkable things happening in the world, in science, in music, in literature, which I believe are compatible with Christianity. We just have to be involved in the conversation.'

'Ooh, don't hold back,' he smiled, looking again to Yoda, who did not return the gesture.

'The world is changing fast,' I continued. 'Governments and businesses shape society without input from the Church, liberalising it at every level, and we can't keep up. We need to be brave enough to change, to evolve, particularly with some of our more oppressive policies.'

'Like?'

'Towards women, especially when it comes to abortion, and homosexuals, other religions – the list goes on. We are too easily knocked into insignificance because of these issues.'

'We *are* looking at these issues, and we have just appointed our first woman Bishop, but the Bible says what the Bible says. That is what forms the basis of our religion.'

'But we don't stone women – we don't cut off hands or pluck out eyes. We don't condone rape, murder or slavery, even though all of that exists in the Bible. We read some of it allegorically and some of it literally, depending on what suits our agenda. The Bible and its teachings are flexible enough to change with the times, but we have to be bold enough and strong enough to take another look, to keep our message relevant today. We need to be open-minded, tolerant to difference.'

'To play devil's advocate, doesn't that make you a hypocrite,' he leaned forward, no longer smiling, 'just changing the story to suit *your* needs?'

'Maybe, but then wouldn't that make the Church itself hypocritical? We follow an interpretation of the Bible, but it was written over the course of centuries, based on the world as it was in those times, derived from many cultures, evolving, changing with each writing in accordance with the issues of the day. It's not just one text, one story – it's lots of different texts cobbled together, told from different viewpoints.'

'Yes, yes, I do know what the Bible is, but that hypocrite word still keeps jumping into my mind.'

'From its inception, Christianity has been splitting off into different branches. The Council of Ephesus, the Council of Chalcedon, the great schism in the eleventh Century, and then the Reformation in the sixteenth century, when the different branches of Protestantism broke away from the Roman Catholics. Five offshoots starting at the same point before growing apart, and now here we are today, Anglicanism, the Church of England, founded because Henry the Eighth needed to remarry because his wife couldn't give him a son. Why can't the religion carry on evolving, be transformative,  an ongoing story adding to what we've got, ever changing, fitting in with modern life?'

'Because Jesus is dead. There, the story ended.'

'Didn't stop Henry from changing things,' I replied, perhaps a bit sharp, a bit childish.

*'Shit answer,'* Peter scolded.

'The story doesn't have to change,' I quickly added, 'just our interpretation of it. If it is fixed then it will fade away into history, the religion of the book in an internet age, and if we don't modernise, we are stuck in the Middle Ages. They'll just think of us as supernatural nonsense, and be as apt to visit tarot card readers and psychics as they are to attend church.'

'It's not as simple as that, though, is it?' he replied, somewhat haughtily. 'You can't just say to a congregation, "Right, today, according to the Bible, it's fine to be gay."'

I nodded, acknowledging that it was a good point.

'This is the bind we are in,' he said. 'How can we change fast without disaffecting our congregations?'

Having no answer, I simply shrugged my shoulders.

'What else?' he asked, his appearance relaxed, but his eyes fierce; his voice a bit too snappy.

'It's all or nothing with the Church. You must accept every aspect of Christianity and its interpretation of the Bible. How can young people buy into that? Scepticism and cynicism are the main traits I see in this society, and yet here we are saying, "This is the full set of rules you need to live your life by, some of which were relevant two thousand years ago, maybe not so much today. Come and join the Church,"' I finished on a sarcastic note, which he clearly didn't like.

*'Punch him in the throat,'* Peter suggested, *'he's a giant.'*

'And what would you do to entice people to "come and join the Church?"' he asked, mimicking my tone. 'It works both ways, you know. People reject the Church on the same basis. One or two things they don't believe or agree with, and they become atheists, rejecting everything, usually missing the most important points.'

There was a tension in the air; Yoda had stopped chewing his biscuits.

*Am I not showing enough respect or humility?* I wondered.

'Flip it on its head,' I offered, 'engage with a soft touch. Just talk to people, let them introduce religion to the conversation and then immerse themselves as deeply as they wish to go. Let people be Christians on their own terms, at a level they are comfortable with. They might be Christian lite, but it's a start – something for us to build on, one step at a time, as opposed to hitting people with a wall of dogma as soon as they walk through the door, making sure they'll never come back.'

'So, why are you still here?' he asked bluntly. 'Why haven't you left?'

'Because I know how the Church can transform a life, a life that was finished before it had really begun. Because the Church has not been replaced, and a massive void has been created in its absence. It's a material world, to which we run parallel, offering something different, a spiritual way of life, where people can become more – oh, I don't know – complete, part of a community. All this technology, connectivity – all of this Facebook, Skype and Twitter, and yet people have never been so anxious and alone.'

'Don't you think this social media pulls people together?' he interjected, disrupting my flow.

'I does both,' I answered, 'pushing groups together whilst tearing the individual apart. I see people's lives collapsing around them, yet there they are on Facebook with a big smile, feeling blessed.' I paused for breath, trying to align my thoughts before continuing. 'I believe that people realise there's something missing. They're still looking for something to believe in, to be part of. There's a longing for understanding and connection that the Church used to provide, and could do again, but we have to change to bring these people in. Preaching at them from the Bible isn't the way. It's about engaging with them, discussing anything – topics they want to talk about, responding from an informed Christian point of view.'

He was staring at me now, but I couldn't tell if he was happy or sad, angry or amused. 'We do have the Alpha course for people interested in religion.'

I shrugged my shoulders. We both knew that didn't address the point.

'I've heard about some of the ideas you've tried to implement,' he said, 'things like the Ministry. Could we talk about those?'

'It's as I've said. People choose the subject, anything, and I discuss it from a Christian viewpoint.'

'Well, let's talk about something, a stick they usually try to beat us with. How about evolution?'

'That's a big subject,' I smiled, 'bottom-up evolution or top-down design?'

'Adam and Eve, where do they fit in? Science suggests the planet is around four and a half billion years old, as opposed to the six thousand years suggested by creationists. On the sixth day, God created man, whereas the fossil records indicate evolution from amoebas and algae through to dinosaurs, through to where we are today.'

'It's about how we interpret Genesis again, isn't it?'

'Not just that, but the whole literal or allegorical reading. Evidence suggests we are the result of an evolutionary process – they are finding early remains all the time. Lucy, Homo Erectus, Neanderthals, all of which suggest that we came from primates, monkeys, great apes, until we somehow got opposable thumbs and started walking on two feet. How does that fit in with the Bible, with God, with Genesis?'

'They are common ancestors, branches of an evolutionary tree. We are

Homos, which split off from apes and gorillas, and more recently chimpanzees and bonobos, five to six million years ago.'

'Homos,' Yoda repeated, laughing.

'I think you mean hominids,' ABC corrected.

'Does anybody want a Garibaldi?' Yoda asked, opening another packet and spilling them out on to a plate.

ABC reached across and took two, oblivious to Yoda's glare, as I politely declined, not wanting to decimate his supplies any further.

'Our brain size grew rapidly,' I continued, 'its architecture changing from Homo Habilis through Homo Ergaster, and then Homo Erectus to Homo Sapiens, where we are now. It was not a single evolutionary branch, though – there were different versions of man evolving simultaneously in different environments. We all originated from the same point, however, in Africa, around seventy thousand years ago.'

'You've got a good understanding,' he held up a finger, 'but you haven't answered my question. Where does the Bible fit in with this?'

It could fit in a number of ways. It could be we are just a result of evolution, or maybe the more dramatic option that God placed man upon the earth literally, a Y-chromosomal Adam and a mitochondrial Eve, the first of the modern-day humans from whom we all descend.'

He was looking at me, listening, the cogs visibly turning in his mind.

'Though it may not be as clean-cut as that,' I went on. 'The traditional arguments are black and white, intelligent design versus evolution, but they never seem to look at the greys. Maybe God blessed Homo Sapiens with an advanced level of consciousness, an intelligence, allowing us to accelerate rapidly from the other branches of the Homo tree.'

'The Homo tree!' Yoda laughed again, spitting out crumbs and raisins onto the floor.

'Oh, grow up,' ABC turned to Yoda, laughing along, as Scruff ran around hoovering up the crumbs.

'Gorillas stopped evolving, chimpanzees stopped evolving and Neanderthals became extinct,' I kept going, undeterred, 'whereas we evolved mentally in a remarkably short period of time. Evolution through intelligence.'

'So, God could just as easily have chosen Neanderthals instead?'

'I suppose so,' I nodded. 'The whole story has been revealed in the Human Genome project. Neanderthals were around at the same time as early Homo Sapiens, and unless you're of a pure black African blood, which of course we are not, you're almost certainly around two percent Neanderthal, even though they were a slightly different species.'

ABC leaned back and looked at Yoda, studying him intently. 'Now that you mention it, hmm.'

Yoda threw a cushion in mock indignation.

'Right, let's get this straight,' ABC turned back to me, 'the first one is a simple application of the Adam and Eve story, fine. The second, are you suggesting something a bit more subtle, like God dabbling with evolution of an existing species?'

'If you like,' I agreed.

'Progressive creationism,' Yoda muttered under his breath, sounding bored.

'Not that direct,' I said. 'Adapted as opposed to created, same common ancestor, so maybe theistic evolution?' I pinched my nose and started speaking in a tinny voice. 'For millions of years, mankind lived just like the animals. Then, something happened which unleashed the power of our imagination. We learned to talk.'

ABC smiled, and immediately began mimicking the opening chords of the Pink Floyd song I was referencing, '*Bow, bow, bow, bow.*'

Yoda also pinched his nose, channelling his inner Hawking. 'It doesn't have to be like this. All we need to do is make sure we keep talking,' he said, before creasing up in laughter, a welcome interlude.

'Most animals have a body and a brain, enabling them to function – competence without comprehension,' I picked up the thread again, whilst Yoda carried on giggling, 'but humans also have consciousness, a world of feelings, emotions, thoughts, inspirations, memories, imagination and love – the soul. Scientists can't resolve consciousness – what it is, where it comes from, because inner experiences are not physical, they are unmeasurable. Why couldn't that be the Adam and Eve moment?'

'Just a network of axons and neurons, electrical and chemical processes, surely?' ABC replied sarcastically.

'Just a virtual manifestation, created by our brain and senses,' Yoda added with a grin.

'The Hard Problem, those tricky little qualia,' I joined the armchair science cock-measuring competition.

'Indeed,' ABC smiled, biting into another biscuit. 'Phenomenal.'

Yoda glared at his greedy friend, narrowing his eyes before eating his own precious Garibaldi.

'This is exactly what I'm talking about,' I exclaimed. 'We have to be able to discuss these matters. We need to be reading and understanding science, theology and modern culture, instead of just sticking our heads in the Bible. To me, all of this only serves to reinforce the beauty of God's work, revealing a little more of its complexity, its beauty, each time.'

'But you also said we could have just been a product of natural evolution, without God's direct intervention,' ABC pointed out. 'How does that fit in?'

'It depends how long you think a day lasts in Genesis,' I said, 'the arrow of time. Time behaves differently depending on where you are in the universe. A day on Venus, for example, is equal to one hundred and sixteen Earth days. We are talking billions of years here, but scientists believe that before creation, or the Big Bang, time didn't exist at all. I'm suggesting that a day of creation time, Genesis time, is infinitely longer than a day of Earth time.'

'Day-age creationism,' Yoda shook his head.

'But still, how do we fit with natural evolution?' ABC asked again.

'They postulate that life started on earth around four billion years ago, the first replicator molecules emerging from a primaeval soup called LUCA, the common ancestor for all life there is and there has ever been on Earth. LUCA still exists in all of us, RNA that evolved into DNA, immortal genes present in everything, from you to a leaf on a tree, to a dung beetle, to herpes, to a tyrannosaurus rex. Every living thing originates from this single point. In my mind, that points towards God.'

'Directed evolution?' ABC suggested, engrossed.

'Maybe, maybe not. Either way, I don't think it really matters,' I shrugged, as a pertinent quote came into my head. '"And God made the beast of the earth after His kind, and cattle after their kind, and everything that creepeth upon the Earth after his kind, and it was so.'

'More Genesis,' ABC smiled. 'I'm not sure the scientists would agree with your finding God at that point.'

'The sciences are as stubborn and dogmatic as religion, but I see them as complementary, shining a light on God's work, helping us to understand a little bit more with each discovery.'

'They'll still beat us with the evolution stick,' ABC said bitterly.

'Evolution disappeared around the same time as belief in God, killed by science – the birth of the Anthropocene.'

'How so?'

'We've taken over. We decide habitats and species, what lives and what dies. We're editing genomes, CRISPR-Cas-nine, and we're even mixing species now, creating chimeras, so who knows where that will end. Natural selection, or evolution no longer exist?'

'Love it,' ABC grinned. 'Not the chimeras, of course.'

'I find it thrilling,' I leaned forward in my seat, hands gesticulating, my whole body talking, actions subconsciously attuned to words, 'but what I don't understand is why I seem to be alone in this. Why can't the Church celebrate when a new discovery is made? Take DNA, for example. "In the beginning was the word, and the word was with God." The Human Genome Project allows us to read God's writing – the very ingredients that make a human.'

ABC flicked his eyebrows, quietly thinking. There was a long pause as he glanced at his watch. 'I think there's a place for this level of discussion in the Church,' he finally spoke. 'I've enjoyed it, though I can understand why Bishop Gordon and many others may not get it. They don't want to consider any variation on the standard message. Whatever the case, we certainly want to keep you, so what now? What are your plans? What are you going to do?'

It all felt a little condescending. He could write books on what we'd been discussing, but had made no attempt to argue, disagree or debate, despite it being well within his ability. I looked down at my hands, feeling slightly embarrassed.

'I don't know,' I mumbled, like a child. 'I don't know what I'm doing. Your advice would be greatly appreciated,' I looked up at him, submissive.

'We want you to come home,' Yoda said.

'What?'

They shared a glance as ABC stood and walked to the window, blocking out most of the light before elaborating. 'We want you to take on the Iron Church.'

'No,' I replied, before he had a chance to go any further.

'Just wait before you say no,' Yoda implored. 'Let us explain exactly what we want first.'

There was a long silence before ABC spoke again. 'We want you to run it the way you think it should be done. You will have free rein, it's yours. The Church as an institution is in decline, and there's nothing we can do to stop it. Congregations are getting older, and there are no youngsters coming through to replace the old. In a few generations, there'll be no one left. We are running out of ideas, you have ideas, so we want you to implement them, to see where they take us.'

'I'm completely the wrong person,' I replied. 'You need someone experienced, a steady pair of hands. That's not me.'

'We appointed a new priest, and he was hounded out within two days. It's a mess,' ABC sighed. 'People are angry, and understandably so.'

'Then find somebody else,' I said. 'I'm the opposite of what you need at this point. I'm all over the place.'

'You're exactly what we want,' he turned from the window, facing me once more, 'and let me tell you why. We need you because you're completely different to anyone we have, and if there's anywhere we need something different, it's here. You're radical and you're naïve, but please don't take that in a negative way. They are strengths – they allow you to try things that others won't. You want to discuss matters that others shy away from, and, just as importantly, you are also of this place. Your roots are here. These are your people.'

'But–'

He held up his hand, stopping me in my tracks. 'It's not just good for us, it will be beneficial for you, too. John cares about you deeply,' he gestured towards Yoda. 'How long can you keep moving on from place to place, running from your past? I completely understand why you do it, but you have to stop at some time.'

'It's different now,' I said, my voice straining. 'People can go wherever they want to go. We are rootless, our life stories are not tied to a place anymore. We can invent our own story.'

'And is that a good thing, do you think? This freedom, this drifting – this severance from home, family, friends and community? It sounds pretty lonely to me.'

'By the same token, is it a good thing to be tied to a place, to a predictable life? How can freedom be a negative?'

'It becomes a negative when people become disconnected from their point of reference – the morals of their upbringing. It becomes a negative when everybody becomes an outsider, part of nothing, caring only for themselves and adjusting their morals to suit. Morals are being hollowed out, mere outlines of the principles people choose to guide their lives by. Nothing more than soundbites.'

'I haven't become disconnected.'

'Then why are you so afraid to come back? This place can't hurt you – the buildings and streets can't hurt you, and *those* people are long gone.'

I sat back, letting out a long sigh.

'Look, I know there's more to it than that,' he raised both hands, palms facing out, as if about to save a penalty. 'I know this place is not just physical, bricks and mortar. You have feelings, thoughts and emotions, and they are real, as are your memories. In some ways, they are even more real than the physical, since no distance is great enough for you to truly get away from them. When you left this city, they went with you. You can't leave a memory behind.'

'You make it sound hopeless,' I said, frustrated.

'We all have our pasts – they make us who we are. Each of us a unique collection of memories and experiences, and, for better or worse, it's your extraordinary past that shapes your thoughts and ideas today.'

'I don't think extraordinary is quite the right way of putting it.'

'I didn't mean it in any kind of positive sense,' he said, apologetic. 'The point is that you think differently than most of the clergy, who, sadly, do tend to be singing off the same hymn sheet. It's a roundabout way of paying you a compliment.'

'You buttering me up?'

'Your past may be set in stone, but your future is not yet written. It's there for you to create, and it could go in any number of possible directions. When you come to the end of your life, do you really want to look back and see it defined by those early years, or would you rather try to change your story, take it on, knowing that even if you failed, you had the courage to try?'

'I'm not doing it,' I said stubbornly, more than a little exasperated. I was in a knot, my arms and legs crossed tightly, my shoulders hunched, as if it might block out everything I was hearing.

ABC huffed in frustration, or maybe disgust, as he slammed his cup down on the tray and strode towards me, becoming more massive with each step.

'I listened to you prattle on about the Church having to be brave, and needing the courage to change. Well, where's your courage?' he bellowed. 'Where's your willingness to change?' His finger was jabbing towards me, his voice getting louder with each word, reverberating around the small space. It felt like I was trapped inside an amplifier. 'I'm sick and tired of people going on, telling me what's wrong with the Church, how it's failing, how it's irrelevant, set in the Middle Ages, but nobody has the bollocks to put their neck on the line and actually do something about it,' he finished with a roar, his face red and spittle flying from his lips.

Ears ringing, I looked over at Yoda, sitting expressionless in his chair, showing no inclination to intervene.

'Why should I sit there and take that sort of criticism from you?' ABC bent over, bringing his furious face close to mine. 'You're no different than the others at the end of the day – negative, hiding behind your intellect, just words, just noise – gutless,' he straightened up and composed himself, lowering his voice to a more measured level. 'I regret having to say it, but all I see when I look at you is a scared little boy who's still in hiding. Hiding from the bad people, hiding from his past – a perennial victim.'

I could feel myself sliding as I jumped off the sofa, Peter squaring up to his towering frame, eyeing his bearded throat.

'Fuck off!' I shouted into his face, not the most articulate response, as I fought to keep Peter down.

'You fuck off!' he responded, leaning forward, our noses almost touching.

'Both of you, sit down,' Yoda said firmly.

Neither one of us moved; our eyes stayed locked, as behind the beard and wrinkles, deep inside, was a young man, a young soul, living in an aging body.

'I'll bang your heads together in a minute,' Yoda shouted, breaking the tension. 'Sit down.'

We both looked at him, and then at each other, as a few deep breaths allowed thought to overtake emotion. I wondered how we'd got to that point, how the dynamic had changed so quickly, as we dropped back down into our seats, and I sat, slightly stunned, loaded with regret, the silence feeling like an eternity before ABC let out a long exhale.

'I'm sorry,' he mumbled, 'I went a bit far.'

I nodded, relieved. 'Me too,' I said, feeling a bit sick, almost tearful, aghast at having ended up on the wrong side of this remarkable man.

'It's alright, just handbags,' Yoda said reassuringly, wearing a wry smile. 'Does he remind you of anyone?' he asked ABC.

'He's slightly taller and much more handsome than you ever were,' ABC smirked.

'Well, one of those statements is accurate, but I'm not talking about me,' Yoda said. 'He's a younger version of you.'

'I think I'd have run a mile if I'd been shouted at like that when I his age,' ABC laughed.

'I somehow doubt that,' Yoda rolled his eyes.

'You're an exceptional talent,' ABC said to me, looking and sounding sincere, 'extremely intelligent and passionate about the Church, so perhaps we're not so different after all.' He laughed at his own wit as he poured himself another coffee from the cafetière, the dregs, which must have tasted cold and bitter. 'I get angry, frustrated, when I see talent going to waste,' he continued. 'especially as a result of barriers that people place in front of themselves, limiting their horizons. I don't want to be looking at you in years to come and still see a victim, Peter, because you are much better than that. You have it in you to be anything you want to be, if you will just believe in yourself enough to have the courage to face your demons – to fight and conquer them.' He sat down and put the cup to his lips, drinking, thinking. 'When you say no, it hurts me. I desperately want to hear you say yes, not just for the Church, but because it would mean you are rising above this thing – that you are going to win.'

I sat staring at him, not sure what to think, my mind empty, save for feelings of remorse tinged with guilt, as another long, drawn-out silence had us all sat looking in different directions, at nothing in particular.

*Is it my turn to say something*, I thought, *to end this awkwardness?*

'Let's go and see this fucking church, then,' I succumbed, offering an olive branch, before quickly adding, 'I'm promising nothing, though.'

ABC's eyes widened, as he turned to exchange knowing nods with Yoda, before giving me a serious look. 'But please, don't do it for me. This needs to be your decision, made with your best interests in mind. I don't want you doing it just because I'm extremely important.'

'Oh, shut up,' I replied, my smile breaking into a laugh; the tone of the conversation did not feel so patronising anymore.

'Well, no time like the present,' Yoda declared enthusiastically, jumping up from his seat and fishing around for his car keys. 'Or maybe "strike while the iron's hot" is more appropriate, considering where we're going.'

Giggling at his own joke, a trait which seemed to be endemic amongst the senior clergy, he was up and out of the door before ABC or I had a chance to stand.

'I thought you were going to hit me back there,' I heard ABC mutter from behind me, as we followed Yoda outside.

'So did I,' I replied.

A small, rickety garage sat at the end of an access path at the side of the house, its wood warped, paint flaking and door not quite closing, allowing a glimpse of two tyres. A high-pitched squealing noise, like nails dragging across a blackboard, filled my ears when he yanked the door up, sending a shiver through my body as I looked in astonishment at what lay within. I had that feeling of sliding back in time again, into my past; it was the same car he had all those years ago, not quite a DeLorean, but an Austin Allegro, caramel with faux-leather coverings, the roof in chocolate brown, and a shiny metal trim surrounding the windows. It was highly polished, and still in immaculate condition.

*Has there ever been a car more loved than this?* I thought.

He climbed in and flicked the key, the engine turning over a few times before it caught and he pulled the choke out, smiling as she purred – or maybe growled or wheezed would be more accurate descriptions. He released the handbrake and pulled out, easing along the path, the tyres crunching as he rolled past us, before stopping at the junction and jumping out to close the garage. Two rubber strips hung down from the boot, covered in little white lightning bolts, no longer making contact with the ground, whilst a sticker in the back window read: *Not leaking oil, sweating power!* He'd obviously enjoyed the eighties, and was determined to stay there.

I opened the passenger door and tilted the seat forward, feeling a firm hand on my shoulder as I was about to climb into the rear.

'I'd better get in the back,' he said. 'I won't be able to get out at the church. Nobody knows I'm here, so I can't be seen down there.'

'I'll move the seat forward,' I said, as he squeezed through the passenger door, pausing with his arse sticking out, the suspension groaning in protest as his body disappeared inside.

I pushed the seat back, bouncing it off him until I heard it click, and then got in, turning around to find his head and beard filling the gap between the front seats. I couldn't figure out how he'd fitted into the space; his contorted shape looked like it might burst out at any moment.

I faced forward, glancing at the green strip across the top of the windscreen as Yoda settled into his seat of wooden beads, his arse abacus. From there, the journey went by in silence, each of us looking out of our respective windows, thinking, as we took the long way around, avoiding my old street, but still getting close enough to bring back memories; the long terraces, old shops and buildings serving as landmarks in the story of my childhood.

I felt morose, but at the same time, I didn't want the nostalgia trip to stop, as old forgotten scenes played like clips from a movie, a different life, a different person, the new me just an observer, until the terraces stopped abruptly and the estates began, taking us into a place that I wasn't accustomed to; one where my childhood wanderings stopped, creating an empty feeling.

As children, we understood how the terraces worked; long roads, some feeling like they went on forever, with back entries, the jiggers, a means of access or escape. The estates were different, curving roads and pedestrian walkways, its boundaries unclear, shaping those who dwelled within them.

A road sign flashed by: *St Domingo*. I wasn't sure if it was sarcasm or contradiction; this felt about as far from an idyllic Caribbean island as one could imagine.

*Contradiction*, I decided, fitting in with this confusing place.

The road opened up before us, a border between two divergent landscapes, their jarring differences amplifying the personalities of each. To the right were blank walls and fences, defensive barriers concealing the inward-facing estates. To the left, open parkland, a green ridge overlooking the centre of the city, framed by large skies and the Irish Sea; the rural idyll of the Welsh Hills visible in the distance.

I could sense the hope draining from Yoda as he searched for positives, something to give optimism.

'Nice park,' was all he could muster, ignoring the estates; words better left unsaid.

'The Lurk,' I dared to name the elephant, as we turned towards its walls.

The estates had their reputations and labels; broad brushstrokes colouring all residents. Domestic abuse, ignorance, sloth, stupidity, anger, hatred, heroin, cocaine, amphetamines, cheap alcohol... whatever degenerate phrase or social vice you could think of seemed to have a home here.

'That name originates from the eighteen hundreds,' Yoda said, filling the silence, grasping at straws. 'The area was christened the Shirk by Catholics as a dig at Protestants, the opposite of work, suggesting laziness. Then it evolved with the nineteen-nineteen police strike, when people ran riot and pillaged shops, the Loot. The Shirk then became the Lurk, something far more sinister, sprouting all the stories and urban myths you associate with it to this day. Just religious propaganda that stuck really. It's not actually that bad.'

I glanced back at the infamous Lurk, *Twinned with Gomorrah* painted proudly upon its walls, radiating threats of decay and violence. Yoda had said that places can't do things to you, they are inert, but he was wrong, particularly in this case, where the blank walls and alleyways were not just an inanimate backdrop, an impassive set for the theatre of life; they shaped behaviour, ways of thinking, setting boundaries and barriers, dreams and aspirations, dictating how people looked at you and spoke to you, determining your opportunities in life.

This place designed its inhabitants, furnishing them with their own unique language and rules. Outsiders didn't enter its black heart, concealed by layers of cul-de-sacs and dead ends, a fiction, buried deep, a no man's land, where one estate collided with another, a Grand Theft Auto car crash of underage sex and single mums, their feral children running wild, covered in dirt, snot and scabs, as benefit-cheat fathers sat chain-smoking forty a day down the pub, waiting for the night, when they would descend upon the city like demons and do what they do. At least that's what the newspapers and daytime television told us, though the drive did nothing to dispel these rumours.

The church gradually appeared before us, like an illusion, its beautiful sandstone form almost stately on the edge of the hill, overlooking the city and river below. Like everything here, it didn't fit; it belonged in a picturesque village, with a village green and maypole, yet here it was, teetering on the ledge with the Lurk looming behind, pushing it towards the precipice. As we got closer, the romance dissipated and the truth of the situation was made clear, *PAEDO SCUM* painted on the boundary walls in big, white capital letters, surrounded by a smattering of smaller efforts expressing similar sentiments: *burn in hell… rapist… fucking nonce.*

I felt a sickness in my stomach, a heavy weight; the beauty of the church now seemed obscene, its innocence gone as it sat hiding behind its walls, labelled, guilty as charged, remaining stoically indifferent as the public took out their anger on it following the abuses of power, the corruption of innocence, that had taken place inside.

Whatever went on in the estates, it was never as bad as what had happened here.

The car was silent again, but I could feel the tension rising as we pulled into a side road. The noisy din of children was coming from an adjacent school, shouting excitedly during their lunch break, girls huddled in groups, boys playing football, their games overlapping in the limited space as the steeple cast its shadow over them, a perversion, reminding them of the existence of evil; of bad people who did unspeakable things.

'Have a wonderful time,' ABC said optimistically as I looked towards Yoda, who pressed his lips tightly together and flicked his eyebrows, as if about to jump from a plane.

'Come on, then,' I murmured.

He replied with a nod, unclipping his seatbelt and checking the mirror before opening his door and clambering out. I joined him on the pavement, slamming the door behind me as ABC peered out the side window from the back seat, looking old and small all of a sudden. I closed my eyes; there was a cool breeze blowing on the exposed slope, and the cacophony of sound from the playground was louder, more vibrant. I took deep breaths, calming my mind.

Yoda was unlocking the gate, drawing squeals of protest from the old metal hinges as it was opened for the first time in a long time. I stepped across the threshold, following Yoda, who was sorting through a large bundle of keys as we walked between the overgrown lawns. I didn't want him to find the right key. It felt like we were entering a crime scene as the church loomed closer. I wanted to turn around and get back in the car, forget about this place.

My vision flashed white. I felt a sharp pain in the back of my head. Turning quickly to see where it had come from, something else flew past, narrowly missing before landing with a whisper in the deep grass. I heard a whizzing near my ear, and then another one above, the stones clattering against pavement further down the path, followed by more and more, filling the air. The noise from the playground increased as I glanced through an opening in the wall to see school children pouring out of their gates, scrambling on the street to gather stones from the potholes and then launching them in our direction, the anger in their action making most go wildly astray.

I turned towards Yoda, who was looking past me, first in confusion, then in shock. He started walking towards the children, only to be hit, and then hit again, the surprise on his face turning to anger as another projectile caught him square on the forehead, drawing blood, giving him pause as the children carried on throwing, emboldened, their shouting incoherent as we made a run for the bright-red door.

Yoda was frantically rifling through the keys as a barrage of stones landed around us, bouncing against the wooden door and ricocheting off the stone walls. We were prone, and they had found their range, well-trained arms finding their target; my hand flying to my ear too late to block a particularly savage blow, leaving a loud whistling that rang around my head as I tucked my face into my arms, hunched over, foetal-like, making myself smaller.

'Fuck!' Yoda shouted as he dropped the keys, the door booming with near misses as he ducked down to retrieve them, shuffling between each one in a panic.

*We're going to get stoned to death*, I realised, thinking it strangely appropriate, pain emanating from everywhere as I contemplated allowing Peter to run towards the children and pummel his way through, before feeling a pull on my collar that took me off balance and then dragged me to the side, into the long grass.

'There's another entrance,' Yoda shouted, scuttling forward as I ran close behind him, up the side of the church, past the regular sequence of buttresses towards the tower; not pointing to the heavens this time, but with a flat top, a battlement, with pointed pinnacles around the parapet.

*'Good for pouring boiling oil from,'* Peter giggled.

We careered around the corner, reaching another bright-red door, the front entrance, where Yoda resumed his frantic rummaging through the keys. I returned to the buttress at the corner, peaking around, and then jumping back as a flurry of stones flew past. They were close, but couldn't rearm quickly in the deep grass so had become more selective with their throws.

'Come on!' I hissed as I ran back to Yoda, before turning just in time to see a boy jump around the corner and take his shot, the stone whistling past my head.

One followed the other, and then another, until the crowd started edging into sight again, boys and girls of different ages, silent, arms cocked, stones in hand. There was a pause as we considered each other; as they decided whether they were really going to do this. We were close, exposed and vulnerable before them.

'Look, this is ridic–' I started, as a brick flew through the air and hit the wall above my head, sending red dust spraying all over Yoda.

It was as if a starting pistol had gone off; arms snapped violently forward, releasing stones, bricks and half bricks.

*Velocity equals displacement over time,* I thought, as I put my arm in front of my face, waiting for the missiles to find their target, but I felt no pain, just a sharp force lifting me off my feet, moving me sideways as I waited for the impact of rock on flesh.

When the pain arrived, it was unexpected, on the other side, as my body tumbled over the threshold, slamming onto the hard flagstone floor, feeling the coolness of the church. I opened my eyes as the door slammed shut; stones and bricks that had made it through were spinning, scattering across the floor, whilst others banged in frustration on the other side, where we were stood only seconds ago.

Yoda was on his back on the floor, one foot still on the door, as he glanced across at me, bloodied, looking pale, his chest heaving. I felt warm lines of tickling sensation travelling down my face, the red dripping on to the dusty stone, taking me back to the village for a moment, to Alf. Gently touching my hand to my head, I winced as it came back crimson, a gusher.

'So, as you can see, the building is in a wonderfully exposed plot with far-reaching views,' Yoda announced, a smirk appearing at the corner of his lips. 'The garden needs a bit of attention, but at least the neighbours are friendly.'

I smiled, before laughing loudly, shaking more blood on to the floor.

'Shush,' he put his finger to his lips, as he started to giggle along with me lying on our backs, trying to laugh quietly, which only made it worse. Through the blood and dirt, his eyes were twinkling, tears cutting clean lines through the grime.

It felt good; we were alive.

'You look fucking terrible,' he said, letting out a huge belly laugh, gasping for air.

'Looking a bit shit yourself,' I replied, unable to contain my amusement. 'It was like Zulu out there – the sky went black.'

I got to my feet, the world tilting for a moment as I went dizzy, temples throbbing and blood rushing to my head. Placing my hand on the wall, I paused until everything became straight again, normal focus resuming, before offering Yoda my hand and pulling him upright. We were both breathing heavily.

'Not going too well, is it?' he asked, a slight understatement, once he had regained composure.

'I nearly shouted out, "Lord Jesus, receive my spirit." Thought we were goners,' I said, dusting myself off as a body struck the door, leaving it shaking in its frame.

'Lord, do not hold this sin against them,' he smiled, shaking his head and laughing quietly as the door rattled again, this time bending at the bottom as the pressure from the other side increased.

I knelt down and slid the bolt into place when the door returned to its original shape. It shook again, a dull thud followed by shouts, a rhythm forming as they tried to barge their way through.

'What are we going to do?' I asked.

'I dunno,' Yoda said.

'We have no right to fight back. We can't go charging into them.'

'I know,' he nodded in resignation, slumping down onto a bench in the lobby. 'I fucking *love* kids.'

The adrenaline was wearing off, and what would have prompted hysterical laughter only moments ago was now hardly enough to elicit a smile, as I tilted my head back against the cool wall, letting out a deep breath. I was hot, agitated, and the stone brought a temporary reprieve.

'Shit,' I suddenly jumped to my feet, 'the ABC!'

It took a second before Yoda processed what I'd said and leapt up next to me. 'Fuck,' he exclaimed, 'my car!'

We looked towards the door, and then at each other, realising that there was no chance as it continued flexing under the children's fury. Without another word, we turned and ran into the church, where I came to an abrupt halt, mid-stride, mouth open, looking up into the space above. Yoda crashed into the back of me, letting out a grunt before appearing at my side, as the danger suddenly paled into insignificance.

It was vast, it was beautiful and it was unexpected.

We stood in the triple-height nave, its red carpet travelling in a straight line between rows of simple wooden pews, an axis pointing to the chancel, leading to a couple of steps that ascended up to the altar, with a three-storey stained-glass window forming a technicoloured backdrop.

*It doesn't belong in this place, in this situation*, I thought, as my eyes followed the impossibly slender columns up to the roof, their delicate arches splaying out at the top like fan vaults, decorative tracery forming gentle curves in between, filling in the gaps.

The design was a lightweight gothic, just the bones, a revival made in factories during the industrial revolution; it looked like it would struggle to hold my weight, never mind the roof and the floors in between. I looked around at the columns that framed the central space, forming aisles to the sides, with first floor arcades above, and a slim tracery to the balustrades giving a light, ethereal feel, almost as if it wasn't really there, whilst large bay windows flooded the space with daylight, pouring in at evenly-spaced intervals down the sides.

'The inside's made of iron,' Yoda explained, after a minute that felt like an hour, 'that's why it's so slim.'

I was still staring, taking it all in, the structure an elegant white, scrolling against a pale blue roof. 'It's beautiful,' I murmured, my eyes darting from detail to detail.

'That's why it's called the Iron Church,' he added.

'What?'

'That's why it's called the Iron Church,' he repeated, 'and not St Georges, because it's made of iron.'

'Oh,' I nodded, getting it at the second time of asking. 'I always thought it was something to do with the place or the people – the area.'

'Nah, they're all soft around here,' he said sarcastically.

I let out a snort as I moved to the centre of the aisle, feeling the power of the place.

Yoda remained where he was, watching, a smile touching his lips, a glimmer of hope, until he remembered himself and cried out, 'My car!'

Yanked back into the moment, I looked around frantically, his panic contagious. 'Upstairs,' I said, 'let's see if we can find a window – see what's happening.'

He nodded, and we split up to look for a flight of stairs.

'Back to the tower,' he called, remembering, 'the stairs are there.'

Once again, I was chasing his tiny form, past the front entrance, still banging as we opened a smaller side door, revealing a stone spiral staircase. His feet disappeared around the bend as I followed him up the smooth steps, into the cold, hard stone of the walls and out on to the arcade, where I found him bent over a pew, breathing heavily.

'You OK?' I asked, concerned.

He nodded, before lifting his head and pointing towards the windows and then doubling over again, putting his hands on his knees.

The floor was dusty, with small fragments of glass, pinpricks of light, shining through as I walked along bays, my footprints suggesting that I was the first to traverse this space for some time. I stopped, estimating the location of the car, the noise of the crowd still coming through. The ugly mesh grilles had protected the windows from serious damage, though a few smaller stones had punctured small holes, giving a view through the stained glass as I pushed the nearest pew screeching across the floor until it touched the wall.

Yoda was moving towards me, pale, holding on to each pew end as he walked along.

'You sure you're OK?' I asked again.

'Just getting old,' he said, taking a seat as I climbed up and peered out of a newly-made peephole.

The car was surrounded, being shook, bouncing on its suspension, as the children took turns stamping on the bonnet. One wing mirror was hanging off, the other was gone, and cracks were spiderwebbing from various points on the windscreen. A teacher stood by, watching impassively, as a rip appeared in the faux-leather roof covering. He was on his own, powerless, as small fingers gained purchase and yanked it away, revealing the bare metal underneath.

'Is it OK?' Yoda asked meekly.

'Erm, yes, I think so,' I said, stepping down from the bench.

'Could you see it?'

'Not all of it, no.'

He stared at the floor, unsure what to do next. If he'd thought there was even a scratch on the car, he'd have been straight out, consequences be damned. He might have been white as a ghost, his face a picture of illness, but those red-rimmed eyes were still glistening, still fierce; still young.

I became aware of the banging at the front door again, a reminder of the angry mob waiting outside.

'I think we should phone the police,' I said, 'unless there's a secret tunnel, of course.'

'No, we're not supposed to be here,' he said. 'No secret tunnels, either, I'm afraid.'

'Why aren't we supposed to be here? It's a church.'

'We're supposed to let the authorities know beforehand, in case something like this happens.'

'Well, we've got to do something, otherwise we're fucked. We're trapped in here, and the ABC is stuck out there.'

'They'll disperse soon enough, when lessons start.'

'They're not going anywhere. The teacher is just standing there watching, doing nothing.'

'We can't,' he said stubbornly, shaking his head.

'Your car's going to get trashed, the ABC–'

'Shit,' he put his face into his hands, despondent.

We sat quietly until the distant sound of sirens became audible over the noise of the children outside, glancing at each other nervously as the electric-blue lights came flashing through the stained glass.

I climbed back on to the pew, peeking through the same hole and seeing two police cars and not a child in sight. The officers were inspecting the Allegro, which suddenly looked its age, damaged beyond repair, when the heavily-dented driver's side door creaked open, and ABC climbed out gingerly, a tartan blanket wrapped around him.

He was speaking to the police, one hand on his hip, the other pointing towards the school, as a small elderly lady joined in the conversation, her movements more agitated, her attention on the church. She looked like Yoda in a skirt, and was probably no less formidable.

'Let's go,' I said.

There came a gentle knock on the door below, followed by another, as we picked up pace and hurried down the stairs, undoing the bolts and opening the latch before pulling the door inwards.

'Bloody hell!' the officer shouted, involuntarily stepping back as the daylight hit our blood-streaked faces.

Even the tough old woman put her hand to her mouth, shocked at the sight before her.

'Is that you, John?' one of the constables asked, the sympathetic tone of his voice suggesting that they were friends, or at least acquaintances.

'It is, Brian,' Yoda replied, head still hanging low, dejected.

'What happened? It looks like something from a Tarantino movie. Is that your blood?'

'No, we've been eating small children,' Yoda snapped. 'Of course, it's my fucking blood.'

'I'm only trying to establish–'

'Just a bit of poor judgement on our part, I'm afraid. We're OK.'

I wasn't sure if I was going to faint as white flashes started appearing before my eyes, leaving purple floaters in my vision, fading, only to be replaced by more. I was still standing, blinking, confused, before I realised there were cameras, as I raised my arms to protect my face from a different type of assault.

Officer Brian raised his hand to block the lens, pushing the reporter back until the flashes disappeared around the corner.

'I'm sorry, John, but I called the police,' the old woman said. 'All we could see was what looked like a riot happening. I didn't know it was you.'

'It's OK, Mo,' Yoda smiled.

'Why didn't you tell me? You know how tense things are right now – how angry people are. All of this could have been prevented, and who's this?' she jabbed a finger at me.

'This is Father McKay.'

'Peter,' I said, holding out my hand, which she ignored.

'We were hoping he might take over the church,' Yoda explained.

'Pfft, well, you've done a good job selling it to him, haven't you. The only thing that could get this church back on its feet is a visit from him upstairs, not another out of towner, unless he can perform miracles. Can you perform miracles?' she asked, turning to me.

'Oh yes, water into wine, no problem,' I shot back, annoyed.

'If I may interrupt,' the youngest of the police officers edged forward, putting his hand between us authoritatively, 'you two gentlemen have been assaulted and require medical attention, which I suggest you get immediately. I've radioed through for an ambulance, and then we'll have to take statements and build–'

'There'll be no need for any of that, officer,' Yoda cut him off abruptly.

'We don't wish to press charges.'

'Whether you wish to press charges or not is irrelevant. A crime has been–'

'It would do more harm than good,' Yoda interrupted again, getting more and more testy. 'The position of the Church in the community is at an all-time low after what happened with Fr Williams. The place would boil over, wouldn't you agree, Brian?' he appealed to the other officer. 'This has to just disappear. We don't want it going any further.'

'I agree, John,' Brian nodded, 'for the greater good.'

The younger officer looked disappointed. 'But–'

'For the greater good,' Brian repeated, pulling rank.

The sound of more sirens announced the approaching ambulance before it pulled up outside the front gate, its flashing blue lights suggesting something interesting to passers-by.

'It's OK, my car's just over there,' Yoda insisted, trying to get out of engaging with the paramedics.

'Erm, well, it is and it isn't,' Brian replied, not sure how to break the news.

'What?' Yoda asked, before breaking away and hurrying around the corner, his feet dragging through the long grass as flashes started erupting from the lingering reporters.

'Anyway, you're in no fit state to drive,' Brian called out, as we followed after him.

'Leave it now, eh?' I suggested, managing to get in front of him. 'Let's get patched up first.'

'I need to see it,' he shook his head, bustling past me towards the side gate, walking down the steps before stopping dead on the bottom tread and staring at the ruins.

'I'm sorry,' I said, unable to think of anything else to say.

'It's only a car,' he shrugged, surprisingly calm, his voice not betraying any emotion. 'It's Fr Williams's fault, not yours, not mine or the children's. Fr Williams.' He stood motionless for a few seconds before turning to face to me. 'Let's go and get patched up, shall we?'

I nodded, and we made our way towards the ambulance, its back doors open, waiting, displaying walls lined with various pieces of machinery, tubes and tools. My gaze looked beyond it to a man standing alone, leaning against a lamppost on the corner, dressed all in black, like a silhouette. There was something about him, about the way he was watching, an intensity, a negativity, a feeling of disapproval.

'The gentleman in the car,' the younger officer said, 'with the bushy beard and funny eyebrows, who is he, and where did he go?'

'Don't know who you mean,' Yoda shook his head and shrugged, before climbing into the back of the ambulance and taking a seat on the padded bed.

Getting in alongside Yoda, I glanced across at Brian, who nodded in response – no further questions – and then my attention turned to the darkened window as we pulled away.

He was still standing there, staring at where we had been, whilst I scanned my memory, wondering if he was real.

∞

My hair dropped to the ground in clumps as the buzzing clippers cleared the areas around the cuts, ready for stitching. I looked in the mirror, at islands of long hair tied up in bunches, surrounded by a sea of pale bare skin, blood-red strips marking the centres, fault lines

'Ow!' I heard from the next cubicle, as Yoda's first stitch was put in.

I smirked, and then said to the nurse, 'Take it all off.'

There was hardly anything left anyway.

'What? Hang on, hang on,' Yoda cried, as the curtain was pulled back to reveal his nurse clinging on desperately to her thread, as he'd jumped up mid-stitch.

He burst out laughing when he saw me, the volume increasing by the second. It was a reaction I recognised; the euphoria following violence.

'You look like a fucking pineapple,' he proclaimed loudly.

'Alright, alright,' I said, embarrassed enough as it was.

'I know how you feel, though. They had to cut my hair off as well,' he gave a mock groan.

'Which one? You're bald as a coot.'

'I've got a few,' he said, feigning offence, 'around the sides.'

The laughter continued as he was ushered back to his seat, only stopping when the nurse resumed the painful treatment.

I looked in the mirror again.

*Fucking ridiculous,*' Peter confirmed.

'Don't think even Herbert could do anything with this,' the nurse said apologetically. 'I'll give you a number one all over once we're done with the stitches. Won't take as long to grow back then.'

I nodded as I felt the first pinprick; the tugging at my skin with the first of many sutures. It didn't feel too bad, though; in fact, it felt good, a cleansing through pain, the discomfort a perverse pleasure as I felt my skin being sewn back together.

Another 'Ow,' followed by a giggle, came from Yoda's cubicle.

I watched in the mirror as the clippers finished their job. My hair was down to nothing, right down to the wood, just a stubble, with seven completely bald strips crisscrossing my head, containing neat lines of black cotton loops that held the angry-looking cuts together.

Yoda threw the curtain open again and strode in, proudly showing off his two stitched-up wounds before erupting with more laughter.

'Fucking hell, you look like you've been scalped by the blind school.'

'I used to enjoy our days out together,' I smiled, 'but they've really gone downhill lately.'

He carried on laughing, pointing at me, 'You look like Nosferatu, like one of Doctor Frankenstein's practise runs.'

He was starting to lose control, finding himself hilarious, as the nurses started to giggle along, dropping their professional demeanour and becoming themselves once they saw that I wasn't offended.

'Well, I think he looks nice,' one of them scolded, coming to my defence. 'I like a man with scars.'

'He looks like his head burst,' Yoda continued, unable to believe his own comic brilliance.

'What have you given him?' I asked. 'Can I have some?'

'You're both fine to go if you're feeling OK,' my nurse declared, once the banter quietened down; quotas and targets from above dictating that they couldn't enjoy themselves for too long.

We gave our thanks and walked back through A&E, drawing surprised glances from the casualties and hypochondriacs, all keeping once another company during the four-hour wait. It felt worse than the prison waiting room.

A welcome smell enveloped us as Yoda opened his front door, a smell of home and safety. Scruff came up to us, tail wagging, wanting attention, which I was happy to give; it was preferable to conversation. The taxi journey had been quiet, slightly awkward, both of us sat on the back seat looking out of opposite windows, seeing nothing, the events of the day running through our minds.

'Cup of tea?' Yoda asked.

'Love one,' I replied, as he disappeared into the kitchen and I sank into the sofa, kicking my shoes off haphazardly before getting up to place them neatly in the corner, remembering where I was.

He came back in and slumped into his chair, cracking open a can of beer and taking a slurp, and then tilting his glass to pour a picture-perfect pint.

I think I might have let out a whimper.

He looked over, catching me staring. 'Kettle will be boiled in a minute, don't worry.'

I nodded, and then slouched down further, feeling parched as he took a long, deep drink from of his glass, letting out an orgasmic, 'Ah!' before adding, 'Gorgeous that,' admiring the golden beauty in his hand.

*'Arse hole,'* Peter cursed.

I sat salivating as he started to chuckle, before pulling a can from down the side of his chair and throwing it over.

'Watch my head,' I protested, catching it with a smile.

'Watch my carpet,' he replied, as I yanked the ring-pull and sent a spray of beer across the floor.

Scruff scampered over to lick the carpet, the quickest I'd seen him move.

*'Fucking alcoholic,'* Peter whispered.

Yoda tilted his glass Scruff's way, and the dog lapped it up greedily, draining the remains, just as the doorbell chimed.

'ABC?' I asked, turning sharply towards Yoda.

'No, he's well gone,' he said. 'That'll be our dinner.'

I felt a mixture of joy and trepidation as Yoda went to the door; joy because it meant he wouldn't be cooking, and trepidation over not knowing who was about to come in. Anxiety increased, like the old days, hearing the mumbling of voices as somebody entered and the living room door nudged open, a plastic carrier bag leading the way, followed by the old lady from the school, Yoda in a dress.

I jumped up, not sure what to say, holding out my hand, which she accepted and shook this time, all the while staring at my shaved head.

'Hello, erm, Mrs–'

'Maureen, love, but just call me Mo,' she said, not taking her eyes off the cuts and bruises. 'Bloody hell, I didn't realise it was that bad. Are you OK?'

'Yes,' I nodded, as Yoda came in carrying three clean plates.

'Look at his head,' Mo exclaimed.

'I know,' Yoda grinned. 'He got battered by a gang of kids.'

'Bloody hell,' she repeated. 'Had the press around this afternoon. Wish I'd kept my mouth shut now.'

'Ah, it wasn't that bad,' Yoda said, passing around knives and forks, 'I've been through worse.'

Mo and I both shared a glance as he set out the little folding tables and returned to his seat, clapping his hands in anticipation.

'Is that what I think it is?' he asked.

She opened the bag and gave us a large, warm parcel each. 'Yep, sausage dinners from Poison Pete's, as requested.'

They weighed a tonne.

Yoda closed his eyes in mock ecstasy and started unwrapping his bounty, revealing a mountain of food sitting in a polystyrene tray. 'You get an extra sausage there,' he said, eyes still closed, looking as though he was praying.

It did smell good, an aroma from the past, a treat on a Saturday night watching the A-Team, as I considered the heap of chips, peas, sausages and onions that lay before me, bound together with coagulating gravy. He was right, I noted, there were *three* sausages.

There was a moment of silent anticipation before we began.

'They don't have gravy down south, do they?' he asked, already scraping his tray.

Mouth full of sausage, I just shook my head.

'Is it true they eat their chips with knives and forks?'

'It is,' I confirmed.

'Savages,' he mumbled, looking towards Mo, who was shaking her head in either agreement or disagreement, as was I.

'I'm, erm, sorry I was a bit frosty earlier, Peter,' Mo said, once we were finished eating. 'I just didn't know why you were there. This dickhead is supposed to give notice,' she added, pointing an accusing finger at Yoda.

'It's alright,' I replied, putting my tray on the floor for Scruff to lick clean, 'we were all a bit on edge.'

'I suppose you won't be having a second viewing?' she asked, going a bit high pitched.

I shrugged my shoulders and sat back, ignoring the heat of their staring eyes. *Another interrogation*, I thought.

There was a long pause as bad cop stood and walked out, returning with three cans of beer.

'You know, love, you shouldn't judge the place on what happened today, or by its reputation,' she said after a while. 'I know that's easy for me to say when you're sitting there with a head like a chewed-up tennis ball, but there's a lot more to the place once you scratch beneath the surface. It'd surprise you.'

'Don't judge a book by its cover?' I smiled. 'Even back when I was a kid, that area had its reputation – we didn't go there. Doesn't seem like much has changed. It's the place that's responsible for the stereotypes that mark the whole city. You can't help thinking negative things when you're there.'

She rolled her eyes, silently dismissing the notion. 'Well, I've been there six years now, and I wouldn't go anywhere else. I had the same preconceptions as you, but they're the same as any other stereotypes – overblown. There are layers that you have to peel back to find the truth of the place, to get to know the people. They're different than the rest of the city, and different from one another. It's like a parallel world, a concentration of big, diverse personalities, each with their own story, which is pretty rare these days. People are so boring now, aren't they?'

I nodded, agreeing that most people are boring.

'It's the history of the place that I love,' Yoda joined in, 'which is why the current situation makes me so angry. It only takes one bad egg to drag the whole thing down.'

He was doing this funny shuffling thing he used to do in his chair before he was about to go on a ramble, like a dog dragging its arse across the carpet, as he sifted through his memory banks, a mental encyclopaedia, staring ahead at nothing in particular, his lips moving slightly, forming words before the sound was ready. I was full and feeling lethargic after the day, so just listening suited me fine.

'The place has always been a focal point of the city, somewhere people look up to,' was his opening gambit, as he finally stopped shuffling. 'Before the church was built, there was a sandstone beacon that used to guide ships coming up the river, built in twelve-thirty. For centuries, sailors looked to that point, which told them they were home after months at sea. It was surrounded by fields, overlooking the old city, with its port and its castle.'

'Remember it, do you?' I quipped.

'Fuck off,' he bristled. 'The beacon fell down, or was blown down, or knocked down, or whatever, at the start of the eighteenth century, and the church was built on the same spot, replacing one tower with another. Everton wasn't even part of Liverpool when it was built. The area used to be wealthy, where all the merchants lived, full of villas when the port was booming. It was called the Montpellier of the county, the prime spot on the hill, looking out at the ships arriving from far-off places stuffed with stories and exotic cargoes – cotton, tobacco, sugar, spice and all things nice. It must have looked amazing to the locals, with its grand architecture and giant stained-glass windows. That was the purpose, of course, to awe with its scale – the light and sound echoing around the space. It's been there watching over the city for two hundred years now, through good and bad.'

'Slaves?'

'No, I think the slave trade was all but over when it was built, and very few slaves ever came here – it was usually from Africa to the Americas, though the city did make big money from it, unfortunately. It was a triangle, alcohol and arms from here to Africa, slaves to America, and then sugar, cotton and tobacco picked by the slaves coming back here.'

He sat quietly for a moment, having lost his flow. The mention of slavery had sent him off on a tangent.

'The church,' I said, nudging him back on track.

'Oh yes, Everton and the church slowly got swallowed up by the expanding city, as the wealthy started to move out. There was a lot of industry, manufacturing and chemical works on the docks and in the city centre, so I'd assume the pollution pushed the money to the outskirts, in search of cleaner air. We were the empire's second city at the time, the gateway to the new world, to New York. Ships were sailing to the Far East, to the Indias, to–'

'All sounds very romantic,' I cut in. He was laying it on a bit thick.

'Nah, it wasn't all good,' he acknowledged. 'Terraces, tenements, courtyards and slums were built to house the poor after the wealthy moved out, covering the area to cope with the massive influxes of Irish immigrants following the famine. A quarter of the city's population were Irish-born, and there were also lots of Welsh and Poles – even a Little Italy off Scotty

Road.'

'They were migrants, not immigrants,' Mo corrected. 'Ireland was part of the UK back then.'

'Alright, you know what I mean,' Yoda replied sharply. 'Anyway, mix all those different accents together, and you probably end up with something like Scouse.' He regained his composure, as befitted his role as chief narrator. 'Times changed during the twenties, as the world moved on and the decline of the city began. Then, the great depression of the thirties hit the city hard–'

'Bloody hell,' I threw up my hands, exasperated, 'feels like I'm on the Magical Mystery Tour.'

World War Two came along,' he ignored the interruption, 'and we were the control centre during the Battle of the Atlantic, making us a prime target. Eighty air raids hit the city, leaving around seventy thousand people homeless. Huge swathes of housing were demolished, and then replaced by council houses, homes for heroes, estates and blocks of flats – modern living. The Piggeries, they were called, falling to bits no sooner than they were built. Once they were demolished, we were left with the crap that's still here today. The estates, and the barren, open spaces.'

'I'm surprised the church survived the bombings,' I offered, trying to feign interest.

'I came through relatively unscathed,' he said, 'as if it had some sort of force field around it.'

'John!' Mo scolded.

'Oh alright, but it only got damaged a little bit. Just one of the stained-glass windows survived. 'Following the war–'

'It's OK, I'm well aware of the city's history,' I had to stop him before he got started again. I was starting to feel drowsy, a combination of the events of the day, the jumbo sausage dinner and the Polish lager taking their toll.

'I was just getting up to skiffle music, Merseybeat, Militant and the Toxteth riots,' he moaned, sounding disappointed.

'I am from here you know.'

'I know,' he smiled at that, 'and it's probably too little too late after today. I was just trying to explain how important that church is to the city – the remarkable history it has witnessed, the changes it has seen. It's probably at its lowest ebb at the moment, along with the area as a whole, but the history is so rich.'

'End of sales pitch, I think,' Mo said, beaming with pride. 'Ultimately, it's up to you to decide. I had to make the same choice, and in the end, I saw it for the massive opportunity it was. Did I want a cushy job making little difference to people's lives? No. I wanted a challenge, which this place gives me in spades. There are too many people living on dead-end street, doing nothing – nine-to-five and then stare at the television, the years disappearing and gone before you know it. I was determined that my life was not going to go that way. I was not going to become one of them.'

'But why are you even here talking to me, after the damage the Church has done to your school?' I asked. 'To your pupils – your community?'

'Because the healing process has to start somewhere.'

Yoda nodded vigorously; I thought his head had come loose.

'In many ways, this place saved me,' she said, coining a phrase that sounded familiar, before sitting back and taking a swig from her glass.

'From what?' I asked.

'A normal life,' she answered, wiping the froth from her top lip.

Yoda offered me another can, which I refused.

'I'm going up,' I said. 'I'm knackered.'

'Sleep well, son,' he said. 'What a day.'

Mo stood and shook my hand.

'Have a good sleep, love,' she said. 'Hopefully, we'll see you again soon.'

I just gave a smile for an answer as I left the room.

'Go on, then,' I heard her sigh, as I walked up the stairs. 'Tell me about skiffle music, Merseybeat, Militant and the Toxteth riots.'

∞

I woke up tired after a fitful night's sleep; the bedroom light was still on, and the muffled sound of the TV was rising up through the floor. I got out of bed and opened the curtains, still confused about where I was, to be greeted by the dilapidated picture-house-cum-nightclub opposite, the Coconut Grove, now boarded up, losing its fight to stay relevant, despite all its many incarnations.

Downstairs, Yoda was sat in front of the television with a plate of toast and mug of tea.

'More tea in the pot,' he muttered without looking at me, as I continued on to the kitchen. 'Do you want a bacon butty?' he called out over the white noise of the television.

'Yeah, sounds good,' I replied, stirring a spoon in my almost stewed tea.

'Great, do us one as well,' he said, no doubt smiling to himself.

*Got me again*, I thought.

The aroma drifted through the house, drawing Scruff into the kitchen, the pan spitting fat as I scooped the bacon onto the bread, melting the butter, a masterpiece.

'Shit!' Yoda cried out. 'Shit, Peter – shit!'

I rushed into the living room, nearly tripping over Scruff in the doorway, to find that he'd spilled tea on himself.

'I'll get a cloth,' I shouted, spinning on my heels and heading towards the kitchen.

'No, not that, look – that,' he said, becoming increasingly agitated.

I turned and looking around, confused.

'That!' he screamed again, pointing at the television.

I nearly dropped the plate at the sight of a smartly-dressed man sitting behind a desk, holding up a newspaper as he introduced me to the nation.

'This story is about two Priests in Liverpool, who came a cropper when walking around an empty church vacated by a certain Fr Williams, who is currently standing trial on charges of paedophilia, alleged to have occurred over a number of years,' a tinny voice announced.

The camera zoomed in on the picture in the middle of the page; my eyes looking wild, hair tangled, blood running down my face alongside a photo of Yoda's battered car. It could have been a scene from Beirut or Palestine: panic, fear, bloodshed, stones, dust and scattered debris.

'Retired bishop John O'Given and Fr Peter McKay were caught out by the strength of feeling of local schoolchildren, and spent the day hiding in the church.' He flicked his eyebrows, smiling. 'Some might call it karma, Debbie,' he glanced over at the glamorous, dark-haired newsreader sitting next to him.

'Well, you reap what you sow, as they say,' she smiled back. 'I don't think we'll be seeing these characters hanging around there any time soon.'

We looked at each other as they moved onto the next story, about the #underclass calling for the abolition of all political parties. We weren't listening; Parliament was prorogued again, so neither were they.

'How did they get my name?' I wondered aloud.

'Maybe from Mo?' Yoda suggested. 'She did say she should have kept her mouth shut. She was a bit pissed off.'

'But…' I started, before realising I was lost for words, stunned. '… how?'

'Ah, don't worry about it – tomorrow's chip paper. Everyone will have forgot about it by the end of the week. Now, get yourself ready and shoot down the shop, get the papers in, and we'll see what the damage is. Oh, and put a hat on.'

He was acting decisively all of a sudden, if not excited.

'Bloody tin hat,' I replied.


I spread the newspapers across the floor. Nobody had recognised me in the shop, though they probably noticed how self-conscious I was feeling, paranoid, twitchy like a smack head, all eyes on me.

'Where's my butty?' I asked, scanning the room. The initial shock had worn off, and now my body realised it needed fuel.

'I ate it, sorry. Thought you didn't want it,' he said sheepishly. 'Make another if you want to do the honours. I'll have one.'

Shaking my head, I sat down and started flicking through the papers, my heart dropping when I came across my panic-stricken eyes looking back at me; it shocked me how bad I looked. We were in one red top and one broadsheet, making page five in both, with each carrying pretty much the same story, detailing how we had got our comeuppance from the schoolchildren, written slightly tongue in cheek.

We were quiet as we read through the articles.

'Ah, most people won't even notice it,' Yoda mumbled. 'It'll get lost in among the other news.'

I wasn't sure if he was trying to reassure me or convince himself, as the phone rang and he reacted with a start.

'That'll be the communications office,' he said, 'Church PR. They'll probably want to give me a bollocking, and then tell us how we're going to handle this.'

It didn't stop; the house was under a communications siege for most of the day: telephones, emails and knocks on the door, whilst trending on Twitter.

'Why should I give a shit about that?' Yoda spat, finding a target for his rage. 'Full of contempt and hate that thing – no empathy. It used to be if you had something to say to a person, you went up to them and said it. Now, it's just anonymous shit bags hiding behind keyboards, losing their inhibitions, saying horrible things. What are they, trolls?' It was a world he was completely disengaged from, as if it wasn't real. 'My worry is that young people no longer have the self-esteem to just shrug it off.'

'Oh, it's not that bad – just different. You sound like a miserable old grandad,' I said.

'It's the new addiction,' he kept going, distracting himself from the journalists shouting through the letterbox. 'I blame that stuff on half the problems the young have today. They're not social anymore, they're lonely, inward-looking, all selfies, headphones and iPads. Remember when everyone used to know everyone on the street?'

I nodded; I did.

'They have all these phones, but they don't actually speak to one another with them. When they do actually have to speak to a person face-to-face, they shy away – it has to be composed, nothing spontaneous. They're like factory-farmed animals, dumb cows, alone in their concrete pens, kept alive, fed and medicated, but psychologically damaged.'

'Luddite,' I laughed, shaking my head. 'It's just another layer of communication. You can talk to the people in the room whilst talking to people on the other side of the world if you want to. How can that be bad?'

'I know I'm ranting here, but in a world where everybody is supposed to be connected, the opposite is happening. They close out the real world, twitchy, unable to communicate, not wanting to even if they could, getting all agitated if you disturb them. The young are supposed to be radical, but they've become passive, fixed to a screen that tells them what to like, what to buy and how to behave – divided and conquered. Where's the next revolution coming from? Where's our Arab Spring? It's life in snippets, quickly forgotten, no place for deep thought anymore. Deep thought is boring.'

The sound of snippets falling through the letterbox ended the conversation. We had made front cover of The Echo, with the same picture of me looking up from the church floor, disorientated, covered in blood; complete disarray.

PRIESTS GET STONED! read the headline, ahead of two pages inside that included an interview with Mo and comments from anonymous locals. Yoda was quickly back on the telephone to councillors, clergy and anybody else who wished to tell him what he should do.

I flicked through my emails; one from Fr Ted:

*Hi Peter, hope all is ok.*

*Saw what happened to you in the newspaper – must have been horrific. Our thoughts and prayers are with you. Think I'll stay in the village, thanks! Speaking of which, things have been eventful down here, but not in a good way. Alf has been served with a Compulsory Purchase Order covering the majority of his land. It has knocked him a bit, but he's trying not to show it. Long battle ahead!*

*Your cottage is still sitting there empty, and we have a cause worth fighting for, if you are up for it? Please give it some consideration. I don't want to see any more pictures of you in the newspaper, black and blue.*

A feeling of anger rose in me, as I slumped back into my chair. *Bastards*, I thought, *why can't they just leave them alone?*

My mind drifted back to the village, the simplicity of it: one church and two pubs, nature, fields, characters; something worth fighting for.

I reread the message again, thinking about the cottage and the walk down the lane to the church, rose-tinted glasses in full effect.

'*How could you not want to go there?*' Peter whispered. '*There's a cause, a fight, a friend in need.*'

Yoda came in and sat next to me on the sofa, letting out a big sigh.

'Any guidance from above?' I asked, staring off into space.

'Just sit tight,' he said, 'no talking to the media. Had a few councillors on the phone as well, shouting blue murder about the yobbish image of the city it's created, reinforcing negative stereotypes, as if the Church hadn't done enough damage already, blah-di-blah.'

'Bit harsh.'

'They have got a point, though. I did completely fuck it up.'

I nodded quietly; they did have a point.

'I spoke to the ABC,' he said, brightening a little.

'Oh yeah, what happened to him? Is he OK?'

'Ah, he's alright, not a scratch. Hid himself under Scruff's rug – thought it was hilarious once he knew we were unhurt, and that the car was insured. He's back home now.' He shuffled uncomfortably and handed me a handwritten list. 'He gave me this – current vacancies around the country for you to consider. He didn't think you'd want to stay here.'

'There's stuff going on in the village that they need a hand with,' I suggested, trying to sound enthusiastic as I shoved the list into my pocket.

He just nodded, patting me on the thigh, saying nothing, until the peace was broken by more harsh electronic ringing; saved by the phone.

The house fell silent in the evening, after six, once everybody had clocked off, probably to resume again in the morning.

'We've not got much in, I'm afraid,' Yoda reported. 'Jockey's rations for us tonight.'

'I can nip down to the chippy if you want?' I offered hopefully.

'Nah, we had that last night. Can't eat too much unhealthy food at my age, and we should be staying in. Got a tin of corned beef there – make some sarnies,' he said proudly, as if suggesting a beautifully marbled Wagyu.

Probably a leftover from a Christmas hamper. Whatever the case, it was well aged.

'I'll take Scruff out,' I said. 'He hasn't been out today – he must be bursting.'

'I let him out in the yard earlier,' he replied, uncomfortable, not wanting to go against official orders. 'He hasn't *really* been out, though.'

I could sense him wrestling with it, trying to break out of the siege mentality.

'Put your hat on and don't speak to anybody,' he eventually decided. 'Just take him around the block.'

It felt good to leave the house, where everything felt so concentrated. Scruff barely made it out of the gate before squatting, his eyes locking on mine as he left me a gift, his relief palpable when I pulled the bags out, my stomach churning, dry retching, as I picked up the hot chunks, cursing him as we walked around the block as instructed, not seeing anybody else.

Once out of sight, we paused under a streetlight and took out the list of potential destinations, trying to decipher Yoda's scrawl under the yellow light: *Hebden Bridge, Marple Bridge, Splott (Cardiff), Farncombe.* I let out a sigh before returning it to my pocket; they didn't mean anything to me.

We continued around the block, up the side of the church, strolling, deep in thought when the door to a parked car eased open, the reflection of street lights moving along its dark grey form, and then shooting off as it opened fully, the interior light illuminating a man climbing out, Dictaphone in hand. I kept walking.

'Fr McKay, we're just wondering how you are?' he called after me.

'Have you got anything to say about yesterday?'

I continued walking, speeding up, the house getting closer.

'Fr McKay, do you think the children were wrong to attack you like they did?'

I was close to the gate when he stepped in front of me, blocking my path; Peter rising.

'We just want your angle on things. What does the Church say in response to what happened?'

'Nothing – no comment. Can I get into the house please?'

He didn't move. 'Can we see your head?' he asked, reaching up to grab my hat as I leaned back.

'No, please,' I pleaded, but he tried again, lunging forward quickly.

Peter stepped in, raising my arm and blocking his hand whilst the other swung up, hitting him with the bag of dog shit. He let out a yelp as it exploded, covering his face in excrement, followed by a scream as he started wiping desperately with his hands, spreading it, before spitting on the pavement, spitting, spitting, as he bent over and then retched, vomited, splashing his shoes, up his legs.

*'I know how you feel,'* Peter giggled.

I stood motionless, taking in this strange one-man show, featuring a noisy, writhing shape covered in waste, wailing as if it was melting, becoming a human puddle. Scruff sat placidly observing the spectacle by my feet, neither of us reacting until I felt a strong hand on my shoulder pulling me towards the house.

'What happened?' Yoda asked urgently, panic evident in his voice. 'You didn't hit him, did you?'

'No – well, yes, but only with a bag of shit,' I said.

'Eh?' he looked confused.

'Scruff's shit, in a bag.'

He stopped and turned to watch as the hack carried on retching, in between attempts at clearing out his nostrils.

'It's in his hair and everything,' Yoda whispered, grimacing.

'Should we get him some water or something?' I asked, starting to feel a bit panicked myself.

'Nah, they've been throwing shit at us all day,' he allowed himself a wry smile, as he ushered me into the safety of the hall, closing the front door behind us. 'What happened? I thought I said–'

'I didn't know he was going to be there. He wouldn't go away.'

'Did you say anything?'

'No, nothing.'

'No harm done, then. I doubt this one will make it into the paper,' he laughed, and he was right.

The rest of the evening was spent sitting on the sofa, doing what normal people do, apparently, watching celebrities trying to dance before good cop, bad cop judges. It was the same format as all the others, a national obsession that I didn't understand, but still I sat staring at it, not thinking, hardly even breathing, until a ping on my phone roused me from my stupor, an email from Meg, hitting me like a slap in the face, making me jump, attracting a sideways glance from Yoda.

*Well, I didn't expect to see your face again so soon. Not the circumstances I was hoping for, I must admit. Are you OK? It said you needed stitches – must have been terrible. What happened? It said you were attacked by schoolkids – not the best time to get your fifteen minutes of fame. The pub seems to have woken up again tonight, there's a cheer every time the news is on!*

*I'm so, so sorry about what I have done to you. I am so ashamed, I can hardly type this out. You must think I'm a prostitute or something. We need to talk, so I can explain things.*

*I understand you leaving. I am disgusted with myself and how I've treated you – secret boyfriends, and taking money to sleep with you. That's not me. How have I ended up like this?*

*It's true that I took Paul's money. There were personal reasons, though they are not an excuse. Dad is housebound with cancer, and I'm looking after him. He's just finished a course of chemo, and we are just about scraping along. I didn't tell you about this as you were my release, letting me get away from it all for a while. I wanted to talk about other things, so kept it from you for the right reasons, I think.*

*Paul threatened to have me arrested for getting his daughters drunk in the pub, leading to them 'exposing themselves'. He even brought two police officers along to reinforce the point. All sorts were going through my mind: losing my job, legal costs, what if I couldn't look after Dad? I had to decide between the money or the police, so I took the money. It was the easiest route, especially since I wanted to sleep with you anyway, you know that, but morally it was completely wrong. I understand that now. I find it hard to look at myself in the mirror at the moment, knowing that I allowed him to buy me.*

*Now for the difficult bit. Dan got down on one knee last night, and with things being so shit lately, and me being pissed at the time, against all instincts I said yes. I've woken up this morning feeling bad, as now that the drink has worn off, it feels like another rope tying me to this place. I do like him, as you know, but engaged, married, a life together? That's filling me with dread, which shouldn't be the case. I know if you were still here the answer would have been no, but...*

*I know this may not be what you want to hear, but look where hiding things has got me. I'm not turning away from you – I don't know what I'm doing. I really miss you. I know it's a mess, but please get in touch so we can see how this plays out between us. It's only when something is gone*

I read it four or five times, hearing her voice say the words, trying to remember her smell, how she felt, how she moved. I thought of the emotions, letting my eyes well up, though not enough to spill out on to my cheeks as I glanced across at Yoda, still focussed on the dancers. I was inviting the feelings in, a welcome escape from the day, wanting to feel their touch, their texture; wanting to control their intensity, taking them to a point, enjoying the sensation, the vulnerability.

*Ted must have relented*, I thought. I could almost see him pinned in the corner, jowls wobbling, refusing to make eye contact with her, and then surrendering as soon as she got near him. I started to type out a response of sentimental drivel, stopped and deleted it, before realising this was probably my perfect relationship, long distance, the little screen giving me all that I needed without the threat of physical contact. Still, I was brooding, raging inside, as echoes from a previous life disrupted this one.

'You OK there?' Yoda asked.

'Yes,' I nodded.

I deleted the email and blocked her address, hoping to feel relief that she was finally gone, but there was nothing

*'She was a slag anyway,'* Peter reassured me.

I pushed myself deep into the sofa, uncomfortable, a heavy weight sitting in my stomach, the perfect ending to a shitty day. It was supposed to be clean, but I kept thinking of her, feeling something I guessed was similar to mourning, a lingering nausea.

*This doesn't happen to me*, I thought, watching the glittering sequins and Lycra outfits spin around for the pantomime judges.

'Did you, erm, have a look at the list the ABC sent through?' Yoda asked tentatively, once the voting was in.

'Hmm, yes.'

'Anything you fancy? No pressure, like.'

'Not really. Don't know where any of them are.'

He gave a little nod, and then sat quiet for a moment, scheming, cogs turning as I stared at the television.

'And the thing back at the village?' he said, casting a line.

'I don't really have a choice, do I?' I shrugged.

'There's always a choice – there are always options. We could get the map out, have a look.'

'Not in this case. I've been plastered all over the newspapers and the television, covered in blood. Look what they did to me,' I gestured, pointing, 'look at my head.'

'I know, I know, but it'll all blow over in a couple of days.'

I just shook my head.

'So, when do you think you'll go?' he asked.

'Where?'

'The village.'

'I'm not going back to the village.'

'Oh,' he glanced at me, confused. 'Where, then?'

'Nowhere. I'm staying here. I've got no choice.'

'I don't understand.'

'How could I come here, get beaten up, get plastered all over the news, and then just disappear?'

'I don't follow.'

'I can't leave. Wherever I go, people will know exactly who I am, a fella who got filled in by a gang of kids and ran away.'

'What will you do here, get a paper round?' he let out a nervous laugh. 'Work in the chippy?'

'I'm going to take the job.'

'What job?'

'The Iron Church. I'm going to take over the Iron Church.'

His face dropped for a moment, and then a smile appeared on the rebound, as comprehension struck.

'What?' he asked excitedly.

'Like I said, I've got no choice,' I repeated, a smile coming to my lips.

He jumped up laughing, doing a jig in the middle of the floor; Scruff barking along next to him, wondering what was going on.

'You're seriously going to do it,' he said, 'after all that's happened?'

'Yes,' the logic was clear to me.

'You fucking loon,' he giggled, before going out to the kitchen, the fridge door opening and closing as I sat sinking into the sofa.

I hadn't known that I was going to say those words until my mouth opened and they came tumbling out, but I immediately realised that a whole series of events, from the village fete to Meg's message and everything in between, had been leading to this moment. There were no coincidences, nothing accidental, this was the path laid out for me; this was God's plan.

'I can't believe it, I'm made up,' Yoda declared, returning with four beers, grinning like a Cheshire cat.

I accepted a can and cracked it open. *Stop thinking*, I thought, *start drinking*. 'To a new beginning.'

# CHAPTER 7

MINISTRY.5

The first day of the rest of my life started full of doubt, feeling what Meg was feeling, the same dread at long-term commitments we didn't really want to make.

*Is she lying, staring up at the ceiling, like me?* I pondered.

*'Fuck's sake,'* Peter spat.

*Feeling the same as me?* I continued, playing the role of a hopeless romantic as my hand reached out, grasping the empty air, imagining her reciprocating my sense of longing. *Are we linked by an invisible cord? A subconscious synthesis of emotions?*

*'The only cord she's getting is physical, and it's not yours.'*

I knew what my staying here meant, its implications; I was putting a match to the final bridge. I wouldn't be going back to the village, and that meant not seeing Meg again. It was a self-imposed bereavement, her life running parallel to mine, but in a different bubble, meeting different people, having different experiences: joy, laughter, sadness; all without me.

'Fuck it,' I mumbled.

This was not supposed to happen. I was not supposed to care.

The days were different now, with the Church Communications Office going into full media assault mode once Yoda informed them of my decision, calling first thing, before I could change my mind. It bothered me having a Public Relations Department, same as any big corporate or government office, creating spin, steering people's thoughts; *'We're going for this angle – let's run with that...'* snaring me in its machinations to manipulate truths and half-truths.

Like a plague of locusts, professionals descended, teaching me about tone and body language; how to position your hands and eyes, or travel down a tangent if questions became difficult.

*'Control it – talk about what* you *want to talk about.'*

For all their qualifications and experience, however, they were still struggling. No matter what angle they tried, with those red lines crisscrossing my shaven head, I still resembled a psychopath, and the fact that I'd stayed after what happened with the kids only coloured the narrative further, reinforcing the impression that my looks gave, suggesting an accurate representation of the person inside. This made press interviews awkward, my image at odds with the answers to their questions, those pre-prepared, all-smiling soundbites.

'I am looking forward to the challenge... I understand the anger... 'I intend to prove to the people that the Church is here for them, to support them through thick and thin… We must win back their trust.'

It sounded hollow, disingenuous; gentle words delivered by a devil.

The press response was positive at least; the heft of the Church ensured it, as my face appeared again on the front page of the Echo, attracting lots of attention, a freak show gaining momentum. It wasn't long before I was appearing on websites and then in the nationals, the same interview regurgitated, my bizarre appearance a point of interest, like a Mad Max extra; the man standing in stark contrast to the purity of his words and his clerical robes.

The charm offensive was launched on many fronts, with radio and television interviews tightly orchestrated; the same questions asked and the same robotic answers given. I even visited the school, where the children sat silent, listening, as Mo watched over them, her threats taken seriously.

'Does anybody have any questions?' I asked, with not a single hand raised.

I hated it, my prepared lines and their toeing the line; there was no self-expression, all just doing as we were told, leaving words unspoken, aware it was an act.

In between media duties, we travelled to and from the Iron Church; Yoda started to clean the inside, whilst I switched my attention to the canned-up vicarage, dismantling the perforated metal panels that covered its windows, removing the aura of dereliction. It now looked like part of the nearby estate, a simple brick box, with a pitched roof and UPVC windows carrying a mock-Tudor diamond pattern. I decided to move in once the church was finished, any lingering fears outweighed by the nightly trauma of Yoda's cooking.

He was more hesitant. 'It's too dangerous right now,' he said. 'Don't you feel the tension?'

'The quicker I move into the community, the quicker they'll accept me,' I said, picturing white fat on gelatinous boiled meat. 'It's no good me just turning up for a few hours, and then disappearing to live somewhere else.'

He ran it by Mo, expecting support, but getting the opposite when she returned the following day.

'You'll be OK, love,' she said. 'You can move in.'

'But–' he started to protest.

'I've spoken with them,' she cut him off, insistent. 'He'll be alright.'

He did have a point, though. We'd been left alone since the incident with the kids, but emotions were still running high. Nothing abusive was ever said when we passed people on the street, but there were no pleasantries offered, either; they simply ignored us. We were being tolerated, nothing more.

'Mo has done a lot of leg work behind the scenes,' Yoda divulged, as we scrubbed. 'Think she feels a bit guilty.'

'They're giving us a chance, then?' I asked hopefully.

'I wouldn't say that, but at least they're not stoning us.'

The only attention we did receive was from the man who would appear each day, standing at the top of the road, a black hoodie concealing his features. I recognised him as the silhouette I'd seen on the day of the stoning, staring, watching, his face a black hole beneath the hood. I'd christened him George Formby, based on the way he leaned on his lamppost, but there was nothing jolly about him; no ukulele or cocky grin. We were under surveillance, our movements observed and reported. My only question was to whom.

Gradually, the church was coming together, its windows repaired, pews polished and carpets cleaned. Each morning, we'd return to find that *PAEDO SCUM* had been repainted on the boundary wall in big white letters, setting the schedule for the day as I collected the scrubbing brush and bucket.

Otherwise, the inside was ready and the house was finished, whilst outside, close inspection of the overgrown grass revealed ancient gravestones lying flat on the ground, optimistic reminders of the city's history, its golden age, when people travelled the world to make their fortunes: Charles Horsfall, owner of a plantation in Jamaica; Mary Piggott of Barbados; Thomas Harman of New Orleans; Netlam and Eliza Tory, also of Jamaica.

*'Slavery,'* Peter observed, giving his usual negative slant.

'We're going to have to set a date for the reopening,' Yoda declared, as we sat in the garden, breathing in the smell of the freshly-cut lawns. 'It's nearly ready now. The to-do list is getting shorter.'

I nodded, although coming to the end of the repair jobs was filling me with dread. I could have happily carried on fixing things, cleaning up and keeping my own company in my own little world.

'Sunday, I suppose?' I suggested.

'This Sunday?' he jerked up in surprise. 'Are you sure you're ready?'

'Yes,' I replied, trying to sound confident, but feeling sick as God's words emerged from my mouth, committing me to a course that I wasn't ready to undertake.

'We'd better start telling people.'

'Issue a press release?'

'No, it needs something more personal for the locals.'

'Stick some posters up, maybe?'

'Could copy what the Jehovies do,' he mused out loud, after a bit of thought, 'start knocking on doors?'

'Oh yeah, because that's a really successful approach, isn't it? I'm sure they're welcomed with opened arms around here.'

'Well, you think of something then, Einstein.'

'What about community groups? We could speak with them.'

'Nah, Mo tried to set up introductions, but they refused. "Just an instant no – they changed the subject. You're on your own, I'm afraid, fellas," is what she said.'

'Door-to-door it is,' I sighed, before lying back down on the grass, enjoying the smell as I closed my eyes, imagining myself back in the village, in swaying fields of corn, anywhere but here.

We entered the Lurk for the first time together, full of trepidation, feeding of each other's bravado. There was a palpable sense of vulnerability and stress as we stepped over the invisible threshold, burdened by the ethereal weight of its sinister fairy tales and physical context, entering claustrophobic jiggers where the pressure was increased by lengths of fencing pressing in, squeezing, choking, constricting, before we burst out into an inward-looking street or cul-de-sac. We were exposed, on trial, as blank, judgmental windows demanded to know, *'What the fuck are you doing here?'*

Everything around us was hard, the people themselves shaped by this amalgamation of red brick and tarmac, the aesthetics harsh, strictly authoritarian; just double-yellow lines and signs dictating *NO BALL GAMES*, high up, out of reach, with crudely-painted goals below, a big fuck you.

Apprehension quickly became confusion, however, as adrenaline tapered off to nothing. It felt like we'd been duped, as we sustained no verbal or physical attacks from feral youths or their drugged-up fathers; no abuse from drunken mothers, taking time out from screaming at out-of-control offspring; no threats of violence from loitering gangs on syringe-strewn pavements. We didn't get mugged, raped or murdered; there was not a knife or a gun to be found. It was as though we were walking through a deserted film set, just a few silent, shuffling individuals, wraith-like, save for a man dressed as a Roman centurion hurrying past.

'Hail Caesar!' Yoda called out, getting no reply.

We were still being ignored, our knocks and bell-ringing going unanswered, as doors remained closed; just an occasional twitch of net curtains suggesting life within.

'I know how they feel now,' I complained.

'Who?' Yoda asked.

'Jehovies.'

Eventually, I gave up knocking and started posting, a long, slow process, punctuated by the occasional dog hitting a glass door, teeth bared, hackles raised, breaking the monotony as they tore the pamphlet to shreds. My feet were getting sore as we pounded identical pavements, passing identical houses; some may have received two or three, others none at all, as we got lost in the warren of streets and back alleys, coming out of the estate to reorientate before going back in, only to be swallowed up by the labyrinth once again; the maze, not a minotaur or golem to be seen.

On our final visit before the grand reopening, we went to the Mere Bank, a black and white mock-Tudor ensemble sat atop ornate brick work, an island in a sea of concrete. It was Saturday night, the place was busy, and I was reminded of the village as suspicious faces looked us up and down as we invaded its cosy interior. Most were smartly dressed, out in groups, exuding a palpable excitement through their animated conversations, regaling one another with tales of past glories, the narrator adding to the drama with a slow-motion punch to the delight of smiling onlookers.

I looked around, glimpsing countless other fight re-enactments, before looking up at the screens and seeing the real thing; two caged warriors covered in blood as they pummelled each other to the ground. I tried to suppress the feeling of nausea as Peter stirred. Violence was permeating everything, like a charge in the air, to which Yoda was oblivious.

'Excuse me,' he shouted, as the barman finished serving a local and then sat back down on his stool. 'Excuse me,' he repeated, louder, but this time the barman picked up a newspaper and started reading. 'Are you fucking deaf?'

'Leave it, they've every right,' I whispered, feeling all eyes on us.

The tension ratcheted up a few notches as I pulled him away from the bar.

'But I'm fucking parched – I've got ID!' he shouted over my shoulder, the barman's mouth turning up slightly at the corners, as he tried to maintain his poker face.

I looked down fondly at him, smiling; Scruff in human form.

'We can pick some up on the way back,' I said, shoving him through the wooden doors, back onto the pavement.

I didn't mind, we were only the starting line; it was clear, nothing vague or ambiguous. We had a point to work from.

'Have you noticed anything?' I asked, as we stood waiting at the remains of a bus stop.

'Erm, yes, they hate us and are ignoring us,' he said, still angry at being deprived of his pint.

'No, look past that,' I persevered. 'Something bigger.'

'What?' he snapped.

'They're *all* doing it, together, acting as one. There's strength there.'

'Suppose so,' he mumbled with a shrug. 'Not much good to me, though. Dry as a nun's nasty here.'


I spent the rest of that evening writing my sermon, and the whole of the night awake, twisting and turning, tangled in sheets; tangled in thoughts barbed like brambles, trying to pin me down, as doubts and fears became irrationally large. I was up with the birds at four, in time to see the sun rising, a new day, *the* day, packing my bags before taking a reluctant Scruff for a walk just to fill the time. I was nervous and agitated; I needed to move.

Yoda got up as usual, projecting calm, just another day, going through the motions matter-of-factly, a bacon sandwich and a mug of coffee placed before me the only indication that he was acting anything but normal. We both felt tense; conversation was short and to the point.

My robes were spread out on the duvet, immaculately pressed; I was getting back on the bike, back to being the Priest, a moral authority, a shepherd of souls, a conduit for God, feeling relief as I dressed, a sense of calm, like the course of my life was set again, no longer moving, with Liverpool mapped out before me. It gave me courage, reassurance, to know that I was part of something bigger; the loneliness briefly receded.

'You look bloody great,' Yoda declared proudly, as I walked downstairs, 'apart from your head.'

We were silent on the bus, which had arrived on time for once. There was nobody else on board, and very few cars on the road or people on the pavement, the city yet to surface, bleary-eyed from the night before. The only activity was on the football fields, where Sunday league nets were being hung and teams were warming up; children in oversized shorts pinging balls around, some of them superstars of the future, as talent spotters milled around, taking notes, the first steps on the path godhood.

The deities-in-waiting occupied my mind until we arrived to the obligatory welcome of *PAEDO SCUM* re-daubed on the wall, which I'd forgot to plan for. The fear started to rise.

'Don't worry, I'll sort it,' Yoda said, sensing my anxiety. 'Go on, you go and open up. Make sure it's all ready.'

'Thank you,' I replied, fighting to keep calm.

I entered the gates to find the grass chewed up in geometric arcs and circles of muddy tyre tracks. I stared in silence, unsure how to react, suppressing the tamping rage that was rising within me.

'You OK?' Yoda called from the other side of the wall, not tall enough to see the act of desecration.

'Yes,' I replied, uncertain, as I forced myself forward, stepping over the gouges. I could almost hear them laughing, mocking, as they committed their approved vandalism, vengeance justified as they spun, spraying dirt, performing donuts on their quad bikes and scramblers.

I dropped my bags off at the vicarage, closing the door and then falling to my knees, collapsing inside at their wanton destruction. I felt vulnerable, alone, as I looked around the empty room, realising that if I didn't gather myself soon, I may never make it out. My legs were trembling as I stood, sapped of strength, feeling nauseous as I returned outside, pausing, breathing in the cool air until the sickness eased, and then heading for the coolness of the church, leaving the front door open for the first time in months.

I was fussing, nervous, putting on the lights, checking that hymn books, Bibles and hassocks were in place. It felt like my first service all over again, as I knelt at the nave and murmured the same prayer I always do, getting into routine, just another service, before standing at the pulpit, observing, as the huge stained-glass window filtered coloured fragments of light all around the space. It felt otherworldly, glorious, and I felt pride in what we had achieved.

*'Sinful pride,'* Peter corrected.

My voice echoed as I shouted, bouncing back at me from the stone walls, and then, 'Testing, testing,' spoken softly into the microphone, the words reverberating as an amplified whisper. Compared to the village church, it was like a cathedral.

With ten minutes to go, I positioned myself by the open door, to welcome the returning congregation. Only Mo had arrived so far, whom I greeted enthusiastically, hiding my disappointment. *It isn't always going to be this way*, I told myself, but it did nothing to alleviate the feeling of failure as I went out to collect Yoda.

'Is it that time already?' he asked, overflowing with positivity at my approach.

'There's only Mo in there,' I replied, my voice flat.

He'd only managed to scrub one letter. It now read, *PAEDO CUM*.

'Come on, let's have a look,' he clapped his hands together, trying to remain upbeat. 'It was always going to be difficult. We could see if George wants to come,' he suggested, indicating the lad stood, as ever, leaning against his post.

'He'll come in when he's ready,' I said, wondering if he was one of those who'd laughed as the motorbike spun.

My heart leapt as we entered the sanctuary of the vestibule to find two more figures sat on the pews.

'Hello, welcome to St George's!' I called out, far too jolly, conspicuous in my relief, as I walked across to greet them.

'Hello again, Father. Good turn out?'

My heart sank as I recognised the dog shit reporter's face sneering up at me, his long haired colleague gurning along with a long lens camera sitting threateningly on his lap.

'I'm very sorry about, erm, the incident with–' I began.

'You will be,' he cut me off with a smirk. 'Looks like the locals aren't too keen, either. Are you growing potatoes in your ploughed field, by the way?'

'They'll come around.'

'You keep telling yourself that. Come on then, get on with it. Get on with your service.'

Yoda appeared at my side as I walked towards the pulpit, each step heavy, dreading the inevitable.

'Just cancel it,' he whispered. 'They're not congregation – there's nobody here.'

'No,' I replied, climbing up the steps and turning on the microphone.

'But – why?'

'Because then they've won,' I bent down towards him, speaking under my breath. 'This is my church, and I'm holding service.'

I read through my prepared script, eyes on Yoda and Mo, defiant, trying to ignore the heckling and laughter coming from Dog Shit and his mate at the back, and the stationary, naked form of the judge sitting on the front row. The hymns were the worst, feeling exposed as I sang before them, my voice amplified through the space, sounding thin and reedy, as my own living judges howled in derision. It felt like one of those TV talent shows where the contestants without talent are as important as the ones who can actually sing.

*'Congratulations, you are through to the next round. Go make a tit of yourself in front of the nation,'* Peter giggled.

I had to keep signalling to Yoda to stay where he was, his bald head turning purple with anger at the commotion from the reporters, both of whom stood and followed me as I opened the vestibule door at the end of the service.

'Thank you,' I said politely.

'No, thank *you*,' Dog Shit replied sarcastically. 'It couldn't have gone any better.'

I closed the door softly behind them, their laughter audible as they crossed the churchyard.

Mo walked over and patted me on the shoulder. 'Well done, love.'

'Yes, well done,' Yoda agreed. 'It was a very good service. Hopefully, in a few weeks, we'll have more people in here to listen to it. Just ignore dick-heads like those two.'

'I think you've picked the right man for a change,' Mo smiled to Yoda, before turning to me. 'There'll be plenty more days like this, but in the end, you may just be the one to turn it around.'

'Thanks,' I nodded, looking down at the floor, not sharing their optimism.

'Do you want to lock up and head out for something to eat, to celebrate?' Yoda asked.

'Nah, I'm going to clean up the rest of that wall,' I said. 'Can't leave it the way it is.'

'I can help.'

I just wanted to hug him as he looked up at me, his eyes momentarily revealing the child still dwelling inside, filled with optimism, an eternal wish to help, even after all these years.

'Honestly, I'll do it myself. You two go and have a nice meal.'

'We can't leave you here on your own, love,' Mo objected.

'I'd rather be on my own for a bit – think things through. I'm fine, though, don't worry.'

'You're sure?' they replied in unison.

'I'm sure,' I smiled, opening the doors, giving them little choice as they glanced at each other before reluctantly passing through.

After sealing off the world off behind them, I slumped down on the nearest pew, exhausted, waiting for the sadness to hit, but it never came. The church still looked beautiful as I turned off the lights and sat quietly in its silence, studying the shafts of light as they cut diagonal swathes through the space, looking heavier than the air, like they could be touched – picked up, bent or smashed into splinters. My hand became illuminated as it moved in and out of the beams, casting an out-of-scale shadow on the floor whilst sending dust motes billowing in tiny swirling currents.

*These are different*, I thought, *made of warmth and light*, as I reached for my hip flask and swallowed its contents, waiting for the numbing warmth.

The brush sent a fine white spray off its bristles, soaking into my robes as I started scouring the remaining letters. I wasn't sure why, but I was still positive, upbeat; perhaps just relieved at getting the first service out of the way, as I stood still, watching the white rivulets run their course through miniature rapids and eddies into the nearest cast-iron grid, and then admiring the fruits of my labour.

*They won't need to bother painting soon*, I thought. *The clean bricks will spell out the message loud and clear.*

Returning to the vestry, I placed the cleaning products in the cupboard until tomorrow, when no doubt I'd be getting them back out to do it all again; my personal Groundhog Day. Then, taking my time, I walked slowly back through the church, feeling sheltered, pensive; at peace here as I admired a column, following its path upwards to where it splayed across the roof in arches, joining others like it, creating a delicate structure, a fragile skeleton. It was beautiful; it was my church, and I felt blessed to have it, despite the naked judge now wandering between the pews.

I went out and closed the front door behind me, turning the key and placing my forehead against the red-painted wood, hearing the heavy clunk as the latch fell into place. I began a silent prayer.

*Thank you, God, for giving me–*

A force hit me from the side, sending me staggering, before pulling me backwards and plunging me into darkness; something was dragged over my head and tightened over my face, deforming my features. Powerful hands grasped me, pinning my arms to my body as I let out a squeal and twisted, pushing us both off balance.

'Just fucking behave, and you'll be alright,' a gruff voice hissed into my ear as I twisted again, lurching from side to side, trying to work free, my breath hot inside the hood, the thin second-hand air stifling, as my lungs were squeezed empty.

I was being smothered, suffocated, restrained by a giant, my jerking movements becoming more frantic as I lashed out with my legs, thrashing, flexing my body, unable to break the grip. I managed to yank a hand loose and immediately threw a punch, hitting fresh air, flailing, grabbing, clawing; failing to make contact with anything.

'Fucking hell, get hold of him will you,' another voice urged from in front, as the arms behind relaxed momentarily, trying to reset their grip whilst I carried on struggling.

Peter was hurtling headlong towards the surface. I let him through, becoming detached as he took over, feeling myself controlled by another, but not another; me, but not me. Planting my heels into the ground, I pushed back until we hit the church wall, the air bursting out of his lungs with an *'Oof!'* as I threw my head backwards, making contact once, twice and then again and again, getting both hands free and yanking off the hood, taking in a huge gulp of air and looking around frantically.

'What are you doing?' I cried, seeing a shaven-headed man standing before me, moving backwards and forwards, keeping out of range, away from my fists.

Arms were scrambling around me again, trying to restrain me, but even as I threw an elbow back, crunching it against his nose, my eyes remained fixed on the man in front. I started giggling as I fired elbow after elbow, landing every time, realising that he couldn't protect himself because his arms were fumbling around me.

He shoved me forward, and I just about kept my balance as I stumbled across the grass, turning in time to see the other one bearing down on me. I landed a punch square on his mouth, making him wince before coming at me again, fists raised.

'We can't hurt him,' a voice from behind him warned.

He paused, distracted, and I lunged, my fist crashing into his nose this time, staggering him; momentum carrying me forward as I jumped, headbutting him, hearing a sickening crunch as his nose splintered. I stopped, hoping gravity would do the rest, but he retained his balance, his nose flat and the swelling spreading across his face, as he wiped away the blood and started marching forward again.

I stepped to the side, shuffling backwards as they both advanced, no time for thought as I put my faith in Peter. They were bloodied and angry, but then one put his hand on the other's shoulder, slowing him down.

'Easy, buddy,' he cooed, 'easy buddy. We can't hurt him, don't forget.'

I didn't understand, my bravado turning to fear as I turned and ran towards the wall, vaulting up, getting my arms and one foot on top, ready to jump over.

'Macca!' one of them shouted. 'Wait, Macca, erm, Fr Macca.'

I stopped, about to drop onto the pavement, surprised to find that they hadn't chased me. They looked identical: shaven heads, black jackets and bloody faces, both breathing heavily, panting.

'What did you say?' I asked, a cold, tingling sensation running up my spine, as a goose walked over my grave.

'Alright, Macca,' he repeated, quieter, calmer this time, as he regained his breath.

*'Don't you say that,'* Peter hissed.

I remained frozen on top of the wall, a feeling of nausea rising in my stomach, unsure which way to go as I glanced at the pavement on the other side; it was clear, empty. I'd be gone by the time they got out of the gate.

'Stay where you are,' I warned, dropping back into the church yard, my curiosity overcoming any instinct of self-preservation, despite my mind screaming run. They both nodded in agreement; they were lifters, strong and immobile.

'Who are you?' I demanded.

They exchanged glances, but neither spoke.

'Are you trying to kidnap me or something? Mug me? And why didn't you just hit me? You had me,' I didn't understand; it didn't make sense. Whatever they were trying to do, they had completely fucked it up.

One of them took a step towards me.

'Don't fucking move,' I shouted, checking over my shoulder, judging the distance to the wall as I took my phone out of my pocket. 'I'm calling the police.'

The other one raised his hands. 'No, there's no need for that.'

'Well, speak, then.'

'It's me – Migsy,' the one on the left said, after a long pause.

The word hit me as hard as any blow, winding me, taking my breath away. It had been over twenty years since I'd last seen him, or even heard the name, and the mere sound of it was enough to plunge me back into the life I'd been running away from ever since. I could picture him as a child, dark hair and freckles, part of the gang; the laughter, the innocence, the pain, the fear, the bravado and the silent tears after lights out. Our paths had come together, taking us through the same experiences; he understood.

Looking closer, although he was nothing like the skinny boy of my memories, the eyes were the same; such beautiful, gentle blue eyes, set in this almost deformed human gorilla shape, all steroids, sweat and testosterone. It was him.

'What are you doing attacking me?' I asked, more upset than angry now. It was like being assaulted by a family member. 'We never had any bother. We were mates.'

He looked down at his shuffling feet, his right foot kicking the long grass. 'We were sent to pick you up,' he said, speaking low, as if making an embarrassing confession. 'Somebody needs to see you.'

'Who's "somebody?"'

'An old friend,' he said guardedly, giving nothing away.

We stood still, just looking at each other, as memories came cascading through. I could see us fighting together, feral boys in the dorm, defending our territory side by side from the older boys, Unit 5, not giving an inch. You couldn't, or they'd take you. There was laughter afterwards, bloody noses and scraped knuckles; sewing kits and stitches.

'You haven't changed a bit, have you?' he said. 'Still an angry bastard. I thought you were a man of the cloth – a man of peace now?'

'Don't turn this on me,' I replied scornfully. 'I thought you were trying to kill me. What was I supposed to do?'

'A leopard can't change its spots, I suppose. I saw the kids had already had a go,' he taunted, pointing to my head.

My hat had come off in the hood, and a couple of stitches must have been pulled out, as I felt a smudge of blood behind my ear.

'Why couldn't you just knock on the door, like any normal person?'

'It's urgent. We can't let you know where you're going, or who you're going to see.'

'You still could've knocked on my door and asked me.'

They looked at each other again, confused, before the other shrugged his shoulders and said, 'We've got to make sure you're there. We're not asking – we've got to bring you. You can't see where you're being taken, and we can't tell you who you're going to see, so this seemed the quickest way of getting it done.'

'Well, what now?' I asked.

'You've got to come with us, there's no choice.'

'You're in no position to dictate anything. I can be over that wall and gone like that,' I clicked my fingers, tempted to add a *poof!* 'So, where to?'

'We can't tell you, but it's urgent. We've got to go.'

'No chance,' I said bluntly, taking another look at the wall behind me.

'Macca, come on, it's me,' Migsy pleaded, pointing towards his chest with both hands, pious, as if he hadn't just tried to abduct me.

'What do you expect?' I asked, incredulous. 'I haven't seen you in years, and then here you are trying to put a bag over my head.'

'Alright, sorry about that, la,' he said, raising his palms up. 'We got it wrong. Can I come closer?'

'Just you,' I nodded. 'I swear, Migsy, if you try anything–'

'I won't,' he mumbled. 'I know what you'll do.'

He walked slowly towards me, stopping, before holding out his hand. Everything was tense, my body rigid, my mind completely empty, fists clenched down by my side. I hesitated before slowly placing my hand in his, ready to pull back. He smiled and drew me into a hug, the grip nice and gentle this time.

'How are you, Macca, lad?' he said warmly. 'It's great to see you.'

'You, too,' I smiled back, my body relaxing as he released me. 'All the years we've known each other, we've never had a bad word, and now I've ended up cracking you around the head. Why didn't you just come and say hello? And where has all your hair gone?'

He let out a snort. 'My brain's got too big – pushed it out.'

'Why didn't you just knock?'

'Like I said, we, erm, misjudged it a bit. It's the world we live in – just becomes habit. Think I got off lightly,' he said, turning towards his partner. 'This is Smiler.'

Smiler wasn't smiling as he ambled over and shook my hand. I didn't know if I should apologise.

'You OK?' I asked.

'Yeah, no problem,' Smiler said, pointing at his nose. 'Been bust a few times.' It was turning purple, the beginnings of black eyes forming on either side. 'Bit one-sided, though – we weren't allowed to hurt you,' he looked accusingly at Migsy.

'Orders from above,' Migsy shrugged.

'I thought I was getting mugged or something,' I repeated, feeling the need to explain myself.

He just nodded, still not smiling.

'Will you come with us, then?' Migsy asked.

'Where?'

'I've already said, we can't say.'

'Oh, just tell me,' I groaned, shaking my head, exasperated.

Again, they exchanged uncertain glances before Migsy let out a sigh.

'Jacko wants to see you,' he said.

In a moment, that world and those times were resurrected, old feelings finding new life, new energy, triggered by one simple name. I felt like I was buckling under the pressure as my mind struggled to cope with the onslaught of suppressed memories, a huge black wave engulfing everything, riotous children sweeping through. I was hearing voices, remembering faces, good and bad, mostly bad.

*Jacko*, I thought, staring, frozen in disbelief. *Yoda was wrong, they are still here.*

'Will you come?' Migsy asked again. 'It's urgent. He's in a bad way.'

I was so deep in reverie, they could have just picked me up there and then, but instead I followed them through the long grass, still strewn with thrown stones, towards the gate, and then climbed into the back seat of a Range Rover, its blacked out windows reinforcing a menacing appearance.

'You'll, erm, have to put the hood on when we're getting close,' Migsy said, passing me the black sack.

'No chance,' I folded my arms in front of my chest.

'You can't know where we're going. Do you know how many people are after Jacko right now?'

'A lot, I'd imagine.'

I'd seen bits about him in the news over the years, and Dad had heard a few snippets in prison, where his influence was still felt.

'It's for your own good. If the bizzies pull you in, you won't have to tell any lies – you won't know.'

'Alright,' I sighed, still feeling a bit numb, but accepting that there was logic in there somewhere.

No one spoke as we headed towards the centre, the city passing by in a blur, and I suddenly recalled the last time I was in a Range Rover, back in the village, being propositioned by Paul's wife.

*The vehicle of choice for the morally unsure*, I thought.

'Do you want to put the hood on now, Macca, please, lid?' Migsy asked, all politeness.

I obliged, lying down on the backseat, even though nobody outside could see through the tinted windows. Not that it made any difference either way; I'd already put my life in their hands.

Silence resumed, and I began trying to trace the remainder of the route in my mind, visualising the traffic lights and bends in the road; the rise and descent over a flyover before slowing down and turning left, down a narrow road. I pretty much knew where we were, one of the narrow service roads off Dale Street, as the wheels crunched over broken glass and cartons, probably passing wheelie bins and service entrances to old brick Victorian warehouses, moss and ferns growing out of the permanently damp walls, as the sun failed to gain access between the tall, claustrophobic elevations.

We came to a stop and the door opened, the engine idling, my senses more alert as my vision was blocked. I could smell piss, a residue from the night before, and hear pigeons cooing, and something was dripping close by. A bus passed in the distance, people going about their everyday lives, unaware of what was happening just thirty metres away, in the shadows.

A large hand reached in and grasped my forearm.

'Big step, la,' Migsy instructed, as I shuffled across the seat, feeling for the pavement with my foot, my stomach curving out, searching.

It was a steep drop; they could have slipped a blade in there at any moment if they'd wished, gutted me, but eventually I hit terra firma and was directed across the pavement.

'Step.'

I obeyed their single-word commands, becoming automated as I lifted my foot and stepped over the threshold. The car pulled away as the door closed behind me, its bolts sliding into place, blocking any outside noise.

'Can I take it off yet?' I asked.

'In a minute,' Migsy answered, turning me. 'Stairs.'

He guided me forward until my foot touched a riser; I lifted one and then the other, taking equal steps until I overshot at the top, nearly falling over.

'Sorry,' he said, catching me as we stopped, squeezed together in a small space, where a door creaked open before us.

This next room felt bigger, the air cooler, and then, suddenly, hands were touching me, rubbing me down as I flinched, pulling back, pushing them away. I could hear others below the gentle buzzing of a fluorescent light, their breathing and tiny, nervous movements, all watching me, blind before them. It could have been one person; it could have been a thousand.

'It's alright, he's alright,' Migsy called off the hands, as I heard the beeping of a metal detector going off, prompting fingers to enter to my pockets.

'I'll do it,' I said, jerking back, almost pleading, before Peter added, 'Get this fucking hood off me.'

'In a minute,' Migsy whispered, as I stopped struggling and felt my pockets being emptied, followed by my belt being pulled from its loops.

A tugging at my shirt told me that the buttons were being unfastened, and I recoiled as a hand came inside, feeling around, front then back, my mind screaming run, Peter shouting fight, as I remained motionless, caught in the equilibrium between the two.

'OK,' a woman's voice announced, saving me from a decision by removing her hand and refastening my shirt. 'You're no fucking Priest,' she murmured.

Migsy gripped my arm again, guiding me forward as another door opened, bolts shooting back before I was ushered through, and finally, the hood was pulled from my head, bright lights causing me to shield my eyes, squinting, blinking, until I slowly lowered my arm and attempted to comprehend the sight before me.

It was like a film set, a hospital bed and a stack of beeping machines, with red and green lines travelling horizontally across their screens, bumping regularly, all within a circle of bright light. Drips were up on stands, whilst plastic tubes filled with clear liquid travelled up and down, in and out of Jacko.

*Jacko.*

I ran to him, forgetting everything. He was dozing, an oxygen mask turning each breath into sound; his torso, bandaged up neat and clean, rising and falling with each regular inhale-exhale, inhale-exhale. He was massive, his arms the size of my thighs, his thick neck indistinguishable from his shoulders, an extension of his back. He wasn't bald, but he had a number one all over; that hadn't changed.

A doctor approached.

'What happened?' I asked.

'Three shots to the abdomen,' he answered, shaking his head gently as my eyes welled up, an automatic reaction after years of practise.

'There must be something you can do?' I said.

'He's barely hanging on. All we can do now is make his final moments as comfortable as possible.'

He looked perfectly fine, as though he could sit up at any moment if he wanted to.

'Is he – can he?'

'He's only mildly sedated,' the doctor said, walking around the bed, injecting something into one of the clear tubes. 'He's been refusing heavier pain relief – says he wants to see you first. Take a seat please,' he beckoned to an empty chair, next to the bed.

The tempo of the beeping started to increase, as Jacko's eyelids fluttered before remaining open in narrow slits, his pupils disappearing then reappearing, staying, moving side to side before his eyes fully opened. He tried to lift his head, but the doctor put a firm hand on his chest.

'Easy now,' the doctor said softly, 'give it a minute.'

Jacko's roaming eyes found me, stopping and focussing, bringing a smile to his lips. 'Macca,' was all he could manage, as his hand came across and I took it in mine.

'Jacko,' I returned the smile.

'Give him a minute,' the doctor said.

I nodded; we just held hands.

'I didn't know if we'd get you here in time,' Jacko said, in between large gulps of air. 'I had to see you.'

'What happened?' I asked. 'Why aren't you in hospital?'

'Got jumped. Fair enough, all part of the game.'

'Who by?'

'Thought it was the Cavs at first, but not so sure now. Things are changing, lots of freelancing going on – guns for hire, know what I mean?'

I didn't, no.

'Anyway, we'll find them. The dogs have got the scent. I might not be here to find out for myself, though.'

'Go to a hospital,' I urged, 'get this sorted out properly.'

'Only one place I'm going, I'm afraid,' he allowed himself a smirk. 'If I survived, I'd be banged up for the rest of my life – not worth living.'

'But if there's a chance–'

'Nah, that's not a life. This is it. I've lasted longer than most in this game.'

'That's not you, giving up. You never give up – *we* never gave up. Where's your fight?' I pressed, my voice cracking, unsure what I was supposed to be feeling: disappointment? Anger? Disgust?

'I'm not giving up, I just don't have too many options available. I'm making a grown-up decision for once in my life. Don't worry, I'm OK with it,' he squeezed my hand.

'Better to die a hero?'

'Something like that,' he gave a little nod, smiling again. 'You know me, I've got to win. Anyway, look at you, a man of the Church,' he teased, switching focus.

I nodded in reply, anger stopping me from talking.

'I didn't know where you'd gone,' he said. 'We all shot off in different directions once they opened up the can of worms.'

'I didn't want to see anyone,' I admitted. 'Nothing personal.'

'No, nothing personal. We were all trying to escape. They just dropped us on the streets, damaged, left to find our own way. We scattered – we were fucked.'

'My dad sent a priest to find me. He blew the whole thing up, hence the Church. It saved me.'

'Whereas I went down the more predictable path – pretty much a continuation of what we'd already gone through. It was made for me, got in at the bottom and then took over at the top. I'm sure you know most of the story.'

I did; he was a source of pride for many in the city, an urban legend, rising from nothing to dine at the top table with the rich and infamous of organised crime, his networks spreading around the world: South American cartels, Russian Mafia, Eastern Europeans, Yardies, Triads, Turks, Afghans; buying, selling, supplying, trafficking; drugs, guns and everything in between. Nothing happened in Liverpool without his approval.

There were always rivals and opportunists that came and went, some old, some young; the next big thing. That was the front line, the coalface, where hands got dirty, gun battles were fought and people died: contracts, hitmen, kidnapping, torture; a war running parallel to everyday life, very rarely breaking the surface beyond newspaper headlines; the next chapters in a never-ending fairy tale.

Speaking of which.

'I suppose you knew I was back because of the papers?' I asked.

'There was that,' he said, 'but we knew you were here before you made the front page.'

'How?'

'Migsy went to the United-Liverpool game, said he saw you at the train station dressed up like a vicar. He couldn't believe it – thought he'd had a bang on the head or something. Said you sort of floated through the crowd, and that he followed you into town. You kipped over in the Hanover – nothing but the best, eh?'

I nodded, remembering the shout; remembering the stragglers at the station. 'Why didn't you come see me then?'

'I didn't need you then,' he smiled, 'I hadn't been shot. And, like you say, we were all running away from one another. I was just glad to hear you were still around. You've always been there, on the edge of my life, out of sight, but there. It was weird, though, you being in touching distance.'

'I've seen your man watching by the Church,' I put two and two together, 'tall fella?'

He tried to sit up, wincing in pain before easing back down again, shaking his head. 'Not one of mine. Like I said, we haven't been watching – we knew where you were. Loads more on our plate.'

'You're sure?'

'Very sure, but I can get somebody to look into it, if you want?'

'Nah, it's OK, probably nothing. Just a local.'

'Well, if anything does come of it, I'll be dead by then anyway,' he laughed.

We sat in silence for a while, listening to the machines beep.

'I nearly cried when I saw your picture on the front cover,' he began, before breaking into a fit of coughing, a racking cough that was clearly hurting, sending shock waves through his body. I looked around frantically for the doctor, who came over with a drink of water, reaching for the mask, but Jacko pushed his hand away.

'I'm OK,' he insisted, taking deep breaths as the coughing subsided. His eyes were losing focus, taking him somewhere else momentarily. 'Not because you'd been attacked or anything like that,' he continued, returning to the room. 'It was just that you didn't look any different – it could have been taken years ago, back in the Pit. Hair wild, blood everywhere and eyes manic. Bets, screaming, the bang of the gate, the bolt – cleaning up with the sand afterwards.'

A tear ran down my nose.

'Some of them didn't come out of there,' he said. 'You remember that, don't you?'

'Yes,' I mumbled through trembling lips.

'It wasn't our fault – it was them or us. It's taken me my whole life for me to be able to say that,' his hand squeezed mine again, tears running from his eyes. 'We were only children.'

I was trying to hold myself together, to stop my body from shaking, convulsing, as my own eyes started streaming. I was a child again.

'You saved me,' he said. 'I remember you jumping in. He had me, but you… he–'

'S-stop,' I stammered.

'They put both of your hands on a table and broke them with a hammer for that,' he carried on, 'but they didn't kill you, because you were entertaining.'

I was sobbing openly now, reliving repressed memories and emotions; the hammer hovering before coming down, as Jacko's hand reached across, coming around my neck.

'The bastards loved it,' he hissed, 'as long as there was blood. It was just sport – we were disposable, no more than fighting dogs, easily replaced by a conveyor belt of new victims. For them, it was just a fun way of killing us – getting rid of evidence. We were never supposed to survive.' He pulled me towards him, my forehead resting on his. 'What chance did we have? How could we ever be normal after going through that?'

'We couldn't,' my tears mixed with his, 'we can't.'

'I should have died there that day – everything since has been a bonus. That's why I'm not worried now.'

I sat back, trying to regain my composure, taking deep breaths, but a righteous anger was beginning to consume me.

'How did you deal with it?' he asked.

'Locked it away,' I said, 'called it a different life. Found God and stayed there.'

'Some couldn't find a way – it was all too much. I know of four that just… couldn't go on,' he paused. 'There could be loads more, though. Those four are just the names I recognised.'

'God bless them,' I muttered.

'So, what brought you back here?'

'I can't carry on running. I'm damaged, and I need to believe that I can be fixed. Like you said, it wasn't our fault.'

'Do you believe that?'

'I do,' I answered sincerely. 'I really do.'

'Do you remember the…' he started, but couldn't bring himself to say. 'Do you remember the–'

I cut him off with a nod, my eyes screaming for him to stop, which, to his credit, he did. He understood.

'It wasn't our fault,' I repeated.

'I want to do confession before I die.'

'You don't need me to do that,' I said quietly, shaking my head, 'that's for Catholics. You just confess in a private prayer with our lot, talk straight to God – miss out the middleman.'

'I don't know what I am, Catholic, Protestant, cat or dog – might be a Muslim for all I know. Does it matter? It's all the same God, isn't it? I just want you to hear my confession, that's all. God can listen in as well if he wants to.' He smiled just as another round of coughing attacked his body, but he raised his hand when the doctor came running with a syringe, stopping him in his tracks. 'I've got more to say before you start putting that stuff in.'

He spoke for two hours, interspersed with fits of coughing that became steadily worse, leaving him smarting from the intensifying pain. The doctor's attempts at intervention became more frequent until, in the end, Jacko could hardly talk, his eyes glazing over, facing inward, seeking out the source of his agony, a fight he couldn't win with his fists.

His story was brutal, a clear progression from the children's home where he had been created, shaped by an institution that had realigned his moral compass, reset the rules; reset Paul Jackman. He'd gone in as a frightened young boy, before being pushed out into a world in which he didn't belong, with no place in society for Version 2.0. He should have been given love, care, so damaged was his mental health, but nobody was there for him; nobody wanted to help.

The underbelly of the city was where he found a home, down its back alleys and dark places, where he could vent his fury, an outlet for blind hatred, achieving notoriety through the brutality of his actions. He knew the potency of a reputation, how daring deeds would be told and retold in the pubs and clubs, on playgrounds and over office desks during lunch breaks; Chinese whispers snowballing exponentially, out of control, invading every home, every ear, until the tale became so embellished, it became unrecognisable.

He was drug dealing, racketeering, running bouncers and rolling over prostitutes and their clients alike; taking any opportunity to mete out violence, sometime going to extreme lengths, reinforcing his status, expanding the brand and the myth. He didn't care if he lived or died in the early years; he would do anything, a psychopath running amok as various groups fought for control over the black economy. His employers gave him free rein; he was good for business, and in climbing the ranks quickly, he moved past the day-to-day brutality; off the streets and behind a desk, as he put it. He had a reputation and respect; he ruled by fear, his lieutenants and foot soldiers loyal and eager to please, though he was not above stepping back out occasionally, doing his own dirty work, as brutal as ever, reminding people what he was all about.

Over the years, he came to know all the important faces, learning about business and managing money, absorbing everything, sponge-like, until one night he killed four male members of the Hooton family, a coup, cutting the head off the snake and taking over.

'They were horrible, loathsome bastards,' he wheezed. 'I knew I was going to kill them as soon as I met them. It wasn't the showing off – the sports cars and the bling all over the place. It was the way they stepped over boundaries. They thought nothing of taking someone out over trivial things, like a girl or a glance in the wrong direction. I'm talking about normal people, not involved, getting their dogs to do it for them, in front of them, for entertainment.'

The killings went on for two nights, determining where loyalties lay as the hierarchy was re-established, shaking out the deadwood.

'I didn't sleep,' he recalled. 'Migsy was with me – we were popping pills and then paying visits. The bizzies didn't know what was going on. It made no sense to them – they were chasing shadows.'

Other families jostled for power, hoping to fill in the vacuum left by 'the Purge' as it became known, entering into local folklore.

'We didn't stop there – we were never going to stop there. We felt indestructible, and the rest were scared. We were running around town, drugged up to the eyeballs with fully-loaded shooters, killing anyone that got in the way. The status quo had been disrupted – they'd got lazy, fat, bloated. We turned most of them over in a few days, got to know who they did business with, who their contacts were. I suppose they'd call it a hostile takeover in business circles. Fair do's, though, some of them fought like bastards, some still are.'

The 'Bouncer Wars' erupted overnight, as Jacko set about seizing control of the whole city. It lasted more than a year, tit-for-tat killings, plenty of guns available from contacts in Ulster, a surplus after the Good Friday Agreement. Eventually, most of the territory was won, and not all through killing; sometimes negotiations took place, forming partnerships, and there was no shortage of coercion and blackmail; buying councillors, police officers and customs officials along the way, until the city was his. He then did something remarkable: he gave it all away, turned it into a cooperative; everybody an owner, a shareholder, from the dealer on the street to the bloke in the docks, to the companies cleaning the money, all the way up to Jacko at the top.

'I didn't want to be looking over my shoulder all the time,' he explained, 'and we were making more money than I knew what to do with. I'm not really arsed about material stuff, and it only made me a bigger target, worth taking a massive risk on, so I got rid of it, spread the wealth and bought people's loyalty, a bit like John Lewis. Everybody was making money – good money, and it was in everybody's best interest that the business remained stable. No more power struggles, it was now about self-policing – poor performers were replaced, infiltrators were killed and grasses were silenced, and others around the world were taking note. Big guns started to approach the organisation, knowing that we were a stable investment. That's when the real money started rolling in.'

'You did OK, I take it?'

'The organised crime industry is valued at around twenty-five billion a year in this country alone, and we were a unique proposition – we controlled a major port. We were the gateway to Europe, and the rest of the world was banging the door down to get access, so we provided it.'

'You make it sound like a legitimate operation.'

'A lot of it is,' he chuckled. 'The idea was simple, based on how bouncers control the flow of goods into a club, a microcosm of what we would do on a global scale. We became a service industry, providing whatever they needed to move their product. This covers anything and everything, mainly drugs, but also tobacco, alcohol, arms, fraud, counterfeiting and money laundering, all the way down to pirated DVDs, music, software, games, perfumes, cosmetics, clothes – even Viagra. The only thing we don't do is people trafficking. We'll move people around, but we've no involvement in the smuggling for sex industry.'

'Corporate Social Responsibility,' I gave a wry smile. 'You'll be telling me you went on sustainability courses next.'

'I haven't had much involvement for a few years now. I'm just on the committee – we meet a few times a year to discuss overall business strategy. There are people a lot hungrier than me doing most of the legwork these days.'

'But it's you, Jacko, public enemy number one.'

'That's because they don't understand the structure of the organisation. I'm just a logo, like Colonel Saunders or Ronald McDonald, and when I'm gone, it'll carry on the same. We don't even have a name – we don't exist. We're a network, impossible to kill off, provided everyone is doing well out of it. We have lots of legit companies under out auspices. I mean, we're building top-end apartment blocks next door to MI5 in London, for fuck's sake.'

'You're retired, then – a man of leisure?'

'Nah, not really. I've just been focussing on more personal interests lately.' There was a long pause as he struggled to arrange the words in his mind. 'I've managed to track down a few of the names involved in what happened. Remember Blakey, who ran the home, basically set everything up and let them in?'

I nodded, feeling sick at the thought of him.

'I killed him. He was seventy, a pensioner, but I killed him.'

'Go on,' my hand went up to my mouth.

'Pigsy, the night guard, who used to bring his lad in to watch?'

I nodded again.

'I fought his son in front of him, and then did him afterwards – not worth wasting bullets on. Then, there was the doctor who used to patch us up, just as long as he could be involved. The two drivers that used to take us backwards and forwards, delivering the meat. That bloke who ran the catering. The ones that brought us alcohol and drugs to pump us up.'

The initial shock gave way to exhilaration. I knew I should have been praying for their forgiveness and salvation, *Forgive and you shall be forgiven*, but I couldn't. Deep down, my heart was still full of hate, not strong enough to forgive.

'There were the club members, the paying clientele. You might have seen reports of a couple of seemingly motiveless murders in Chelsea – *"They were such nice people, we can't understand why somebody would do this to them"* – as if living in Chelsea makes a person nice,' he scoffed. 'There was the Judge in Oxford, the retired minister in Spain, the granddad on his allotment in Nottingham–'

'All you?'

'All me.'

'You've been busy,' I observed, smiling, wondering if it was right to take pleasure from murder. I was thrilled.

'There are more that I haven't got to yet – more difficult to reach. The politicians, the general, the police commander – you know who they are, and then there were those who were just faces. I couldn't put names to them, but they must have known what was happening – that I was coming.'

A coughing fit tore through him; his teeth clamped together, distorting his features in a pained grimace. I handed him the oxygen mask, and he took deep, greedy breaths, moaning as he inhaled, and still the coughs came, forcing him to lie back and close his eyes.

I looked over at the doctor, back at the bedside, syringe in hand, as panic rose inside me. *Not yet*, I thought pleadingly.

At last, his breathing steadied enough for him to open his eyes and take off the mask.

'I know that in society's eyes, I've done wrong,' he wheezed, 'but my only regret is that I won't get to finish the job I started – that they started.'

'Nobody else was going to do it. Some have tried pursuing them through the courts, but they're fobbed off for as long as it takes for the bastards to die of old age. Justice only travels from the top down – doesn't go the other way.'

'Ah, you don't have to make excuses for me. You went towards God, whereas I've got more in common with the other fella. Hate and revenge drove everything – I'm black inside, I know that. The things I've done in my life, and my only regret is not killing more people. Pretty much tells you what a horrible bastard I am, but I don't think I was always this way. If there's anything after this, I'll be going to see him downstairs. Might be better off there anyway, amongst my own kind.'

'Everyone's got good and bad in them, Jacko. It's not for others to pass judgement on you now. They'll be down there themselves for what they did.'

His hand came across, and I clasped it in mine. It still felt strong, tightening as another wave of pain went surging through him.

'Thank you,' he whispered. 'You're proof that something good could come out of what happened.'

'It was pure luck. We're no different, you and I. I was picked up, patched up and guided in a particular direction. I could have easily been you, doing what you've done.'

'What a team that would have been.'

'Come to the hospital with me,' I pleaded quietly, just about managing to say the words. It was coming to an end, I knew it.

He smiled back at me, before signalling across to the doctor, who had the needle waiting on a tray.

'I won't leave you now,' I continued. 'We'll get through it together, like we always did.'

'I'm ready,' he said, lying back, pain etched on his face.

I kept going, but he was just looking at me blankly, his features changing as another wave of pain crested and then crashed down inside him. He gave a small nod as the doctor slid the needle into his catheter.

'See you on the other side,' he winked, as the plunger was pressed and the syringe emptied into his veins, his grip remaining tight for a few minutes before gradually slacking off as he slipped deeper into his unconscious.

*At least he's not in pain now*, I kept saying to myself; some sort of comfort blanket to wrap around me; some sort of positive sentiment that seems to work for everybody else.

*'Fuck that'*, Peter was screaming, *'fuck that,'* to the steady rhythm of the machine, the only sign that he was still alive.

'Is that it?' I asked the doctor.

'He may come around again, he may not,' was the unhelpful answer. 'It could be hours, or it could be a day or two – but no more than that.'

'Could a hospital bring him back?'

'Probably not, no.'

'But maybe? He'd have a better chance, surely?'

'Yeah, maybe.'

'Then let's get him to a hospital.'

'It's not what he wants.'

'Fuck what he wants, he's going to die,' I shouted. 'Get him to the hospital – I'll take any comeback for it.'

'We can't,' the doctor said softly. 'It's not what he wants.'

'I'll fucking take him myself, then,' I roared, as the door flew open and Migsy appeared, grabbing hold of me, this time more gently than before.

'It's what he wanted, Macca,' he said quietly. 'We can't do anything else – It's what he wanted.'

I looked at him, and it was obvious that he was struggling to hold it together. His features were tense; he looked vulnerable.

*They're right*, I realised, my anger abating. *Who am I to turn up after all these years and say what's what?*

I slumped back down into the chair, submitting, watching his chest rise and fall, his pulse still beeping away.

*'You're giving up on him,'* Peter hissed, his voice full of loathing. *'You're letting him die.'*

I ignored him, entering into my own internal dialogue, trying to rationalise Jacko's capitulation.

*How could he choose death when there's the possibility of life? Because he's not afraid. Whether he's going up, down or forward, into an eternal nothing, he's not afraid. Most people are terrified of death, and fight to hang on to life to the last, their belief in God irrelevant as doubt comes kicking and screaming, yet here he is, ready to push open the door and go face to face with whatever's behind it. He's not afraid.*

For the first time since I'd arrived, I looked properly at my surroundings. Behind the glare of the medical lights, the room was actually a recording studio, clinical and soundproof. I sat staring into space, the beeping almost hypnotic, Dylan Thomas resonating in my head.

*'Do not go gentle into that good night. Rage, rage against the dying of the light.'*

I was awoken by a shake on the shoulder; the machines still beeping, Jacko still breathing, as Migsy looked down at me.

'Time to get you home, mate,' he said. 'You, erm, need to say your goodbyes.'

'I'll stay.'

'There are others who'll want to see him. You can't be here.'

'Just give me a couple of minutes,' I said, exhausted, my mind numb.

With a nod, he left us.

I held Jacko's hand and acted out emotion, mimicking what I'd seen from others many times before, as tears of grief silently streamed down my nose, dripping onto the carpet. I prayed that he'd be in God's hands soon, waiting at the gates whilst they carried out their checks and balances, not an easy decision; the contradictions, the cause and effect.

*From one Peter to another, please look after him*, I made a silent request. *What chance did he have?*

I stood as Migsy returned, holding the door open whilst I took one last look, seeing Jacko as a child, alive, running and laughing, his innocent optimism still there, despite the things they were doing to us; we didn't understand. Life failed him, and this is what they created, the righteous, a product of an extreme environment, a Frankenstein's Monster.

*Would they ever ask how he ended up this way?* I thought, as I bent over and kissed him on the forehead, before turning and walking out of the room. Migsy closed the door behind me, the beeps and Jacko's breathing becoming inaudible, left to bounce around the sealed echo chamber, confined to a closed environment.

*On his terms.*

I understood.

We were silent in the car, Migsy driving, 'I'll let you know,' the only words spoken as he dropped me off outside my new home, if it could have been called as much.

It was dark, around three in the morning, when I reach the front door and struggled to get the key in, looking around nervously after the day's events, and then finding my bags sitting in the middle of the floor where I'd left them. The naked bulb was too bright, so I switched it off, returning the room to darkness, feeling the loneliness creeping in, trying not to think as the black waters started rising, the tide just coming in.

*'It'll be a long time before it goes out again,'* Peter cautioned, *'should have stayed in Yoda's'.*

I lugged my bags up to the bedroom, finding the bed unmade, without sheets, but still I undressed, lying naked on the lightly-stained mattress, staring up at the ceiling. I'd had to get out of the clerical robes; they felt wrong, out of place in this place. I didn't want them tainted by history, my history, polluted by the old me.

The room was empty, walls bare; just a clean white box, no quirks, no details, like being inside a perfect white cube of sensory deprivation. I checked my emails, looking for distraction, an island of light illuminating the space before the room returned to darkness, nothing in the inbox, leaving no option but to lie down and drift, feeling awake whilst vivid dreams suggested otherwise.

It was Jacko.

Memories returned in glorious technicolour, complete with soundtrack in Dolby Stereo, breaking through their bonds of repression. I could see all the old faces again through an alcohol- and drug-fuelled haze, their voices becoming slurred, their laughs echoing, intermingling, indiscernible from the crowd as I became detached, withdrawing from myself. I curled up and started crying, or was it a memory of crying? I couldn't tell. My body was trembling, remembering pain, causing me to jerk out of bed, waking up in fright as I looked around the room in a panic, looking for something, someone, but finding no one. I took deep, deliberate breaths until I settled down and drifted off again, only for it to keep happening over and over, a never-ending hellish cycle.

A large bang woke me up, a thud, a tremor, the house shaking as I found myself face down on the floor. I sat bolt upright, looking towards the bedroom door, disorientated, staring ahead, listening intently for any sign of movement, any sign of a presence, but there was nothing, just silence. I looked out of the window, finding the streets empty, sepia under the glow of the streetlights.

*Just on edge*, I reassured myself, as I climbed back on the bed, lying awake, waiting for the dawn. *It's nothing.*

A knock on the front door drew me back to consciousness; I felt like I'd only just fallen asleep, my eyes red raw as I checked my watch; seven-thirty.

*Must be Yoda*, I thought, lying back and revisiting the previous day, Jacko, until more knocking blocked that avenue, spurring me into action as I unzipped one of my bags and pulled out the first clothes that came to hand, a T-shirt and jeans, still bearing their price tags, before running down the stairs as the knocking started again, more like a hammering now.

'Alright, alright,' I shouted, pulling open the door and squinting in the morning sunlight, expecting to see Yoda, but it wasn't him; it was the police.

'Hello Father, are you OK?' the male officer asked.

It was Brian, from the stoning.

'Erm, yes,' I replied, confused, looking along the street, seeing nothing, just the police car parked outside.

'Why didn't you call us?' he asked. 'You must have been terrified.'

'What do you mean?' I asked, feigning confusion, feeling protective over Jacko and Migsy.

'You should have called us,' he said, 'we're here for you.'

'I, erm, don't really know what you're talking about.'

Brian looked at me, perplexed, and then started laughing as he looked to the female officer at his side, who dutifully joined in.

'Jesus, you must sleep like a log,' he said, as I stood scratching my head, not getting the joke. 'Look behind you.'

'What?'

'Look behind you.'

I turned and saw it immediately; the front door an explosion of splinters and bare wood, a ragged circle of pockmarked paintwork.

'What happened there?' I gasped.

It looked like it had been chewed up, gnawed by a giant rat.

'Shotgun,' Brian answered matter-of-factly. 'We had reports of a possible shot being fired early this morning, but patrol cars couldn't see anything, so assumed it must have been an exhaust backfiring or something. It appears that there *was* a discharge, though.'

'Somebody shot my front door?' I asked doubtfully.

'Looks like it,' Brian said sombrely.

'Why would somebody shoot a front door?'

'It's what they do,' the WPC chipped in. 'It's meant as a warning.'

'They shoot your front door?' I frowned, still not really understanding.

'Yes,' Brian said.

'Who? Who shoots front doors?'

'Usually gangs – to warn somebody off, or to let them know that they don't like what they're doing.'

'The High Rip,' the WPC added.

'The what?'

'That's the name of the gang that runs the show around here,' she said.

'Why don't they just knock? Doesn't anybody know how to ring a doorbell anymore?'

'It's to intimidate,' Brian said.

'I still don't get it. They shoot your front door if they don't like something you are doing?'

'Yes,' Brian repeated, getting a little frustrated.

'I'd have been far more intimidated if they'd knocked and showed me the shotgun,' I said. 'They'd save on bullets, too.'

'Cartridges,' Brian corrected. 'The question is, who? Why would they shoot your front door?'

'I don't know,' I shrugged.

'Well, what have you been doing? Have you upset anybody?'

I closed up. 'I don't think so – I've only just moved in,' my version of the truth. 'Nobody is speaking to us around here. I had my first service yesterday, but no locals came – just a couple of reporters.'

'I know,' he said, 'I've seen the paper. Anybody suspicious been hanging around? Anybody said anything to you?'

'There's somebody who hangs around at the top of the road a lot.'

'Who?'

'I don't know. I just assumed it was a local lad.'

'A description?'

'Erm, tall, wears black.'

'Could be a Cornerman,' the WPC suggested.

'A what?' I asked.

'They're a gang around here.'

'I thought you said the High Rip–'

'What the fuck's happened here?' a voice interrupted from the opposite end of the garden.

It was Yoda.

'Someone has shot his front door, John,' Brian answered, as if it was a normal occurrence.

'Are you OK?' Yoda asked me.

'Yeah, but I don't think the door is going to pull through,' I grinned, but nobody shared my amusement. 'I only found out just now.'

'You didn't notice somebody shooting your front door?' Yoda looked at me in disbelief.

'No,' I mumbled, as he and Brian exchanged glances.

'This is all we need,' Yoda groaned, dismayed. 'Have you seen these?' He held up a bag full of newspapers.

'No,' I said, before remembering my manners. 'Come in, everybody, come in.'

We sat in the lounge as I gave my statement, being careful to make sure everything I said was true, albeit with some omissions. I described George Formby to them, but there was very little to say: a man, a shape. Forensics inspected the front door whilst Yoda was on the phone to Mo, talking with his hands, excitedly emphasising a point.

'We need to find out who your mysterious admirer is,' Brian said. 'That's our starting point – any ideas?'

'I think he may be something to do with what happened here in the past,' I said. 'Possibly a victim, or maybe a victim's relative?'

'What makes you think that?'

'Just a guess – a feeling I get from him.'

'Well, there's certainly motive. There's also the local community, some of whom are still upset.'

'You really have to handle this with kid gloves,' Yoda interjected. 'We can't go around pointing the finger. It's such a fragile peace at the moment.'

Brian nodded in agreement.

'Don't do anything for now,' I suggested. 'Let's just see how it all pans out.'

'We can't do that,' the WPC said. 'This is a serious firearm incident – it could be you next."

'You can't stay here until we've resolved the issue,' Brain said. 'It's not safe.'

'I'm alright,' I said.

'Seriously, somebody has sent you a warning. You need to move out.'

'I can't,' I argued. 'I won't.'

'Will you tell him?' Brian implored Yoda. 'Pull rank or something, make him see some sense.'

Yoda looked at me, but he knew he was wasting his breath. 'Just a couple of nights?' he asked.

I shook my head. 'We've just got to get through this bit. If I leave now, it'll never stop. It's just a front door.'

'These could be dangerous people,' Brian said. 'We don't know who they are.'

'Or they could be kids,' I countered.

'Kids with a shotgun?' Brian threw up his hands, incredulous. 'That's even worse.'

'Alright, just let me think about it,' I said. 'Let's see how the day goes. Who knows, you might have caught them by tonight.'

The two officers glanced at each other then stood to leave; we had reached an impasse.

'Cup of tea?' I asked Yoda, as Brian and the WPC joined their colleagues outside.

'Yeah, go on then, before I show you the next bit of good news,' Yoda spilled the newspapers onto the table, spreading them around.

'What's happened now?' I moaned. 'We're not in there again, are we?'

'Afraid so. They've got their teeth into you now.'

He flicked through the pages of one before stopping on the headline: *FOOL ON THE HILL*, set above a picture of me, a bizarre-looking creature in the pulpit, and another of the graffiti.

'They do have a point,' I laughed.

Yoda looked back at me, confused.

There was a link, so I typed the address into my phone and found myself on film, a demon singing to an empty church. Flicking over to YouTube, I saw there were a quarter of a million views already, with plenty of comments forming below, all that vitriol Yoda was talking about. I switched it off.

'I've gone viral,' I laughed. It all felt like a joke after what had happened to Jacko.

'Bastards,' Yoda growled, too angry to see the funny side.

'I've never been viral before.'

'I don't know why you're laughing,' he spat, 'this is serious. I've had the Communications Office ranting in my ear already this morning.'

'But you do understand that this is why I can't leave? What sort of message would it send out?'

'You could be in danger. You–'

'The world is watching,' I cut him off. 'What was it you said? "Where are the men who went out on ships? Men who fought for their beliefs?"'

'But–'

'We always knew it was going to be difficult.'

He hesitated, but then nodded in agreement.

'I'm really not bothered,' I said after a long pause, and I wasn't. 'I did hit him in the face with a bag of dog shit. I still think he got the worst of it.'

'I'm not so sure,' he allowed himself a smile. 'Your singing sounds terrible there.'

'I'd better get some practise in, then. I'm going to the church.'

'Go on, you do that, and I'll sort you out a new door.'

The police had left, replaced by the local press taking photos of the shattered wood as I stood next to it, giving a cheesy smile and a big thumbs up, projecting as much sarcasm as I could muster.

'Can I get a few words?'

'No.'

'Why not? It might help.'

'The Fool on the Hill?'

'That wasn't us.'

'No,' I repeated.

'You're on the front of the Echo again,' he called after me, once he realised that I wasn't going to answer any of his questions. His tone was starting to sound almost apologetic.

'Surely, there's something more interesting than this going on in the world?' I replied over my shoulder, not breaking stride. 'We're becoming a dictatorship, and the prime minister has just arrested his own brother, yet here you are harassing me again.'

'We just go where we're told to go,' he complained with a shrug, as I entered the silence of the church, gently closing the door behind me and sitting on a pew bathed in sunlight.

I said a quiet prayer before emptying my mind, entering a state of untrained meditation. I just wanted to be alone.

I had become used to my own company over the years, finding comfort in it way too early in life; the stillness, silence, solitude. I was calm, not caring about the whirlwind going on outside: the press with their stories, the murdered front door or the endless karaoke that was social media.

Jacko had put everything into perspective; into its proper playground context.

I sat for hours, enveloped in silence until the creaking of the door announced Yoda's arrival.

'Lunch is ready,' his voice echoed around the space, rousing me from within myself.

'What are we having?' I asked, standing up and following him across the grass.

He sat down and emptied the contents of a carrier bag onto one of the flat gravestones; Charles Horsfall, 1846. It was a bright day, worthy of a picnic.

'Just been to the petrol station,' Yoda said, pointing towards a small pile of sausage rolls, Pepperami, Red Bull and Quavers.

'Is it OK to eat off a grave?' I asked, feeling slightly uncomfortable.

'I'm sure he won't mind.'

A strangeness came over me as I lay back on the grass, suddenly tired as energy was diverted to my stomach, digesting the feast, and yet I was wide awake, restless, owing to the caffeine from the energy drink. Yoda, on the other hand, was having no such problems, snoring away next to me, resembling some kind of cold-blooded amphibian trying to warm itself in the sun, mouth open, a silvery line of dribble falling onto Charles Horsfall.

I looked up at thin wisps of white cloud moving slowly across the blue sky, all at the same speed, the same height; all the same type, cumulus, nimbus, cumulus-nimbus... fuck knows. I felt guilty for lying there, as though I should have been doing something productive, but the caffeine was wearing off and a heavy tiredness was washing over me, a different tide this time, lethargic, pulling me under after a restless night.

I succumbed, submerging, drowning in a deep, dreamless sleep, and then awakening with a jerk as a shape stood over me, blocking the sun, its features concealed by the surrounding glare. My eyes tried to adjust, unsuccessfully, before flicking across to Yoda, who was still snoring peacefully. I felt vulnerable as I stared up into the impenetrable black where I thought the eyes must have been, my foot twitching, ready to swipe through its legs.

The shadow stepped back, allowing the full glare of the sun to hit my face. I covered my eyes, recoiling from the brightness, and used the momentum to flip over, pushing myself up to my feet and taking a sharp step backwards, expecting a blow to land, but nothing happened.

I studied the man in front of me. He was elderly, but massive, stocky, tattooed swallows decorating the backs of his hands, whilst regimental insignia covered his forearms, the ink blurred slightly with age. His grey hair was slicked back, and there was a hand-rolled cigarette tucked behind his ear as he stood there in a plain white T-Shirt, his stillness uncomfortable, forcing me to break the silence.

'Hello,' I said extending my hand. 'Fr McKay – erm, Peter.'

He accepted my hand, giving it a brief, firm shake.

'Jim.'

There was a pause as we stood considering each other, and I felt the need to start talking again, the silence becoming uncomfortable.

'Nice to meet you, Jim. Are you from around here?'

'The gunshot was nothing to do with the residents,' he replied. 'Nobody from around here was responsible.'

'O-K,' I answered slowly, a little taken aback.

'Would you be able to attend a meeting tonight?' he asked, making me wary, setting alarm bells ringing. 'With representatives of the community,' he added, apparently sensing my apprehension, but the clarification did nothing to allay my fears.

I had images of being set upon in a dark alley, pulled into a doorway; my body washing up in the river weeks later.

'Sorry, who are you again?' I asked, an edge to my voice.

I felt intimidated; it sounded like something from a paramilitary, the inner council of an abbreviated organisation. I could feel my anger rising as I watched his fists opening and closing by his sides, those swallows, suggesting fast hands. We didn't need words; it felt like we could fly at each other at any moment, that we *should* fly at each other; that feeling of peace was coming to me.

'I'm Jim,' he spoke a bit warmer this time. 'I was asked to come here by the local community representatives. We're known as the Know-alls around here because we're a gang of auld-arse pensioners who know everything about everything. We want to clarify that the gunshot didn't come from anybody in this area, and to ask what your plans are – where we can go from here.'

'Can you guarantee my safety?' I asked. 'I won't get hurt?'

'We're not the mafia,' he laughed, an almost soundless wheeze, 'we're pensioners. The only way you'll get hurt is by words, if you're a bit of a soft lad that is, but you won't come to any harm, no. Speak to Mo, she knows who I am.'

Mo's name settled my nerves, and the tension started to recede.

'We can meet at the church,' I sd, 'and I'd quite like Mo to be there, if that's OK with you? She knows us both.'

'Fine by me,' he agreed with a shrug. 'What time's best for you?'

'Eight?'

'Eight,' he nodded, and then turned towards the gate.

I glanced across at Yoda, still snoring away, drooling, blissfully unaware, deciding to leave him to his dreams as I headed for the coolness of the church. I texted Mo, asking if she could make it, before returning to my meditative state, only emerging when she arrived with Yoda in tow.

'What's going on?' he demanded, bald head reddened by the sun, unsure whether to be angry or concerned, so going with angry.

'I've had a visit from some local residents,' I said, 'the Know-alls. They want to meet with me here tonight. Can you make it, Mo?'

'I can, love, yeah,' she replied. 'Who was it that came to see you?'

'Jim.'

'Ah, Big Jim. He's alright him – fought in the war on Crete. He was a POW, I think, kept escaping then getting caught again. Ended up on that Lamsdorf Death March.'

'Sounds interesting.'

'They're all quite interesting, though, like most old people, they don't really like to talk about the past,' she shrugged. 'Our loss.'

'Who else is likely to be there?'

'Depends who turns up, love. We'll find out when we find out.'

# CHAPTER 8

FIRST WAVE IS THE OLDEST WAVE

I heated the urn and put the cups out ready; tea, coffee, sugar, milk and biscuits – chocolate biscuits – before stepping back and looking over the spread at least ten times. It felt new, and yet somehow familiar.

"Pink wafers, fuck, no pink wafers," I cursed, worrying it wasn't perfect.

I'd been fussing, taking care to make sure the church looked its best, spending an inordinate amount of time flicking switches, trying to create the perfect atmosphere, eventually settling on a limited number of lights providing a dim glow, strengthened by candles in the alcoves; their warm, flickering flames reflecting in the windows. It looked beautiful.

Empty chairs waited around the wooden table in the vestry, probably too many, as I sat on the cold stone within the alcove by the door, my dark robe cascading down the steps, fidgeting with nervous tension until the latch rattled, followed by a shaking of the door, the abruptness of the noise making me jump. Two heavy knocks drew me off the step, and I hurriedly undid the latch and pulled the door open.

'Father,' a monotone voice said, as I was met by the outline of a group, Big Jim its highest point in the centre.

I felt a twinge of panic; I was off-guard, expecting Mo and Yoda first. The residents had turned up half an hour early.

'Erm, come in, wel– welcome,' I stammered, stepping back and opening the door wide; offering my hand, but immediately sensing that a jovial smile would be out of place.

There was a seriousness in the air; they were not here to be smiled at, so I kept my face sombre, my voice polite, as they remained outside for an uncomfortably long time.

'I said I'd never set foot in this place again,' one of them cursed, before reluctantly stepping over the threshold, ignoring my hand and walking past.

The rest of them followed in single file, each leaving me hanging.

'Erm, just go through to the vestry please. There are drinks and biscuits in there,' I called after them, trying to assert a modicum of control, but nobody gave any indication they had heard as they continued forward.

My heart sunk as I closed the door behind me.

*'What did you expect,'* Peter whispered mockingly, *'a hug?'*

I followed them inside, watching as they arranged themselves around the table, all sitting in one row, with a few empty seats left over in front of them.

*'An interrogation,'* Peter confirmed.

I'd be getting off lightly if that was the case.

'Erm, tea, coffee, anyone?' I asked, getting no more than a few headshakes and a frosty, 'No, thank you.'

'Coffee, white, six sugars please,' a man with an oversized head spoke up, prompting the others to turn to him as one, tutting. 'No coffee,' he quickly changed his mind. 'We're not here for coffee.'

I poured myself one, glad of the opportunity to stall for time, before taking a chair opposite them.

'I'm Peter McKay,' I started, as means of introduction, 'and I'm the new priest for the parish, though I think you already know that.'

There were a few grunts and nods.

'We just want to clarify that no resident of the estate was involved in what happened to your front door,' the man with the big head announced, now looking stern faced.

'Yes, Jim said as much,' I replied. 'Any idea who it could have been?'

Shaking heads came back, a closed shop, as again we sat facing each other in silence.

'Does anybody mind if I smoke?' a man wearing thick-rimmed bifocals asked, pulling a pen-like electronic cigarette out of his pocket, its little canister of yellow liquid sloshing about in the middle.

'Erm–' was all I could manage, before one of them kindly replied for me, 'Go on, Alan,' overruling what I was about to say.

Most of them followed Alan's lead, the awkward silence continuing as they put pens to lips, a little light appearing on the top whenever they inhaled before exhaling a thin smoke. I saw blue lips, blue teeth, a memory from childhood flashing through my mind.

*'Stop chewing that fucking pen!'* Peter teased.

The old lady in the centre drew me from my thoughts, scrambling around in her handbag, with her gaunt, yellowing face below a bright-blue rinse, like a cloud of candy floss; she looked familiar.

'There's a man who stands at the top of the road occasionally,' I said, 'watching the church, dresses in black. Any idea of who he is?'

All heads turned to the youngest amongst them, a man in his mid-forties, sporting a centre part, as the old lady pulled a huge hand-rolled cigarette from her bag.

'You?' I asked, unsure.

He responded with a shrug, before spitting on the floor.

*'Fanny head,'* Peter mocked, as I tried to remain calm.

'Residents of the estate were not responsible for what happened to your front door,' was repeated again, like a mantra, this time in a slightly sharper tone by a thin man with a grey moustache and a bright tan; his open mouth revealed a single tooth, like a can opener.

*'Summer teeth,'* Peter giggled, in a jovial mood, revelling in the tension. *'Summer there, summer not.'*

The old lady lit up and blew out a large cloud of smoke, giving a big sigh as she leaned back in her chair, as if a huge weight had been lifted from her.

'Anyone want a bang on that?' she leaned back in her seat, offering the spliff up for sharing.

'No thanks, Madge,' came the reply.

*Madge*, the name stirred something in me, but I wasn't sure what.

'But do you know who he is?' I asked again, my question met with silent stares as strata of smoke were forming in the room, floating between us. 'I, erm, wondered if he might be something to do with one of the victims?'

This did provoke a response, mostly gasps and tuts.

'Don't you dare,' one muttered, the tension ratcheting up a few notches as the sweet marijuana smoke wafted over me.

I looked around at the glowing pens before settling back on Madge, who was inhaling another lungful, lips puckered and cheeks collapsing inwards, the red tip glowing before she exhaled, leaving just her blue rinse visible behind a thick cloud of smoke, a blue cloud making a white cloud.

'You know, we asked the council if they could knock this church down,' another man said, leaning forward, his grey hair combed conspicuously over an obvious bald patch, his face aggressively red.

'*Bobby Combover,*' Peter cackled.

'Or if we could get it turned into flats or something,' a large lady chimed in from the side.

'We don't want the Church around here. We don't want people like you around here,' Bobby Combover added, getting warmed up.

'Yeah, I've noticed,' I replied, indicating the cuts on my head. 'The newspapers have been supportive as well, and now somebody shoots my front door. I understand that I'm not welcome, but I want the opportunity to prove that we can be a force for good in the community.'

'Bit late for that,' came the stubborn reply.

'Look, I'm not here for you to tear strips off me. This needs to be constructive,' I suggested, in a low voice. 'Terrible things have happened in this church – disgusting, inexcusable things that make me feel sick to the pit of my stomach. For that, I can only apologise on behalf of the Church again and again and again until I'm blue in the face, but the fact is that the man who did those things has been arrested and is going to prison, and rightly so. He's a man who abused his position of trust within the community in the most cowardly, despicable way. The Church has not tried to protect him, we are as disgusted as you are. I am as disgusted as you are.'

'We can't trust you, and we can't trust the Church, so there's no point in you being here,' Bobby Combover said, sitting back with his arms crossed.

I looked around, seeing that all arms and legs were crossed, like a series of human knots, apart from Madge's.

'I just want to try,' I replied, shaking my head, denying them.

'That's not up to you, it's up to us,' Fanny Head said, standing up, jabbing his finger at me.

There was general murmuring and nodding, but there was also a tension between them.

'What do you mean?' I asked.

'I mean, when we decide you have overstayed your welcome, we make sure that you leave,' he sneered, banging his finger on the table repeatedly, like a sewing machine.

I was still unsure if he was George Formby. 'Is that some sort of threat?' I asked, noting how their comments were becoming more pointed, insinuating.

'Is right,' he answered, still standing. 'You'd have been spending a lot longer in hospital if it was up to me, you fucking paedo.'

'Sorry?'

'*Let's go,*' Peter was rattling around, excited, filled with glee.

'You heard,' he continued, his jabbing finger now hitting his own chest, 'and I'll be the one to do it, when we decide it's time for you to jog on.'

It felt like a pantomime, as they performed their roles before me. It was threatening, but I didn't feel threatened, since I recognised him from Stanley Park, on those long adolescent summer nights.

*He doesn't remember*, I thought, as I recalled chasing him down, watching my fists pummel his stricken face.

We sat facing each other, at an impasse, the lights of their e-cigarettes nervously blinking on and off as they took diluted hits of nicotine, something to fill the empty space.

'*Planet of the vapes,*' Peter quipped, as I tried to stifle a grin.

'What are you fucking laughing at?' Fanny Head screamed, standing up again, fists clenched, with everyone seeming to ignore him.

'Look, I don't want any trouble,' I said, raising my palms. 'I'm not going to fight you, I'm a Priest. I just want an opportunity to bring the Church back – to be beneficial to the community. One man has dragged it down, but before that there was a good congregation here, which tells me there's a need for a church in the area.'

'*Was* a need.'

'St George's has been serving this community for hundreds of years, and Fr Williams has undone all of that with his horrendous acts. I understand there's a lot of work to do, and I do accept that the damage may be irreparable, but I want to give it a go.'

'Where are you from anyway?' Bobby Combover asked.

'I'm originally from Anfield,' I replied. 'From the terraces, just by the ground.'

'That explains why you're still here, then. Shit hole down there – makes Mordor look like Mothercare.'

I smiled again, but there was nothing coming back. I was starting to feel a bit giddy, looking at Madge as she stubbed out the last of her joint, her pupils dilated as she reached forward, grabbing a couple of biscuits before fishing around in her handbag, presumably for another smoke.

That's when it clicked.

'Margaret!' I shouted, bolting up in my seat. 'It's Margaret! How's Stan?'

'What?' she looked up with a start, confusion etched on her face.

'What do you mean, how's Stan?' the large lady at the back asked, standing up, a frown forming on her forehead below the fringe. Her huge, meaty arms trembled, their freckles and moles cascading down the dimpled, swaying red flesh, speckled like corned beef.

'I met you both at the hotel above McCartney's a couple of weeks ago, at breakfast,' I went on, enthusiastically, smiling broadly.

Her eyes opened wide in surprise, in recognition, as a hand reached over and pulled her off her chair by her blue rinse.

'The Hanover?! He's my husband, you slag – you dirty fucking slag,' the big lady bellowed, as she started grabbing, punching and slapping in a wild frenzy.

I sat back, stunned, letting the show unfold as Margaret gave as good as she got, teeth bared, scratching and clawing at her assailant, the two seventy-year-olds shouting and screaming incomprehensible insults as they grappled.

Eventually, Big Jim stepped between them, holding them apart, giving me a curt, 'Nice one,' as he dragged them out into the church, bumping into pews, sending them clattering, their howls only stopping once the front door closed behind them.

When he came striding back into the room, it felt as though the situation could explode. The dynamic had changed; they'd seen that violence could happen inside a church.

'I don't understand,' I said, holding my hands up in surrender, feeling more and more light-headed. I could have started giggling again, as the weed mixed with clouds of strawberry cheesecake and butterscotch emanating from the vapes.

'It's not his fault,' Summer Teeth argued, trying to diffuse the situation, 'they've been fighting over Stan for fifty years. He's been married to them both – our own Shakespearean tragedy.'

'Seen more bell-ends than weekends them two,' Bobby Combover agreed, grinning as a couple of them nodded, smiling, rolling their eyes.

*Good*, I thought.

'It *is* his fault,' Fanny Head blurted out in disagreement, back on his feet once more, looking to the others for support. 'Distractions, divide and conquer – I know what you're doing. I think your time has come, Father.'

'Look,' I said, trying to act serious, but feeling drunk, 'why even come here unless you believe that we could be able to fix this?'

'To stop Mo phoning us up, bending our ear every five minutes,' Summer Teeth answered with a straight face.

This knocked me over the edge, laughing out loud as they looked uneasily between themselves. I reached forward and grabbed a couple of biscuits off the tray.

*Shit*, I thought, *concentrate!*

'What's so fucking funny?' Fanny Head took a step forward, trembling now, his top lip curling up above his teeth, too far gone. Big Jim put a hand on his chest, holding him back.

'Nothing's funny,' I shook my head vigorously, before bursting out laughing again; I couldn't help it. 'I'm sorry, it's just when he said about Mo–'

I felt his hand on my throat, furniture crashing around us as I was tipped back onto the floor, the air knocked out of my lungs as I landed with a thud.

'Twat him,' somebody shouted, as Peter took over, grabbing the hand to stop him throttling me, and then noticing the other, cocked and ready to come down as I jerked my knee up, catching him between the legs. His eyes opened wide as the pain hit, giving me the chance to roll him off and climb to my feet, leaving him curled up below.

A powerful arm came around my neck, drawing me backwards. *Big Jim?* I wondered, going limp, letting him take me without putting up any kind of struggle; I didn't want this. We kept going until we came to the wall, where I realised that Big Jim was amongst those stood watching me in shocked silence. Slowly, the arms holding me slackened off.

'What are you doing here?' Bobby Combover asked.

'I'm here to speak to Macca.'

My knees buckled at the sound of his voice.

'Macca?'

'Peter – Fr McKay. Whatever you want to call him.'

'You know him?'

'Yeah,' Migsy said.

'He's gone, hasn't he?' I asked, the urge to laugh vanishing.

'Yeah,' came the soft reply.

'Who's gone?'

'Jacko,' I whispered, staring at the crowd. 'Jacko's dead.'

I watched their bodies react as if they'd received a physical blow, a simultaneous impact from a sound wave, landing like a punch in the gut. They went limp, some sitting, some still standing, looking forward, shock showing on their slackened faces, followed by a chorus of denials, demands and laments, as they struggled to comprehend a simple two-word sentence. I was surprised how much it affected them.

*Did they even know him?* I thought.

'We need to make arrangements,' Migsy said quietly, placing a hand on my shoulder.

'I'll do it,' I said. 'We'll do it here.'

He nodded in agreement.

'You can't do it here. What fucking right do you have to do it here?' Fanny Head shouted, shaking with rage, having managed to get back up.

Before I could reply Migsy stepped forward and hit him square on the chin, returning him to the floor, out cold. Nobody seemed to notice; too far gone in their own thoughts.

'Cheers,' I murmured.

'It's alright,' Migsy said, as the door opened and Yoda and Mo stepped in, their faces transforming from painted-on smiles to stunned surprise.

'What's going on?' Yoda cried, flabbergasted as he surveyed the scene; the table on its side, chairs scattered with biscuits and cups strewn across the floor. 'There are two old women fighting outside the front door, and– and what's he doing down there?' he groaned, pointing at Fanny Head.

'Having a little sleep,' Migsy confirmed.

'He gave him a fluke's gob,' Summer Teeth explained, gesturing towards Migsy.

'And who are you?' Yoda demanded. 'And what's that smell?'

'Skunk,' Bobby Combover answered.

'Oh no, please no,' Yoda cried. 'What happened? The meeting isn't even supposed to have started yet.'

'They came early,' I said, still in a bit of a daze.

'Didn't want him too well prepared,' Bobby Combover grinned.

'But, why?' Mo asked imploringly.

'We'd better get off,' Summer Teeth suggested, to nobody in particular. 'Good meeting – look forward to the minutes. Somebody pick him up,' he nodded down at Fanny Head as he made for the exit.

Big Jim pulled the stricken man up with one hand, pushing him through the doorway as he tried to regain his feet, staggering like a new-born lamb, as they shuffled out in single file until there was just the four of us left.

'I'd, erm, better be going,' Migsy said, almost bashfully, 'lots to do. I'll be in touch.'

I leaned over and gave him a hug before he followed the residents out into the night, before slumping down into one of the few remaining upright chairs.

'Who's that?' Yoda asked, still looking bewildered.

'A blast from the past,' I said.

It took him a moment to comprehend, and then he almost jumped when he realised. 'Hang on, you don't mean from–'

'Yes,' I nodded, as he picked up a chair and dropped down next to me.

'What's going on love?' Mo asked, concerned. 'Are you alright?'

'Yeah, I'm fine. Went well, I think,' I gave an empty laugh.

Yoda was looking at the floor, stony-faced, understanding. The past had met with the present.

'Got my first booking,' I joked, feigning optimism.

'Eh?' Yoda was back to being confused.

'Jacko died.'

'Who?'

'Jacko – Paul Jackman.'

'The gangster Paul Jackman?' Mo asked, looking surprised.

I nodded, squeezing my palms together, knuckles turning white.

'So, why are…' Yoda started, but the answer came to him before he finished the question. 'You knew him from–'

'Yes.'

'Oh, fuck,' he moaned, burying his face in his palms.

'God help us,' Mo whispered, sitting down and then standing up again. 'I'll go and get some chippy, shall I? Sounds like you two have a lot to talk about.'

'Special foo-yung, half and half,' Yoda said into his hands.

'Beef mushroom, half and half,' I said, standing up, handing her a ten-pound note. I was starving all of a sudden, and the biscuits were all over the floor.

∞

We ate quietly around the table, knives and forks clanging loudly, the long break in conversation punctuated by the slurping of beer, and crunching of complimentary prawn crackers turning to dust.

'Was it as bad as it looked?' Mo asked, once we were all sat back, looking into our empty trays.

'Nah,' I said, 'eventful, but not too bad. It's a start – something to work from, a baseline.'

'I should've known they'd pull a stunt like that,' she huffed, 'turning up early.'

'Ah, honestly, it was fine. There's plenty they need to get out of their systems.'

'They're just testing you,' she said, patting me on the arm, 'seeing what you're made of.'

'I thought for a horrible moment there that you might have sparked that bloke who was on the floor,' Yoda grinned, joining in.

'That was Migsy's handiwork.'

'He's a little shit – they call him Knock Out,' Mo said. 'Fancies himself as a bit handy, slaps his wife around, apparently. Built like a brick shit-house, but his chin is like an off button – press the switch and he's out like a light. His kids are an absolute pain as well. He wants them to be everything he is not, so they're always scrapping in the yard, a pair of bullies.'

'I think he's learnt his lesson,' I suggested.

'No, he bears a grudge that one,' Mo shook her head, 'so keep an eye on him. He'll be feeling a little bit humiliated at the moment.'

'I'd be more worried about Big Jim,' I said, 'even if he is a pensioner.'

'Ah, he's a gent, and fair, too. If he has a go then you must have done something wrong.'

'What about the others, who were they? None of them introduced themselves.'

'The main one was Alan, but I doubt he'd have said much. He'll just watch, taking it all in, seeing how you behave. His nickname's Lucky.'

'Which one was he?'

'He was the one with the long hair, beard and thick-framed bifocals.'

I recalled him passing me on the way in, first across the threshold, only to then disappear behind the more vocal ones.

'He pretty much heads up the committee. They all look up to him, and to be honest, he's probably the most normal of them.'

'Normal didn't show up for the meeting,' I smiled. 'Why is he called Lucky?'

'He was sunk six times on the Atlantic Convoys during the war. People wouldn't get on a ship with him in the end. Did you hear about the Laconia, where the U-boat sunk the ship, and then the German captain surfaced and rescued the survivors?'

'Did Bleasdale make a film about it?'

'Yes, that's the one. Well, he was on it. The Americans bombed them, too – happy to kill the survivors to get to the U-boat. I think it turned out that the same captain had sunk him a few times - they got on like a house on fire. I'd love to get inside his head,' she paused. 'How could you get back on a boat after being torpedoed once, never mind six times, and then left floating about in the freezing Atlantic?' She shuddered.

'Who else was there?' I asked, intrigued.

'The one smoking pot with the blue rinse is Margaret. Her grandkids drugged her up with some sleeping pills, and put the blue rinse in while she was asleep, for the derby. She's a massive Liverpool fan, you see.'

'I put my foot right in it there.'

'Ah, those two can't be in the same room without fighting, even though they live opposite each other, so don't blame yourself. They've both been after Stan since they discovered hormones. She's an interesting one,' she leaned in close, speaking quietly. 'She invented the inner-city cannabis farm, all for medicinal purposes, of course,' she raised her eyebrows sarcastically. 'She's the go-to person in the city for setting them up. She charges a lot, but the increased yields make it more than worth the cost, so

I hear. The systems she puts together are supposed to be amazing – hydroponics, lamps, fans, fertilisers, pollination – she knows everything. Jacko even used her for quality control. She's known as Space Cadet on the streets – the police have been after her for years, Operation Green Badger, but they think she's a twenty-something black fella, our very own Gangsta Granny.'

'And the one she was fighting with?'

'That's Sharon Williams, AKA Poison Ivy.'

'Poison Ivy? Why is she called that?'

'Because she poisoned someone called Ivy. Did her time for it.'

'Oh,' I said, trying to appear unmoved, 'and what about Stan?'

'Stan Williams. He used to work in ship building, one of the Cammell Laird thirty-seven.'

'Sounds like a terrorist cell.'

'And you sound like Thatcher. They were jailed in the eighties for striking, to set an example to anybody else thinking of doing the same. Sentenced in absence, they spent a month in a category A, and had their redundancy and pension stripped from them. These days, he's known as the Blue Diamond – swaps Viagra for similar Chinese versions and sells them online. It's his son who's the interesting one, though, a proper little chemist. He messes about with things, inventing. Very nice lad as well, all things considered.'

'What's his name?'

'Ste Williams, or Willow – Willow Wonka, to give him his full title. He works in a call centre during the day, and tinkers with his chemistry set at night – creates all sorts of magical treats, apparently. Jacko sorted him out with some lab equipment.'

'Jacko?'

'Yes, he was very interested in what Willow got up to. A few weeks ago, he created Sextasy, combining the effects of ecstasy and Viagra in one pill. He said the trials had gone well. God knows who the volunteers were.'

'I think I know who,' I grimaced, remembering my night in the Hanover. 'It definitely works.'

She looked puzzled.

'Next?' I asked, keen to move on.

'There's Mekon Don. He's the one with the combover. He used to work on the docks before they shut down. He was involved in a big accident there, apparently, lucky to be alive. He's got a huge steel plate on the top of his head where he smashed his skull, hence the combover. His head's a bit of a funny shape – they ask if Stan made the plate for him in Cammell Lairds. The kids call him Chrome Dome – he'll let you knock on it when you get to know him better, it makes a funny noise, like there's an airgap somewhere. They always knew if he was there fighting with the police during the dockers' strikes, as his head made a bonging noise whenever he'd get hit by a truncheons – they used to call him the Gong. He's also certified medically insane following the accident, but he's fine as long as he takes his medication.'

'What happens if he doesn't?'

'He can get violent,' she frowned. 'He gets a look on his face – the kids start teasing him, calling him Terminator or Robocop, and run away, but only certain things set him off.'

'Like?'

'It's pretty random. One time was because a mate didn't wash his bowl after eating Weetabix, but I can understand that. Another was because somebody walked diagonally across a zebra crossing, cutting him up.'

'I'll remember to avoid doing either.'

'Then, there's Elvis.'

'Which one's Elvis?' I couldn't imagine.

'You don't know?' she grinned. 'The skinny fella with the moustache and the fake tan.'

'The bloke with one tooth, built like a pipe-cleaner with a little pot belly?'

'That's him,' she laughed, 'got a face that could scare a police horse. The pot-bellied twig, he's an Elvis impersonator, available for parties and functions. It's hilarious, he puts on this Lycra suit – you can see every bone in his body.'

'Is he any good?'

'No, he's terrible, but nobody's got the heart to tell him. The suit reveals a few other things that appeal to the ladies in the audience, so he gets a lot of hen night gigs.'

'What?' I almost gagged.

'He's, erm, slightly out of proportion in certain areas,' she winked, laughing again.

I felt a bit nauseous.

'He also has a bit of a side graft going, full-body spray tans for pensioners, though, between you and me, I don't think spray tans are the only service he provides.'

'He should link up with the Blue Diamond.'

'You can spot his groupies a mile off,' she grinned. 'Orange pensioners with big smiles on their faces, shuffling around like happy Oompa Loompas.'

'And these are the people on the committee. I can't wait to meet the rest of them.'

'It's like our own House of Lords. The committee seems to attract the cranks – they get in there mostly because they're old,' she joked. 'The majority of people around here are nice, normal people just trying to live nice, normal lives, but we do have a higher proportion of characters than most places. These estates breed them different. I'm from the terraces, like you, where everything is ordered, we think in straight lines, whereas their thoughts are all over the place, curvy, often leading to dead ends or going down unexpected tangents and alleyways. They'll take you to places you've never been to before.'

'Sounds like something from Alice in Wonderland,' I held up my can. 'Down the rabbit hole.'

'Down the rabbit hole,' she replied with a grin. 'Cheers.'

∞

I spent most of the following week preparing the church for the service, burying myself in the sermon whilst people left me alone, which suited me; everything else felt petty. Yoda was battling with the Church's internal hierarchy, its committees and departments, fighting for my right to carry out the service.

*'What image are we portraying?'*

*'How will it be perceived?'*

*'How will it affect the brand?'*

He had similar doubts, and we quarrelled over it, turning on each other as the pressure increased.

'He was a murderer,' Yoda argued. 'Why can't he just go straight to the crematorium?'

'So is my dad,' I replied childishly, over-aggressive. 'It's my church – we agreed we do things my way.'

'You're a pain in the arse,' he threw his hands up, exasperated. 'It's painful working with you, like shitting a hedgehog.'

'I won't be dictated to.'

There were brief respites where we'd laugh together, but then the phone would ring again and we'd resume bickering, until finally I told him the full story of Paul Jackman, the boy before Jacko, detailing who he was and what happened to him. From then on, Yoda was onside, fighting tooth and claw, often screaming down the phone, slamming the receiver back into its cradle; he understood.

'Fucking gobshites!' he'd exclaim.

In the wake of national jubilation following Jacko's death, the media turned on the Church, an editorial in a broadsheet getting us on the front page again:

*Sympathy for the Devil*

*In a desperate attempt to attract a congregation following the disgusting abuse of minors within St George's Church, and the failed sermons of 'the Fool on the Hill,' Fr Peter McKay has agreed to hold a funeral service for Paul 'Jacko' Jackman. How can the Church celebrate the life of this*

I read them all, but I couldn't take them seriously, their dramatic words
trying to whip up moral outrage with a version of the truth, spun to
generate anger, despite being written by large-scale consumers of Jacko's
product as they burnt the midnight oil, hitting deadlines.

'Where's the investigative journalism?' I slurred at them, drunk.
'Where's the alternative angle? What about his early life?' I shouted,
tearing them up, scattering them across the room. 'Who's going to give
them the Gospel of Jacko – the Gospel of Migsy?'

This was just the beginning; the pressure increased, the Church
squirming in the spotlight as politicians jumped onboard, opportunists
littering the airwaves with soundbites, scrambling up the slopes to the
moralistic high ground until at last the Church relented, buckled, a diktat
coming down from some faceless meeting, decreeing that the service was
not to go ahead, which I tore up and threw in the bin. We hadn't been
invited.

Yoda was spending more time screaming down the phone, before
eventually throwing it across the room, smashing it against the wall,
providing much-needed respite for the first time in days. He was shielding
me from the maelstrom, from my own church, my own religion, giving me
the space that I needed to think.

The battle soon expressed itself externally, as congregations from
surrounding churches became caught up in the whirlwind of negative
media attention and internal disapproval. I walked to the church, past
elderly protesters with their placards and vitriol, finding it difficult to align
them with the religion as they spat out insults, their faces contorting in
anger and hate, before settling down to their packed lunches and tea until
another poor soul walked past.

'You disowning Jesus again, Peter?'

'Cock-a-doodle-doo.'

'How much are they paying you, Judas?'

'Cut off his ear!'

*They'll all be dead soon,'* Peter cackled.

A placard lay inside the church: Revelation 21:8. I kicked it to one side,
my anger rising as I stood in the centre of the aisle, trying to stay calm, to
empty my mind of their words. I held out my arms and looked up at the
stained glass, bathing in its multi-coloured glow, letting it drown out the
anger and recharge me with positive energy, powered by light.

Once the din had quietened down, I sat in the cool silence of the vestry,
writing the sermon, hearing the conversation with Jacko, his voice clear in
my mind. As shocking as his story was, one sentence kept coming back to

me:

*'I don't think I was always like that.'*

It made me consider myself, the person I was before that time, finding there was hardly anything, just barely discernible memories of a family life, a childhood, buried in the darkness at the back of my mind, superseded.

*What if those things had never happened?* I wondered. *What sort of people might we have become? Why is it still those years that define me, shaping my identity, silencing the before and creating the after?*

I made the sermon short and concise, not overly religious or dressed in flowery language; no frills, no tugging at heart strings or appeals to emotion; no mention of forgiveness. I centred on Matthew 7 and James 4:12, *'Judge not, that ye be not judged.'* Jacko had never told others about his earlier life, and it was not my place to do it for him.

Flowers arrived the day before the service; the church was decked out lavishly without being ostentatious, each bay filled with cascades of yellow and gold, with smaller arrangements placed upon the pew ends; it looked exquisite.

I sat in the silence as the last rays of the day mixed with the perfumed aroma, accosting the senses, overwhelming, sublime. I felt at peace at the thought of the coming service, at the prospect of bidding farewell to my friend. There was sorrow, too, of course, but the emotion receded with each day. Our relationship was never based upon sadness, pity or self-pity, it was about resilience and inner-strength, and those were the qualities I needed to display. I'd ran through the sermon with Yoda, who mumbled that it was 'fine' before locking up, as dusk turned to darkness.

The Wirral Peninsula and Welsh mountains were barely perceptible in the gloom, as stars and their constellations began to appear, like they always do, as the world keeps turning, oblivious.

∞

A light snapping sound drew me from my sleep, like twigs being broken, and then there was a large crack, followed by another, and another, as I sat up and listened, immediately alert, a hair trigger jumping out of bed, scrambling around for my clothes whilst the noises continued. Somebody was doing something, I knew, up to no good, as I looked out of the window to find the usual sepia light, only this time it was different. Shadows were moving, trembling, hinting at some unseen activity, hidden out of view.

I ran downstairs, pausing behind the front door, listening, before stepping back as I imagined somebody on the other side, shotgun raised, about to shoot, the faint snapping still audible.

*There must be a few of them*, I thought, remaining still until the sound of breaking glass spurred me forward.

I opened the door a crack and peered outside, and, finding nobody there, I inched it wider, wincing as it gave a creak. I stopped, holding my breath, but there was nothing; they hadn't heard.

Another shattering of glass made me open it wide enough to poke my head out and look up and down the road; still nobody, but the noises, which seemed to be coming from the churchyard, were getting louder, an occasional flash of light leaping over the walls, sending shadows shooting across the pavement.

I walked cautiously over to the wall, staying in the black of the shadow, my eyes fixed on the church gate ahead, waiting for somebody to come out.

*Might just be kids*, I thought, *drinking and smashing bottles.*

'This isn't *fucking* kids,' Peter whispered.

I paused by the side of the opening, listening for voices or movement, but there was nothing, just that same snapping sound, wood breaking.

*He's right, it's too quiet for kids*, I thought, as I tried to put an action to the sound.

The night before it had been motorbikes, loud, blatant and aggressive, but this was something else, quiet, sneaky, insidious.

'They're inside,' Peter said. '*Devils defacing your church.*'

A loud crack impelled me to move, running through the gateway before freezing at the top of the steps, overwhelmed by the sight before me. The churchyard was clear, illuminated by the stained-glass windows as they flickered like lanterns, with loud pops and another heavy rumble from inside, as if the walls were struggling to contain a violent storm. I looked up to see thin lines of smoke billowing between the roof tiles, and then a much larger plume of black mushrooming out, the storm escaping as a small section of roof collapsed, its void filled with delicate tongues of fire, growing larger, lapping up the plentiful supply of air. A long groaning sound preceded a deafening crash, breaking me from my stupor.

'Fire!' I started shouting, unable to really comprehend what I was seeing. 'Fire!' I cried out, again and again, my voice weak, pathetic, as I turned on the spot, looking for help, before running around to the main entrance as another section of roof collapsed.

A thundering sound came from within, followed by the delicate cascading of glass, creating an almost ethereal feel, a sprinkling of magic dust, as I fumbled with the key, luck intervening when the hot handle made me leap backwards, just as the door opened and a jet of flame and scorching hot air came bursting out, travelling the full width of the churchyard. I peeked tentatively around the stone doorway, seeing a vision of hell before me, an interior of glowing red embers and spreading fires. Covering my face with my T-shirt, I stepped inside, my skin stinging, eyes streaming, hairs shrivelling to nothing under the intensity of the heat, as I purveyed the scene before me until I broke down in a fit of coughing, the acrid smoke filling my lungs. I staggered backwards, tripping over the threshold and falling onto the ground outside, the cool air hurting my skin as much as the heat as it contracted. I was like an insect or wounded animal, pushing back on my heals, scuttling along the ground, whimpering, until a strong pair of hands hooked under my arms and pulled me onto the grass. Glancing up, I saw Big Jim and Lucky looking down at me, the flames reflected in the latter's bifocals.

'Is there anybody in there?' Big Jim was shouting. 'Is anybody inside?'

'No,' I replied, once I realised he meant the church.

'Then what the fuck are you trying to get in there for?' he bellowed, lifting me to my feet as I bent over coughing, tears streaming down my face.

'I don't know,' I replied between gulping breaths, shaking my head. 'I don't know.'

A crowd was gathering, a collection of pyjamas, nighties and bloodshot eyes come to admire the spectacle, as the sound of sirens approaching from the distance gradually increased, filling the night. The residents stood around me in a semi-circle, some in shock, others laughing.

Knock Out pushed his way forward, meeting my eyes, smirking as he pulled out a Zippo and flicking it open, its flame stuttering in the wind.

'First time the old fire beacon has been lit for hundreds of years,' he shouted, laughing. 'Spanish Armada must be on their way to turn us into Catholics.'

I took two strides towards him before Big Jim's arms came back around my torso, restraining me.

'Easy now, lad,' he whispered into my ear.

'I'll fucking kill him,' I hissed, Peter lunging forward, but Jim's arms stayed firm, restricting my movement.

'It won't have been him,' he said, as Lucky appeared in front me.

'We'll find out who did it,' he promised, placing his hand on my shoulder. 'This is too much. If he did do it, we'll find out.'

'*Jim'll Fix it,*' Peter said sarcastically.

I looked back at the crowd, the target of my fury no longer there, as my anger turned to shock and I slumped, dropping to my knees, hands going to my face.

'We put so much into it,' I lamented, crushed.

'Come on, soft lad,' Big Jim, clearly not one for weakness, pulled me back up by my collar, 'get a grip.'

Another huge crash made us pause, before a ball of fire and smoke billowed out of the door, sending glowing embers floating down around us, a gentle shower of light, like fireflies whirling around on warm currents of air, soon to be joined by the pulsing blue strobe of the fire engines pulling up on the road.

'Is everybody OK?' a Perspex visor shouted at me, flames dancing in the reflection, mocking me.

'Yes,' I confirmed, feeling just the opposite.

'Is there anybody inside?'

'No, I locked up. There's nobody in there.'

'Get to the ambulance,' he instructed, as more blue flashing lights arrived to join the others.

'I'm alright.'

'Get to the ambulance,' he insisted, as the hoses came past, leaving a steaming path up the stone walls before cascading into the open roof. 'I'm not asking.'

Big Jim manhandled me towards the paramedics.

'Get off me,' I protested, attempting to struggle, but lacking the energy to get away.

'There's nothing you can do here, lad,' he said calmly, as hands pulled me up into the bright, clean portable room, and then slammed the doors shut.

'No!' I yelled, looking for a handle, thumping the glass, trying to open them up again before a more gentle hand landed on my shoulder.

'Come on, let's take a look at you.'

Turning, I was met by the wide blue eyes of a young girl in a medical uniform. There was an innocence about her, a sense of goodness, something pure. 'I'm Ruth,' she smiled.

I stared at her for a moment, then acquiesced, slumping onto the bed as I felt the vehicle moving, taking me away, feeling filthy in this clean, sterilised environment.

'I'm OK,' I kept repeating again and again, her hands gentle as she prodded and inspected me, lights shining into my eyes as an oxygen mask was fitted to my face.

The air tasted cool and clean as she eased me back, nothing forced, just gentle touches, directing my body until I was lying on my back staring up at the ceiling, exhausted.

∞

I was released at five in the morning, the sun already rising as I flagged down a black cab with my bandaged hands. Minor burns covered the exposed parts of my body, my hair was singed, gone in places, and my chest felt heavy, breathing laboured and voice gravelly, breaking as I spoke. I hadn't felt anything whilst it was happening, but now my body was aching, my skin raw.

A single fire engine was there when the cab came to a stop outside the church, and as I struggled to get the money out of my pocket, the door opened and Smiler poked his head in, handing the driver a ten-pound note.

'You alright, la?' he asked.

'Yeah,' I nodded, stepping out onto the kerb, looking up at a ruin.

Everything felt heavy all of a sudden, like an unseen force was pushing me down, as I stared at the smoking shell, weight after weight being piled upon me. Only the walls remained, the windows nothing but charred, blackened holes; the roof completely gone, wisps of smoke still rising from the embers inside.

I felt the same, just a shell.

Migsy appeared next to me, repeating Smiler's question, 'You alright, la?'

'Yeah,' I gave the same answer, this time over my shoulder, as I walked through the church gate, entering the grounds.

'It's fucked,' he shouted after me, as I went past firemen sitting on the lawns, equipment scattered around them, each looking exhausted, coated in soot. There were a few of them in conversation near to where the door had been. I headed for the one who appeared to be in charge.

'Hello Father,' he greeted me.

'Hello,' I replied, 'I just want to thank you and your men for all your help with this,' I gestured, waving my hands before me. 'This.'

'I'm sorry, Father, but we couldn't save it,' he placed a hand on my shoulder. 'It was already too far gone when we arrived.'

'It's OK,' I nodded, 'I understand. Any idea what caused it, or would it be too early to tell at this stage?'

'There'll have to be a full forensic investigation before we can say for certain, but it's pretty obvious that it was an act of arson. Come with me,' he beckoned, entering the doorway, which had been reduced to a charred opening beneath the massive stone tower looming above.

Inside, it was like hell had visited a sacred place, perhaps because it had, rending its destruction, leaving everything black. Now, with daylight illuminating the large, cavernous space, the reality hit that it was all gone, the columns and ironwork twisted and buckled, lying at strange, contorted angles, like sculptures portraying pain. The balconies had disappeared, only occasional, twisted pieces of metal indicating where something used to be, a few arches at roof level doing the same, supporting nothing, a silhouette, the remains of something long dead.

*'This fucking church,'* Peter suggested.

'What I don't get is, how could it burn like this?' I asked. 'It's stone and iron, non-flammable.'

'My guess would be that somebody stacked the wooden pews around the columns,' he said, pointing to uniform piles of embers around the bases, 'added an accelerant, and then *poof,*' he splayed out his fingers, like a firework. 'The fire's got to such an intensity around the columns that the iron went soft and melted, taking the structural support from the roof and balconies, causing the whole thing to come crashing down.'

'It couldn't have been an electrical fault or something? A candle fallen over?'

'No, that would have meant small, localised damage. The only way to bring the whole thing down was by doing exactly what they did, a fire on every column.'

'And the external walls, the tower, are they alright?' I asked, indicating the charred shell around me.

'I think so. They're structural walls, self-supporting – the internal structure was independent of them. We'll need a surveyor to take a look, but it all looks pretty sound out there.'

'The forensics people, when will they start?'

'They already have,' he replied, pointing to a team of people in masks and paper suits around the base of the furthest column, flicking amongst the ashes.

'I've got a service at one.'

'You can't do that,' he smiled, shaking his head, probably assuming that I was still in shock, 'we're boarding it up. There can't be any public access.'

'I've got to,' I whispered to myself, as I walked back towards the doorway, finding Migsy waiting outside.

'What are we going to do?' he asked urgently. 'Can we move it to a different church?'

'Nobody will take it,' I said. 'We'll do it here.'

'What? Are you–'

'We'll do it here,' I repeated, a smile touching my lips as I left him standing.

I slept the rest of the morning, deep and dreamless, waking at eleven, actually feeling good as the course of the day was laid out before me. All I had to do was go through the motions, act out emotion.

It was busy outside; the fire engine had left, but there were police milling around amongst a mixed crowd. I ignored the repeated knocks and switched off my phone; there could be no distractions.

Putting on the robes, I felt more focussed than I had done in a very long time, becoming somebody else as I struggled to fasten buttons with bandaged hands, eventually succeeding, before I looked in the mirror one last time, scarred and burnt, practising grief before heading out the front door.

The noise of the crowd hit me as I stepped outside, the road solid with people, throbbing and swaying. The police were stood in lines, trying to direct and restrain, standing no chance, their human chain breaking as the crowd moved in different directions. The press was out in force, perched on top of their vans to avoid the throng, talking into microphones, gesturing for the cameras.

Elvis was the first face I recognised as he came towards me through the crowd, his skinny form slipping its way through, like an eel.

'You'll need to go in the back way,' he said. 'The Health and Safety, the police and whoever else are waiting up there to tell you the church is unsafe. Get these on,' he held out a hat and jacket to cover my clerical outfit.

Nodding, I put on the disguise, allowing myself to be led away from the church, around the block where it was less busy, as he pointed towards the boundary wall and cupped his hands together. He was going to give me a bunk over.

'Thanks,' I said, placing my foot into his upturned palms, doubting he would be able to support my weight.

'It's not for you, it's for Jacko,' he replied as I lifted off the pavement, swaying as he grunted below, until I regained my balance and managed to scramble up the wall, pausing as a sea of faces looked up at me from the other side, and then rolling over the top and dropping to the ground

There were murmurs from the crowd as a route opened up, carefully choreographed, with locals lining its sides. Mekon Don was crouched, waiting at its end on the back wall of the church, his combover fallen to one side, exposing his oversized head. I bent over, making myself small, and ran towards him as he readied himself to give me another boost up, this time towards the triple-height opening above his giant dome, where the stained-glass window used to be; too big to be boarded over.

I gripped his freezing-cold head as he started lifting, snorting as he peeled my hand off his eyes, steadying us both, allowing me to stand as he raised me towards the blackened opening. A low whistle came, a signal sending the crowd shuffling left, its density impeding any approach as another low whistle came, urging me to hurry up, I assumed, as Mekon Don extended his arms, a jerk and lift, raising me up quickly.

I was in.

Rolling over the stone sill and dropping onto the floor, I considered the empty black shell before me. Ashes were still spread in mounds around the twisted iron columns, writhing like snakes through the space, but the flowers had been replaced, their cascades of white and gold vibrant against a matt-black everything else.

I removed my disguise and waited at the altar. The police had sealed off the entrances with wooden boards, but I knew that they wouldn't last long; like King Canute trying to hold back the tide, the will of the people would eventually overcome. It always did.

The sound of the crowd steadily increased, causing a light fluttering in my stomach as the rumble of applause approached from what must have been the cortege, making its way slowly along the road. Voices were becoming louder, more agitated around the openings, shouting out instructions, sounding panicked before banging started on the wooden panel that filled the charred entrance. I could hear scuffles, the sound of bodies hitting bodies, of struggle, as the battle for access began. A part of me wanted to be out there, in the thick of it, as the sound reached a peak and a corner of the wooden panel was broken off, a Biblical shaft of daylight piercing the shadow before the hooked tip of a crowbar filled the hole, violently yanking and splitting the remaining timber.

A helicopter appeared overhead; I could feel its camera pointing, observing, the flowers fluttering in its downdraught as I stood motionless, staring at the opening below the tower, whilst the final pieces of timber were pulled away from the entrance. There was a moment of silence as we made eye contact; they were breathing heavily, some bloodied after confrontation, as they stepped back, parted, forming an aisle.

The whole crowd was silent now, heads bowed, as a white coffin came into view, Migsy, the first pall-bearer, tipping me a wink as the others followed around the corner, slowly walking forward together until they reached the front of the church, where two stands appeared and the white and gold-topped coffin was gently lowered, as people began filing in behind, looking around in shock at their surroundings. They all looked immaculate, beautiful in their suits, dresses and hats, carefully making their way through the debris and standing in orderly lines, silent.

Raised voices came from the doorway; Migsy put his hand into his jacket pocket, as a grey-suited elderly man stood still in the entrance, not crossing the threshold.

'Who's that?' I asked.

'It's Sean Cav,' Migsy answered, with a look on his face that I recognised.

'Come with me,' I said, striding towards the entrance, taking control.

'What?'

'We can't have this today. Come with me,' I repeated, and this time he followed

Sean Cav looked like any ordinary elderly gentleman, his grey hair slicked back, suit sharp, smart, with slightly outdated gold-framed glasses, like a Scouse Yankee, fresh off the ship. He was flanked by two younger men, presumably his sons, but was otherwise alone.

'Fr McKay,' he said, in a soft voice, bowing his head as we approached. 'Migsy.'

'What are you doing here?' Migsy asked, his hand still in his jacket pocket.

'We've come to pay our respects,' the old man replied, 'a professional respect. Nothing more, just us, no guns.' He opened his jacket, inviting inspection. 'He was a man that we admired greatly.'

'There'll be repercussions for this,' Migsy hissed, moving forward, unable to deduce whether Sean was speaking honestly or boastfully.

'Not today,' I put my hand on his chest, halting his advance, as a group of shaven-headed bouncers closed in around us.

I recognised this silence, everything on pause, the stillness as they breathed in the bad blood, their minds emptying to that split second of inner peace, of bliss, when the heart sends adrenaline coursing around the body, before the rush into the red.

Sean didn't flinch.

'We didn't do it,' he stated authoritatively. 'We didn't shoot Jacko.'

He was a bigger character than Migsy, old school, with a calm voice that you strained to listen to.

'And the fire?' Migsy asked, his eyes never leaving Sean's.

'Not us – not our style. You know that.'

Migsy looked down at the ground, a tug of war going on in his mind.

'There are things happening in the city,' Sean continued, 'things that neither of us are responsible for. The unknown is no good for either of us. We need to parley.'

Migsy looked up and gave a slow, deliberate nod.

'If you ask us to leave, we'll go,' Sean said. 'We're not looking for trouble – we'd have come with a crew if we were. Let's just put things to one side and admire Jacko. He was never a friend, he was a rival, a most dangerous rival. I've never been more afraid of anyone than I was him as a young man, but he had rules in his later years, and we could all learn from that.'

He stopped speaking and waited for an answer, looking patient, like he was made of stone; like he'd stand there all day if necessary. Migsy eventually relented, stepping to one side, allowing them through.

'Thank you,' Sean murmured modestly on his way past, joining a row at the rear as the palpable tension, a static charge that I could almost taste, evaporated through the air, its energy fizzling out into nothing.

People continued flowing in until the hall was full, standing in rows, as if the pews were still there, as a line of bouncers blocked the doorway, the police and any other authority kept at a distance.

My voice was loud, echoing through the space before floating out through the openings, where crowds had gathered, my white bandaged hands visible as they moved against the black backdrop, like a wailing mime artist. There were no hymns – I couldn't imagine Jacko wanting hymns – and the congregation remained silent, save for the occasional 'Amen.'

Wet spots started falling from the sky midway through, singular scattered drops landing noiselessly in the ashes, gradually increasing in frequency, a contribution from God to offset the lack of tears perhaps, for these were hard people. Nobody moved when mascara started to run, streaks forming in foundation, flattening hair and soaking through clothes, their masks washing away to reveal the real faces concealed behind, laid bare, exposed before His eyes. The rain intensified as I continued through the sermon, shouting to be heard, waiting for the clap of thunder, the flash of lightning, the voice of God, '*Thou shalt not*', like a scene from the Old

Testament, but the rain continued steadily until we finished with the Lord's Prayer, from the more genteel Sermon on the Mount, with its words of mercy, love and humility.

I nodded to the pall-bearers, and the white coffin began its final journey, floating through the black church in silence, the congregation peeling off in lines, synchronised, flowing out solemnly, as Smiler walked against the flow towards me.

'I'll take you to the crem,' he said.

I nodded, following him out with the bedraggled crowd, hoping the police would nail the boards back up again to finally close the place, as we walked through an aisle of people, soaked to the skin, standing silently, heads bowed.

'Peter!' a voice called out.

It was Yoda, his small frame wedged between larger bodies as I pulled him out of the crowd, allowing him to walk alongside me.

'You're in so much trouble,' he whispered, as we climbed into the back of the blacked-out Range Rover.

'Why?'

'The fucking church burnt down to the ground, in case you hadn't noticed.'

'Well, I didn't do it, did I? Arson, apparently.'

'Any idea who's responsible?'

I shook my head.

'You're mixing with some bad people,' he said, his voice full of reproach. 'I know your reasons for doing the service, and I respect them, but what are we involved in here? What world have we entered? Your door getting shot, the church burning down – you could've been killed.'

'You've changed your fucking tune,' I snapped back. 'This was never going to be a pleasant journey. It was never about going to nice places with nice people – there are no cups of tea in the garden centre with pensioners. If you want that then you can fu–'

'Alright, I'm sorry,' he interrupted, holding up his hands in surrender. 'It's not your fault, it's just the church –  it'd been there for hundreds of years, and now it's gone.' He looked despondent.

'Look, I've no intention of going any further down this road. Once the service is over, it's over, and I'll have no reason to mix with these people any longer. I just want to get on with being a normal priest.'

'But you haven't got a fucking church anymore,' he shouted, Smiler's head turning sharply to look at him admonishingly.

I hadn't thought of that obvious issue, the realisation hitting me for the first time, turning my stomach sour.

'And then there's the police,' Yoda said quietly. 'You held a service in a dangerous building. It could've collapsed.'

'The fireman said it was sound,' I answered sharply; he was getting hysterical.

'You could be arrested.'

'For what? Nobody told me I couldn't do it.'

'That's because they couldn't find you.'

'I was in the church all day. If they couldn't find me, they can't have looked very hard. Nobody mentioned anything.'

'I couldn't find you, either, and your phone was switched off.'

'I was there to do the service – they could have spoken to me then.'

'Nobody could get near the place because of these fucking gorillas,' he jabbed a finger towards the front seats.

'Could you two shut up,' Smiler interrupted, looking back again from the front seat. 'Everyone's been quiet and respectful all day apart from you two, bickering like a pair of auld women.'

Yoda looked like he was about to explode, stewing as we waited in the queue, on the conveyor belt of cremations. When he did eventually explode it was more of a rant, a torrent of words tripping over each other as he detonated, his face crimson, trembling, spittle flying.

"You've fucked it," he shouted, "you've fucked it up in record time. At least the last bastard didn't get the place burnt down. What were we thinking? What planet were we fucking on, to think you were the one to fix this almighty mess?"

"But…" was all I managed in response as he jerked his door open.

"And now, this, THIS!" he wailed, "the cherry on the fucking cake, a full funeral for Britain's most wanted, all on national TV. You're finished, we're finished, we're both fucking FINISHED," he finished as the door slammed shut and he stomped away, raging.

Smiler chuckled as we both watched him disappear into the crowd, people moving out of his was as they sensed the on-coming fury. Of all the things that had happened, it was Smiler talking down to him that tipped him over the edge. I leaned back and let out a sigh, raising my hands then slapping them down onto my thighs in frustration.

"Bell-end," Smiler mumbled, as I struggled to contain my rage until two white horses appeared in the rear-view mirror, their coats shining brilliantly against the black shadow coming up behind them, a crowd of people forming a silent straight line covering the width of the road, stepping solemnly forward, Goodison Park the backdrop.

All traffic had stopped as I stepped out of the car, standing on the broken white line in the centre of the road, on a collision course with the oncoming horses, their white plumes bobbing as the glass carriage approached. I entered the crematorium before them, leading them in as the last of the previous staggered out from this place of desperate embraces, where men were allowed to cry. There was that smell in the air, like candyfloss, which most attributed to the roses, thriving in the Garden of Remembrance.

I waited behind the lectern, watching as the pall-bearers trailed into the red sandstone chapel, placing the coffin on the shelf before the open curtains, about to complete its final journey to the storage area and furnace beyond. I took a moment, placing a hand on the casket, whispering a silent farewell to my friend, allowing myself to feel the force of emotion before switching it off again as the congregation followed in, silently taking their positions.

The service was very short, a final goodbye.

*'All go unto one place. All are of the dust, and all turn to dust again.'*

There was no weeping, no music, as the curtains started closing and the coffin disappeared from view. I didn't watch, just stared ahead, over the congregation, letting my mind go elsewhere, into science books, to dust, electrons, the building blocks of everything: me, the podium, the planet, as well as the tens of billions of galaxies expanding through space. It was wonderous, everything in existence constructed from the same identical ingredient, our temporary configuration blessed with life, a soul, consciousness for a brief time.

Jacko was about to be set free, to become something else, a sweet smell of candyfloss for us all to inhale, but what of his soul?

I wasn't sure if it was sight or sound that dragged me from my thoughts; the sudden jerk of a man standing at the back, and then an incredible bang, an explosion, everything going white, silent, disappearing, before zooming back into focus as another bang erupted and I hit the wall and then the floor, landing with Migsy on top of me. Through the ringing in my ears came screams of panic as we lay there, surrounded by chaos as people moved in slow motion, scattering in different directions. I looked down to find blood soaking through my robes, the linen sucking it up like litmus paper, sending me giddy for a moment before I regained focus, trying to feel my body; trying to see where it might be coming from. There was no pain.

I sat up and looked at Migsy; his shirt and suit were crimson, his hands pressed against his shoulder. He was pale, but conscious.

'Been shot, la,' he said.

I stood up slowly, just looking at him, leaning in, unable to comprehend as people came rushing over, pulling us apart, trying to get to him.

'Smiler, take him,' he instructed, pointing at me, then pulling a gun out of his inside pocket and handing it over. 'Make sure he's OK.'

'What are you worried about me for?' I shouted, alarmed by the presence of a handgun.

'Just run,' Migsy screamed, as he disappeared behind a pile of bodies.

I spotted Yoda in the crowd, looking panicked, as Smiler pulled me through a doorway and down a magnolia-painted corridor, that colour again, before opening a door that led out to a lawn. He looked around cautiously, and then started dragging me across the grass, both of us running, hunched over, careering towards the wall, just maintaining balance before vaulting over into the cemetery, where we paused, scanning the headstones for movement. It felt like we were two grown-up kids playing army.

'Come on,' Smiler barked, getting ready to run again.

'What happened?' I asked. 'Who shot Migsy?'

My ears were still ringing; I was probably shouting.

'Don't know,' he said, looking around, nervous.

'The Cavs?'

'Don't know.'

'Where are we going? Why are we running?'

'Jacko woke up again before he died – said you've got to be protected.'

It felt like a blow to my stomach, knowing he'd been conscious again, and that I'd missed his last words.

'Protected from what?'

'Dunno, probably nothing – he was high as a kite, like. Come on,' he called, crossing the exposed path.

I followed his lead, crouching low, like we were about to storm the enemy base, until we stopped, panting, amongst the cover of the headstones.

'What else did he say?' I asked. 'How long was he awake?'

'I don't know, he just spoke with Migsy,' he said tetchily. 'We've got to keep moving.'

Off we went again, running through the cemetery, stooping down, though I was sure we were in no danger. It was peaceful, just birdsong, as we slowed to a walk before sitting down on the ground, watching the helicopters circling over Stanley Park in the distance whilst Smiler called for a pickup.

I leaned back against a headstone, reading the one opposite, cracked down the middle, James Maybrick, feeling the hairs starting to creep up the back of my neck as I looked along the line to see a man standing there, dressed in black, staring towards us from a distance. He stood motionless, quietly watching, before disappearing between some of the taller monuments to the dead.

'There's someone down there,' I said.

'What?' Smiler looked at me doubtfully. 'Where?'

'He was just there,' I said, pointing down the now empty grave-lined avenue.

He stepped back through the lines, looking along each in turn before returning.

'There's nobody there,' he shook his head dismissively.

'He's dressed all in black – it must be him.'

'Who's him?'

'Him who did it.'

'We're in a cemetery, for fuck's sake. Everybody is wearing black. Anyway, why would anyone be after you?'

'Why are we running away?'

'Because Migsy wanted you out of there.'

We sat in an uncomfortable silence, on tenterhooks, until Smiler received a text. For all his supposed scepticism, he'd sat with the gun in his hand, looking around anxiously, jumping when the *ping* told him that the car was waiting at the gate. Perhaps it was the cemetery, something built in, instilling fear as he stood up and glanced over his shoulder before leading me towards the intricate sandstone gateway, calmly entering its central tunnel, but hurrying along towards the arch of light, where the Range Rover could be seen idling on Cherry Lane.

'How's Migs?' Smiler asked, hopping into the front passenger seat.

'Alright,' the driver replied, 'just flesh – shoulder.'

'Any idea who?'

'Not yet,' the driver reported calmly, before performing a swift U-turn and accelerating away.

Smiler was clearly struggling, wondering what to do with me as we cruised past the terraces.

'Drop me home,' I said.

'I can't,' he said, 'it might be–'

'I'm not involved in your gang wars. I'm not a target.'

'I know, but…' he was trying to call a number, presumably Migsy, getting no reply. He tutted as lowered the phone to his lap.

'It's fine,' I said. 'This is nothing to do with me.'

'I know, but–'

'But what?'

He relented, agreeing to drop me off just past the church, away from the police cars parked up outside. I climbed out opposite the pub, where the wake had spilled out onto the pavement. They stopped talking and looked over, but it didn't feel quite as negative as before; they seemed unsure, cracks forming, as I turned and walked back towards the blackened shell of the church, where I found Yoda and Brian deep in conversation, laughing, until they saw me and put their serious faces on.

'You OK?' Yoda asked, this afternoons rage apparently a memory.

'Yeah,' I said casually. 'Hello there, Brian. I suppose we need to have a chat.'

'We do,' he agreed softly. 'It's been a traumatic few days for you, I'd imagine, so why don't you go and get showered, and then we can talk.'

They were sitting in the living room when I returned downstairs, with a hot cup of tea waiting for me on the table. It all felt very relaxed, very reasonable.

'There are a few issues on the table that we need to talk about,' Brian opened. 'You're not in any sort of trouble at this stage. If anything, you're a victim.'

'Oh?' I was surprised.

*'Always the fucking victim,'* Peter chuckled.

'First of all, John has told me there are very good reasons for you wishing to carry out a funeral service for Paul Jackman.'

My eyes flicked across to Yoda.

'He hasn't given me any details,' Brian hastened to add, 'though he's assured me that your acquaintance was formed long before he went into crime, and that you'd had no further contact with him until very recently. Would you like to tell me the story? It's completely up to you.'

'We were in the same care home together, that's all,' I shrugged. 'When it was closed down, we all went our separate ways. John brought me into the Church, and Jacko went wherever he ended up.'

'And the recent contact?'

'He'd seen the articles in the paper. He'd been shot, and he knew he was going to die. He wanted to say goodbye.'

'Did he know who shot him?'

'No, he said there are a lot of things going on at the moment – outsiders trying to get a foothold.'

'OK,' Brian nodded. 'We're treating the shooting at the crem as a gang-related attack. This often happens when a big player departs the scene, so we're expecting more in the coming weeks, as new business opportunities present themselves and other organisations move in. Did you see who fired the shot?'

'No, I only saw a quick movement before hearing a very loud noise. I was on the floor before I knew it.'

'How did you get home? We couldn't locate you.'

'I ran across the cemetery. A member of the public picked me up, dropped me off here.'

'Who?'

'I don't know.'

'You don't know?'

'I'm in fucking shock here,' I snapped, wide-eyed for dramatic effect.

'What about the church? Any idea who might have done that? Can you think of anybody that could have a motive?'

'I suppose there are the other gangs, victims, their relatives. Jacko probably had plenty of enemies that might have got a kick out of disrupting the service.'

'Go on,' Brian urged, taking notes.

'There's also Fr Williams's victims, and their families.'

'Uh-huh.'

'The locals. Some of them have been a bit threatening.'

'Oh, like who?'

'I met with the Know-alls, who made it clear that faith has been lost in the Church.'

'Anybody else spring to mind?'

'Plenty of traditional-minded church goers were against the service going ahead.'

'No, no, no,' Yoda objected.

'They formed picket lines outside,' I continued, 'and a placard was left in the church, carrying a biblical reference.'

'What did it say?' Yoda asked.

'Revelation twenty-one eight.'

'Which is?' Brian asked, pen poised.

'But the fearful, and unbelieving, and the abominable, and murderers, and whoremongers, and sorcerers, and idolaters, and all liars, shall have their part in the lake which burneth with fire and brimstone.'

'That could be a goer,' Brian nodded.

'It's not the fucking Da Vinci Code,' Yoda replied angrily. 'It's not a goer.'

'Anything else?' Brian asked.

'No,' I said.

'Jesus,' he sighed, leaning back and blowing out his cheeks. 'How can the Church have so many enemies?'

'Ah, there is one more,' I recalled, smiling. 'The bloke who stands at the top of the road. I don't know who he is, though.'

'You've mentioned him before.'

'Yeah, I get the feeling he's one of the victims. It's just the way he carries himself.'

'We have an idea who he is, and he's our chief suspect at the moment. His house is being watched, but we don't have enough evidence to make a case at this stage. You're right, by the way. He is one of the victims.'

'So, what are you going to do?' I asked, concerned.

'We'll bring him in for questioning at some stage, I imagine.'

'But you've got nothing on him.'

'He's got strong motive, not to mention past arson convictions from his youth.'

'Woah there,' Yoda interjected, 'we have to be very careful with this. The whole place could erupt if you go in heavy-handed.'

'The church erupted last night,' Brian said. 'There's nothing left to be concerned about on that front.' He turned to me. 'And you, what are you going to do now?'

'I've no idea.'

'Move to another local church?' Yoda suggested.

'We've already burnt our bridges there, if you'll pardon the pun.'

'We'll worry about that tomorrow,' he frowned.

'The final issue is the holding of a service inside a dangerous structure,' Brian said, a sterner tone tinting his voice as he leaned towards me. 'What you did was extremely negligent, and it was pure luck on your behalf that the structure was sound.'

'The firemen–'

'Don't give me any of that shit!' Bad Cop Brian interrupted. 'You were nowhere to be found, and then all of a sudden you pop up in the church just in time for the service. You could face charges for what you did, but for the moment, I'm willing to put it down to naïve stupidity.'

I was about to answer back, but Yoda held his finger up, stopping me.

'Don't say a word,' he said. 'He's helping you out here, and he's right. You *were* naïve and stupid.'

'Thanks,' I muttered, as Peter silently pulled a knife across his throat.

'We'll chat more tomorrow,' Good Cop Brian returned. 'For now, I'm sure you'll want to get some rest.'

'Can I speak to him first?' I asked, as Brian stood to leave.

'What?' he looked confused.

'Your suspect. Can I speak with him before you make an arrest?'

'Why?'

'I'll be able to tell you if he's the character who stands at the top of the road. There's also somebody else it could be.'

'Who?'

'Knock Out, from The Know-alls. Can't you arrest him instead?'

'He's connected to the High Rip,' Brian said, his interest piqued. 'What makes you think it was him?'

I recounted his aggression towards me, and his mocking performance at the fire, before turning my attention back to the chief suspect.

'Maybe it will soften the impact if I speak with him first?'

'This is official police business. It's not like the television shows, where all and sundry get involved – Silent bloody Witness.'

'Rosemary and Thyme,' Yoda added with a smirk.

'Do my fucking head in them two,' Brian complained, packing his bag to leave. 'Keep your nose out, I mean it.'

'If he didn't do it, he doesn't need the police knocking on his door, accusing him of destroying the church,' I called after him, as he went into the hallway.

'Keep your nose out,' he repeated, his final say on the matter, as he gently closed the front door behind him.

'It hardly seems fair,' I said.

'What?' Yoda asked, slumped in his chair, looking more tired than I'd ever seen him before.

'That being abused in the past justifies further pain in the future.'

'When you put it like that,' he replied mindfully. 'Motive is a much cleaner phrase.'

I crashed down in the chair opposite, decompressing, wondering if I could keep going until I disappeared.

'What a day,' I mumbled, letting out a childish giggle.

'I'm meeting with the ABC tomorrow,' he said. 'See what we can sort out.'

# CHAPTER 9

OF THE END OF THE BEGINNING OF

I tried the doorbell twice, getting no response, all the while glancing nervously at an unmarked car parked further up the road, knowing that they would be calling this in, so I'd have to move quickly. I pressed the bell again, nothing, so reverted to the knocker, a huge brass lion's head on a white UPVC door, making a hollow banging sound as I rapped urgently, small splits becoming visible in the plastic beneath. A light came on, revealing blurred movement through the frosted glass before the door was pulled open, catching on its chain, and immediately starting to close until I pushed my foot into the gap.

'Get the fuck away from my door,' a woman snapped, as she tried to kick my foot out. 'How dare you come to this house.'

'I need to speak to Danny,' I said pleadingly. 'The police are coming for him – they think he burnt down the church.'

'It wasn't our Danny, but I'm glad somebody put a match to it, now fuck off!' she shouted, succinct and concise.

'Please, I need to speak with him.'

I heard the chain rattling before the door swung open, a smile automatically forming on my lips as a man flew out and struck me on the chin; Danny, I presumed. I raised my arms to protect myself, crouching as lightweight blows rained down on me, stinging when touching the still tender burns, but none scoring any points as he vented his anger.

Patience was the key, I decided, as I heard his breathing become ragged, his fists gradually losing power, so I started to speak.

'Danny, I'm here to help. Danny–'

I was about to stand up when something hit me on the back of the head, hard, like a hammer, my vision flashing white for a second as I staggered backwards.

'Ow!' I cried, recoiling, and then looking up to see the head of a brush swinging towards me again.

'Fuck off, you dirty little bastard,' his mum screamed, as I ducked out of the way, hearing it whoosh through the air above me.

Her eyes were wide, wild, she looked deranged, like a berserker, swinging the brush in big arcs above her before she released it, like a hammer, spinning towards me, barely missing, before she ran back into the house.

'Danny, the police are coming,' I continued, trying to sound calm, 'we need to talk.'

He had his hands on his knees, breathing heavily. He only looked around nineteen; he wasn't George Formby. He shook his head as he carried on panting, before launching a kick that flew through the air, missing like the broom.

'We haven't got much time,' I implored, stepping back into the road and flicking off my dog collar. 'We need to talk. Forget that I'm a priest – there's no church now anyway. I just don't want the police storming in and dragging you off down to the station. You don't deserve that.'

'Just leave me alone,' he said, breathless.'

'You don't have to talk, but please listen to what I have to say.'

His mother reappeared in the doorway and launched a bucket of water in my direction, the translucent liquid seeming to hover for a split-second, deforming and changing shape, before crashing onto the pavement, leaving splash marks on my trousers. I leaped to one side as the bucket itself came flying at me next, her anger ensuring that it strayed off target.

'*Fuck off!*' she screeched again, leaving little space for doubt.

'*Going well,*' Peter giggled.

'OK, OK,' I conceded, backing off, picking up my collar, 'but if you need to speak then I'm here for you, Danny. It doesn't need to be as a priest.'

I turned to walk away, his mother continuing to hurl insults down the road as I went, with neighbours emerging on to their front doorsteps to join in.

'Shame.'

'Shame on you.'

'Wanker,' shouted a little girl with pigtails and no front teeth.

Curtains twitched, as voyeurs followed the commotion; the bucket skidded past me, breaking into bright-coloured splinters as I turned at the end of the road.

'*We need to speak,*' Peter mocked. '*Talk to a Priest?*'

I stopped by the church, staring at it for a while, now just a charred shell, a ruin, standing proudly above the city, still beautiful, but I could also see its truth. Its beauty was perverse, an illusion, concealing the corruptions that had happened within. It had always been a shell, forever tainted.

'*There's nothing here for you now,*' Peter said.

I'd been too eager to hear its sweet words, I realised; to see the images it had painted in my mind with promises of a future, of salvation, in flickering candles and stained-glass light. I should have gone with instinct, stayed strong and never entered its doors, but like a fool, I'd been blinded by its splendour, a hypocrite, taken in by its polished veneer.

*I've achieved nothing here*, I thought, a smile coming to my lips. *It's just been constant fighting for weeks on end.*

I walked to the step to find a stack of newspapers waiting for me, images of the funeral and the burning church making for a dramatic front cover:

*ATONEMENT*

I rolled them up and put them in the bin. There was nothing to be gained from reading.

Within minutes, I'd gathered all my belongings and laid them out on the bed; back to living out of bags, with no idea what I was going to do or where I was going to go.

*'Running again,'* Peter jeered, as I looked in the mirror, watching my face contort, mimicking the look of rage, the fury of Danny's mother, scrunching my features, eyes narrow and teeth bared, until I was interrupted by a thumping on the door.

*Who's first?* I wondered, walking down the hallway.

*'Round one,'* Peter giggled.

'What the fuck did you think you were doing?' Brian spat, barging in, pushing me into the hallway and then slamming the door closed behind him.

No sign of Yoda.

'I couldn't just let you go in and arrest him. You've got nothing on him, he's a victim,' I shouted back, matching his anger.

'He's our chief suspect. We told you that in confidence, and then you go around there like a loose cannon, telling him we're on our way.'

'I went around to see for myself – to see if he's the one who's been watching me.'

'And is he?'

'No.'

'That doesn't mean he didn't torch the place.'

'Even if he did, I'd forgive him.'

'Oh yeah, love a bit of forgiveness you lot, don't you?'

'You've got absolutely nothing on him. How can you barge in and arrest him when you've got nothing? And don't give me that intent bullshit. Something bad happened to him in the past, so it must be him?'

'It makes no difference what you think,' he screamed. 'He could have destroyed vital evidence by now. What were you thinking?'

'I was thinking he needed protecting,' I screamed louder.

'Bit late in the day for the Church to start caring, isn't it, after what you people did to him?'

'It's all I can do.'

He lunged at me, reaching forward, grabbing me by the collar, his knuckles under my chin, lifting my head as he pushed me back against the wall.

'These people don't need protecting,' he said through gritted teeth. 'They don't feel things like normal people. They're not afraid – they're feral.'

I could feel the spray off his spit hitting me in the face, tasting his breath as he came in close, squaring up to me. A face pushed into mine had always been a weakness, a hair trigger, so I put my hand to his chest and pushed him back hard, sending him staggering backwards, landing on his back, a look of surprise briefly crossing his features before the anger returned. I walked after him, standing over as he climbed back to his feet.

'He's not the man, standing, watching.'

'I know,' he hissed. 'That man is from a much higher authority. Just because they knocked the home down doesn't mean they went away. They're coming to take you back.'

I felt dizzy, reaching out for the wall, something solid, as the ground beneath my feet started to shift.

He knew.

'Get – get out,' I stammered.

'John's not here to look after you now,' he taunted.

'He's not here to look after you, either.'

'You need to decide which side you're on, sunshine.'

'What do you mean, "side?" I'm not on anyone's *side*, sunshine.'

'You know exactly what I mean. We can't protect you from them if you don't play the game. There are rules.'

'Who's them?'

'The people you're mixing with. The people who are shooting your front door. The people who are burning down your church. The people you are tipping off. The people from this fucking estate. I swear, this city would be a million times better off if they dropped a bomb on this place.'

'Just close the door behind you on your way out,' I said, turning my back on him, walking into the living room.

'I don't know why I'm wasting my breath. You'll be gone in a few days anyway, or beaten up, or dead,' he shouted after me.

'Don't waste your breath, then, just fuck off,' I replied, waiting for the door to slam; it slammed, and the house returned to silence.

*'What are you waiting for?'* Peter whispered. *'Just go.'*

'Where?' I asked, open to suggestions.

Another knock drew me from the conversation. This one was different, gentle.

*'Round two, ding-ding!'*

'Alright Migs,' I brightened, opening the door wide, beckoning him through to the living room, 'you're alive. Should you really be out?'

'Yeah, I'm OK. Bullet went right through, came out the other side. Just another scar to impress the ladies with,' he winked, waving his arm in its sling. 'Just got to wear this bloody thing for a few weeks. What were the bizzies after? I kept my distance until they were gone.'

'Ah, they're just pissed off because I tried to speak with their suspect. Probably fair enough, I suppose.'

'Upsetting everyone as usual,' he grinned.

'Any idea who did it?' I asked, gesturing towards his shoulder.

'Not really,' he shrugged. 'Nobody seems to be making any moves yet. It doesn't really make sense.'

'What do you mean?'

'Well, we thought it might have marked the start of something big – someone trying to move in while we're supposedly at our most vulnerable, but,' he shrugged again, 'nothing. Are you going somewhere?' He glanced down at the bags piled up in the corner.

'Not much left for me here,' I said. 'I haven't even got a church anymore.'

His smile dropped into a frown.

'Can't you just work in another church, until they've fixed this one?' he asked.

'Not after Jacko's funeral,' I said. 'Maybe I was only supposed to come back for a short time, say my goodbyes. Who knows?'

'Just wait a bit,' he said, lifting a bag on to the table, 'wait, wait, wait. I don't know if you're aware, but Jacko woke up again before he died.'

'Yeah, Smiler mentioned it. When was that, the day after I saw him?'

'Yeah, he died a couple of hours later. He wasn't conscious for long, but I think you being there had a massive effect on him. He went peacefully, without anger, without hate, if that makes sense. Before that, it was as if he was getting ready for battle, the way he used to get.'

'Was he with it? Could he talk?'

'Yeah, and the main talking point was you.'

He looked up at me before taking a package out of his bag.

The breath went out of me as I looked down at the plain folder on the table, as Jacko came back from the dead, the panic rising – *breathe, breathe* – but I couldn't. I slouched down in a chair, feeling those weights of the past returning, piling up on me, invisible cords tightening, constricting me.

'What is it?' I managed to ask, terrified to hear the answer.

'He left you a type of trust, I suppose you might call it, or a donation.'

'He left me money?' I said, thinking that it didn't sound like Jacko, but then perhaps it did, as it occurred to me that I hardly knew him as an adult.

'No,' he said, 'he left you a club that he was about to open. He thought the Church could probably do with the profits, and that it would allow you to build something good here – to implement all your ideas.'

'A nightclub?'

'Yes.'

'What would I do with a nightclub?' I laughed.

'You take the profits and do some good for the community, for the estate, for the city,' he frowned, looking slightly offended.

'I can't do that,' I said, shaking my head, 'it's mad. I don't know anything about running a nightclub.'

'You don't have to. We'll put people in there to run it – you just spend the profits.'

'But I'm a priest. The Church can't take money from Jacko. They'd never accept it. It's wrong on every level.'

'They'd never be able to trace it back to him. Besides, most of his businesses are legal now. Half the people running them don't even realise who owns them. It's all clean.'

'I can't.'

'You've got to, he left it to you. These were the last words he spoke.'

'The Church would never accept it – the alcohol, the dancing, drugs. They'd think it was depraved.'

'Who gives a fuck what they think? It's an opportunity for you to create something new, and anyway, the Church has been brewing alcohol for centuries. What about those Trappist Monks? They make the best ale there is. Strong, too.'

I leaned back in my chair as nausea rose through my body. I felt like vomiting.

'It's not even a nightclub yet,' he said, 'it's still not finished. It's a building, and you do need a building at least?'

'Where is it?'

'Down on the industrial park. It's basically a massive shed between Greaty and Scotty Road. It's even in your parish.'

'So, it's a shed, not a church.'

'Is there a special way a church has to look? Does it say in the Bible that a church has to look like this?'

'Well, no, but–'

'Do you even need a church to talk to God?' Can you be religious without going to church?'

'Yeah, of course, but you'll miss out on the sharing aspect of–'

'So, it's more of an institutional thing, then, the Church? A brand selling God, a few competitors doing the same?'

'Fucking hell, Kierkegaard is alive and well in Liverpool.'

'What?'

'Nothing, just religious joke,' I said, disappointed in myself.

'Oh, I don't know, it's all over my head,' he sighed. 'Would make a nice change from the pubs taking over old churches, though.'

The corners of my mouth turned up.

'There is something attractive in that,' I agreed, concealing the spark of excitement he'd lit in my mind, at the prospect defying the flow of churches slowly being absorbed by the city, turned into bars, apartments and leisure centres, the slow death of religion. 'Keep hold of that for now,' I said, pushing the unopened folder back across the table towards him.

'You weren't planning on leaving tonight, were you?' he asked, changing the subject. 'Fancy a pint?'

'You've just been shot,' I smiled.

'So?'

'Honestly, I'd love one, but I'm not exactly welcome in the pubs around here.'

'Things might have changed after the service.'

'Any credit I gained with that, I lost by going to Danny Morgan's house. Him and his mum went berserk.'

'Well, what did you expect?'

'I was trying to find out if he was the bloke at the top of the street, and to warn them that the police were on their way to pick him up.'

'Your heart was in the right place, but you definitely fucked up there.'

I could only nod in agreement, letting out a small sigh.

'Come on, what's the worst that can happen?' he clasped me on the shoulder with his good hand.

'In this place, I dread to think.'

'Let's go,' he marched out into the hallway and threw the front door wide open. 'Let's go,' he repeated, almost goading me, speaking with a bit more urgency. 'If you're leaving, it might be our last chance.'

We entered the Mere Bank, its chatter boisterous until I walked through the door. People looked across, silent, before resuming their conversations.

'See what you mean,' Migsy murmured, as we made our way to the bar.

'Peroni please, Jack,' Migsy called to the barman, who nodded and then looked at me.

'Same for me please,' I added quietly, looking down, too nervous to ask for Stella as I inspected the slop trays and mats, expecting to be ignored.

Surprisingly, two pints were placed in front of us, in their tall, elegant glasses, vase-like, with condensation running down the sides.

'On the house,' the barman announced, his cheerful voice not matching his appearance; skin slightly yellow, nicotine-stained and old for his age. 'Your service was outstanding, Father. Everyone's been talking about it, a great send off.'

'Thank you,' I replied, rather taken aback.

'And, you put your neck on the line to make sure it went ahead,' he added, 'which a lot of people around here appreciate.'

'Thank you,' I said again.

'You're blushing,' Migsy teased, as the barman left us to our drinks.

'It's been so long since anyone gave me any praise,' I allowed myself a smile, 'I've forgotten how to handle it.'

The pints kept flowing, as the locals took turns sending their offerings to our table whilst buying their own rounds. They didn't come over to speak, just tipped a glass when the barman pointed out who'd paid, and though I didn't recognise most of the faces, it still felt like a step forward, a rare moment of optimism, despite all that had happened. I dared to think I'd won their trust, a bittersweet thought, considering the high price I'd had to pay.

*'Or perhaps they're thinking that this is goodbye. Close the door behind you on the way out,'* Peter mocked, parroting my words to Brian.

Lucky was the first to come over and break the deadlock, his bifocals glinting like shells in the light.

'I erm, spoke to a few people,' he said, 'and it wasn't Knock Out that torched the church. He was out with the lads.'

'We were all a bit emotional,' I replied noncommittally, a sit-on-the-fence comment, the best I could muster.

'If he was here, I'm sure he'd come over and apologise for his behaviour when it went up,' he shuffled his feet, looking a bit awkward.

'You reckon?' Migsy laughed, taking another swig of his pint.

'He was bladdered,' Lucky scratched nervously at the back of his head, 'but that's no excuse, I know.'

'It's alright,' I smiled, wanting to put him out of his misery.

We both knew the truth; our mouths were saying one thing whilst our minds thought another, but we were keeping the conversation cordial as we tried to lay foundations.

'Same with Danny Morgan,' he said. 'His mum said he was at home that night, and,' he paused, his tone lightening, 'I believe her.'

'Please pass on my apologies to her,' I said bashfully. 'That was poor judgement on my part today.'

'It was, but I think people realise that you were doing it for the right reasons, so don't beat yourself up.'

He was giving me space, the benefit of the doubt, on points that he might previously have seized upon. It made me want to smile and laugh with him; to find common ground.

'They took Danny in earlier today,' he said, serious again.

'It's not him,' I shook my head.

'He'll be alright. This is nothing compared to what he's been through in the past, and he's got good people around him. Anyway, what's next for you?'

'I don't know, now that there isn't a church to serve.'

'It was nothing personal, you understand. It's the institution that people are angry with, and you just happened to be there to take it out on.'

'It's OK, they've every right,' I accepted the olive branch.

He nodded, turning to leave before turning back. 'Oh, while I remember, we may have something on the bloke hanging around at the top of the road.'

'Really? Who?' I asked urgently, excitedly.

'It's a bit far-fetched,' he looked to Migsy, 'not much more than a guess, I'd say.'

'Who?' Migsy echoed, impatiently.

'One of the lads reckons it's the Nightman.'

'Who?' I asked.

'Nah, what would he be watching a church for?' Migsy tutted, sounding irritated, dismissing it out of hand.

'Like I said, someone seen him and reckons it's him, but,' Lucky sighed, 'it doesn't make a lot of sense.'

'He has been quiet for a while,' Migsy allowed, lifting his head, looking pensive.

'Who's the Nightman?' I asked.

'A pain in the arse,' Migsy replied. 'He basically taxes the dealers – skims cash from them. Does the same with prostitutes, security, that sort of thing.'

'And what happens if they don't pay?'

'They do,' Migsy answered. 'He's horrible. Tortured a few of ours. We've been trying to take him out of the game for years, slippery bastard,' he ranted, as he took one of his phones out and started texting.

'Great,' I gulped.

'Ah, don't worry, it won't be him,' Migsy said. 'No money in burning down churches, is there?'

'Suppose not. Would he do it to get at Jacko, though?'

'Nah, not his style. It's just business with him, pure and simple. He'll be in a dark hole somewhere, upsetting somebody else.'

'Well, just passing on what I heard,' Lucky said, shrugging his shoulders. 'Don't forget, somebody did shoot your front door.'

'That's true,' I glanced at Migsy.

'Cheers, Alan, let us know if you hear anything else,' he said, frowning as Lucky returned to his group of friends.

'Not a very scary name, is it?' I said.

'It is in this city,' Migsy laughed, still tapping away at his phone. 'We've managed to get a copy of the police surveillance videos of the procession from the church to the crem. I'll ask them to take a look, see if they can spot him. Just can't see it being him though.'

'Any reason he'd want to shoot you?'

'Only if I was in his way,' he paused for a second, 'or if there's a price on my head. That could tempt him, if it was big enough.'

He swapped sim cards and continued texting.

Eventually, the curtains were closed and the door was locked, as drinking continued after last orders. Pints kept arriving whilst we talked about Jacko, and what we'd been doing since we left the home, avoiding the times before, our shared histories. More people had started approaching the table, their inhibitions lowered, emboldened by the sight of others doing the same.

'This is Judy,' Migsy announced, introducing a pale, waif-like girl who appeared at my elbow. In my pissed-up state, her long blonde hair appeared to be made of light.

'I just wanted to say thank you for the service you did for Jacko,' she said in a low, timid voice.

She seemed fragile, delicate, like she was made of glass.

'You knew him?' I asked, surprised.

'He helped me out,' she nodded, 'got me back on my feet. I owe him a lot.'

'Oh, that's nice,' I said lamely, nervous, my mind empty as I kept putting the glass to my lips, taking little sips.

'When's your next service?' she asked. 'I'd like to come.'

My heart started beating that little bit faster, wondering if she was taking the piss.

'Erm, I'm not sure. The church is…' I just stopped talking, staring at her.

'You'll figure it out,' she replied, touching my arm, flashing her white teeth in a big smile, crow's feet forming at the corners of her eyes. 'See you later,' she floated off to rejoin her group, all men, crowding around, predatory but she seemed confident around them, her body language self-assured, incongruous with the brittle, easily breakable first impression I got. She'd been to dark places in her life; there was an inner strength that I recognised.

'You're catching flies,' Migsy said.

'What?'

'You're catching flies,' he repeated, interrupting my thoughts. 'Your mouth's hanging open.'

I slammed it shut and looked at him, not having to ask.

'She was a heroin addict,' he explained. 'Jacko made sure she got cleaned up. She works in one of the companies, doing well for herself.'

'A drug dealer helping a drug addict?' I asked sarcastically.

'There was nobody else. The refuges were closed down, so she was homeless. He's helped a few off the streets, usually victims of domestic violence or with mental health issues.'

'There must be some sort of official support structure they can use?'

'All gone,' he shook his head, 'there's nothing now. The only way she could get a bed for a night in a safe place was by committing a crime, until Jacko stepped in.'

'Wouldn't be because she's quite attractive, by any chance?'

'Nah, he wasn't like that. Could have had a different woman every night if he'd wanted to, but he wasn't really interested.'

'And you?' I asked.

'Nah,' he looked down at the floor. 'You?'

I just shook my head as my eyes flicked back across to Judy, who was laughing with her group.

'He tried to turn a blind eye to the bad stuff – the damage it caused to ordinary people, and he helped out where he could,' Migsy picked up again, getting us back on track.

'That's a bit, erm–'

'Hypocritical. Yeah, it is, but then who isn't?'

'Who's she with?' I asked, noting that they all looked around my age.

'Ah, they're alright them lads. The one with the dark hair, that's Willow – Willow Wonka. The younger lad next to him, dressed as a wizard, is Moat the Quote, Jeff Moat.'

'Why is he dressed as a wizard?'

'He runs a fancy dress business – wears the costumes he hasn't rented out. He's a different character every day.'

'I think I saw him dressed as a Roman Centurion the other week. Where does "the Quote" come from?'

'I don't think anybody has ever actually heard him say anything he's come up with on his own – he talks in quotations. The lad on the end, the ugly bastard with the big quiff, is Trev, also known as Discharge. He's one dirty dog.'

'Oh,' was all I could think to say, feeling slightly repulsed.

'I think we'll be seeing a lot more of his type in the future – the first generation raised on internet porn. They go one of two ways, numb or the opposite. He'll stick his dick in anything, pay for it if he needs to, keeps pushing boundaries. Name any STD, he's probably had it. Was getting treated for brothel sprouts, last I heard.'

'What?' I grimaced, scrunching up my features.

'Genital warts,' he laughed. 'Some of the places he's been, he's probably the bravest bloke in here.'

'Who else is there?' I asked, looking around.

'Plato is over there, or Craig Platt, to give him his proper name,' he nodded towards a man in the corner, with a large beard and Fedora, who was talking to a group of similarly-dressed friends; extended adolescents, wearing skinny jeans, Buddy Holly glasses and either checked or paisley shirts; hipsters, their beards quivering as they spoke in a huddle, avoiding the status quo around them, even though it was anything but normal.

'After the Greek philosopher?'

'Yeah, he's a really intelligent lad – could have been anything he wanted to be with a bit of direction.'

'They look like a gang of Amish that found a time machine,' I laughed. 'What does he do?'

'Nothing – whatever he wants to do, he's free, as he'll no doubt tell you. If you want to lose half a day, just say hello to him, and he'll gab the leg off you with his philosophies on life, hence Plato.'

The speaker system hummed into life, seemingly out of nowhere.

'Fuck, they've put the karaoke on,' Migsy looked over at the side of the bar.

Suddenly, Mekon Don's voice was everywhere, amplified, interrupting all conversations, 'Testing, testing,' before going quiet again.

A burst of laughter erupted from the far corner, followed by another, getting more hysterical.

'That'll be Degs in the middle of that somewhere,' Migsy pointed towards a gathering crowd. 'He's had it tough. Used to be in the army, fought in Iraq, lost his eldest in Afghanistan, though never talks about it. Now he basically flits from job to job, zero hours contracts and agency work for peanuts, works all hours trying to support his family. Whenever he has a skinful, he can only laugh so much before he pisses himself – loses control of his bladder, just a little bit at a time.'

I grimaced again.

'He's alright. He got injured during the war, but he's never told anybody about it. The others have clicked on, though, so it happens every time he comes out. It's become a bit of a competition.'

'Can't he go to the doctors or something, get it sorted out?'

'I'm assuming there's nothing they can do. He has the choice of either going out or staying in and letting it get on top of him. He spends most of his night with people trying to make him laugh, and with so little to laugh about in his life, maybe it's not a bad way to be. He was wearing nappies for a while, but then he'd never go the toilet. Just went quiet every now and then, staring off into the distance.'

'You're winding me up.'

'I'm not,' he laughed.

'It sounds humiliating. How does he live like that?'

'He's had all sorts of issues, but he's a strong man. When he first got back, he was trouble – wanted to fight the world, full of rage, wanting to show he was still a soldier, a man. We thought he'd end up going down. Him and Big Jim fought for an hour once, nonstop. Forget Ali and Frazier, *that* was the fight of the century. In the end, he internalised everything, stopped talking with his fists, stopped talking all together. He's been to some very dark places, but now, hopefully, he's through the worst of it. His battle is to keep his family fed and clothed these days.'

'And that?' I asked, pointing to a lady at the bar, just as she was downing a bright-pink shot.

'That's Joyce. Her husband works nights in the tunnels, so she comes here and gets drunk most evenings.'

'What's she drinking?'

'Gaviscon chaser. She's got a hiatus hernia – they all have around here. It's like Alien, they breathe acid.'

The first bars of a familiar song started playing; Mekon Don had the microphone, and was doing jerky movements with his arms and legs.

'Oh, baby, baby,' he sang, before lowering the microphone to dance again, as though electric shocks were coursing through his body, sending his limbs into spasms, all independent, doing their own thing.

'Oh, baby, baby,' he repeated.

I burst out laughing; I couldn't help it.

'You don't want to see this,' Migsy said, indicating the dozen-or-so empty pint glasses. 'Shall we get off?'

'Yeah, go on,' I agreed, standing up, reaching out to the bar to regain my balance, the local Britney singing us out as we walked towards the door.

'Hit me, baby, one more time…'

I started laughing again as we left the noise of the pub behind, staggering into the empty road.

'I'm fucking hammered,' I confessed, the world swaying as I put my hand on the nearest wall.

'Moi aussi,' Migsy grinned, 'but we needed this after the last few weeks. A release valve, essential to our mental well-being.'

'They're all a bit mental in there, aren't they?'

'Nah, I only pointed out some of the more interesting characters, and they're why I love it here – I *fucking* love it here,' he shouted down the empty road, laughing. 'There's difference here, real characters, and people accept what they are, creased and wrinkled, not ironed out – not the same dull, homogenised folk, trudging along within their parameters, bored out of their minds.' He staggered back and raised up his arms, flinching before lowering the injured one again. 'This place is rich, instinctive, raw. This is where footballers come from, where boxers come from, where real culture comes from, whether it's music, art, writing, politics – whatever. It never comes from comfort, it comes from the shitty end of the stick. The rest of society is a desert, a *fucking* desert! These people are free, creative, imaginative – they refuse to toe the line, doing things their own way. They'll tell you where to shove your societal norms.'

He put his arm down, lowering his voice along with it.

'At the same time, these lives are precarious, vulnerable, with no money or work – or not enough money, doing shitty, menial, dead-end jobs that grind them down, take their pride and barely support them, giving them just about enough to live on. They die young, and their children enter the same cycle, taught in the same shitty schools with nothing at the end, repeating their parents' mistakes, natural talent pouring down the drain. They're hard as nails, but they're also being walked on, bullied, by somebody they can't fight.'

'Who?'

'The government,' he slurred, 'who else? This place might not even be here in a couple of years if the developers get their way. The Council's been told they have to sell their prime-value properties, and they're fucked for money with all the cuts. Everything else has been shut down – all they can do now is sell things. The same people who did town have got their eyes on this, the best spot in the city, to bring back the wealthy, the Everton Villas.'

'You mean regenerate it?'

'It's not regeneration, its social cleansing,' he snapped. 'The people around here won't be the ones living in those houses. They'll be cast to the wind, ending up in some shitty estate on the outskirts, where nobody knows anybody.'

I stood swaying on my feet, wondering if Migsy was one of those people that started crying when they were pissed. I was surprised by the eloquence of his sermon.

'I've got a few in the fridge, if you fancy it?' I offered, hearing the slurring in my own voice, feeling like I could be sick at any moment.

'Nah, fuck it, let's go to town,' he pulled himself together, putting his hands on my shoulders. 'You up for it?'

'But you've just been shot.'

'Just a flesh wound – helps you get pissed quicker.'

I could hardly stand up; my vision blurry as the streetlights left streaks in my eyes.

'Yeah,' I said, 'go on then.'

A taxi dropped us outside the doorway of a large brick Victorian warehouse on the Ropewalks, part of the city's merchant past, a toast rack of long, straight streets built for twisting ropes, now appropriated by bars and clubs, a twenty-four-hour party, with all of its hedonistic associations. There were people everywhere, beautiful young people making their way to the next neon sign, alive with the fearless, drunken optimism of youth. The sailors of old would have approved.

Migsy marched straight to the head of the queue, the bouncers nodding their heads in deference, as if saluting a lord, Sir Migs, who nodded back and then ushered us into the darkness.

It felt hot, sweaty, as a room of writhing bodies emerged before us. The music was loud, its bass vibrating through my soul, as a beer was placed into my hands and I took a mouthful.

'Cheers,' I raised it high, as we stood there shouting, unable to hear each other as the music coursed through us.

Without realising it, I'd started moving. *Fuck it, I'm going to dance*, I thought, whilst Migsy was busy shaking hands with an entourage of people that wanted to be seen with him, hoping his infamy would enhance their credibility, pump them up in front of their Facebook peers. I wanted to scream in the middle of the dancefloor; it felt primitive. I could feel my soul emptying, an exorcism, as I cast aside the demons, the weights and ties that defined me, restrained me, allowing myself to be lifted by the music. I was lost to the crowd, a beautiful crowd of smiling faces, silhouettes revelling in the lasers and lights, as we all became one, our limbs moving in a euphoric frenzy, forgetting everything about ourselves, only the music mattering as I merged with them.

People were taking pills, swigging them down, faces gurning, grinning, teeth grinding as the effects kicked in, an austerity-driven release. The toilets were a more private affair, a different market of self-proclaimed VIP's following formal rituals; gentle snorting sounds preceding their emergence from closed cubicles in ones and twos, focussed, wired, all rolled up banknotes and traces of powder, the ultimate versions of themselves.

*'A night on the lemo, lid.'*

Hours passed, and the crowd gradually thinned until the music came to an abrupt stop and the harsh lights came on, announcing an end to the revelry. People wore slightly stunned expressions, like they'd just woken up here, blinking as their red eyes adjusted to the light, as their bodies stopped moving, our shared experience proven temporal, fragmenting in different directions, souls flying back into individuals, back to normal lives. I wanted to stay with them, talk, carry on, but they were walking out of the door. My ears were ringing, and I was soaking with sweat, shaking with exertion, but I was the happiest I had been since I could remember. Migsy was standing at the end of the bar; handed me a shot of something as I joined him, followed by another.

'You look like you enjoyed yourself,' he smiled.

'Was great,' I replied, jubilant, 'really needed that. What time is it?'

'Just gone six,' he grinned, raising an eyebrow.

'Fuck, I'd better get off.'

'I'll come with you,' he said, downing another shot before staggering away from the support of the bar, leaning on me as we headed for the exit. 'See you, Niall,' he called over his shoulder, to no reply, as we walked past the bouncer, his forehead resting on the black-painted brick wall, as a pair of slim bare knees poked out from between his legs, a girl praying, no doubt, the lucky one chosen to make an offering to this muscular, deformed deity.

We opened the door into the daylight, blinking, our pupils dilating as we left the depravity of the night for the purity of early morning, standing, taking a few deep breaths before smiling at each other. People were sitting or lying on the pavements outside, quiet and at peace after a night of exertion.

'Let's go and see the club,' Migsy said.

'I can't do any more, Migs,' I shook my head, defeated, shivering, trembling, 'I'm done.'

'I don't mean carry on, I mean *the* club,' he jangled a set of freshly cut keys in front of me. '*Your* club.'

'Now?'

'Why not? You won't be good for anything later. Let's get brekkie up there, and then we'll go have a look,' he pointed towards a little greasy spoon, its window a magnifying glass, showing dishevelled clubbers tucking into mugs of coffee and full-English breakfasts, like bugs in a petri dish, on the tail end of whatever stimulants they'd put into their bodies.

I looked back at him; he could see I was about to say no.

'Please,' he implored, 'I made a promise to Jacko.'

'Alright,' I gave in, accepting that I had no choice.

We ate our breakfast rolls on the way to the taxi rank, my body appreciating its sparse nutrients, making me feel warmer, providing an element of control after the chemical-fuelled exertion. The reprieve proved temporary, however, as I stopped the taxi mid-journey, scrambling out before it had come to a complete halt, sending me sprawling across the pavement. I climbed back up to my hands and knees as the waves of nausea overwhelmed me, vomiting out the barely-digested food in a most unclerical manner, all over the dog piss-stained pavement.

*That smell*, I thought. *What the fuck am I doing?*

Migsy came up behind me, chuckling. 'Forgot to shout one thousand, two thousand, three thousand, you lightweight.'

'Travel sickness,' I replied, grinning, tasting the acid, as my fingers found purchase between the bricks of a wall and I tried to pull myself up, clinging like a free climber on El Capitan.

He burst out laughing, and then bent over and started vomiting right next to me, the sound of it setting me off again, as I glanced across at a silver thread of spittle hanging from his mouth, connecting him to the floor.

'Fucking lightweight,' I murmured, once I'd finished gagging, smiling, as the taxi sped off behind us, cutting his losses.

I felt good, cleansed, as we walked silently towards the industrial area on a relentlessly straight, featureless road. It was empty, with only the birdsong accompanying us. I was on autopilot, placing one foot in front of the other, automated like the traffic lights ahead, which came steadily closer, changing from red to amber to green, marshalling an empty road, just functioning for functioning's sake, a bit like me.

*If we weren't here to see them, would they exist?* I wondered.

The monotony was putting me on edge, the endless pattern of grey paving slabs bringing back the nausea. I could feel my mind beginning to unravel, thread by thread.

'Down here,' Migsy said, saving me from myself as he turned off down a narrow street, into the detail and decay of old dilapidated industrial units, with their crumbling brickwork and iron-framed windows, shards of broken glass shining, like jewels or jagged teeth. It was pure, unadulterated dereliction, something this area specialised in, as corroded corrugated roofs sent lines of rust and algae pouring down walls on to the pavement below, making them seem as one, merging with old cobbles poking out from beneath tarmac underfoot; the relentless passage of time.

'We bought all of these,' he declared, waving his arms around. 'The idea being, if the club takes off, we can do something with them.'

They were in such a piss-poor state, I couldn't have been less impressed. Hardly even buildings, they were mere elevations covered in fly-posters, their accumulated layers probably holding them up. He could sense my negativity; it must have been emanating from me, radiating in waves.

'I know what you're thinking,' he said, 'it's a dump. You can't polish a turd, all that sort of thing.'

I smiled apologetically, feeling guilty.

'You can put glitter on it though,' I joked, trying to lighten the mood as he looked at me inquisitively, confused, trying to figure out what I was thinking.

I turned, surprised to see movement ahead; other people, a few tired, pale-looking women standing in doorways, leaning on walls, alone or in pairs; short skirts, tight tops and flesh, lots of flesh. I looked back at Migsy.

'Skanks,' he said, 'coming towards the end of their shift, I'd imagine. There used to be a cat house down there, but everything's just falling apart here now.'

'Prefer "brass" myself,' the nearest one called, lifting her top, exposing her breasts. 'A happy ending to your night, lads?' She put her tongue over her top lip seductively.

I nearly jumped out of my skin, making her abandon her pose and break into a giggle, as I nervously walked to the other side of Migsy.

'What's wrong, never seen tits before?' she said, trying to look around him, to see where I was hiding.

'I have seen tits before,' I replied, regretting the words as soon as they left my lips.

We all paused and stared at one another for an uncomfortable moment.

'You're alright, thanks, love,' Migsy said calmly, 'we're not here for any of that.'

'What are you here for, then? This is all that's on offer around here, love,' she frowned, her small breasts pointing out in front of her, covered in goosebumps in the cool air.

I kept my eyes firmly on the ground, the scene transporting me back to the village, even though the girls couldn't be more different, at opposite ends of the spectrum; breasts that had everything, wanted for nothing, bored, rebelling against their privileged upbringing, ready to be caught in their safety net; the other breasts hoping I'd want to touch them, to put food in their mouths, a roof over their heads.

Without making eye contact, Migsy handed her a twenty-pound note. 'We're here to look at the club,' he said.

The money disappeared into her top as she pulled it down, covering herself. 'Cheers, love,' she said. 'any fags?'

He offered a cigarette, even lit it for her, before sending her back to the doorway, no business, no banter; her heels clattering on the pavement as we continued walking, none of the others approaching, as if some invisible signal had been given.

'There it is,' he announced dramatically, as we turned the corner to find a huge industrial shed looming before us.

It was strange, a hybrid, with original brickwork on the ground floor, and new matt-black metal cladding along the roof, resembling a curved shell. Like the church, it took my breath away, but in a different way; this place was without detail or craft; without artistic or historic influence, and yet it had a beauty. It was monolithic, minimal, brutal, its clean lines offset by the desolation of the surrounding estate, slowly decomposing in the background, giving the appearance of it having been picked up and dropped there.

'It's not finished yet,' Migsy said, trying to gauge what I was thinking. 'The whole thing is going to be covered in screens.'

'Eh?'

'You know, lights. The whole thing is going to be covered in lights or screens, or whatever.'

'Really?' I laughed, not sure if he was joking.

'They pretty much let us do what we wanted. It was going to take something big to get people out here, so we're going to cover it in its own technicolour dreamcoat,' he beamed. 'They design it all on a computer, and then you can make it do almost anything – change colour and all that.'

'Sounds like Blackpool,' I said, trying to picture it in my mind.

'Think more Vegas.'

'In Everton?'

He pulled the keys out of his pocket and unlocked the front door, a chemical smell of new materials wafting out, leaving a toxic taste in my mouth. I took a few deep breaths outside to keep the nausea at bay, before entering a lobby full of stacked boxes and packaging, with three sets of double doors in front. There was a counter to the right-hand side, and a room to the left.

'For the door staff,' Migsy explained, following my gaze.

The walls were exposed brick, giving the space a warmth, and as he pushed open the double doors and entered the main club, pausing on a tiny, dimly-lit area of floor, we contemplated the pitch-black void before us. Nothing was perceptible, we were on the edge of nothing; it felt like it could go on infinitely in any direction, up, down, left or right, like stepping into outer space, until he pressed a control panel and the lights slowly came on, illuminating the room. It was vast, a triple-height space, sleek, smooth and modern, housing single- and two-storey exposed brick structures, buildings removed from their original contexts, to be preserved like archaeological relics.

Essentially, a roof had been placed over the estate, changing the buildings into abstract, stand-alone objects, sculptures, pieces of art to be contemplated, interrogated for meaning against the clean blank surfaces. They had been manipulated to function as seating areas: a bar, a DJ booth and toilet blocks. The dance floor must have been a parking area in its previous life, a huge, empty swathe of land now dressed in a sprung wooden floor, with lighting booms and acoustic panels sailing overhead, to focus the experience on to revellers below. Huge, deep-purple velvet curtains and double-height mirrors completed the look, allowing for views into side areas away from the main dance floor. Whereas the church had been delicate and refined, this was a modern, tough, powerful blend of old meeting new, of soft velvet meeting decaying brick and exposed concrete.

'It's stunning,' I gasped, taking it all in, deja vu striking with a vengeance, as I recalled similar feelings with Yoda standing next to me only weeks before.

A huge smile illuminated Migsy's face, as he struggled to conceal his pride. 'A couple more weeks are needed on the outside,' he said, 'but the inside is pretty much there. Then, it's ready to open.'

'What's it called?'

'The Temple.'

A smile came to my lips, which quickly became a grin.

'Did you just make that up because we need a church?' I asked sarcastically. 'I'm surprised you didn't call it St Peter's.'

'Nah, that's nothing to do with it,' he laughed. 'It's because of the street names – Great Homer Street, Iliad Street, Virgil Street, all that Greek mythology stuff, hence the Temple.'

'It's not a good name for a church, actually,' I began, but he ignored me, cupping his hands around his mouth.

'Odin!' he shouted, his voice echoing off the hard surfaces, reverberating around the space. 'Odin! Send the wind to turn the tide, Odin!'

'That's not Greek mythology, you tit. That's Vikings.'

He was laughing hysterically as he started shouting again, 'Odin! Odin!' bending over, putting his hands on his knees.

I wasn't sure if he was going to be sick, as he swayed between silence and mirth.

'Ah, they're all the same, aren't they?' he giggled quietly, looking up as he regained control. 'All just pagans.'

'Polytheists,' I corrected, 'multiple gods.'

'Whatever,' he shrugged, putting an arm around my shoulder, walking us back towards the doorway, shifting from laughter to serious in two steps. 'There's, erm, one more thing I want to show you.'

'What?'

He looked agitated; the smile had changed to a look of mild panic, as he switched off the lights and locked the doors behind him.

'It's back at your place, in my bag,' he said.

'What is it?'

'I still don't know if I should show you,' he said, as we stepped back out into the morning, 'but I need to show somebody.'

I put the kettle on when we arrived at the house, the click rousing me as I stared at the bags lying in the corner, wondering whether we'd be staying or going. Migsy went into his bag and pulled out a large folder, looking nervous as I sat next to him at the table, exchanging it for a cup of coffee.

My apprehension was rising as I opened its cover, finding a neatly organised file, the brightly coloured tabs poking out of the side as I flicked through typed documents, lists of meaningless names, my present mental state preventing me from focussing, until I opened the first tab and leaped back off my chair, knocking my cup off the table, sending it smashing onto the floor as an arc of coffee sprayed against the wall. I wasn't sure if I'd let out a scream as I looked at Migsy, still seated at the table, looking down, fingers interlinked, face pale.

'This is my inheritance,' he said tonelessly, 'what he left me.'

I looked at the file again, seeing a face I recognised from the home, albeit much older. Reaching forward, my hand shaking, I turned the page, trying to control my emotions. It had addresses, employment details, maps, photographs and pictures of family: wife, children, grandchildren; each the same as I flipped between tabs and recoiled, seeing a face that I recognised immediately, one that my mind had blocked out. I could feel walls breaking down inside, smelling the tobacco and whisky on his breath as I slammed the folder closed, unable to bear the sight of it. We both sat in silence, the buzzing of the fridge the only sound in the room, the horrors of our shared past in one neat little file.

'There are thirty of them,' he said quietly. 'Each tab a different person.'

'I can't look at it,' I said, my head spinning, teetering on the edge, like my mind was about to collapse in on itself, implode, and there was nothing I could do to stop it.

I wanted to lie down and close my eyes, but I knew what would be waiting.

'Is it…' I started, not finishing the question.

'A kill list, yeah.'

I sat back down and put my head in my hands, swaying slightly, rocking. 'Maybe it's not,' I said. 'Maybe we could go to the police with it.'

'It's a fucking kill list. There's no way he'd have been interested in going to the police.'

'We'll never know now. It's up to you – to us,' I stammered, correcting myself quickly.

'We do know. Jacko was working his way through them, *killing* them.'

'Jesus,' I whispered.

'I just want it to go away,' he mumbled softly, looking down at the table. 'I wish somebody could just cut it out of my head – stop me thinking about it, remembering.'

'You don't have to do anything. Jacko's gone.'

'At the same time, I want to see every one of them dead for what they did.'

*'Every fucking one,'* Peter agreed.

He picked up the folder and put it back in his bag. I was relieved to see it disappear from sight, but I couldn't bear to see him take on the load alone.

'We can't do anything now,' I said, 'we're both a mess. Let's look at it properly when our heads are straight.'

'Will you even be here, then?' he glanced at my bags. 'You look like you're about to fuck off.'

'I'll be here.'

'I don't just mean the next few days.'

'I'll be here.'

'You haven't got a church.'

I smiled, and he returned it, both knowing I'd been outmanoeuvred, put on the spot.

'I'll be here,' I said again.

'Yeah?'

'Yeah.'

'I'm gonna get off,' he stood from his seat, looking relieved. 'Stuff to do tomorrow – today.'

'Crash here if you want to,' I offered, secretly pleading, not really wanting to be alone.

'Nah, something's come up.'

'Something's always coming up. What is it?'

'I got a text – they reckon it was the Nightman at the funeral. They've got him joining the crowd as we entered the crem, all dressed up, like, but they think it's him. I'm going to take a look.'

'What's he doing hanging around here?' I asked, suddenly feeling vulnerable.

'It won't be related,' he shook his head, 'that'll be someone different. There must be a price on me – big enough for him to take a risk. He'll have gone to ground now, otherwise he'd have nailed me last night – probably let my guard down a bit too low.'

'Why would he be watching me?'

'It won't be him,' he insisted. 'It could be the police, the government – anything. They've extended the Snoopers Charter to allow them to intercept threats to public order before they can develop. It means they can basically do anything they want.'

'Seriously?' I replied sarcastically. 'It's a church – I'm a priest.'

'It happens around here. Undercover police for the obvious, government officials for the not-so, and then a whole range of agencies in between. A lot of the time, it gets outsourced to third parties. Could be one of those.'

'Probably the Church,' I grinned, before realising there could be some truth to it.

'It's always been like this around here, though they usually get the people to do it for them. They get into the cracks, become a weapon that people can use against one another when disagreements happen. "He's got an extra bedroom," or "she's claiming disability and going wrestling," all that sort of shite. It keeps the community fragmented, distrusting.'

'I'm not sure any of that is applicable to me.'

'I'm just saying, surveillance around here isn't just about CCTV cameras on poles. It's much more subtle.'

'So,' I sighed, unconvinced, 'what now?'

'We ask around, find out where the money has come from, see which hole he's hiding in.'

'I don't want to know.'

'Better that you don't,' he smiled. 'Thanks for a great night. Definitely needed that.'

'Same to you, mate,' I pulled him in for a hug. 'Shame about the ending,' I added, as he unclasped himself and picked up his bag.

'Like you said, let's sort ourselves out first. Get down the road if you want a happy ending,' he laughed. 'You've got twenty-quid credit down there.'

∞

I slept fitfully throughout the day, my hangover waking me at times with its intensity, sending me stumbling from the bed to the toilet, to the kitchen. I was a simple machine, a series of processes, guzzling water and then sweating it out on the bedsheets, as my mind took me on a familiar journey with the usual script and cast. I was on repeat, waking in a state of intense terror before the fear disappeared in a split second, as consciousness returned. I'd almost laugh with relief in a bipolar swing, before the pendulum reached its fulcrum and began slowly swinging back, its velocity increasing, panic welling up again at my vulnerability, the defencelessness of sleep.

The cycle was broken in the afternoon, as I sat at the table, looking at my bags, my head throbbing as I continued to work my way through a box of cereal. I was still a machine, a nodding donkey, my jaw rhythmically swinging from left to right as I tried to eat my hangover into submission, when a light knocking on the front door, barely audible over my crunching, gently demanded my attention. I ignored the first two, wondering who it could be, feeling fragile, in no mood for yet another fight.

On the third knock, I managed to raise myself from the chair and shuffle gingerly towards the front door, pausing before opening it to find Elvis, his broad smile curving out from beneath his greying moustache, revealing his single tooth.

'Fucking hell, you look rough as a badger's arse,' he declared, his grin getting wider.

'Good morning,' I said, despite it being well past midday.

'You smell worse than a Muslim's knob,' he continued, laughing at his own comments.

'Alright, alright,' I groaned, before he could come out with the next one. 'What is it?'

'Lucky has got you a meeting with Danny, if you want it. You know, to apologise and that.'

'Really?' I asked, surprised. 'Where?'

'The View, in an hour,' he replied, my stomach flipping at the mention of a pub, as I found myself staring at his tooth, appearing and disappearing as he spoke.

'I'll be there,' I said, closing the door over before opening it again, calling after him, 'and thanks.'

'No problem,' he turned around, flashing that tooth again. 'Get a shower first. You stink like ye ma's–'

I closed the door before he could finish, smiling as it clicked shut. The fact that he'd been here, that they'd gone out of their way to speak with Danny, and that Danny had agreed to speak with me, meant a lot. Walls were starting to come down.

Armed with a purpose, I rushed to the bathroom and considered the grey apparition in the mirror. Elvis wasn't far wrong in his critique, I looked like shit and probably smelled just as bad, but the hangover was receding, the power of good news pulling me from my lethargy as my heart began to soar. Good things were starting to happen.


There was a cool wind coming off the sea, blowing over the city before hitting the exposed ridge. It made me walk quickly, hunched over, hands in pockets as it cut through my jacket, my blood running thin, the hangover making it impossible to keep warm. Wildflowers echoed the white horses of the distant sea, swaying in colourful waves as they were buffeted by the wind, the same force sending huge white clouds cruising across the sky above, their weightless forms seeming solid and monolithic, casting fast-moving shadows over the hills in the distance.

My mind was racing, the initial excitement tempered by the subject matter, as I paused at the park gate, observing the View beyond. It was a contradiction, an irony, or perhaps sarcasm: a squat brick bunker on a high point overlooking the city, without a single window, just bricked-up openings. Its form was defensive, like a wartime lookout post with nothing to look out of, its front door like a back door, set within a narrow slot between two single-storey, mono-pitch blocks, with walls of matt-black anti-vandal paint. Coils of razor wire were its only decoration, giving that welcoming, homely feel.

I pushed the heavy door open, the smell of stale beer hitting me straight away, sending my stomach lurching as my eyes adjusted to the lower light levels. A pink dinosaur was sitting at the end of the bar, Moat the Quote, I assumed, wearing one of his outfits, and then there were two others nursing their drinks, separate, stooped individuals who didn't look up when I entered.

The barman floated towards me, making me nauseous as he slowed and spun, stopping with a grin.

'Do you want to buy a Segway?' he asked.

'What?'

'This Segway – do you want to buy it?' he asked again, ticking all the stereotypes.

'Erm, no thanks. It's got Helsinki Tours written on it.'

'Oh yeah, just ignore that.'

'I'm here to see somebody.'

'Oh, right,' he replied, touching his nose and then nodding towards a side door. 'They're in there.'

An uncomfortable feeling settled in my gut as I looked at the door, all positivity gone, now nervous and twitchy, afraid of what I was going to say.

'Drink?' the barman asked.

'What?'

'Drink. Do you want a drink?'

'Stella please,' I said, feeling sick as soon as I said the words, following as he glided ghost-like behind the bar to pour.

He reminded me of Paul, back in the village, as my gaze returned to the door.

'Are you going in?' he asked irritably, after a long pause.

I took a mouthful and nodded, pushing myself off from the bar, the feeling of dread increasing with each step.

As the door creaked open, two familiar faces looked up, their eyes fixed on me. I felt like running as it closed behind me, trapping me in the small, claustrophobic room, bathed in artificial yellow light. I wondered if they could sense my panic in this concentrated space, dense with emotion, nowhere for it to escape.

Revealing nothing, they continued staring at me, Danny's mother trembling slightly, perhaps with anger, or was it hate? I could feel the tension, the air thick with it, as I placed my drink on the table and sat down, feeling like the accused, their eyes never leaving me throughout the silence.

'Thank you for agreeing to see me,' I said, the only thing I could think to say by way of an ice-breaker.

It felt like I was vomiting words instead of speaking them, emerging incoherent as they stuck in my throat.

'Lucky said we should speak,' Danny's mother replied flatly. 'See if we can iron things out.'

'I want to apologise for what I did,' I said, 'for just turning up. I had no right.'

They said nothing.

'I knew the police were coming, and I wanted to warn you,' I continued, feeling sick as I reached forward and took a sip out of my drink.

*'You can't even say it,'* Peter said scornfully.

I sat back and closed my eyes, taking three deep breaths.

'There's a reason I felt that I needed to help, which has nothing to do with the Church,' I began slowly, each word an effort. 'There is something that… links us.'

'What are you going on about?' Danny asked in a low voice, his first words.

'I'm going to tell you about myself. I just want you to listen,' I replied, leaving another long pause as I tried to compose myself. 'I wasn't brave enough to do what you've done,' I swallowed hard, feeling like I was having to reach in and drag the words out. They were slow, heavy, thick and viscous, like treacle.

'What?' his mother barked, creases forming on her forehead as her features scrunched up. I could sense the anger rising up in her.

'Go to the police – I couldn't do it,' I added quickly. 'I ran away. I'm still running.'

'From what?' Danny probed, irritated, before a look of realisation spread across his face, his mouth hanging open below his unblinking eyes, in an almost comedic look of shock. 'Wait, are you saying…?'

'It happened to me,' I said quietly, tapping the table nervously, rhythmically, with my fingers, a metronome dictating the speed of my speech.

'What?' his mother exclaimed loudly, as if she had misheard. Her hands were clenched into fists, her face red and trembling, eyes bloodshot, large in their sockets, cartoon-like. She was there to fight, imagining what she was going to say, what she was going to do, but this wasn't going according to script.

'It happened to me,' I lifted my head and looked at her, speaking quietly, a finger tap for each word. 'I was sexually abused.'

She shuffled uncomfortably in her seat, her mouth opening to say something, before closing abruptly as she thought better of it. The anger was still there, searching for an outlet, something to attack.

'Are you telling the truth?' Danny asked, after a long pause, looking down at his tightly clasped hands. I could hear the emotion in his voice.

I hesitated before answering, barely a whisper, 'Yes.'

'Oh, God bless us,' his mother sighed, her body losing its rigidity as she slumped back into the chair, before springing upright again, her index finger pointed at me. 'If you're fucking lying,' she warned, unable to find words to match her anger.

'I'm not.'

Her anger abated as suddenly as it appeared, sucked up by the softness of the answer. She slumped back down again, shaking her head, seeing no place for her rage to go, not knowing how to react.

'When?' Danny asked, just a single word question, anger colouring his voice again, as a tear ran down his cheek.

'I was sent to a care home when I was young,' I replied. 'My mother died when I was born, and my father was sent to prison.'

'And it happened there?' he asked, fighting to hold himself together, his mother's hand moving across to his.

'Yes,' I looked down at my feet, a natural, uncontrollable reaction that I could not fight.

Shame.

'Who?' he asked. 'Who did it?'

'There were lots of them,' I said, also trying to fight back rage, a tear running down my cheek, betraying my anger, as I frantically tried to reconstruct those walls in my mind, but I could hear a voice escaping, an elderly man:

*'Come on, sunshine. Big boys don't cry…'*

I felt my body jerk involuntarily as I closed my eyes, squeezing them tight, pushing out more tears, sending them rolling down. I placed my head into my hands, taking another three deep breaths. It seemed to be the magic number, three, to compose myself, to allow me to speak again.

'There were celebrities, judges, civil servants, police officers,' I murmured, pausing to think. 'Businessmen, solicitors, social services, Home Office, Foreign Office, intelligence agencies, and just well-connected nobodies with the same tastes. There were lots of them.'

The defences had fallen, and what started as a trickle was now coming out in an uncontrollable torrent of disgusting memories and words, my life story, a black, bitter-tasting bile that my body was trying to discharge, spit out, as my mouth continued talking, saying things I'd never said before to somebody I hardly knew.

'I can't remember all of them,' I went on, my eyes still closed, 'but some of them are still around. I see them in the newspapers, on the television – everywhere.'

I opened my eyes, and they were both staring at me, eyes wide, but the stares were no longer hostile; they were looks of shock, disbelieving, dumbfounded.

'We should go,' she said softly, the anger momentarily gone from her voice as she pushed into him, around him, placing her palm on his cheek and turning his face towards her. 'This is too much.'

It made me envious for a split second, before an intense feeling of emptiness took over, a chasm of self-pity, bottomless, as I thought of my own life, without the love of a mother. The strength of their bond, her urge to protect, the instinctual motherly love was overwhelming, as was her instinct to flee, to unhear the disgusting base words describing the evil in the world.

'No,' he said, taking her hand away, kissing her on the forehead and then turning back to face me. 'Where?' he asked, sticking to the one-word blueprint.

'The care home. It was a supply line of children, as were many others,' I answered, surprised that I could actually say the words, but struggling to stop the slight stutter as emotion tripped my tongue. 'There was a network of organised rings, one ring linking to another, and then another. They traded us, like football stickers.' I took a deep breath, just one this time. 'Sometimes, they would come for an hour, or stay for a night at our home, pick from a menu.' My chest tightened, heart pounding, lungs struggling to inhale. 'Other times, we travelled to them – North Wales, the Midlands, once we went to Jersey, but it was mainly around London, where the power is. Pimlico, Barnes, Westminster.'

I stopped and focussed on my breathing, realising I was looking at my feet again, my arms and legs crossed in a defensive posture, trying to make myself as small as possible. I looked up to see them both still looking at me.

'Go on,' he urged quietly.

'They created this tiny space,' I explained, showing a one-inch gap between my index finger and thumb, 'an exclusive bubble of moral exemption into which we were thrown. A space where rules and laws need not apply, where they could fuck and kill children without guilt.'

I heard a sharp intake of breath from Danny.

'But how could that happen?' his mother asked. 'How could they get away with that?'

'You know how it works,' I said, looking to Danny. 'You're terrified to talk. You think no one will believe you, and most of the time, they don't.'

There was no response; he just looked down at his feet, twiddling his thumbs nervously.

'It was governed by powerful people, who kept it exclusive,' I continued. 'We were kept there by fear, a daily prescription of mental abuse, reminding us how hopeless our position was. You just took whatever alcohol and drugs they gave you to get through.' I reached forward, adjusting the position of the glass on the beer mat in front of me. 'Sometimes, we would all be in the one room, passed around, but other times we were locked in separate rooms.'

I stopped talking as another tear ran down my nose, dropping onto my foot, my breath catching like a hiccup, breaking up my words.

'You don't have to say any more,' Danny's mother said, her teeth clenched, the muscles of her jaw protruding, as if she were going through some sort of endurance test.

'That was the worst,' I persevered, 'just lying there, alone, terrified in the silence, until you heard the key in the lock.'

Danny let out a sound of revulsion as I paused again, trying to hold back the emotion, my body starting to jerk as I held my breath, battling to keep the tears inside, swallow them down.

'Sometimes, one would come in, sometimes two,' I blurted out. 'Some would hurt you, some were more gentle, as if they cared for you, trying to be tender, saying "I love you," some sort of self-justification. It could go on through the night, lying there alone, listening to the noises coming through the walls, waiting for the key to rattle in the lock again.'

My voice was starting to crack, my throat becoming dry. I reached forward and took a swig of beer, its coolness diverting me for a millisecond, a welcome respite before my mouth started talking again.

'Once we were older, they started to lose interest, and fresh meat arrived, so they had to get rid of us. Some would follow the standard route – a child taken into care, broken in, passed to a paedophile ring, and then into the whole network of fixers, brothels, hotels and bars for child prostitution and pornography. Children they deemed less compliant or attractive simply disappeared, or in my case, they made you fight.'

'What?' Danny cried, shock registering in his voice as another disgusting twist was added to an already disgusting tale.

'They used to take us to a round pit in some basement, like cage fighting before it was invented. The same people that used to fuck us would sit above, betting, drinking, spitting, pissing, screaming and shouting, as two of us were thrown in.'

'Oh, I feel sick,' his mother groaned, putting her hand to her mouth. 'They can't have.'

'Only one would come out, most of the time,' I continued, as a fresh series of tears began their brief journey. 'Sometimes, it was fists, and sometimes they put weapons in. Sometimes, they would just drop one weapon in, or a bottle, like Caesars, the power of life and death in their hands. The only reason I'm still alive is because they enjoyed it so much, but they got careless. Once I was past my sell-by date, they should have just killed me.'

'But how could they cover that up, the death of a child?' she demanded, hoping I'd got it wrong, hoping it was just a story.

'Do you realise how many children disappear from care homes every year? I asked her. 'Nobody gives a shit about them. Society wants them to disappear – they don't fit in. They made sure to choose children who wouldn't be missed. We were segregated.'

'Fucking hell,' she cursed, shaking her head, looking down at the floor, her jaw muscles still flexing as she ground her teeth.

'I'd imagine the majority ended up in paupers' graves,' I said, 'or were cremated by the people they'd placed in key positions. Invited to partake, their involvement guaranteeing silence.'

'Nothing stays secret forever,' she reasoned, 'it always gets out. Why didn't you report it – do something about it?'

'The main reason is that I can't bear to go through it again,' I admitted, talking to my pint glass. 'I can't stand up in front of a room full of strangers and recount the physical and mental abuse.' I shrugged, again looking down at my hands, interlocked, my thumbs rubbing up and down nervously. 'I'm a coward. This is the first time I've even spoken about it. I keep it locked away, even from myself. Another reason is that there's nowhere to go with it. Braver people than me have tried, but they get nowhere. The system doesn't allow them to be touched – they're well protected.'

'What about the police? Why don't you go to the police?'

'The police are in it up to their necks, cover-up after cover-up, their detachment vital in order for the networks to operate, to keep them untouchable. Because of their corroboration in the past, they continue the cover-up into the present. I don't know how they sleep at night, how they've allowed these people to stay free. They're all involved to varying degrees – the police, the judiciary, Crown Prosecution Service, hospitals, councils, even social services, the very people we were supposed to go to for help.'

'Surely, somebody would have said something?'

'I'm amazed that there have been so few whistle-blowers over the years, considering the number of organisations involved. So many people who must have known, but chose to look the other way. No doubt, they sate their conscious with "just obeying orders from above," like guards at Auschwitz.'

'They're looking into it, though,' Danny said, clinging to his illusions. 'They've made arrests, like Operation Yew Tree.'

'They've sacrificed a few ageing celebrities, but it's gone no deeper than that. An establishment figure is only mentioned once they're either dead or deemed unfit to stand trial. Why do you think they waited for Savile to die before allowing him to be exposed? He would have brought them all down with him.'

'No, they couldn't hide something like that,' Danny's mum said forcefully.

'They give the impression that they're doing something, that justice is happening,' I explained, 'but it's just a charade – it never goes anywhere. They use inquiries with deliberately limited scope to close down all further investigation. They're just damage-limitation exercises, with evidence tightly controlled, the press restricted in what they're allowed to report. There's a massive, heavily-compartmentalised structure in place to protecting the so-called elites.'

'There have been arrests made,' Danny repeated.

'Just the tip of the iceberg,' I shook my head, 'the minimum that they can get away with. It's happened so many times, it's amazing that they still manage to pull it off.'

I had more control over my voice now; the tears had stopped, the primary emotion becoming anger. I raised one finger.

'There was the Westminster Dossier, which was handed to the government, listing high-profile paedophiles, but it disappeared without any action being taken, allowing them to carry on.'

'I've heard about that one,' Danny said quietly.

'Over a hundred other incriminating documents regarding high-ranking paedophiles also disappeared from government files, and after a "review," they found nothing suspicious about it.'

I put up a second finger.

'There was the Jillings Report, of which only a redacted version was published, the names of the accused blacked out. The full report and its contents were classified, and then it was pulped, unreleased, as the Council's insurance company was concerned about the cost of potential litigation. The same happened with the Cartrefle Report, the insurers requesting its destruction with no action taken against the accused paedophiles.'

'The insurance company?' Danny's mother shouted in surprise, her features scrunched up again.

'Yes,' I nodded, 'allowing the paedophiles to remain anonymous, to carry on doing what they do, so they don't take a financial hit.' I sighed, moving on to the third finger. 'Then, there was the Waterhouse Inquiry – where to start with this one? Same again, a few serving sentences, none of them establishment, and the majority escaping any sort of justice, allowed to continue. In this case, they only permitted the naming of care home staff involved, not the high-profile visitors that were accused by hundreds of witnesses. They granted anonymity to those alleged to be part of the paedophile ring, lots of big names, and the press were prevented from exposing them.'

I looked towards them both, but no words were coming. Danny's mother was still trembling; this time it looked like anger.

'There was even photographic evidence at the care home,' I said, 'but the courts ordered the destruction of the file, unseen, preventing any further investigation. It seems that the whole point of the Waterhouse Inquiry was to accumulate and destroy any existing evidence against the paedophile rings.'

'Surely, they couldn't get away with that,' she exclaimed, 'destroying evidence?'

'They did more than that,' I said. 'The accused were allowed legal representation, witnesses were not. There was also pressure on witnesses to amend statements, not to mention certain names, not to mention certain places. They were told what they could and couldn't put in their statements.'

'Sounds like Hillsborough.'

'In the sense of a repeated miscarriage of justice, inquest after inquest, designed to deflect, you're right, but the families of Hillsborough pulled together and did something remarkable. We, on the other hands, are a disparate group of damaged individuals, spread out across the country, who just don't want to remember. The other issue is, Hillsborough was a single, definable event. This is something diverse and ongoing.'

We sat quietly for a moment, just looking at one another. There was a feeling of despair in the room.

I held up fingers four, five and six.

'Operations Fairbank, Fernbridge – I'm not even sure if the new one has a name yet. They just keep rolling them along, more of the same, as the offenders get older, the evidence against them more faded,' I raised a seventh finger. 'Operation Pallial was the main one around here. Again, hundreds accused and only one or two sentenced, none of the elite circle. Most cases never even got this far – most were ignored or brushed under the carpet.' I smiled for the first time, a humourless, bitter smile. 'The announcement of a new inquiry is their way of telling you it's pointless. They'll go through the motions, making the victims relive their experiences, going through hell again and again and again, but you can never win. In the meantime, they use every trick in the book, putting out disinformation, using the media to create doubt and undermine the process. They label the victims claimants, as if they're scroungers looking for compensation, a subtle change of identity, a sleight of hand creating a label, utilising public bias against them.'

'But,' Danny started, pausing whilst he thought, 'why would the government allow it to continue?'

'Because of the involvement of their own, an establishment to be protected at all costs. Because the corruption spreads through the very building blocks of our society, permeating the institutions that we should be able to trust, preserving the illusion our "civilised" country, with justice, democracy and freedom for all. Also, because it's useful, a resource used by agencies that groom paedophiles into positions of power, film them in action, and then use it as leverage to manage them. Most of the rooms in the care home were bugged.'

'But they're human beings,' he cried. 'How could they justify it to themselves?'

'Probably classed it as being for the greater good, in the national interest. They give themselves all sorts of excuses for not speaking out, for letting it go on. Criminal inertia.'

'How high do you think it goes?'

'To the very top,' I answered immediately. 'Prime ministers have known about it, and all of them do nothing. From there, it cascades down through the rest of them, which makes them all complicit in my book. It makes you think how powerful these people are, and how widespread it must be, if even prime ministers are afraid to allow a proper investigation.'

'Nothing would surprise me when it comes that lot,' his mother snapped, 'they've always fucked us over. I remember what's-his-face sticking his cock in a dead pig. That perversion hasn't even got a fucking name, necrophiliac bestiality?'

'I dread to think how deep it really goes,' I said, 'but suffice to say, it's big money. The child sex industry is intertwined with other branches of organised crime, the illegal arms trade, terrorist groups – the list goes on and on.'

'Sounds more like Jacko's area,' Danny suggested.

'He never touched the sex industry,' I replied, a little sharply. 'Look, I know I sound like some sort of unhinged loon, going on about a big conspiracy theory, but the cover-up is still going on, the extent of which tells you a lot about the power of those involved. They hide behind status, respectability and wealth. The government could choose to stop it at any time – their agencies could hand over their information, the photographs and recordings, and justice could be done, but they won't. Paedophilia was, and is, allowed to happen by the government, with decades of cover-ups enabling it to continue on an industrial scale, a state-sponsored child abuse and pornography industry, subsidised by the taxpayer.'

'Has anybody ever taken them on – tried to expose them?'

'The press have tried in the past, but they get blocked with D notices, and if the risk becomes too great, the rings will take things into their own hands. They'll kill their own if they feel threatened – way down the pecking order, of course, the guest house owners and such. Then, they'll kill others who try to do the right thing, a politician shot in the head on a remote country road with a briefcase full of evidence, no official inquiry into his death. An ex-MI5 officer had to flee to South America after she tried to shine a light into these dark places. They smeared her all over the papers, but it was so transparent it was laughable. She's still in hiding.

Then, of course, look what just happened with Epstein.'

'And the victims?'

'The cover-ups allow for the persecution of survivors who are seen as a risk. They slip on railway lines or fall into roads. A twenty-one-year-old found dead of natural causes. Some have died in fires, other of overdoses or hangings. Lots of suspicious circumstances, but it's hard to prove.'

'And you, have they approached you?'

'No, I've stayed quiet, like a good little boy,' I confessed, feeling my cheeks burn with embarrassment. 'I'm no trouble.'

I was looking down at my feet again.

'How did you escape?'

'The whole place was shut down, just like that,' I clicked my fingers. 'The Church came and collected me. Some went to other homes, others just ran. It was knocked down a week later, as if it had never existed, erasing the memories, like all those terrible things never happened. All records were destroyed.'

'No, how do *you* escape? How do you get it out of your mind?'

'It gets easier,' I lied.

Peter was raging, screaming.

'*How about words like empty, hollow, guilty, bitter, breakdown, self-harm, panic attack, trust? ... What about the anger, the hate? What about the fear of going to sleep, of staying awake, of being alone, of being with other people? Tell him about the help groups, the parasitic agencies living off abuse. Tell him how it's hard to like, hard to love – how you're always distant, transient, living a false existence. How you don't know who you are any more, schizophrenic. Tell him how it was a living nightmare, and still is. Tell him how you still feel it, smell it, taste it...*'

'You learn to live with it, and you move on,' I said. 'You can't let it define who you are. Your case is different, it's against one man, a priest, who has admitted the allegations. It's no less horrific, no less disgusting, but because you've been strong enough to stand up, there can be closure.'

'How did you manage to hold it together?' she asked. 'How can you believe in anything anymore?'

'For me, it was the Church,' I said. 'I found something greater to believe in. I can't see any other way I could have coped.'

They both glanced at each other, and then back at me, just the word eliciting a reaction, a stepping back, the atmosphere immediately changing, becoming charged.

'Maybe it's just a comfort blanket,' I said. 'Maybe it's because I know there'll be no justice in this life, but my faith tells me they'll face it in the next.'

He was looking down again; she was glaring at me. I'd lost them.

'When are you going to do something about it?' she asked quietly, abruptly, before standing up, pointing that finger again. 'Do something in this life, instead of hoping for something in the next.'

'What?'

'When are you going to stop crying, acting like a victim, and do something about it?' her voice started to rise, the anger returning. 'You're not going to end up like this,' she said to her son. 'No way are you going to end up like this.'

My mouth dropped open, the red rose in my cheeks again; humiliation this time.

'Mum, that's enough,' he said, trying to quiet her.

'You sit there, a grown man, with tears running down your face, saying how the people that allowed this to happen are complicit. Are you not also complicit? Doing nothing, allowing them to continue?'

'Have you not listened to anything?' I asked, standing up, my voice now rising to match hers. 'It's not possible to get any sort of justice.'

I was trembling. *It's not supposed to work like this*, I thought.

'I'm sorry about the things that have happened to you,' she said, calmer now, 'I truly am, but where's the anger? Where's the passion? You act like you're the guilty one in all of this. I don't even know you, and I'm furious about what they've done to you.'

I slumped back down and sat looking at her, waiting for the next sounds to come out of her mouth. *Perhaps this is the only way she knows how to respond*, I considered, *with anger, confrontation. Maybe this is her life.*

'There's nothing I hate more than little frightened people who whine and complain, and then do nothing to change things. There are people who have had a go, they call themselves survivors, not victims, and every time they get knocked down, they pick themselves up. You're right, you can't win if you stay like this. You're exactly what they want you to be – meek, timid and lonely, the perfect Priest,' she finished sarcastically.

'That's enough,' Danny insisted, stepping in front of her, but she ignored him, leaning around to see me.

'People around here won't come to you unless you stick your neck out, fight for what's right. You'll get plenty of pity and sympathy, but what fucking use is that? You'll stay lonely, a creature of their making, weak. Around here, you fight – you fight, fight, fight,' she hissed, her finger jabbing the table with every 'fight.'

'I've no problem with fighting,' I replied, starting to feel irritated.

'You can fight with your fists,' she said, 'but have you got the bottle to fight without them? All I'm hearing are reasons not to do something.'

*'She talks like it's a playground fight,'* Peter whispered.

'It's more difficult than it's ever been,' I sighed, shaking my head. 'We're buried under an avalanche. They've made chaos the new normal, creating outrage after outrage until people become numb to it, accepting. They've invoked the Emergency Powers Act, suspending the rule of law – they prorogue at will, preventing the debate of anything that could threaten their agenda. The troubles have returned in Northern Ireland, Scotland has gained independence. They pass racist, sexist, homophobic comments without consequence, and when anybody mentions historic abuse, they say it's money wasted – spaffed up the wall.'

'That's just noise,' she argued. 'We've never been able to rely on the institutions.'

'Look at that the last inquiry, where they followed the allegations of a liar, a fantasist, debasing the claims of any real victim, casting doubt upon every future allegation.'

'Was it a set-up?' she asked.

'Who knows, but it was certainly a gift. Perhaps they could, or should, have stopped it at the beginning, once it became apparent that he was a fraud. Maybe he was convincing, and they were doing everything they could to bring justice. That's where they hide, in the maybes, the plausible deniability that makes any prosecution risky, prohibitively expensive.'

'But why would anybody do that?' Danny asked.

'I think he was looking for meaning to his existence, now God has gone.'

'Will you stop bringing God into it,' she snapped. 'God wasn't there for Danny.'

'Imagine, how empty his life must have been to do something like that. It's like a distorted route to fame, fabricating a life story, filling a void by claiming somebody else's trauma.'

'Sounds rigged to me,' she said.

'The abusers don't have to rig it, some desperado will do it for them, pulling it down from the inside.'

'It was a bloody set-up,' she insisted.

'Maybe, but again, it's all maybes. They reckon the Prime Minister is just a puppet, and all power lies with his advisors. Who knows who they're working for. It's not beyond the realm of possibility that they represent the interests of the very same people.'

'You're just giving yourself another reason not to do anything,' she scolded, standing again. 'It doesn't matter if you win, you just have to try – give them a black eye, be a survivor. If you do that, people around here will back you for as long as it takes, and I'll be the first to stand with you,' she declared, prodding herself on the chest. 'It's up to you, at the end of the day, but all you have at the moment is my sympathy, love.'

She sat back down, finished, her eyes directed across the room, unwilling to look at me.

*'What the fuck was that?'* Peter laughed, *'Some sort of cruel to be kind act?'*

'I take it you don't work for the Samaritans,' I joked, after a long pause, but they were not in the mood for humour; another defensive device honed through a traumatic childhood, mistimed, transparent, pathetic.

Her presence was dominating me; I felt unable to speak, to stand up and leave, as though I needed her permission. I was confused, unsure; I'd never been spoken to like that before. The words should be gentle, to sooth, to pacify. I kept leaning forward, taking sips of beer as we sat, fidgeting, focussing on different points in the room.

'I didn't burn down the church,' Danny eventually said.

I was glad he had broken the silence, changed tack; it was a route to getting out of here, any final business.

'I know,' I said. 'I knew as soon as I saw you.'

'Because it didn't happen in the church.'

'What?'

'It happened in your house.'

My stomach twisted, a wave of revulsion washing over me. I felt the ground move as I swayed.

*'How could you even contemplate taking on that church? Living in that fucking house?'* Peter berated me.

'Can you be at the pub tonight, seven-thirty?' I asked. 'There's something I need to show you.'

Danny looked perplexed as I glanced across at his mother, who raised an eyebrow and nodded.

'Please could you…' I started, standing up, not finishing the sentence.

'What's been said stays within these four walls,' she said, anticipating my words. There was no anger to her voice now; she had said what she needed to say.

'Thank you,' I said, turning to Danny. 'If you ever want to talk, please do come to me. I don't mean as a priest, but as somebody that understands.'

'I will,' Danny nodded, before standing up and shaking my hand.

'Same goes to you love,' his mother said, getting up and walking around the table, embracing me, adding to my confusion. 'And think about what I've said. Sorry if I come over aggressive, but sometimes people need that to get them thinking straight. When you're ready, we're here for you, and we've got a lot more to give than just sympathy.'

I walked back the long way, along the ridge, with its far-reaching views and massive skies, finding a spot to sit amongst the flowers, like I used to in the village, a meadow of poppies, foxglove, buttercups and countless others, previously labelled weeds, now rebranded, allowing people to open their eyes and see their beauty. I had to admire them, their tenacity, their toughness, trampled and walked over, yet still flourishing.

Survivors.

Purple thunderheads were cruising in the distance, but I wasn't really looking. I already knew it would be my last visit, that I'd never spend another night there, glancing at the charred shell of the church as I passed.

*'You made a promise to Migsy,'* Peter reminded me.

It was the house than caught my attention now, looking humble, innocuous, innocent. The church had been an easy metaphor, an abuse of power, but the house was a symbol of normality, the everyday, giving no hint as to what had happened behind its closed doors.

*Do they all have such secrets?* I thought. *Stories hidden behind their humdrum facades, washed away by time?*

I went inside, looking at it through new eyes, like a crime scene, exactly what it was. It felt different, dirty, offensive, as I studied unnoticed detail like a forensic scientist, crouching, looking at scuff marks on the wallpaper, chips in the woodwork and light stains on the carpet, wondering what they were, how they got there, what scenes they had witnessed, shadows of memories. I could smell the light undercurrent of bleach, of cleaning products concealing something imperceptible, something vile beneath the appearance of normality.

*'How have you not noticed this before?'* Peter reprimanded me. *'The whole place is rotten.'*

I strode up and down the living room, pacing, as if trapped in a cell, my stress levels rising, thoughts relentless.

*'How must it have looked to see a new Priest arriving, living under this roof? To see you cleaning up the church, washing away their protests every day before opening up, business as usual? How empty must your words of optimism have sounded to them, a sales patter of trust and togetherness, community?'*

'Shut up!' I shouted.

*'To think, you saw this as a home, a refuge, somewhere to get straight, to chastise your demons and achieve your ambitions – you, you, you – only to find that similar demons resided here, in plain view, hiding in the corners, sitting on the same furniture, lying on the same stained bed.'*

I started sorting through my bags, choosing what I needed and what I would leave, Peter still talking to me, admonishing me.

*'Of all people, how could you be so blind?'*

'Shut up!' I screamed in a whisper, afraid somebody might hear.

*'Unsighted by hope? By pride? Relying on time, the great healer?'*

There was almost nothing amongst the luggage that could qualify as important, with the exception of a few faded photographs of my mother, just black-and-white smudges, her features faded, our only link, other than her genes, 'the good half,' as Dad would say. I sat and looked at them, trying to put a voice, a personality, to the static blur, but I knew it was futile, just mind games, trying to convince myself that there was a truth, a memory hidden somewhere in my subconscious, but our lives had only overlapped by minutes, hours. It was impossible.

The rest of my belongings were clothes, as transient as I was, soon to be discarded through the repetitive cycles of fashion; profitable obsolescence.

I couldn't truly see them, my eyes too busy flitting from logo to logo as I packed a bag and then started going through the cupboards, emptying out the piles of old newspapers, junk mail, rubbish just kept. I crumpled, twisted, tore it up, releasing pressure as I snarled, baring teeth, my arms lashing out, leaving a trail of mess as I searched for anything useful: kitchen roll, toilet paper, a bottle of Sambuca, its aniseed smell making my stomach twist as I took a swig and tipped it out, the aroma filling the room.

Looking outside, I saw it was getting dark. My stomach was growling, I hadn't eaten. I heaved a single bag on to my shoulders, looking back into the living room one last time at my abandoned belongings, making sure the curtains were closed. I was feeling shame, for there *was* a future here, hope, but hope always led to pain. I was too weak, seeking safety in the familiarity of the unfamiliar, my life returning to its ever-repeating pattern, running from myself, this place, becoming anonymous, a stranger, as if I were the offender.

*'Coward,'* Peter taunted.

He was right; I would not be leaving on my own terms this time.

I slumped, kneeling on the floor, amongst the debris, reflecting on the sheer hopelessness of it, this never-ending cycle of moving on, wondering at which point you just give up, lie down and die. Eventually, I roused myself, my mind emptied, the thoughts stopped, voices silenced, as tended to be the case in such times. I wished I could stay there, in the clear, but it was always a precursor to action, a violence with a beauty all its own, as I lifted up my bag and entered the hallway, grabbing the Sambuca, unscrewing the lid and spilling the last remaining drops over the crumpled newspaper below the front door, before turning around and surveying the mess behind me.

There was a crackle as I struck the match along its box, sparking a blue-yellow light as it flickered and then took, illuminating the hallway, staying lit as it dropped, the paper igniting with a gentle *poof*, followed by a light blue flame racing across the floor, along the Sambuca, turning yellow as first the paper and then the carpet caught. It was hypnotic; I wanted to stay and watch as it rushed around the corner into the living room.

Stepping out into the street, I locked the door behind me and glanced up at the house, still innocuous and innocent, stubbornly keeping its secrets behind that plain façade. I felt like I was squaring up to it, taking it on.

'Got a leaflet for you.'

I spun around quickly to find a teenager dressed in black, my stomach lurching and my heart leaping in my chest. He was shaven-headed and covered in acne, each red spot wearing a little yellow crown, and like their owner, they looked like they were holding back intense pressure, ready to erupt at the slightest touch.

His face looked angry, everything narrow, curving downwards, like he had never smiled. He had a frown on his forehead, and a bundle of leaflets in his hand, as two others appeared, followed by three on mountain bikes, Cornermen, dressed all in black, circling like rooks, looking for carrion.

'*Bonjour,*' Peter giggled, as I tried to suppress a grin, reading Balmain, Louis Vuitton and Givenchy in bold letters across their chests.

'*Just stepped off the fucking Champs-Elysees,*' Peter mocked.

'It's about the eviction notices,' Balmain said.

'What?'

'The eviction notices,' he mumbled, walking towards the door. 'I'll stick it in your letter box.'

*No,* I thought, and then I shouted it, causing him to pause and look at me, his frown sinking deeper as the mountain bikers stopped their passive-aggressive circuits, placing a foot onto the ground, focussing on me, sensing something. Three other garcons appeared from around the corner at the top of the road, hoods up, black silhouettes, standing, just watching, as that beautiful tension was creeping into the air.

'I'll take it with me,' I suggested, holding out my hand.

He hesitated for a second, looking at the front door and then back to me, one hand in the pocket of his tracksuit bottoms, fidgeting with his balls, figuring out how to maintain status in front of his pack.

'You need to be careful how you speak to people,' he warned, unzipping his tracksuit jacket, revealing the handle of a blade. 'God isn't in charge around here.' He placed the leaflet in my hand, his eyes locking on to mine.

I'd have happily stayed and let the scene play out had I not set my house on fire moments before. He amused me, a contradictory mix in a teenage body, the immediate threat of violence paired with delivering pamphlets for his mum, as I crammed the leaflet into my pocket.

'Thanks, mate,' I replied, submissive, giving him what he needed as he turned away.

My eyes flicked towards the door as he walked past, up the road, where he was joined by his comrades, their shoulders swinging whilst arms hung limp below. He turned, taking the expected final glance before disappearing around the corner, the bikes following, swarming around them like defensive drones. Only one remained, motionless, leaning on the lamppost.

George Formby.

I looked at him, wondering if he was real. My visions were usually perverse, naked, from my past, but whilst he was not from my past, he was quite possibly perverse.

'*Just because they knocked the home down doesn't mean they went away,*' Peter shouted, mimicking Brian's words. '*They're coming to take you back.*'

'No,' I mumbled.

'*He's the reason you're running, at least be honest with yourself.*'

'They'll leave me if I go,' I replied, not disagreeing with him.

I glanced at the house, hearing a light snapping; not enough to indicate of the inferno within, and as I returned my gaze to him, I realised it didn't matter who he was, where he was from or who he represented. He was abstract, an analogy of this place, this bubble, this fluid balance of internal and external pressures. They attacked from inside and out, setting the boundaries between which normal people lived their lives.

He could have been Police, Church or a lackey for any one of the outside authorities that Migsy had mentioned; some random agent of government policy or media spin, creating the resulting prejudice imposed on people and places like this.

*Then again, he could just be from around here*, I thought. *High Rip, Cornerman, the Nightman – some other superhero or supervillain, or just a random local, defined by internal pressures, unspoken rules, binding them in its rituals, keeping them where they are.*

*'Let me take him,'* Peter pleaded.

'No.'

*'Put him in the house, with the fire.'*

'No.'

*'A leaving gift for Migsy,'* he whispered. *'He tried to kill him – he'll try to kill you.'*

'No!' I shouted.

George Formby continued staring as I argued with myself, but it didn't matter now.

*'Fucking coward,'* Peter cursed, as I turned my back on him and the church, walking down the road at a fast pace before stealing away across the park.

Entering the darkness of back streets, I heard the distant sound of sirens. I paused and smiled, hoping that they were stepping out of the pub, drawn to the commotion as windows shattered, roofs and floors collapsed, flames emerging, consuming all the scuff marks and stains, the underlying stench of perverted corruption.

I pulled up my hood and continued towards the bright lights of the city centre, my destination anywhere, somewhere, nowhere.

*'You promised Migsy,'* Peter whispered.